WOLF TONES

WOLF TONES

a novel

IRVING WEINMAN

John Daniel & Co., McKinleyville, California, 2009

Copyright © 2009 by Irving Weinman
All rights reserved
Printed in the United States of America

Published by John Daniel & Company
A division of Daniel and Daniel, Publishers, Inc.
Post Office Box 2790
McKinleyville, CA 95519
www.danielpublishing.com

Distributed by SCB Distributors (800) 729-6423

LIBRARY OF CONGRESS CATALOGING-IN-PUBLICATION DATA
Weinman, Irving, (date)
 Wolf tones : a novel / by Irving Weinman.
   p. cm.
 ISBN-13: 978-1-56474-480-7 (pbk. : alk. paper)
 ISBN-10: 1-56474-480-9 (pbk. : alk. paper)
 1. Novelists–Fiction. 2. Interpersonal relations–Fiction 3. Self-realization–Fiction.
 4. New Mexico–Fiction. I. Title.
 PS3573.E3963W55 2009
 813'.54–dc22
       2008033177

*This book is, eventually,
for Alexander, Nicholas, Sophie, and Chloe*

WOLF TONES

I. FLIGHT

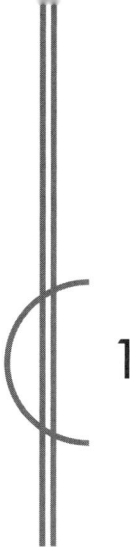

1

HIS FLIGHT TO ALBUQUERQUE is annoying, but at least it's daytime. He hates night flights. Flying in daylight, he can still imagine his country has a countryside. There seem vast spaces without roads or houses. Even the crowded East gives unbroken vistas of spruce, or maple, or southern pine. By daylight he looks down on a patchwork of fields quilting East Texas, big enough to cover Denmark. He sees glades and glints of lake the whole green length of Florida. But he can't kid himself at night. What he sees from the sky at night are the lights. Lights clustered at farmland villages, lights strung out along the highways, lights from traffic, the close and further towns glowing their oranges and yellows, lines of light from Denver shot into the Rockies, lights from Kansas heading west up to the Sangre de Cristos, Moab showing and the canyons lit right out to Las Vegas, city of clogged lights. What he sees illuminated when he flies at night is the sad arteriosclerosis of America.

The Boston–Dallas flight had been long but not unpleasant. The people he sat among were sober, clean, and, best, were silent. But on this leg from Dallas to Albuquerque, he gets a talker. He can't switch seats because those vacant aren't, like his, on an aisle with an empty seat beside him. This provides the opening for the talker by the window. "You need leg room even more than I," he says with a foreign accent. Ethan nods and looks away, usually a talk stopper. The man reeks of cigarettes. Ethan sets the a/c nozzle to blow away the stench. He trusts the stinker notices. He anyway stays quiet for the remainder of boarding, so Ethan lets his eyes half close to a pleasant blur in which a realtor shows him a reasonable adobe rental. And there's a good used car in view; cars are supposed to last forever in the dry Southwest. Ethan considers himself, despite this flight—and here he acknowledges its other meaning, *to flee from*—an optimist. He remembers Albuquerque being cute.

The minute the plane takes off, the man beside the window takes off talking. It isn't English; it must be his name. Ethan turns his head. The man's hand is out. Ethan considers refusing it, so little does he care for in-flight bonding. But the man's expression—narrowed eyes and twisted smile on a broad, creased face—as if anticipating the rebuff, makes him take the handshake. Ethan reasons the man is foreign, and we are, Americans, a superficially friendly people, after all, up to a point. He says, "Ethan Baum. I didn't get your name."

"Stucic, Miroslav. Miroslav Stucic." Ethan can visualize the accent marks because of Sandy Milocic, from whom, among others, he's taken flight. "You are from Albuquerque?" Stucic asks, putting an extra syllable between his rolled "r" and the "q."

"I will be. I'm going to teach at the University." Ethan wonders if the pretentiousness of "I will be" is linked to the precariousness of his job.

Stucic says, "Aha. I, too, Eaten. It is Eaten, as in Frome?"

"Exactly. Ethan."

"Eee-than," says Stucic, sticking out his tongue. "What is, may I ask, your field? I am myself heading to European languages. Also I am a translator. Also I was a playwright and diplomat."

"I have a year's contract to teach Cultural Studies in the Honors Program. I'm also a novelist." He feels it would have been more accurate, considering his writer's block, to say, like Stucic, "Also I was a novelist." He asks, longing to close the chat, where Stucic is from.

"From... How I wish for a cigarette. I am from what I still insist on calling Yugoslavia, now that it is, of course, Bosnia. When there was a real Yugoslavia, I would say I was from Bosnia, but without chauvinism. You know of Nicolas Chauvin?"

Ethan says, "A popular fellow," and is immediately sorry he's spoken.

Stucic's hand loops forward in a mock bow. The middle fingers are tanned from tobacco. "I was," he says—and Ethan knows the man will never stop—"a type of classical Bosnian Sarajevan: my mother was Catholic Croatian and my father Orthodox Serbian, and I grew up on a delightful street of very nice Sarajevan Moslems and Jews. So you will excuse me please if I react too much to you asking where I am from, since I cannot get back there probably forever, and this is because all the sides now regard me as their implacable enemy since, by their standards, I am, it is true, guilty of the highest crime—impartial humanism."

The man's hard smile reminds Ethan of Sandy Milocic's smile as she sat on the bed pulling her stockings off and stopped to look up at him, her breasts already swollen, the understanding in her tight smile that he didn't want the baby nor, in fact, her, on her own terms. He sees that what has made him flee Boston she might call his partial inhumanism.

His flight-buddy is saying, "This is the *reductio ad…* You are a scholar of Latin?"

Ethan isn't, but as a graduate of Boston Latin School he rises to represent New World learning and completes, "*ad absurdum.*"

"*Absurdum,*" Stucic nods, "of fundamentalism in religion and nationalism. This curse What happened, in short, was that I attempted to be of assistance to everyone who suffered—Serb, Croat, Bosnian, Catholic, Moslem, et cetera, et cetera. For which I lost everything, until, with my family, I was forced to flee for my life. But you would not wish to hear this story."

Rather than saying, "How right you are," Ethan foolishly says, "Please."

They turn to each other across the empty seat. Stucic starts the story of his war against the war in Bosnia. The plane climbs above the suburban lakes of Dallas. Just to the left of Stucic's talking head, Ethan has a clear view out the window. After a while, he sees the long arm of the Brazos River bending west. Stucic is explaining his ambivalent position. Below, the plains begin to rise and yellow. Some time later, the pilot announces they're over Lubbock. In the foothills, the shadowed ravines look like bare trees. Stucic continues his conflicted talk. The hills below pucker with erosion. Somewhere down there, the land crosses from the endlessness of Texas into New Mexico. Stucic talks on. Ethan nods, deciding a line of green below is the Pecos River going north into high mountains. He imagines the sparse greens as separate juniper and piñon. Stucic continues. Here comes the wall of the Sandia Mountains, and Ethan looks out to the white desert just beyond the green slash of the Rio Grande valley. Albuquerque comes into view. Stucic goes on. The airplane turns. The passengers are told to prepare for landing. The airplane banks over the city's southwest plateau and drops to its airbase-airport. As they touch down, Stucic finishes and says, "So."

"So?" is what Ethan's thinking, because even though he's sympathetic to this narration of injustice and carnage, he's had to play aerial reconnaissance to keep awake. It's as if someone, not close to you, were talking about his illness. You have some concern, but after a while you think: Yes, he's ill, his sickness consists of such and such, and this or that way is how it may or may not be cured. But what can you do? How are you to engage in what is essentially an internal monologue which happens on you as its audience? What Ethan says is, "That's awful. Let's stay in touch when we settle in on campus." Then the plane stops and he stands to get his laptop from the overhead.

He last sees Stucic where the dockway joins the terminal, stopped to put an unlit cigarette in his mouth, blocking the passengers behind him.

At his motel, Ethan finds an invitation to a University party taking place this evening. The cut price motel is in an uncute part of Albuquerque consisting of other cheap motels, pawn shops, grubby fast-food outlets, derelict buildings and used car lots. The party offers company, the opportunity to make a good impression and some time away from his room, this dim dump. He gets ice, takes vodka from the suitcase and pours a long one. Stretching over the short sagging bed, Ethan imagines what sort of place he'd be in had he come with his ex-wife Helen, whom, when tense, he thinks of as XHelen.

Black Forest *gateau*. They would have stayed at some heavy downtown hotel for heavy businessmen and sat in a restaurant where the brass-plated dessert trolley would have as its centerpiece an uncut Black Forest *gateau*—never straightforward chocolate cake in these places—which XHelen would insist on ordering and then would not eat, merely breaking it to bits on the plate with the side of her fork as she drank cup after cup of coffee, whose effect, though he drank none, would be to keep both of them awake all night. As opposed to Sandy, his sweet grad student Sandy Milocic, good democratic Pittsburgh Croat who wouldn't mind this Indian Chief Motel up the shabby end of Central Ave. in Albuquerque, as she hadn't minded the seedy Putnam House in Scituate, Massachusetts, nor the truly abysmal Tabrisky's Cabins in Watervliet, New York, nor, indeed, a ground sheet and blanket anywhere flesh was roused or sleepy, and the spirit sang or snored. Sandy, he thinks, pouring more vodka, with whom he'd broken his vow of chastity with students because he was a year and a half divorced and horny and lonely. Not that it did either of them good, especially not her. Sandy with her flat, round face and deep, quick mind, her laugh and shining teeth which he'd kiss carefully, one by one, which made her laugh, which made her teeth shine.

No laughter that last time. "Yes, I'm having the abortion. No, I don't want you there or paying for it. No, I won't reconsider, because you know I only want the child of the man who wants my child." And though he was not what's called a tit man, nor a leg man, but more your all round *mens-sana-in-corpore-sano* man, he almost, from an insane love of her growing breasts and darkening nipples, from thinking how, when she lifted them one in each hand as if offering fruit, his breath caught and his legs went weak, he almost told her he did want the baby. Which would be as mean and selfish as the truth. No, he thinks, putting ice in the drink and seeing it now requires more vodka, somewhat less selfish. His bad feeling—might it be guilt?—about this is a chief factor in his flight from Boston. But thinking about it, he finds, has given him an erection.

Maybe he'll meet a woman at the party. This thought is inspired by his vodka glow, brighter than the room's one bulb. He has been drinking on airplanes all day, eating only pretzels and nuts. He should grab a sandwich: he's not a good drunk. But there's plenty of time. He'll rest for half an hour. He feels he has done the right thing to come out west. He's even content to have lost the house in Somerville to XHelen, content in that although it's close to Cambridge, the house is in Somerville, and not, as XHelen puts about, in Cambridge. He closes his eyes. XHelen whom he also flees, not to mention his father.

Ethan wakes up three hours later, drunk. He calls a cab and showers. He puts on clean clothes, starving. He'll eat at the party. Who will he know there? His teaching job is so last-minute, his one and only interview was a phone conference. He's heard of only one faculty member, their star writer Lucy Evans. And, yes, Stucic, the airplane bore. He has a quick vodka to relax, and then the taxi's there and he's slumped against the back seat as they drive up Central. He doesn't recall Albuquerque sprawling on and on like this. Was there so much so ugly? Then they're driving into mountain foothills. The taxi swings south. Up above is a rising, white-silver, full summer moon. He remembers he has to make a good impression. The cab pulls up in a hilltop grove of ponderosa pine. Ethan pays and turns to the big stone and log house. Dozens of cars are parked around. He doesn't know who's giving the party. What is he doing here? Music and voices. Shadows moving behind big window curtains. The air up here is cold, and he's dizzy from vodka. He sits on a slate step, his head in his hands. A voice from the door says, "Are you okay?" He says something about something to eat.

He lifts his head and sees the city spread before him. What breaks his heart from airplanes here thrills him: the city drops from plateau to plateau in great steps of light, a landscape intricate and glittering as a robe by Klimt. Above Ethan, the moon has faded in the clear sky into a faint gray disk. Is he losing his eyesight or his mind? A bad omen. He should not have married XHelen, not taken up with Sandy. He tries to swim his mind to a place from where he can experience his life directly, unmediated by literary analogy, revisionist daydream, or his father's learned voice. Here?

Someone taps his shoulder. His eyes shut for a second and he immediately falls into an old argument–dream with XHelen. She's wearing a beige cashmere sweater stained with printing inks. The tendons on her neck stand out like the roots of a small ficus. He's saying, "*I'm a hypocrite? I'm not the one who lives in Somerville and says she lives in Cambridge.*"

She whispers, "I don't. I say 'near' Cambridge."

"Somerville," he says. "Somerville is where it is."

She says, "We're two blocks from Cambridge, and more people have heard of Cambridge."

He says, "By that logic, 'near Boston' would be even better." This gives him some pleasure. It is the high point of this dream.

She says, "But we're nearer Cambridge. Besides, if we lived in Dorchester, I'd bet you'd say 'Boston.'" This is where the dream swings XHelen's way.

He knows what's coming. He knows he's dreamt this before, but he cannot alter it. He says, "That's different. First of all, Dorchester is part of Boston."

"And second?"

Ah, the contest is now over and he should cut his losses. But he must dream it through. He says, "Second, what?"

She says, "You said 'first of all.' You mean, second, Dorchester is such an awful, Black slum that it would be okay to say you didn't live there."

He says, "I didn't mean that. That wasn't second. I didn't say that, you did. Maybe that's what you believe. I grew up in Boston and don't have that racial—or is it racist—association with Dorchester. My parents remembered it as a Jewish slum."

She says, "I know, and Bobby Doer was playing second base for the Red Sox then. Oh, you're such a hypocrite."

The image of XHelen—baggy doe eyes, bony shoulder-blades, smeared cashmere—disappears, and Ethan dreams thoughts. XHelen has no right to the Doer expression, is no baseball fan, would not know Doer from Yastrzemski or Yaz from big Mo Vaughn. But, having somewhere heard the Doer expression, she's annexed it as her own metaphor for living in the past. A typical XHelen Van Leyden usurpation of *his* character: to invoke baseball, and the Red Sox in particular, and thereby his memories of left field in great detail, as seen from the bleachers, where his courtesy uncle Phil Friedman takes him as a small boy and tells him stories about cheering Ted Williams at bat, and, better, about booing him in the outfield as he refused to hustle after hits, and, best, about how Williams eventually scowled up his way and gave him the finger…. And that XHelen should appropriate even *this*—little Ethan Baum's stories of his Uncle Phil being personally signaled "fuck you" by the greatest batter of all time, the Splendid Splinter himself, something which could happen only in America, as Uncle Phil points out, laughing and pounding little Ethan's thigh—is outrageous. How dare she! Ethan is so angry. He feels her shaking him and whacks at her hand on his shoulder.

Someone says, "Ow!" A woman squats beside him, rubbing her hand. She's holding a sandwich. "Swiss cheese. You said you were hungry, not angry."

She's a middle-aged woman, square faced, with heavy eyebrows, dark red, like her hair. He's drunk, aware they're staring at each other. Her eyes are small and very pale blue. She lifts the sandwich to his mouth as if feeding a child. He puts his hand over hers and takes a bite. She doesn't withdraw her hand. She says, "What's your name?"

"Ethan Baum. You have me eating out of your hand."

She smiles and says, "If only. You're going to be teaching here, right? *Jack at Bat* is such a good book. I think someone teaches it here."

This someone is obviously photocopying his long out-of-print first novel and handing it out free. He knows the woman is trying to be nice, but all he can think of is to sue the copyright-infringing bastard. He concentrates on holding her hand and the sandwich. He lifts his hand, her hand, and the sandwich and asks if she wants some. She nods and takes a bite from her end. She holds a finger up to indicate she'll speak after chewing. Ethan finds this charming. Sexy, even, though she's not really pretty and she's pretty old. She swallows and says, "I thought I recognized you. You're so tall and we read together once, in Minneapolis, five or six years ago."

Now he remembers: this is Lucy Evans. She must be at least forty-five, thirteen years older than him. Maybe more. He can see she has a crush. He feels some comfort and a vague distaste. Still, here she is, the big writer on campus. It can't hurt. He says, "I'm a little drunk and you're Lucy Evans, so I can say you're a terrific writer and I'm jealous of your completely deserved success because you write in fire. On fire."

She stares at him and smiles, at her end of the sandwich. They eat from each end until there's not enough left to hold, so they eat around each other's fingers at their mouths. The sandwich drops to bits between their lips. They kiss.

Lucy says, "You're so wonderful looking, you smell like heaven. I'm older than you and don't want to make a fool of myself. But—" They kiss again. She unbuttons the top of his shirt and kisses his chest. She says, "I have to go in now," and leaves him.

Ethan's mouth tastes of Swiss cheese and this stranger's saliva. He thinks why not pursue some happiness? He's drunk, sure, but how well did it go with XHelen his own age, or with Sandy much younger?

He takes a few deep breaths of the cold, piney air and goes inside.

In the entrance hall he picks up bits of conversation from around a corner. He hears "Irish" and "freedom" and "Wolfe Tone." Figuring eighteenth-century Irish history might be as good as any other way to impress his cultural credentials on the University, he steadies himself and enters a lodge-sized living room and says to the group around the fireplace in a voice he hears as too loud: "I heard you speaking of Grattan's Parliament and the 1798 French invasion of Ireland." Good, he's caught their attention. He goes on, "Interesting to speculate, isn't it, that if Wolfe Tone hadn't killed himself in prison..." He stops. He realizes they're looking at him as they would at a six-year-old who insists that he could too sing Schubert *lieder* if you told him what it was.

A woman says, "We were talking about music."

"But the Irish," he says, "Wolfe Tone. Didn't someone mention Wolfe Tone?"

"I was, you see," comes the original voice, from the center of the group, "speaking of tonal freedom in music such as the Gypsy and Irish, in which eccentric overtones aren't shunned, as in classical music. And this is known as 'wolf tones,' though, of course, my friend, originally applied to the organ."

It is Stucic who is speaking, patronizing. Stucic the exile, the immigrant airplane bore, the nobody who has already slithered into the collegial heart of the University. Ethan despises him, says, "Miroslav, my buddy." He pushes through the throng of Stucic worshipers. "Did I tell you about Sandy Milocic, my grad student, my Sandy?"

Before Stucic can answer, Lucy's hand comes onto Ethan's arm and leads him from further humiliation. She's saying, "The best road map for out here is called 'Indian Country.' I'll show it to you, later." She goes to find someone she wants him to meet, and he finds a bar and gets a vodka. Lucy returns and takes him through a series of crowded rooms to someone he hears her say is Dock End. Ethan apologizes for being drunk. She tells him he's perfect.

He's on a sofa beside this Dock End fellow. They get talking about funny names like Dock End and Ethan. Ethan says someone once told him Ethan sounded like a chemical. Dock End says, "I knew someone, man's name was Bobby Jim John Smithers. Called Bobby Jim John for short. Name out of redneck heaven. His kids, legit and otherwise, were called the Smithereens."

Ethan says, "Here are three funny names: *Jack at Bat, Jack Off First*, and *Who's on Second*." Naming his novels makes him feel less drunk.

Dock End says, "Who's on first."

Ethan says "Not on the cover of my third and seemingly last novel, he's not."

Dock End says, "I see: jack off, first." His big face drops its grin. "Had you slotted into conventional Abbot and Costello wisdom. Yuh, by way of the perils of slottism, get this: Years back, doing my residency in Boston, I had a breakdown, big time. One day, this beauty comes to visit me in the bughouse. I was amazed. For three years I'd tried to date this woman, with perfect unsuccess. So after half an hour of small talk and silence, she asks if there's anything she can do for me. And in my what-the-hell craziness I say, 'Yuh, you could fuck my brains out.' And she does, just like that, right there in my broom closet of a room. And other times in the actual broom closet down the hall, and, once, behind the torn curtains of the wreck room while the other inmates digested their afternoon Thorazine and TV. She did it everywhere with me: behind the bushes on the hospital grounds, on the steel table in the kitchen where it smelled like stale tomato soup. What a woman! I fell in love. I got better. But then, when I left the hospital, she wouldn't look at me, wouldn't answer my phone-calls. I got worse again and went back into the nuthouse. And, yuh, bingo, she goes back to being my insatiable visitor. This time, knowing what to expect, when I got out, I stayed out. I never saw her again. Strange. I can't figure it, except she was nuttier than I was, or maybe it was the race thing."

"Because you're oriental."

Dock End laughs. "Maybe thirty thousand years ago. I'm Navajo."

Lucy appears from the crowd and squats before them, a hand on each man's knee. "Isn't Doc N great? He's legendary: a doctor, a psychiatrist, a great social healer. You'll be friends." She bangs their knees together.

Ethan doesn't find her attractive now, though, looking up her dress as she squats, he sees her legs are nice. Maybe she's the opposite of the woman in Doc N's story—only able to make love in public. He realizes how he's misheard and says, "Oh, Doc N, N, Doctor Navajo."

"John Wauneka, but, yuh, Doc N."

Lucy says, "I think the 'Indian Country' map must be in the car. It's a good one, isn't it, Doc?"

Doc N says, "Yuh. Especially if you're looking for all the worst, most waterless land out here. The Anglo term for it is 'Indian Reservation.'"

Lucy takes Ethan with her, but she's instantly pulled away into an impenetrable knot of large people in fancy western dress—cashmeres and silks, and leathers so soft-looking they might be tanned cherub. Ethan is sorry there's no one with him to hear "tanned cherub." At another bar he gets another vodka and wanders out to a vast back deck that looks towards a forested hillside across a canyon. He shivers in the sudden cold and sidles behind two women for a windbreak.

One is saying, "At least Viv Acious is her own chosen name, not like those names, you know, like Caresse. Caresse Crosby, wasn't it? What can be the intention of naming a baby Caresse, for pity's sake, except that she become some man's pet?"

The other woman says, "What if she wanted to be caressed and petted by a woman? What if Viv Acious wanted to change her name to Caresse? I'm Roberta, obviously my father's second-best name for the little Robert he never had. But now it's my woman's name and I own it. Anyhow—we mustn't let Lucy hear us—what about 'Embrace?'"

The first woman says, "Who? Oh my god, is that her Emmy? I assumed it was 'Emily.'"

The other woman sees Ethan and says, "Hi, I'm Roberta Palmer and this is…" Ethan loses the name in the wind.

Roberta says, "And I'll bet you're Ethan Baum."

"Yes."

Roberta says, "Lucy described you to us."

The other woman says, "She said you were tall and very good looking."

Roberta says, "She was right about you being tall. How tall?"

"Six four," he says.

The other woman says, "As for being very good looking, I don't know." She cocks her head. "Maybe a lopsided Gary Cooper."

Roberta says, "Cooper as painted by Francis Bacon."

The other woman says, "Or Cooper and a bit of Montgomery Clift."

"Clift after the car crash," Roberta says.

Ethan says, "Ha-ha."

Roberta says, "Oh, look, the poor boy doesn't like being teased. We're only joking, poor boy."

Ethan says, "Are you at the University?"

Roberta says, "No, I'm a judge."

The other one says, "I do inner city stuff."

He says, "But this is a University party?"

Roberta says, "Definitely. Everyone is here."

The other woman says, "Except Carlos."

Roberta says, "This is far too minor an event for Carlos."

Ethan says, "Is he the President?"

The other woman says, "No, he's a satanic presence."

Roberta says, "Or angelic, depending. Carlos Alvarado is Vice President and Special Advisor to President Klotz. President Klotz smiles. Carlos raises the money."

The other woman says, "Carlos raises the stakes. Lucy says she's finding a map for you."

Ethan says, "She must think I'm lost."

Roberta touches his arm: "I hope you're not lost. Lucy's smitten with you, Ethan."

"Really?" He can think of nothing else to say.

"In my judgment, yes. And I'm a judge."

The other woman says, "Be kind to Lucy."

Roberta says, "We all love Lucy."

Ethan smiles and moves away from this uncomfortable conversation. He wanders the very large, crowded house and gets another drink. He looks at old Navajo rugs and kachina dolls, at signed Charles Lavery photos of a desert. He finds himself in a library, desperate to pee. He scouts around, but all the bathrooms are occupied. He retires to the empty library. Soft light comes from behind the ceiling of arched beams. He thinks of an overturned ship's hull. Through an open window, he hears the splashing of running water, a waterfall. He takes a wide-mouthed jar from the library table. It's obviously decorative, some sort of art deco design on it, but he can wash it when a bathroom comes vacant. He turns to the window and pees.

A man's voice, behind him, says, "The Great Leviathan that maketh the seas to seethe like boiling pan."

Ethan gets the message but can no way cease seething.

"Avast!" Then, directly behind him, "Hey, knock that off!"

Now able to comply, Ethan zips up and turns to the man with the nautical vocabulary. "I knew it wasn't a chamber pot, but I didn't want to piss on the floor."

"You should have. You've just pissed into a perfect, twelfth century bowl from Chaco Canyon." The man is tall and bony, with gray-blond hair and a lined face. A lined, angry face.

Ethan says, "It's not very smart to leave something like this around at a party."

"It's always around at parties, but no one before you has had the wit to piss in it. It's part of this collection of Anasazi and old Acoma pottery. My collection. I'm Will Dixon. Your host, sir."

Ethan sees niches in the bookshelves with spot-lit jars and bowls. "Damn, I am sorry I peed in your collected pot." He sets the jar on the table. "Or should I—"

"Just leave it."

Ethan asks, "What was that Leviathan business?"

"From Melville's glossary to *Moby Dick*. The room you're in has probably the best collection of Melvilliana outside the Library of Congress. I teach Melville at the University. Behind my back they call me 'Moby Dixon,' jealous little assholes. And who are you?"

Ethan thinks of saying "drunk," thinks of saying "potted appearances to the contrary." He manages, "Spotted appurtenance to the contrary, I mean, I'm a little bombed, here. Ethan Bombed. Baum. Bummed out, here to teach a Comp Cult, that's Comparative Culture course in the Honors Program on an intensely dinky year's contract. Still, it got me away from Boston and the Eastern Skiboard. Whoosh."

A smile appears on Dixon's face: "You owe me one for that pot business, Ethan. Come on into the *sanctum sanctorum* and have a drink with me. I keep the good stuff there."

He follows Dixon through a door of bookshelves into a study. An armchair and sofa flank a window looking out to the canyon. Dixon waives him into the armchair and says, "I have some fifty-year-old tequila here. Okay?"

Ethan does not love things so Mexican, but he nods. He won't be surprised if the man hands it to him in the only glass left from Hernando de Soto's expedition. He takes the snifter and puts his face into it. It smells of bad dreams from Mexico. He toasts: "Nice party, Will."

Dixon sits back on the sofa, drinks deep from his own snifter and smacks his lips. "Bunch of jerks and jerkoffs, for the most part."

Ethan says, "I met nice people. Doc N and a judge, Roberta."

"Goddamned socialist Indian. As for Roberta Palmer, she's a stupid cunt. Bleeding heart who gives killers probation and thieves citations of merit. My wife's dear friends, both. You married, young man?"

"Divorced."

"Stay that way. This is my fourth marriage. It's a goddamned bad habit I can't break. Not, I have to say, that I much liked seeing you play kissy-kissy with my wife on our front doorstep."

Ethan decides it's best to finish off the priceless tequila. A mistake. Dixon immediately re-pours both snifters. Ethan begins his apology: "I'm sorry—"

Dixon interrupts, "But then, given the choice, I think perhaps I'd rather you fucked my wife on the front steps then pissed in that pot. Do you have any idea what the pot is worth?"

Ethan sets the drink down on the coffee table between them and says, "To collectors or to Indians?"

"Oh, Jesus, not another guilty liberal from back East. Okay, let's forget it, Ethan. This is a party and I want us to be friends and be festive. Girls. Let's talk about girls. Do you like girls?"

"Girls."

"Yes. No, not old bags like Lucy. Girls, Ethan. Young girls."

Ethan feels a bitter comfort in talking with someone he's wronged twice before meeting and to whom he's taken an immediate and deep dislike. He says, "Yes. I unfortunately liked one a lot. Sandy. It went bad. Maybe she was too young. I don't know."

"How old? How old?"

"Twenty-one, when we met."

"No, no, no. I mean young girls."

"Like teenagers?"

"Like *young* teenagers, Ethan. Younger."

"No. Not my style, Will."

Dixon goes to a desk drawer: "Don't knock what you haven't tried." He holds a photo at Ethan's face. "Better than a pot, I promise."

The photo shows two clothed men urinating into the mouths of two barely pubescent naked girls whose arms are tied with rope.

Ethan says, "Not for me," and gets up. Dixon pushes him back into the chair and shows another photograph. Ethan looks away, but not soon enough to avoid seeing a little girl, of eleven or so, in pain, anally penetrated. The man is Dixon.

Dixon says. "Don't like it? Poor you. Well I don't like you pissing in my pot or kissing my wife. Now if you'd pissed in my wife and—"

Ethan jumps up. His shoulder grazes Dixon's cheek. Dixon shouts, "How the fuck dare you!" and slaps Ethan's face. Ethan twists away, cheek and eye burning. Something about Dixon's smile reminds him of a Mexican policeman. Ethan's right fist draws back defensively as he tries to move past Dixon, but Dixon's arm is drawing back to punch. Ethan steps forward on his right foot and swings his fist into Dixon's smile. He hits high and can feel Dixon's nose at his fist, bending; he hears the sharp crack and feels Dixon's cheekbone and eye socket at his knuckles. Dixon is falling back over the coffee table and onto the sofa as Ethan gets away.

He walks through the party, and when he sees Doc N he tells him he's had a fight with Dixon and thinks Doc N should check the study. Ethan walks out and someone going back to town gives him a lift. He falls into the seat and is woken at his motel. When he drops onto his bed, he has no memory of where he's been.

He wakes before dawn feeling weak as the proverbial child, the kitten, the limp dishrag. He's sick in the bathroom. He throws water on his face, strips off his clothes and falls back on the bed. He wakes to a cracking sound in his head. Someone is knocking at the door. The knocking stops.

Someone is in the room. He doesn't care: he's too drunk and weak to keep from being robbed. The bedsprings shift. Mexico: he doesn't want to be murdered in his bed. A hand comes down over his mouth.

"Shh. Shh."

He opens his eyes. There is, he finds, no need for hushing since he is speechless. Lucy Evans is kneeling over him, naked, and neither child, nor kitten, nor dishrag. She says, "I'm sure Will had it coming to him. He's such an awful drunk."

Ethan remembers. He says, "You don't mind?"

"No. His nose is broken, but that's not the problem."

Ethan says, "That's not? What is?"

"You couldn't have known, poor darling. The party was to celebrate Will's just becoming Chair of your Honors Program. But don't think of that now. You are such a beautiful darling. You know that, don't you?"

Ethan has nothing to utter, other than a sigh. He finds, as Lucy's arms and breasts and long, strong legs stretch over him, that he's becoming more mature, unkittenish, and not very limp at all.

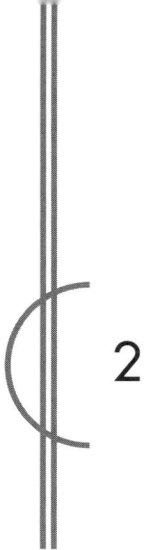

2

HIS EYES OPEN. His ears ring. It's the telephone. Lucy's smell is still in his bed, yet the entire night is unbelievable. He picks up the phone.

"Ethan? It's seven-thirty your time. I wanted to make sure I caught you. You said you'd call when you arrived. I've been thinking about my funeral."

Ethan says, "Good morning, Meyer," to his father, the philosopher Meyer Baum, who occasionally revises the details of his funeral. Ethan sighs, without thinking why.

His father continues: "Small, I'm thinking now, by invitation only. Even family. Especially family by invitation only."

Ethan says, "Will I be among the invited?"

"Who do you imagine will send the invitations? I'm thinking small not only because throwing the funeral open would give so many people the opportunity of not attending, but also to reduce the chance that the wrong grouping would turn up and that the Meyer Baum they'd—what's the word, here, Ethan: evoke, concoct, apostrophize, effigize—is there a verb from effigy—would be so little like how I see myself as to be grotesque. Worse, slightly farcical. And I mean regardless if this concoction were better or worse than the so-called 'real' me. Why didn't you call?"

Because of this, thinks Ethan, because you haven't said hello or asked how I am, because... He says, "I had a strange night. One minute there was a full moon, the next, there was no moon. Yet the sky was cloudless. That's something about out here, the clear night."

"Another thing is the eclipse of the moon last night, especially visible in the southwest."

27

"Thank you for clearing that up, Meyer. You've restored my faith in my vision." Their conversations are often tests of wit, paradox, and allusion. Illusion, he thinks.

Meyer says, "How about your vision of the rightness of your move out there?"

Ethan remembers the party, the debacle of decking his boss. "It was right. It is, absolutely. As a matter of fact, Meyer, I have to get ready for an appointment with my boss. I promise to call soon." He puts the phone down thinking my dear, feared, famous father.

After a cold shower, several bottles of water, and two black coffees, Ethan feels able to make his appointment at the Honors Program office. The assistant says, "Dr. Dixon is expecting you," in a perfectly neutral way, encouraging Ethan to believe it will only be a matter of apologizing and then getting on with his new life.

Honors Program Chairperson Dixon sits behind his desk. Where his nose used to be there is a casket-shaped cast. Ethan can't help finding it odd that though the sound of Dixon's voice is what anyone would call speaking through his nose, that organ, so encased, is completely incapable of such activity.

"Bister Bomb, I dote wish to dough *why* you broke by doze."

Shocked, Ethan forgets his very good reasons, recalls only Dixon's naked wife moving on him. He says, "I'm so sorry. So very sorry." He sounds to himself like Tokyo Joe in the war films, thinks he may even have said "solly."

"Be that as it bay, you caddot work here. Our legal officer tells be we have *bore* thad apple cause to break our codtract. Udder the circubstadces, I'b being kide dot to press charges. Good bordig."

Ethan sees it will be Dixon's word against his. He has to think of something brilliant. He comes up with, "You hit me first."

Dixon says, "Out," and Ethan leaves.

He sits on a bench. He's been fired before starting his job. And nothing could have been more infantile than his "You hit me first," except perhaps to have burst out crying. The idea is so preposterous that he bursts out crying. Then he notices how quickly the tears disappear in the dry southwestern air. He laughs: there is something hilarious in being so loosed from all he knows, from any expectation.

Yet it's too disorienting. So he resorts to talking to XHelen in his head, rationalizing that it might not be so bad to have been fired, that is, to have been finally, if forcibly, weaned from alma mater. How is he not to set his standard against XHelen's after their exasperated years? They were too young, too reactive. He shuts his eyes against the hard morning sun. Not, he thinks, that he doesn't respect and even admire his ex-wife, though in ways that grow ever more abstract.

His father pointed out—probably after Meyer's last bout of Derrida—that Ethan's divorced name for her, XHelen, was very close to "exhaling," but that far from signaling an expelling-from-himself-as-respiratory-waste-product, the metaphorical ideal actually contained its deeper obverse: to exhale necessarily required to inhale, to inhale her. Breathing being perpetual, XHelen was therefore the *signature* of Ethan's breath, synonymous with his life itself. *Ergo*, Ethan actually wanted to get back together with Helen.

Ethan remembers countering to the effect that eating was also necessary for life. Had he renamed Helen the waste product of that process, would Meyer argue that his life-itself's signature was *doodie*?

At which, Meyer noted that he hadn't; he'd chosen exhaling.

At which, Ethan said that, no, what he'd actually chosen was XHelen, as in Helen his ex-wife, for heaven's sake.

He doesn't like thinking of old arguments with his father. He returns to thoughts of respect and admiration for Helen as a painter, what he thinks of as the Pollock–Miro paradigm. It goes like this. Eight or nine years ago, when they're twenty-four, Helen becomes fascinated with Jackson Pollock. She buys books of his paintings but says the colors aren't right, and there's not enough indication of texture or density. Deciding she has to photograph some Pollock paintings herself, but knowing little about photography, she takes a three-month intensive color photography course at the Boston Museum School and sets up a color darkroom in a corner of her studio.

Her studio is this big industrial shed in, of all places, classy Lexington, just beside Route 128. It's on the property of a dark-glass biotech outfit called Haemotics, which has some corner of the hemoglobin market to itself. Helen calls it Blood Lust. Ethan suspects she's stolen the name from him. She has this studio courtesy of her father, Van Van Leyden, who, by some tax quirk of his palmy days in industrial real estate, has been able to give her its lease. And the owners of Haemotics for some reason—taxes, or PR, or probably because they're two nice brothers from Braintree who collect Helen's work, named Alex and George Goulatis (the artificial blood counts, the hemogoblins, thinks Ethan but keeps these to himself) never pick up their option to annex the studio.

So Helen, using friendships, contacts, charms—Ethan isn't saying to himself she's without any of these—gets to set up her lighting and large-format Hasselblad to photograph the two Pollock action paintings she's chosen, one in a New York museum, the other in a private collection outside Chicago. Then, over six months into the project, she begins making blow-ups of her photographs. After another six months, the photos are reproduced in hundreds of sections, two-foot square, making up two giant composites, seventy foot by twenty foot.

Then, for maybe another six months, Helen focuses on one or two of the small sections from each painting, transferring their images in a process she works on in a Watertown print lab. This results in four huge sheets, thirty by twenty foot, hung two each across the long sides of her studio. What happens in the following six months, Ethan learns only from the few words she says about it and two visits—not invitations but the two times when Helen's car is being serviced and he goes to pick her up, and, curious, arrives early. He looks in through the small wire window in the door. Helen is pacing back and forth in front of one of the big prints. She frowns, she lights another cigarette, she stops, she walks up to the three-foot orange blob with its ten-foot tail, and she stares. She stares, blowing smoke from her nose and mouth like a small dragon in trouble. The second time he comes, there's smoke even without the cigarette, on a bone freezing, black February afternoon, the impotent heat blowers either end of the studio only accentuating the cold. Helen is wearing three or four very long sweaters, originally elegant, their stained and shredded mohairs and alpacas unraveled at her wrists, elbows, and hips. From time to time, before a particular blob of color, which to Ethan's eyes is no more than a photo dot magnified as in a dream of elephantiasis, Helen's empty right hand begins to move, making brushstrokes on the canvas of pure air beside her. Then she exhales, water vapor or Marlboro, and her already knotted brow furrows deeper into whatever work—and he can see it is hard work—is going on inside there.

How can he, shivering at the window, help being in love again with Helen as he witnesses her courage to go alone out of the known and over the edge, the only place the really big fish swim? Eventually, because his ears and ass are burning cold and wake him to the rush-hour roar of Route 128 traffic down behind him, Ethan walks in. Helen switches into her "Let's go—Where've you been—I'm freezing—Let's get out of here" mode.

In the car, Ethan tries to work up the naturalness to tell her he's been moved by her work and loves her.

She says, "Start the car. I'm freezing."

He says, "Lee Krasner."

She says, "What about her?"

He says, "That's who you reminded me of, in there, wed to Pollock as you are. How you smoke, too. Wasn't it the way she smoked and smoked, they both did, and always asking if what they were doing worked? Worked, my god, how you worked."

Maybe there's not enough love in his voice, because she says, "Were you standing out there watching me? What did you think, that I didn't work? That what I did out here was, what, like sneak off to the de Cordoba or over to look at the Minuteman Statue?"

Then he says something back and it's all gone.

At any rate, only then, over two and a half years into the project, is Helen ready to start painting. Ethan gets to see her work in this phase because, from time to time, with all the grace a paranoid workaholic can muster, she invites him to the studio: "If you aren't doing anything better, you can come over to see what I'm doing. But only if you want, and, whatever you think, no comments. Bad or good, no comments. Okay?"

He goes to the studio. What she's doing is three large canvases, and it's here that Miró comes in. Ethan's reaction is deeply disappointed amusement, he's sorry to say, though he plays fair and says nothing. What has begun from a fanatical focus on the tiniest sperm-sized splatters of Jackson Pollock has turned, through Helen's hands, into gigantic Miró amoebas, nothing much more. Helen, always wise in her work, sees his smile and says, "I know what you're thinking, but they won't end up looking like this."

He says, "Like what?"

She says, "You know, so stupidly Joan Miró."

And she's right. The next time Ethan visits, months later on a steamy, late September day, the shapes appear thickened by many layers of paint. No longer like Miró, though with the same general outlines, they make him want to duck, so near are they to exploding off the canvas. Another effect is their pathetic, yet revolting force-fed quality.

She says, "Okay, you can say something. Short."

He says, "Sick. Thick. Threatening."

She gets the compliment and smiles at the canvas they're facing. Helen is barefoot, only in wine-colored, silky boxing shorts. Her small breasts are sweaty. She hugs herself and her bony shoulders curve like wings. He wants to touch her but feels it would disrupt her pleasure.

The next time he sees them, the paintings are finished. The shapes, in red and orange and light greeny blue, are now chipped, striated, scraped—"strafed" is what he thinks. The effects of these layers and levels, pinks and whites appearing through the red and orange, is astonishing. The huge, scarred shapes of color have become nothing less than human—full of feeling and ignorance, knowing and neurotic. After some time standing before them—Helen has brought them home and the three canvases fill all the open-plan first floor—Ethan backs onto the sofa, staring. When he looks away, he finds he's still staring in his mind. Then Helen paints two more, very quickly, the strangest of all. They're like full-scale portraits of the other paintings; two in one, one in the other. These are portraits which take nothing for granted, which—and if it sounds weird, it's pretty much what the *Art in America* critic writes later—Ethan feels show the original three paintings in all their vanity and grace and viciousness, especially the one entitled "Double Portrait," with its crippling, brave loneliness.

It takes Helen four and a half years to produce these five paintings. By this time, the marriage is essentially finished. Helen for these years is impossible to be with. This is mostly a literal statement: she's mostly away from home. Maddening yet admirable. Entirely maddening is that this same damn-anything-or-anyone-who-interferes-with-my-work painter is, away from her art, the most boringly conventional person in—you name it—in dress, food, décor, in social thought. This tattered, sweaty muse is in everyday life the uptight Bonwit-Teller-for-brains "Oh, god, not politics again!" Helen. Is XHelen at whom Ethan rages, "Let us for sanity and the fuck's sake just switch the house and studio. Then you could honestly say you live in fucking Lexington and only work in Somerville." To which XHelen says, "There's no need to swear."

Sitting jobless on the bench in the middle of the shining University campus, Ethan is aware that his head arguments with Helen are an attempt to hold on to Boston. He even considers that he might get his teaching job back at Thoreau College. But he will not slink back to Boston. He will give this place a try. He needs work and somewhere to live. He thinks of the Indian Chief Motel and decides to first look for a place to live. And he will not call Lucy Evans for help. Not, at least, for a place to live.

Two days later, by working hard with a realtor, that is, by working hard against the realtor and the higher-priced and horrible condos she tries to rent him ("But, Ethan, this is brand new, and it has a communal pool and putting green, and it's almost *on top* of two good malls.") he holds the keys to 17 Copper Place, a few blocks south of Central near the university. It's over a bike shop storeroom, the second floor of a two-story adobe style building: one large room of long windows with kitchen and dining bar, and off it a small bedroom and bathroom. After calling the Boston moving company to ship his books, pictures, and few bits of furniture, he sits by the motel room telephone in the afternoon realizing he's counted on the University job to find friends. There is Stucic, of course, but his pride rejects chasing after him, like being the displaced person's displaced person. Which leaves crazy Lucy Evans. Crazy, old Lucy Evans. Was she, he wonders, good in bed? She was certainly active, proactive in bed, but he can't remember his feelings. Nevertheless, he remembers her ankles and legs. He shouldn't be so harsh. She was friendly: she left her card on his bedside table two days ago. She's there at her University number.

"Lucy, it's Ethan. I should have called sooner. I've been busy sorting things out, like what I'm going to do and where I'm going to live."

She says, "I wanted to call you. But I didn't want to scare you off. I've been trying to get Will to change his mind about your job. But I couldn't. I told him how I felt about you, but that didn't work."

Ethan says, "That we made love after I broke his nose didn't make him want to re-hire me?"

She says, "You remembered. About us, I mean."

"Of course." He sees Lucy rafting across the current of his conversation. He tells her of his decision to stay, of finding an apartment, of his idea for running a fiction-writing workshop to make some money.

Lucy says, "You're staying. That's wonderful. I know it's not because of me. It's because you can't go back. Besides, I'm sure I scare you a little."

Ethan says, "More than a little, which isn't to say I don't like you."

She says, "Ah, a double-negative declaration that you like me a little. Would you think I was throwing myself at you if we met this evening for a drink?"

Ethan says, "Throw away."

Lucy says, "I won't be so scary. For one thing, you couldn't have known how finished my marriage to Will has been for some time."

After the call, having agreed to meet at a hotel bar downtown, he thinks this might be a big mistake, what Hemingway said about never waking up in bed with someone crazier than yourself. Then he thinks what could be crazier than Hemingway on women? Or could this be what XHelen called his "insatiable need to charm"?

He lies back on his broken mattress, remembering that this belief of Helen's is the example he's given his father of how infinitely irreconcilable they are, to Meyer's last minute appeal, the night before Ethan leaves Boston, that he might still be reconciled with Helen. Divorce has proven deeply disturbing to his father. They're in the large living room of Meyer's apartment off Beacon Street in Brookline, having just returned from what they call a "toofer" dinner—two lobsters for the price of one—at the Shamrock Tavern in Allston. They do this together, hunt out the toofer ads for bars, grills and taverns in the Boston area, and go once every week or two during the past ten of the sixteen years since the death of Ethan's mother, Marion. It isn't the bargain per se: they figure that with the time and travel spent on a Tuesday night toofer at Angelo's Café in Brockton or at the Sunday night Seafood Ceilidh at John Ryan's in Haverhill, they may as economically go lobstering at Lockober's. Not the point. It is their ritual time together. Helen had gone with them twice before suggesting it might be nicer for Ethan to go on his own with Meyer. Which it is, as well as not being her thing, her thing being more the lobster Savannah at Lockober's.

Ethan's shoes and socks are off: he toes the Persian carpet's tree of life on its wine-red ground. Meyer pours a cognac for his only child and takes a soda water for himself. He sits in his reading chair, turns the lamp to low, and says he's never understood Ethan's aversion to argument. "You were raised in a home where argument was honored."

"Worshipped," Ethan says.

"I trust not," says his father, philosopher and atheist by profession. Meyer regards his cordovans and lifts his shoulders.

Ethan notices how scrawny his handsome father has come to look, doing this: a turtle retracting its head, drawing attention to its thin, ropy neck.

"Your mother and I enjoyed argument. We engaged in it seriously but never with rancor. It was a stimulus for our minds and our bodies. It refreshed us. One could say argument was our countryside. Sometimes, afterwards…" Meyer stops and looks into his glass.

Ethan envies him. His own years of argument with XHelen have been consistently banal and vicious. Nor leading to any sexy afterwards.

This reminds him of his date with Lucy. Lucid or goosey, she'll be his first actual date—he can't count the other night's drunken tumult—since his breakup with Sandy, months before, in early spring. So, he thinks, shaving and showering, how should he act with an older woman? Easy, act younger. He remembers hearing at the party that she has a daughter. Dixon's, he guesses. Dressing, he reasons that his bad luck in losing his job is offset by this sudden—lover? protector? mother? He feels elated in not having a clue. His new life is certainly news to him.

He somehow arrives at the hotel half an hour late and walks through its ordinary hallway into a central Spanish courtyard, complete with plashing stone fountain, banked flowers, and Lucy at the mirrored bar, turning to smile at him. She's in a tight, flowered dress, and her long, good looking legs re-cross as she turns. What follows is not seduction, neither of them requiring leading on or drawing out, both already so ductile.

They say Hi. He says he's sorry he's late and orders vodka. Everything he says and does seems trite yet thrilling. He's looking at what they look like in the mirrors. He says his apartment in Copper Place could do for a writing workshop. She says she knows it. It used to be a coffee shop with poetry readings. She went once. It was awful. The poetry, she means. She says she'll get him a rug as a house warming. He says it should be ready to move into, just, by Saturday or Sunday.

She says maybe he shouldn't run workshops where he lives. He says he has the keys to the apartment and maybe she's his new alma mater. He knows he's parodying the dialogue in her novels. An instinct to tease her. She says, "You have the keys."

When she says this, he puts money on the bar for the drink that hasn't yet been served and they leave. They wait for her car to be brought around. She says that this was Hilton's first hotel. Her dirty, white SUV pulls up. She puts money in the valet's hand and tells Ethan to drive. And giving him road directions, and with the valet still touching his cap to them in the rearview mirror, she leans over the console and undoes his trousers.

There isn't a great deal of traffic at seven-thirty of a mid-July weekday evening at the edge of downtown Albuquerque, but neither traffic jam nor SUV of clearest plexiglass could have stopped them. At Copper Place, they fall up the stairs, through the door, and onto the floor, his trousers down, her flowered dress bunched to bouquets up at her waist. In her orgasm she moans deep and loud, and her head arches back to show her neck shining with sweat in the streetlight through the windows. Ethan doesn't come; something will not let him loose. They fall back alongside each other, her head on his arm. Oblongs of light fall on the floorboards.

Lucy says, "Once, just after marrying Will, I panicked and had a short affair. This is nothing like that. You smell so, so good." She buries her face under his arm. Shadows of windowpanes move on the damp red ropes of her hair. She's murmuring, "You will, you will." He assumes she means he'll come, but he hears it as "You, Will, you, Will."

Then, the sweat drying on his chest, because he knows he should say something but can't say he loves her, he says, "Is your daughter angry about me hitting her father?"

"Oh, no. She's not Will's. She's the daughter of my first husband, Perry. He died. Emmy doesn't like Will." Lucy stretches out on top of him. She says, "The night of the party, the minute I saw you there on the front steps with your long legs stretched out... You were staring off somewhere. You were something. You looked like a lost heron, so beautiful..."

His looks, he thinks, his looks that he can't take seriously yet expects women to notice.

She says, "I never did this before, falling for someone at first sight. I wish I had more hair down here for you. I think lots of hair down here is lovely in a woman."

He has to say something.

She says, "And I know I'm old for you. Forty-six. But I was so wet.... Not for years."

Ethan pulls her head down to his and says, "Old isn't so wet." He hopes it sounds gallant

Lucy turns her body head to foot on top of him, saying, "Do you really like my—" He hears "ooks" as her head moves between his legs, so that he answers "Yes" into where she wishes more hair, unsure if the question is her looks or her books.

Again they make love, and again his final pleasure is in her long moaning. Afterwards, feeling the floorboards in his back, he's uneasy with Lucy's sudden confession of marital infidelity. Perhaps it's his resentment at not coming; perhaps it's his unwillingness to share an intimacy not purely physical.

She says, "You were married to Helen Van Leyden the painter. How long have you been divorced?"

"Separated four years, divorced three. We married way too young and had too much success too early. I think I was more affected by it than Helen. Then Helen withdrew for years and came out an even better painter, but I was stalled after my last novel, am still stalled. Maybe I haven't been able to grow up."

Lucy says, "But your character Jack Fisher was starting to grow up at the end of *Who's on Second*."

Ethan says, "It could be I've come out here to try and catch up with him. To step out of those shadows…"

Lucy says, "You've come to the right place. It's all bright sunshine here."

He turns on his side and looks at her. "Really?"

"No," she shakes her head, "of course it's as dark as anywhere else. But it's not back there. Not Boston for you or Butte, Montana, for me." Later, dressing, she says, "What exactly happened between Will and you at the party, I mean besides you peeing in his precious bowl?"

Ethan says, "He said he saw us kissing on the steps. I know you said the marriage was gone, but I guess he felt that it was his house—"

"My house, actually," she says.

"Yes. And we were drunk." He's not going to mention the child pornography, not so much because he doesn't want to shock Lucy, should she not know about it, but because it might involve him in her private life more than he wants. He says, offering emotional recompense, "What I just told you about my marriage and myself in Boston, I've never told anyone before, not even myself."

She smiles and says, "That's good. I like that. I can come back here on Sunday and help you fix the place up. And mess it up some."

At the motel, just as he's falling asleep, Ethan realizes that what he's told Lucy about not having talked about these things before is, surprisingly, the truth.

By Sunday afternoon, when Lucy comes to Copper Place, he's bought a used red Jeep Cherokee, and the apartment has a stocked kitchen, stools at the dining bar, and a bed with linen. She looks around and drops a large package by the door. "You're going to be all right, here," she says. "You're going to be king of the castle."

Lucy sits on a stool and her jeans move up her legs. He definitely likes her ankles. He's going to hold on to that. He stands beside her and strokes the back of her neck.

She says, "Remember I told you the house was mine? My first husband, Perry, inherited mining money. He died in a climbing accident, two years after we were divorced. But he left me the house and Emmy got a trust fund. I don't care about that big house. I'm staying at my friend Roberta's until the University finds me something. I don't want the big house to screw us up, Ethan. Maybe something else will."

Ethan says, "No," and thinks of her ankles.

"Anyway," Lucy says, "you'll come." She then explains in mythophallic detail how. In her telling, there are flash floods in which they save themselves by surfing on breakers of his sperm. She kisses him and unwraps the package. "My housewarming present," she says, rolling out a Navajo rug. It's in black, gray, and brown on faded white. Two black-outlined brown triangles are at its center. It is simple and startling. "Two Gray Hills," she says, "from the nineteen-twenties. Do you like it?"

"It's wonderful," he says, "and beautiful of you to give it." He senses that accepting such a gift is careless of him, because he'll never be able to give her what she wants of him. He doesn't want to name what that is, yet he feels more tenderness for Lucy because of this unspoken, future wrong. They undress and sit cross-legged on the rug like Indians, and they stroke each other's face. He sees lines around her eyes and mouth he hasn't before noticed. As they begin to touch each other's body with their fingertips, Ethan thinks of the stiff-legged, slightly splayed way in which Meyer has recently been walking, who has been forever lean and lithe. He feels bad to have had to move so far from his dear, despised father, almost eighty now, an old father, forty-six when he was born—exactly Lucy's age.

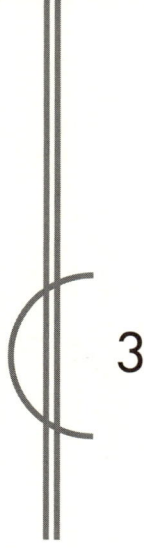

3

TWO WEEKS LATER, in the hot afternoon, Ethan is walking with Doc N from a community center classroom to Doc's office on Yale Boulevard. At Lucy's urging, Doc has found Ethan this cut-price classroom for his workshops. Ethan, having remembered the instantly friendly and funny man from the party, has to re-adjust to this taciturn Doc N too busy to give him time, other than on this exercise walk back to his work.

Doc turns them off the avenue through an open gate marked Fairview Park.

"A short cut?"

"No, but there's some shade and it gets whatever breeze is going."

Ethan has learned to wear his Red Sox cap and long sleeved shirts in the southwestern afternoons. The park is an old unkempt cemetery. Avenues of spruce and cottonwood stand in brown, knee-high grass. There's enough open space to give a view of the mountains. Ethan says, "I haven't been out of town yet."

Doc N doesn't respond. They pass skewed headstones in weedy plots. Minutes later, Doc N says, "Your first time here?"

"No," Ethan says, "I was here once, years ago, with my ex-wife. One of those see-everything trips: Arizona and New Mexico—the Grand Canyon, Navajo country, Canyon de Chelly. Very beautiful." He wonders if this sounds callous. He adds, "But you could see how poor it was."

"Poor," Doc N repeats. Ethan can't make out any feeling in his voice. They're walking between gravestones whose inscriptions are mostly weathered away. A few hundred yards on, Doc N says "What you can't see on the rez from your car window are the dependencies, the alcoholism and self-loathing. Pandemic diabetes, TB, even some plague. Tribal leaders owned by the BIA—Bureau of Indian Affairs—Our White Father who art within the Beltway. Yuh."

Everything has been said without emotion but the last word, "yuh," sounding from somewhere deep in Doc's barrel torso. Ethan decides to stick with aesthetics. "Canyon de Chelly is about the most beautiful place I've ever seen."

Doc N bends to the path and scoops a fist of gravel without breaking step. With his thumb, he flicks a pebble at the gnarl of a cottonwood trunk. He says, "We only met once, drunk at that party. I don't know you, so excuse me for saying yes, Canyon de Chelly is beautiful and you've been there and read the guidebooks and had the tour, and you don't know shit about Canyon de Chelly."

"Really," says Ethan, slightly shocked. "What don't I know?"

Doc N looks at his watch. "I guess I have ten minutes. You got the classroom because Lucy asked me and I owe her. She's put good things the way of the rez, so I'll give you my standard intro to the real history of Indians for Anglos. When the Civil War came, the Navajos and other Indians took advantage of white soldiers fighting each other to get back some of the lands stolen from them. Not all Navajos, just some bands. Navajos didn't have centralized political traditions like some other large tribes."

Ethan says, "Oh," but he knows this.

Doc N says, "Truth was, the Civil War was the end of Indian hope, because the huge army it organized stayed together after the war to police the westward land-grab."

Ethan knows this, too.

Doc N says, "Towards the end of the war the U.S. government decides there's been enough Indian raiding and recouping lost land out here, and it gets its favorite Indian-killer, Kit Carson, to be in charge. Carson was commissioned into the war under a general called Carleton, and he'd learned his tactics under Sherman. It was Carleton who set up the Fort Sumner death camp."

Doc N flicks another pebble. It clicks off a windswept stone angel. Ethan stays serious-looking, but he's heard it all. Doc says, "So the word goes out for the Navajo to surrender, and some do and some don't. They send the army after these, and one of the bands decides to hide in Canyon de Chelly, thinking maybe it was impregnable from the east, or that no one would think of looking in the old cliff dwellings, or, I don't know, maybe old Spiderwoman would protect them."

Ethan hasn't heard of this.

"And Carson, yuh, sends out a hundred soldiers under a Captain Pfieffer who brings them into the canyon over a trail down its eastern rim. There's a small battle: twenty Indians killed, forty captured, and about two hundred surrender voluntarily. No big deal as battles go, yet after that, all the other rebel bands of Navajo gave themselves up, and all the Navajos are put on the death march to Fort Sumner. All that's now in the history books. Except none of them explain *why* the Canyon de Chelly fight broke the rebellion."

Ethan says, "Maybe the Navajo were essentially peaceful."

Doc N says, "No, we'd been a warrior people. We swept down with the Apaches eight hundred years ago and pushed out the old enemy, the Anasazi. But from the Canyon de Chelly fight we were a broken people and did just what the white man told us to do."

"Why?"

"The burning. After the surrender, Pfieffer did a Sherman—had his men burn Canyon de Chelly: burnt the apple orchards, the pear and plum orchards, burnt the trees, the bushes, the shrubs, the grass. Yuh, burnt every living thing. Hey, Navajos weren't angels: we'd taken land by force and even, way back, taken captives as slaves. But to destroy the land itself was out of our thinking. When word spread that after the battle the white men had burnt the land, we all surrendered. Only demons would destroy the land, their own mother. We couldn't fight demons who didn't have souls."

Doc N flings out pebbles. Ethan looks at a headstone, just able to make out: RICHARD HITCHCOX, 1848–1884. The brown stone has worn so thin it seems the sunlight could pass through. What's Doc N waiting for, his apology? Ethan says, "Some story. More white men beating on Indians."

Doc N says, "It's a story of land. You want to find out about New Mexico, find out about the land. Today it's ripped off by big lobbies buying legislators."

They've come out of the park onto the higher end of the boulevard. Commercial and industrial sites alternate with run-down houses. Signs say: SKWEEKEEKLEEN CARWASH ADULT FILMS MAGS PEEPSHOW

50C BLUEBOY DRESS JEANS MADE HERE FACTORY OUTLET PARKING AT REAR. Doc N points across the street. "My office is in there, the 'Bud' Brandon Mental Health Center, Bernalillo County. The guy Brandon who gave the land and money for the building is a philanthropic gangster. A pal of Carlos Alvarado."

Ethan says. "Who is this Alvarado? Everyone mentions him."

"Like I said," Doc says, "a matter of land. He brings in funding to the University through the Hispanic and state historical institutes he runs, but his power comes from being from an old land grant family. He and his wife both inherited eighteenth-century Spanish royal land grants, over a quarter of a million acres each. Carlos is tight with everyone: mining and logging interests as well as the environmentalists. But maybe all this political stuff bores you."

"On the contrary," says Ethan, not knowing exactly what contrary he means.

They cross the street. Doc says, "The word is, Carlos found it pretty funny that you socked Willy Dixon. Carlos is an old friend of Lucy's, though you probably know that by now."

"No," Ethan says, "but it seems you know about Lucy and me."

Doc N says, "Yes, but not from Lucy. Hey, you've been seeing each other for a couple of weeks now, and this is not really a big city, and the University is one of the biggest employers, and Lucy is one of its stars. Don't let it bother you."

"It doesn't," Ethan says, though it does. He knows he wouldn't be bothered if he liked Lucy more, was in love with her, was crazy about her, was... He says, "Thanks very much for setting up that classroom for me."

Doc N goes to the front door waving goodbye by wiggling his fingers at the back of his cap. It looks like two feathers on a headdress.

Ethan crosses back to the cemetery. The afternoon is beginning to cool from the low hundreds to low nineties. What if he'd just come right out and asked Doc N if, in his professional opinion, Lucy was crazy? He does not like the fact that he and Lucy are an item. In a year and a half with Sandy, he'd lived in a cloud of erotic anonymity worthy of Virgil's Venus. But here, just weeks, just nineteen days after they've met, everyone knows. He imagines a photo of the two of them, entwined and smiling, in the Albuquerque newspaper and, beneath, the caption:

SLEEPING TOGETHER. Professor Meyer Baum, 79, of Brookline, Massachusetts, reluctantly announces the adulterous fornication of his son Ethan, only 32, barely moved in to 17 Copper Place, with considerably older Lucy Evans, famous married, divorced, widowed, remarried writer, of Albuquerque, New Mexico, daughter of May Evans, of Butte, Montana. Mrs. Evans, 83, a homemaker, had no comment on her daughter's immoral union with a man far too young for her, but her pale blue eyes were more watery than usual. Dr. Baum, who continues to be 79, an internationally renowned philosopher at Brandeis University, commented that his son's liaison was, "as the man remarked, undreamt of in his philosophy," and characteristically stretched his neck, recently more scrawny and tortoise-like.

What is he playing at? He doesn't know Lucy's mother's name, or age, or even if she's alive. Why does he care so if people know about them? An easy question, he thinks: Because it will be more embarrassing when he dumps her.

Back at Copper Place, sitting among the unopened crates of his books, he checks the list of places where he still has to distribute his workshop fliers. He decides to do it tomorrow and have an early night, since Lucy's out of town, reading at a writers' conference, something he did when he was a writer. Pure envy, though at the same time, he's grateful for all the help Lucy's giving him in talking up his workshop at the University and in getting him the classroom. So, though he's looking forward to the weekend they've planned to meet at someplace Lucy calls "a hideaway," north of Santa Fe, he's happy for the few days on his own. He has an early supper, returns and unpacks his CD's and tapes, and goes to bed before ten.

    He has a dream. He's hovering cherubically over a map of New Mexico, which is the size of New Mexico. North of Albuquerque, the Rio Grande is filled with ice cubes up to the Colorado border. To the south, the river runs fuming with bergs of dry ice down through unlabeled desert landscape into Texas. He knows it's unlabeled because the Indian Country map he's bought ends at Socorro County, sixty miles south of Albuquerque. He moves north and drops lower:

the ice cubes are entire mountain slopes, with ski lifts. Lucy is skiing in a bright blue parka, naked from the waist down. Her eyes are completely white with reflected snow. She has a big bush of red pubic hair that the rushing wind can't flatten. He rises and floats south. Clouds of freezing mist surround him. He begins to plummet like a lead weight. Streams of freezing wind sear his legs: he, too, is naked below the waist. He can't see what awaits his crash. Then he's in the Rio Grande, but the river is all sand, a warm silt he's able to swim and see through. Pods of white dolphin dip before him. They arch and break the surface in perfect synchronicity that he finds somewhat boring. A boat comes rushing over a vast wrack of cottonwood trees, as if over waterfalls. At its prow, harpoon in hand, stands Moby Dixon. Ethan tries to shout that these are dolphins, not whales, but Dixon harpoons them, and with such terrible force that he pierces six at once. They hang like skewered shrimp. When Ethan opens his mouth to scream, the sand rushes in and chokes him.

He wakes up sweaty, gasping. He's certain his father is dying. He turns on the light. It's three-thirty in the morning, five-thirty in Boston. He'll call later. Not Meyer, he could never confront Meyer so directly. He'll call his father's old friend and doctor, Haskell Perlmutter. This decided, Ethan goes back to an untroubled sleep. In the morning, his premonition seems neurotic, part of his bad dream. He will not give in to homesickness or to fear of the new.

In the next two days, he distributes his workshop fliers and continues to fix up the apartment. By Friday evening, though the books are still in crates, tall bookcases line much of the wall space. He catches himself packing for the weekend and wonders why, since he isn't meeting Lucy until lunch tomorrow, he hasn't waited for the morning to do this. He puts it down to compulsive neatness and lust.

On Saturday, Ethan wakes early and loafs. He finally has the sense of possession. His sheets, his bed, his morning. He picks up his city's newspaper and reads it at his desk, over coffee. Its lead article reminds him of Doc N about the land: it reports the State Legislature moving a bill through committee which will "dramatically relax" logging and mining lease restrictions on state land. He opens the Indian County map and sees there is a great deal of state land. He supposes he's against such a bill being passed. He skims the rest of the paper, takes another cup of coffee and goes out to the deck at the top of the stairs. The sky is a fresh, endless blue, the kind, he tells himself, that might be called halcyon without too much pretension, and he looks out over Copper Place with an air of comfortable possession. As if materialized by his mood, a man walking down the street, carrying a small suitcase, touches his Panama hat up to him. Ethan waves and turns to go in.

"No, hello! Yes, Ethan, no, wait! It is I, Miroslav."

It's Stucic, sweeping off his hat. "I am, good morning, so glad to find you at home, since I did not call. You have, may I ask, not as yet taken breakfast?"

Stucic's improbable dress and demeanor—white hat in hand, suitcase propped on the bottom stair beside his two-tone spectator shoes—and his slightly loopy syntax make Ethan forget his earlier dislike. He calls down that he hasn't had breakfast and asks what Stucic has in mind.

"Ah, wonderful, wonderful. A custom not so much ethnic as Stucic in origin, my own, you see," he says, coming up the stairs, "or shall see, shortly." He sets the suitcase on the deck. It's one of those old leather ones with battered elegance, the kind Ethan occasionally sees coming around on the airport carousel to make him disdain his own clunky petrochemical luggage. As they shake hands, Stucic grips Ethan's forearm and scrutinizes him. "Ah, so you are well, physically, I see. I apologize for not having communicated sooner, but I only this week found your address. I should have better befriended you at the fateful party. Perhaps it would have changed the course of your evening and kept you from the loss of your employment, for which, my real condolences."

Ethan says, "Maybe it was for the best. Come in. I can do toast and coffee or coffee and toast, or we could go out, though I have to leave in about an hour and a half. I see you're going somewhere, too."

"To be perfectly honest..." Stucic puts his suitcase down inside and spreads his arms. "But this is, though small of scale, magnificent. The space, the light, these—I assume—still unpacked books. Ah, and the rug! It is I believe transitional period, Twin Hills of Gray, no? *Une merveille!* And the fireplace, and the balcony from the French windows. You are, I see, as everyone tells me, a most sophisticated fellow. And modest, Ethan. Your novels, I find, have cult status."

"Yes, they're out of print. Where did you find one?"

"Ah, as yet, I have not actually had the time, what with preparing for my teaching and all the settling in, to read for pleasure. May I be permitted?" He points to the kitchen side of the dining bar. Ethan assumes he's looking for an ashtray. "How did you get my address?"

"From the Vice President. Carlos Alvarado is a most remarkable gentleman. He is, I'm certain, one of your fans. But now—" He sets his suitcase on the dining bar and opens it. "Have you a frying pan? Everything else, except coffee and plates is with me. I may please wash my hands?"

Ethan points him to the bathroom and looks into the suitcase. It's full of plastic containers. One is shaped and holds six eggs. He makes out an onion and some peppers. A small bottle of clear liquid in a holder, a loaf of dark bread, a leather knife holder in the top with four knives.

Stucic returns. "As I was saying, the balcony, so charming. I am reminded of our former summer cottage on Hvar, an island off the Dalmatian coast. Yet, as you say of your job, Ethan, perhaps what is gone is best not yearned for. Yes, yes." He sets down Ethan's new chopping board and goes into his suitcase. "I had intended this breakfast for my daughter Elena. I thought, you see, she would appreciate this, a gesture, a memory of home. I say 'gesture,' as you doubtless infer, to indicate a motion on my part of reparation."

"I didn't know your family was here with you."

Stucic selects a thin knife and begins to deftly clean out and slice the red pepper. "Ah, family. Elena was in Albuquerque before me. An intensely independent young woman for whom, alas, our war has had typically disquieting effects, one of which is an alienation from her father. My wife Vera remains at her information technology job in Dallas. We hope her company will soon transfer her to its offices here. But to my morning: I appeared earlier at my daughter's apartment, thinking to surprise her into a breakfast of reconciliation. It was not to be. So I thought, Slava Stucic, don't be a fool and make yourself completely miserable. Nearby lives your new friend Ethan Baum." He looks down at a small green pepper, says, "Aha!" and, drawing a short knife from the suitcase, begins taking small, furious nicks off its skin. "Never mind, *mon vieux; tout va bien.*"

Ethan brings out plates and cutlery. "What does your daughter do here?"

"Elena has been good enough to inform me she has some sort of telephone work. As for details, well, that, of course, might suggest to her an intimacy out of keeping with her breakaway regime." He laughs and chops the onion into bits. "A Yugoslav obsession, one might say. A bowl, please, for the eggs?"

Ethan finds him the bowl. He has the feeling that much of what Stucic says is rehearsed: his statements seem too organized, "Twin Hills of Gray" is just too cute. And he's not smoking, yet there are the nicotine-stained fingers holding the bowl. There's something strange about stopping cold such heavy addiction. Change of identity? Ethan catches himself being melodramatic and unfair. The man is cooking, and thoughtful enough to remember his dislike of smoking from the plane. He says, "You're not smoking."

"Well, it's not done at the university. A good incentive to stop." He finishes beating the eggs and pours some olive oil from a cut-glass bottle out of his case into the pan on the stove. He says, "It is actually difficult as damned hell to give up. But Elena has always disapproved of it, and I thought this might impress her. What fools we are for our children, eh, Ethan?"

"I don't have any."

"Ah, but you're young. You would certainly make an excellent father." He pours the beaten eggs into the pan. The cut red pepper, bits of green chili, and chopped onion are on the board in three neat mounds. "Yes, despite the misery our children can give us, it is we who are civilized by being their parents."

Ethan imagines how completely Meyer would demolish this proposition.

Stucic draws a flat foil packet from the suitcase. "And this," he says, opening it to show its papery, red and white streaks, "is the Dalmatian ham I cut this morning." Stucic spreads the red pepper on the eggs, then the chopped onion, then drops in the chili. He lays on the ham, lifts the pan, folds the eggs over with the spatula, sets the pan back on the stove for a few seconds, lifts it and says, "And now if you will be so good as to take the bread and slice it, *à table*."

Stucic now takes the small bottle of clear liquid and sprinkles some over the eggs, takes a lighter from his pocket and lights it over the pan. Pale blue flames play over the omelet as he halves it and slides the halves on the plates. "*Et voilà*, omelet Stucic, or *l'omelette au diable de Bosnie.*"

Ethan tastes it. He says, "An angel, not a devil. And the ham is sensational."

"Ah, the ham," says Stucic, offering a slice of bread on the flat of the knife. "The ham I have carried with me from home with the reverence that Aeneas carried Anchises. The 'devil' of the *flambé* is, of course, slivovitz, this, the last of a batch made by a good friend."

Ethan re-evaluates Stucic: How could a dubious character make such good food?

Stucic says, "I believe that Carlos Alvarado is not overly fond of your *bête noire*, Professor Dixon. I also believe that being a good friend of Lucy Evans, he may yet find work for you…" He stops and looks guiltily at the piece of bread in his hand.

Ethan says, "Don't worry, Miroslav. Why should you be the only person in Albuquerque who doesn't know about Lucy and me?"

Stucic smiles. "Ah, yes. So why might you not get another appointment in the University? Not, I hasten to add, that I haven't seen the notices for your fiction writing workshop up and about. Of course, this would not preclude the omnipotent Don Carlos from also finding you work."

Ethan says, "I hear that could be anything from orphanages to strip-mining national parks."

Stucic grins and offers Ethan a shot of slivovitz.

"No, thanks. What will you be teaching?"

"My dear fellow, they are plugging every academic gap with my poor self. Serbo-Croat, beginning and intermediate, advanced German, right now to a rather dull summer seminar, except for one pale urban exile from Chicago who burns to do a paper on Rilke. And in September there will be beginning Czech and a small graduate seminar in French classical theater. I shall in all this be recommending your workshop to those who reveal themselves as would-be authors."

"I'd be grateful."

Stucic wags a stained finger: "Grateful is not a word we need use with one another, else I would be embarrassing you with my feelings upon your being, once again, as on the airplane, such a sympathetic listener to my no-doubt quite stupid tale of *paterfamilias* woe. I also should like you to know that, without knowing the details, which are naturally none of my business, I am completely convinced that Dixon must have been the provocateur in your fight."

Ethan thanks him, deciding not to give him the details his disclaimer of interest so clearly begs for. Why should he tell Stucic what he doesn't see fit to tell Lucy?

Stucic says, "I also wish for your literary opinion. I have just finished reading Lucy Evans' remarkable novel *Crybaby*. You know it?"

Stucic has minutes before said he was too busy to read novels. His novels, he meant. Ethan says, "Yes, it's very good."

Stucic says, "Well, here is my problem, perhaps a European's problem. There is a heartlessness in her writing which is not of this world, not true. That is to say, although sentimentality is a delusion, it is a delusion of the human condition, and though the writing—the novelist—must not have it, the characters must. Think of Flaubert."

Ethan says, "Think of Kafka. I'm not comparing Lucy to either, but in Kafka the great effects come from the ironies between the *reader's* sentimental expectations, not always the same as the character's, and what happens in the book. And then, Kafka's funny. *The Trial*, for instance, is full of sly humor, though it won't save us or Kafka's characters from ending badly. Lucy's writing has a certain American deadpan humor, a literary Buster Keaton, though we know the train won't get through. That's at her best."

"And at her not-best?"

Ethan shrugs. Would he be disloyal to go on? He says, "Her writing can be mannered and empty, as you suggested. But she's willing to take the necessary risks."

"Thank you. I shall continue to read her with your comments in mind. And you, Ethan, you are yourself working on a new novel?"

"No," Ethan says brightly, refusing to sigh, "I've come out here in some part to shake myself into starting one. What about you, why Albuquerque? I mean, besides your daughter being here?"

Stucic narrows his eyes. He says, softly, "Trying to reunite my family is enough reason for me. And also there was no real work in Dallas. But I have kept you long enough." Ethan thanks him for the visit and the omelet. Stucic rinses the knives and repacks his suitcase. He tells Ethan he must call him Slava. They shake hands, and, with a bow and sweep of his hat, Stucic leaves. Ethan watches him walk up Copper Place, slightly ashamed at still feeling there is something devious about the man.

Inside, remembering that nights at high altitude are cool, he's just added a sweater to his bag when the phone rings. He considers not answering and then picks it up to hear a loud, "Hello. Is Ethan Baum there? E-t-h-a-n B-a-u-m."

He immediately recognizes the voice he hasn't heard in years, the heavily pushed out, chewed-down-on syllables of Dr. Haskell Perlmutter. Ethan's heart drops. He hasn't called his father; he's been eating the Bosnian devil's omelet as his father died.

"This is Ethan, Dr. Perlmutter. What's happened?"

"Ethan, how are you, boy? I got your number through Albuquerque directory, a new listing, I told them."

"How's Meyer? What's happened to my father?"

"Luckily, you're not unlisted. So many nowadays, my own Joseph, for a for-instance, with their unlisted numbers like movie stars. You think the Police Benevolent Fund doesn't still find the number and call Joseph in the middle of his dinner for a twenty-five buck contribution?"

"For heaven's sake, Dr. Perlmutter, my father!"

"Sha! What, you're going deaf, you have to shout? Meyer's okay, don't worry. Nothing's happened."

"You're sure?"

"Who should be sure if not his doctor? Sure, I'm sure."

"That's a relief."

"On the other hand, when I say nothing has happened, I don't mean that nothing is happening. But you know your father: he'd *plotz* before he'd say a word."

"About what?"

"About what we're talking about, about what's wrong with him."

"Dr. Perlmutter, tell me, tell me what is wrong with my father."

"I'll skip the medical terminology. Not that I think you couldn't understand the words, because who should understand words better than a wordsmith like yourself? But to make it short and—I'm not going to say 'sweet;' what could be sweet about any health problem— short and to the point, that's it. Okay, your father has ankylosis spondylitis. What this condition is, is a stiffening of a couple of your dad's neck vertebrae, the ankylosis part. And then there's the spondylitis, which is the inflammation of these vertebrae. Okay, so the inflammation, thank God, doesn't affect the carotid arteries, because that would do it—curtains, *kaput*. But it's affecting the smaller vertebral arteries. You following, Ethan, boy?"

"Yes, the smaller vertebral arteries are affected." He wishes Perlmutter didn't have the voice of a plumber.

"Right. Usually this is no big deal. But sometimes, and this is your dad's bad luck, the slightly decreased circulation can affect the brain. Blackouts, memory loss, brain dysfunction, symptoms consistent with, say, Alzheimer's. What we used to call dementia, no one home upstairs. Now the good news. You with me, Ethan?"

"Yes, Dr. Perlmutter. The good news."

"Is that this process can be very slow. Varies case by case."

"And is there bad news? I mean in addition to all the other bad news?"

"Bad is that in the current state of medical knowledge, it's one way—degenerate. There's nothing we can do about it."

"And you're certain this is what Meyer has?"

"Am I certain? Why would Mass General keep on an old fart like me if my diagnostic skills had gone? A lot of tests I put your father through. And done by younger doctors, hotshots with good eyes for reading data. What, I'm going to send my oldest friend who I've known since Boston Latin to a bunch of sleep-deprived *interns* for something like this?"

"I'll get on a plane today."

"If you care for your father, you'll do no such thing. Don't even call him today. He knows I'm talking to you this weekend. You call now, you'll depress him to hell, though he wouldn't admit it. And he'd be sick thinking he caused you worry. Give him a ring during the week, like you would anyway. If he brings it up—and by then I think he'll have worked it out and will—good, the two of you talk about it. If not, give the man some time here, some dignity. Eventually, he'll want to talk to you about this. He's philosophical. And why not? He's a philosopher, right?"

"Right," Ethan says, stunned.

"Ethan, sorry I've made you sad, boy. Don't be. Meyer could be bright as a button for another ten years. Hey, we're old guys: we expect to get it in the neck, you'll pardon the expression, and in lots of worse ways than Meyer. It's the miserable way of the world. Who said that?"

"Congreve, Dr. Perlmutter. *The Miserable Way of the World* was the draft title of his play before he figured there was no future in Restoration tragedy."

"That's the spirit, Ethan: knowledge, scholarship! You taking care of yourself out there in the wild west?"

"Good care, thanks." There's no pleasure in making fun of the doctor.

Perlmutter says, "Wonderful. My Joseph is always asking after you. You kids were at Harvard together. So, lots of love and *nachas*, boy."

"The same, Dr. Perlmutter."

Ethan is thinking how Haskell Perlmutter, crass as he is, could be a substitute for family, even for his father, Perlmutter at least being warm and demonstrative. He thinks of Joe Perlmutter, a super geek undergraduate he ignored. Now Joe owns a chain of homes for the aged and is worth many millions and should get life in prison for robbing and maltreating the old and demented and dying, like his father. Meyer isn't like that yet. But what a disease, this imperceptible strangulation. A disease straight from Kafka's "In the Penal Colony" into his father's neck.

He doesn't care that, as usual, he's ducking his feelings under an allusion; the allusion is horrid enough. What he should do is immediately call Tesuque and leave a message about why he has to cancel the weekend. He sits on the bed and looks at his packed bag. What would Meyer do in the circumstances? Ethan decides with a sigh that it's best to let Lucy see him as he is—heartbroken at the news of his father's creeping death, but not allowing that to spoil his weekend.

4

AS HE DRIVES OUT OF ALBUQUERQUE, Ethan realizes he hasn't called Meyer not because of Perlmutter's warning but because of his own fears. To name his father's mortality to himself is not much more than a metaphor; to discuss it with his father would be death itself. Not that it wouldn't have its ambiguities. Ethan is reminded of his father's best-known work, *The Ambiguity of Opposites*, about which Meyer is himself ambiguous.

Meyer had made that clear the first time he spoke of his funeral, the day after Ethan introduced him to Sandy. Meyer phoned him at his Thoreau office and said, "It's Dad. Are you busy?"

"Dad" was no good omen; he never called himself Dad.

Ethan said, "I'm marking student papers, grateful for the interruption."

There was a silence, but silence was a feature of their talk.

Ethan said, "What did you think of Sandy?"

Meyer said, "As I said last night, I think she's very nice."

There was another silence.

Ethan said, "'Very nice' is what you say when the Bruins score out of a power play."

"Are you fond of this girl?" Meyer asked.

"Head over heels fond. Tell me what you think of her."

Ethan was neither angered nor abashed by the ensuing silence. He was used to Meyer thinking carefully before he spoke. It was Meyer who had told Ethan the joke: Two philosophers meet in a corridor of the university. One says, "Good morning." The other says, "Define your terms." Sometimes these defining silences of Meyer would last for months. Then he'd say, as if out of the blue, "I've been thinking of what you said..." This silence was shorter than months. It was forty seconds long. Ethan knew it without looking at his watch, so practiced was he in this speech gap assessment.

Meyer said, "First impressions, by definition. A sensitive, intelligent girl. A sweet smile, for sure. And a knockout figure, to these old widower's eyes. Also, it's obvious she's very taken with you."

"So you like her."

"Yes. She was reserved, as was I, under the circumstances of a first meeting. I believe I'll like her even more, as I get to know her better."

Ethan said, "But? There's a 'but' in there bursting to get out."

The silence now, though not so long, was intense.

"Since you ask," said Meyer, "I cannot in the long run see you being happy with a twenty-one year old. You'll say eleven years is no big difference. That was sometimes the case when I was your age, but these days, each decade is a cultural generation with a different world view. Put another way, the teacher-pupil relationship is fine — for teachers and pupils. For life partners, it's intolerable. I know how intense you are, Ethan, how much you want. The girl will tire of you as her teacher and you'll get hurt."

"I'm more Sandy's student than she's mine."

"Very gallant, and, I have no doubt, true, in this head-over-heels phase of the relationship. Besides, there's the ethnic business to consider."

"Ethnic business? Last night, you seemed to find her thesis on the American Croat experience fascinating."

"Well, yes, as cultural idea. But this deconstructing local American politics to find European patterns worries me at the personal level."

"Meaning?"

"My father didn't flee the Old World so that his grandson would spiritually re-emigrate."

This silence, Ethan's, did not have a cognitive cause. He was just speechless. Then he said, "Meyer, that's preposterous. If one of my grandfather's reasons for coming to America was to found a make-believe Yankee dynasty, that was his problem, not mine. Frankly, I'm shocked. I didn't expect neo-con xenophobia from you."

Meyer said, "Nor did you get it. My beloved Marion and I named you Ethan because it's an Old Testament *and* a New England name. I had you circumcised *and* I took you to Brooks Brothers for your first suit."

"Yes, and that was *your* social experiment. What I know is that I love Sandy. She makes me happy. Happy. I hope that's all right, inasmuch as the perfect ethnic and generational-compatible XHelen made me miserable. Do you, at least in theory, approve of my being happy, for a change?"

Meyer's voice softened: "Of course I do. I'm only thinking of your happiness. I apologize for offending you."

"Me, too. I shouldn't have raised my voice."

An understandable silence occurred.

Meyer said, "Ethan, Sandy is a fine young woman, and I'm sure I'll be very fond of her. Are you thinking of children?"

"Not thinking of it. Thinking no of it."

After a pregnant silence, Meyer said, "Ah."

Ethan, trying to lighten the mood, said, "Sandy's a Pirates fan and doesn't like the Yankees. I think we could turn her on to the Red Sox as her American League favorite."

Meyer said, "Yes, we'll all go to the ballgames. Ethan, I want to ask you something. What would you say my best work was?"

"Besides what you're working on now? I'd say *The Ambiguity of Opposites*."

"I was afraid you'd say that."

"Why afraid?"

"Because I wrote it so long ago, and it's so popular—for philosophy, that is—and because it fixes me so narrowly."

"It's not just popular. That's the one Quine raved about."

"Yes, Willard was generous about it. But you know, I'm almost seventy-eight. Your kindness about current work notwithstanding, I'm not... Well, we all know one's best work is done before thirty, in philosophy, or fiction, or physics."

Ethan looked away from the receiver. How could his father say this to him, thirty-one with writer's block?

Meyer said, "The point is, I'm thinking of how I'll be assessed at my funeral."

Ethan, still cowering from his father's last blow, was unable to shift to this new idea. Where were Meyer's two-month pauses when he needed them? He said, "Don't be morbid."

"Not at all,' said Meyer, enthused. "It focuses my mind, to paraphrase. I'd like some later work mentioned at my funeral, like *An Aesthetic of Questions*. And they're sure to speak of where I took up from Wittgenstein, but I'd like you to make sure that my debt to Husserl is mentioned. And, of course, Thoreau, in another context."

"Dad," Ethan said, his own anxiety surfacing in the unfamiliar name, "please, leave it. Anyhow, who am I to speak for you, now or later, qua philosopher? Talk to Mossler. He's the disciple and biographer."

"The very reasons I can't trust him for this. He'll have his career to think of. Not that I'm not fond of Jerry, otherwise. But not for my funeral."

Seeing himself as no more than the mirror-polisher for Meyer's self-reflection, Ethan thought to take a new approach. "I can understand your concern for your reputation, but not this funeral business. Are you not telling me something about your health?"

"No, I'm in perfect health. My funeral, Ethan, is how I conceive of my life's end, its *summa*. And since I won't be around to consider it at the time, it makes sense to consider it beforehand. *Not* to consider it would be morbid."

Ethan had fallen back on the old formula: "Once again, Socrates, I see that you have said only what is so," but added, "and at the funeral, what's to be served—hemlock or chopped herring?"

Turning onto the highway approach road, Ethan notes that Meyer first talked of his funeral after hearing that he'd have no grandchildren. Ethan is locking down on a hideous scene of razor-fenced trucking lots, beer billboards, and sign after sign urging him to turn at Route 40 for GIANT CRAFT MARKET LOWEST PRICES IN THE WEST MOST STALLS IN NEW MEXICO KACHINA DOLLS! TURQUOISE! SILVER! RIDES! He finds it difficult to believe in Meyer having patriarchal aspirations, by way of generation, at least. He doesn't want to think of Meyer.

He thinks of the city he's passing. He hasn't yet been to a Dukes ballgame, the Dodger's triple-A team here. Does Lucy like baseball? He sees himself carrying a cardboard tray of beer and hotdogs. Lucy's legs cross as she takes her seat. A man in the box in front of them, wearing a red Dukes cap, turns and looks up her legs. It's Stucic, already so at home with America's national pastime, as opposed to Yugoslavia's, which is major league ethnic cleansing. Beer spills onto Ethan's hands.

It's sweat; he's forgotten to turn on the a/c. The suburbs stretch north along Route 25, both sides of the Rio Grande. As the car cools, the city thins. On his right, the ridge of the mountains bristles closer. A sign says he's entering the Sandia Pueblo. At last he's in Indian country, like on the map. He makes out a small herd of buffalo. Doubtless a tourist lure, yet he can't help singing. "Oh, give me a home, where the buffalo roam—" Roam inside an acre of barbed wire. "And penned deer and stuffed antelope play—"

He passes a small sign saying: NM BOSNIAN ASSOC. He was mean, thinking that Yugoslav slur about Stucic. He'll tell him about the NM Bosnian Assoc. He keeps the Cherokee at sixty-five. Even the car name becomes exciting here. The road swings northwest along the river valley, and then the river disappears, the Sandias sink into the plateau, and the road plunges down into, the sign says, the San Felipe Pueblo. Dry arroyo follows dry arroyo. Then the road becomes a long, long uplift, and Ethan sees the West he's had in mind. Those years ago with XHelen, he must have seen this: there were quiet times among the arguments, but they must have been times of depression, when scenes like this edge of the Colorado Plateau were emotionally leveled flat. But this...

This! Ah, the mountains and valleys back East behave themselves; the land back East is a pet. What he's looking at now is a wild beast; the land lifts, buckles, splits, the land rears up like something live—sea monsters, dendritic dragons in the sky that breathe red canyons. This landscape is a dry ocean whose insane waves crest half a mile high in a furious catatonia of stone.

Ethan pulls off the road and gets out, thinking to offer some homage, lithage, his own ethnic whooping it up; that is, a circumspect, circumcised Brooks Brothers snake dance. His begins with a hail to the place, a stretching of his arms that, to anyone passing in a car, looks exactly like someone getting out of his car and stretching his arms. But his arms drop. The landscape won't be patronized. He grows cold and shivers. He sweats, his breath comes short. He squats in the Jeep's shadow and shuts his eyes. The land on his retina isn't beautiful. Such gashed, gouged, slashed, cracked, split, riven, fissured, blown, fractured land is horrifying. He opens his eyes. It's beautiful. Lines, folds, these labyrinths of orange-blue receding, these pockets of green, the sheer white-gold outcroppings. It's something beyond beautiful: gigantic jut and crumble, the eons visible. He stands up and stretches full out. He looks at his watch. He's late.

Ethan drives elated, light-headed. Is it the landscape or something to do with his father dying? He decides that one thinks the worst to have done with it. He hopes what he's experienced with the landscape was Joycean epiphany rather than St. Lawrence of Taos hysteria. His pal and Thoreau colleague Pete Walsall said of his fellow Nottinghammer: "You can't blame Lawrence too much for going potty out there: poor consumptive bugger wasn't used to more than a few Midland hills and Cornish cliffs."

Ethan mistakenly turns off at the first Santa Fe exit into suburbs which have bred sub-suburbs. Mock pueblo spreads like fungus over the hills. He concentrates on looking straight up the road or out to the far mountains. Back on the highway, he turns off correctly to Tesuque. He instantly dislikes the place with its contrived air of the seedy-genteel, its one-time farms and ranches now gussied up in hovel chic, Anthony Caro sculptures visible through a coyote fence, the E-type Jag in British racing green angled to an old log gate. He cannot wait to leave for Lucy's hideaway. He can imagine it straight from her fiction: lone, bare, and intimate.

He pulls up to Café Tesuque fifty minutes late, hoping that Lucy's interest is piqued by the wait. The café's patched door predictably opens to a fashionably dim interior where stone walls and abstract oil paintings are picked out by pinpoint spots.

Lucy smiles at him from a banquette. She frowns. She smiles again and reddens. A margarita glass is before her, its salt high and dry. He assumes it's not her first.

"Hi," she says. "You're—"

And before she can say "late" he slips in beside her and kisses her ear, and as she says "late," he puts his hand up under her dress onto her underpants and feels the crinkle of pubic hair under satin.

"Oh, my god," she says pushing his hand away. "There's no tablecloth; anyone could have seen."

But he knows he's made a great hit. He's her Errol Flynn, her feral fling. He says, "Blame it on the landscape, a spiritual hit-and-run. Are the margaritas any good? Will you have one with me?"

Lucy says, "No." She says, "They're good." She says, "Why not?"

A waitress takes the drink order. A young man puts warm tostados and green chili salsa on the table. The drinks arrive; Ethan resolves to have two to her one. He tells her this, says it's atonement for his lateness. His arm around her waist, drink in hand, he begins to recount his vision of the landscape but stops a few statements in, saying, "The words are falling short and shorter."

Lucy grabs his hand at her waist and says, "Don't apologize. I'm crazy about you."

This is what he wants yet is not crazy about. He says, "I know. Having ridden in on the white stallion, I can't fall off and become a verbal stumblebum."

They drink and don't say much. Lucy asks what he's thinking. What he's thinking is that his spirit, as Bessie Smith called it, is way up high. What he's thinking is how the blues are mixed with this shining white knighthood bestowed by Lucy. What he says is nearly true: "I'm thinking of you in your hideaway." He can almost smell its dry wood, see the sliver of sunlight through chinks in the wall. At one point—they go on with margaritas through the lunch of New Mexican *nouvelle*—he finds it important to tell Lucy: "I hear our conversation reel away to its own music. Emotionally Stravinsky's *Le Sacre du printemps*, intellectually some *Little Songs* of Virgil Thompson."

Lucy says, "Ah, I thought we were talking."

He's not sure if he's offended her. Although she's smiling at him, he senses he'd better talk about her, and says, "You told me you were going shopping this morning in Santa Fe, with your daughter. Emmy? How did it go?"

"Great. You have to meet her. She is such a good kid. She's eighteen, taking a year off before starting college. We were shopping for the kitchen in her first apartment. I wanted to give her a present of this nice set of copper and cast iron pots and pans, but she had me buy a much cheaper set and contribute the difference to an animal rescue center she works for."

"She sounds nice. What do they rescue?"

"Wild things. Everything wild needs rescue here: eagles, elk, ravens, snakes. Up north, wolves. And bears, everywhere. After hard winters the poor bears come down off the Sandias right into the outskirts of Albuquerque. A few years ago, one had to be rescued off a telephone pole. They get run down on the roads. People shoot them from their kitchen windows. It's awful."

Ethan doesn't want this conversation. He says, "Let me rescue you from the awful. Where's this hideaway of yours?"

Lucy says, 'We'll get there soon enough. Aren't you interested in the environment?"

"Yes, yes. As I was trying to tell you when I got here. But I want to know about you in the environment. I read somewhere that you hike and camp all over the state."

"Not for the past few years, but yes. I like to go off on my own for days with a sleeping bag."

"And you're not afraid?"

Lucy says, "Not out there. Though, one time, a creepy guy turned up, in the Tusas, near Break Off Mountain. I gave him coffee, and he started saying how cold it got at night, even in the summer, and how body heat was best for warmth. Not subtle."

"What happened?"

"Nothing. I told him I liked it cool at night. I took out a hunting knife and told him it shared my sleeping bag; it kept me cool. He thought about it for a while. Then he left."

"What if he'd had a gun?"

"He didn't," she says. Her thumb moves lightly back and forth over a vein in his wrist.

He says, "It's strange: we've been seeing each other for three weeks and we haven't talked about our writing."

Lucy says, "What is there to say? You write. I write. We both know what it's like: it's hard and the work is private. I'm working on a first collection of stories, if that's what you mean. And you?"

Ethan is hurt, certain he's told her of his block. He says, "On nothing. Nothing has been my work-in-progress for a few years now."

"Just sit down and write anything. Do what we tell our students. Keep a journal, write a long letter."

Lucy's matter-of-fact tone strikes Ethan as unsympathetic and insensitive. He'd hoped... But he won't whine to her. Whining's not much good for keeping his spirit way up high. He makes a joke of it; he says, "If I started a letter, I'd imagine a great epistolary novel and get depressed. If I started a journal, I'd think of Defoe and rationalize that it's not a plague year."

Lucy leans her head to his and says, "It's always a plague year." Then, brighter, "When I was away this week, I reread *Who's on Second*. I love how it decomposes, how it sneaks up on you that Jack's lost it."

He likes the compliment; it puts her comment about plague from his mind. When Ethan insists that he pay for lunch, Lucy reminds him that the rest of the weekend is on her. They look at each other and laugh.

Outside, he sees only one suitcase in her white Jeep and assumes she already has supplies at her place. He follows her north out of town. After a few miles, she turns right and heads towards the mountains. He's relieved to be out of the cities and the too-crafty village. Ahead, green mountain slopes rise from the upland desert yellow. He's going ninety, but Lucy is a dot way out in front. She drives too fast for an environmentalist, but he figures she's high on hormones and margaritas. He sees by the rising dust that she's turned onto a dirt road. He passes a sign when he gets to the turn, but he's going too fast to read it. The dirt road to her hideaway feels smoother than the paved road, but he puts this down to testosterone and margaritas. He brakes as the road swings into a cactus lined drive. Flowers ring the cactus. There's Lucy, getting out of her Jeep at wide, stone steps. He pulls up by a sign: ←CASITAS→ He still doesn't get it. Where is this? Men appear at her door and his, in black and yellow striped porter's jackets, as at the grand hotels of Europe. He finally gets it, sees the name in stone. Rancho Escondido, the grandest hotel in New Mexico. Why should Lucy resort to a resort as a "hideaway?" What happened to the genuine, sexy, scraggy shack of her novels, the place he's set his heart on, his hard-on? Rancho Escondido means "hidden ranch," of course, but, damn, he has been one romantic dumb bunny. Well, here he is, and he can't let her down. He gets out and grins at her, putting his arms out in a gesture of Wow, all this!

Their luggage is wheeled away. He gives her a big hug and says, "I'm speechless." At the top of the stone steps, between big blue cascades of periwinkle, they turn to look at the mountains. Ethan says, "What a view!"

"What?"

"A view!"

"No, what's wrong?"

"Nothing at all." Ethan smiles and squeezes Lucy's waist as they enter.

While Lucy checks in, Ethan wanders the lobby, hoping to stimulate or simulate enthusiasm. Maybe, like Lucy's daughter, he should ask for the weekend in a sleeping bag and the thousands Lucy's spending on Rancho Escondido to go to wild animal rescue. He sits in an armchair and tries to unsullen. Across the lounge is a massive stone fireplace. Over its wood beam mantelpiece a surround has been created of swagged fruit and festooned flowers, all real—apples, pears, lemons on their branches, roses, lilies, orange blossoms—so that its effect is wonderful, a Grinling Gibbons come to life. He's cheering up when he considers how it would have to be reconstructed every day or two, and he thinks of the work and the waste involved and decides he hates the place even more.

As he sits, trying not to scowl, a young woman in a white tennis outfit comes to the fireplace, puts a shoe on the fender and bends deeply forward to retie it. Ethan's expression turns to rapt concentration as he looks the length of her legs, her calves' curve, thighs' thrust, now the buttocks break! and the, ah, white ribbon of her panties' perfection!

"Looks good enough to eat, doesn't it?"

Startled, Ethan sees at his side the voice of his thought, a man smiling brilliantly under a broad white moustache.

"The fruit around the fireplace, delicious. You can almost taste it." With which he crosses to the now straightened beauty, and the two of them go off to or from tennis. The man is in white tennis shirt and full-length white flannel trousers. He is tall and extremely elegant and old enough to be the woman's grandfather, though, patting her behind like that, appears to enjoy a different relationship. And this is where Lucy thinks to take him to be *Escondido*, where old men parade their mistresses, this… He walks back to the desk not wishing to find the right name for the place. Where Lucy is so crude as to… Where older women parade their young… To bring him someplace like this Rancho Hanky Panky.

Ethan puts his arm around her as they leave the main building and walk the delicate, desert-garden path to their casita. He kisses her ear and says, "Our little house," relieved she can't see his unhappiness.

Lucy seems crazy in love with everything about their weekend *perdido* at Rancho Escondido: their two room casita, the views from its French doors and windows, the painted peasant furniture, the 1890's Spanish saddle blankets on the walls, the tin and silver crucifix, the 1930 School of Taos painting of Taos, the Andalusian tiles in the bathroom, the sprays of flowers in their silver pitchers, the carved oak four-poster bed, his penis.

They spend the rest of the afternoon in and around these last two. Ethan despises the designed loveliness of the place and observes his feeling of aesthetic superiority transform to moral superiority, the resulting guilt from which makes him, he sees, a charming companion and sensitive lover (the ideal kept man?) who finds, at Lucy's second orgasm of the day, that he achieves his first of their affair, which, though not the fabulous cataracts of her imagination, is so good as to have him atypically shouting in tongues. He drifts to sleep in her arms and wakes to a rose-colored sunset filling the room, streaming on the bowls of cut roses as if the blooms, pink and cream and carmine, were themselves the source of the luscious light. Lucy sits in a white silk robe by the bed, a bottle of champagne in her hand. Ethan notices it is the most expensive type he knows of. He says, "What a study in pink: the sunset, the roses, the Roderer *Crystal* in your hand."

Her head slumps. "I'm sorry you find this so awful, or phony, or whatever it is I've done so wrong. Please, Ethan."

He says, "What could be wrong? I can't find a single bad proportion or fake decoration or even a shade too much or too little of *anything*."

She says, "I'd already ordered this and it's open, so we might as well have it." She pours two glasses but holds on to them. "Please tell me what's wrong. This is humiliating."

His instinct is to continue the denial, but as he throws off the covers, Ethan catches reflected in the champagne bucket an image of Lucy and him so rounded into the room that they, too, might have come from the mind of its interior designer. He can't deny his disdain. He says, "I had the wrong idea. When you said 'hideaway,' I thought of someplace simple and natural, not…" He swings his hand out to the room.

Lucy's eyes follow past the bedposts. She stands and turns as if trying to see everything as he does. She turns back and holds out his glass, and he thinks, so that's all right. As he reaches for it, she throws the champagne in his face. He sits up and she tips the bucket—ice, water, and bottle—into his naked lap. He watches pink champagne run down his thigh.

Lucy's eyes are shut. She whispers, "You're mean. You're smug and arrogant and mean. Why don't you just, please, leave. Please get out and take your precious authenticity with you."

He says, "I'm sorry."

"You're sorry I'm onto you."

Her eyes remain closed as he goes to dry off in the bathroom. Then she's in the bathroom door: "You're not sorry for your feelings; you're sorry for expressing them. Or are you sorry for the lines in my face?"

He shakes his head no as he passes her to dress.

Lucy says, "No, I don't think it's because I'm older. Why can't you let go of this little glass case you stick yourself in?"

He licks his lips. The taste of flat champagne is bitter as perfume. "You really want me to go?"

"Yes."

He dresses and packs his bag and doesn't believe her. He has not said anything rotten, and he knows she's crazy about him. Perhaps what's getting to her is that he is not so crazy about her. But that's not his *fault*. She's on the edge of the bed with her head in her hands. Her red hair streams over her forearms. If he really were rotten, he'd look for gray roots. He says, "Let's make it up."

"Just go. Please."

So he goes. He goes to his Jeep and sits in the parking lot. To the west, the top of the sun still shows over the mountains. The foothills behind the Rancho are in purple shade and black shadow. He doesn't deserve this. He can't understand her. But he hasn't come all this way just to scurry back to town. He'll go for a walk.

Path lights have come on. He passes floodlit tennis courts. He doesn't look towards the casitas. Beyond the stables, a sign points him up to the trails. He wishes he had a horse to ride off into the mountains. He feels ashamed to come up with such a Lawrentian image, disgusted to have his feelings so culturally filtered. Lucy's "glass case." He walks faster. The path lights end.

He walks. A moon is up. The trail rises, a pale line into the mountains. He walks in a landscape of low scrub stuck with twisted pines — piñon, he supposes. Lucy would know. Her writing pricks with detail of cactus and weed. Oh, great: now he's using *Lucy's* writing to sort his experience. He shakes his head at himself. He doesn't want this, nor does he want any of Mexico to come back at him.

He walks faster and, because he's forbidden himself to think of Lucy's writing, he thinks of it, of how most of it is no more than an arm's length from the narrative eye. He's trying to know the difference between her character and his own, but he can't quite get it. He looks to the dark blur of trees along the trail. Why can't he even take a moonlit mountain walk without worrying about narrative stance, without... What is the word? Ah, yes, *recontextualization*, as horrible a word as anyone could want. Is that his glass case? He hasn't told her about his father. Ethan nearly walks into a boulder around which the trail splits. Typical. Of course he has a personality: charming and even kind, in small detail, and quick to get the joke. But personality is not the same as character, is character's overcoat or glass case.

He walks and walks from moonlit dark to darkness. Does he worry about narrative because he's been listening his lifetime for his own voice, he means the one that will accurately narrate him? Some of these thoughts come, he knows, from his father's paper "The Logos and the Prosopaea," which he likes but hadn't dared mention when Meyer asked for his favorite, because the world—the handful of philosophers who matter for Meyer—didn't like it. Didn't the critic Richard Apther call it "pop Freud meets pop Plato?" Ethan walks in the cool wind. The trail tips up like a ramp to the stars, ridiculously large stars out here, stars with eyeliner. The stars make him desperate not to think of Saint Exupéry, but this is like trying not to think of de Brunhoff, of elephants, he means. In this way, the actual trail with its real luminescence and bona fide stars above conflate with ideas and images in which little prince Ethan feels touchingly lost. Wost.

At the top of a rise he comes to a sign: RANCHO ESCONDIDO (DIRECT) 2.5 MILES. As he turns to take this path, he sees up above him the full moon. It's either four weeks since he arrived or there wasn't a full eclipse. Of course Lucy was right. It is his own false idea of her that has made both of them unhappy. Is he frightened of what she gives of herself in bed? She gives everything, naked, open beyond... He's afraid of her so skinless. No wonder she's so hurt.

He walks down the trail looking up at the moon. He moves past juniper which come to his peripheral vision as faint blue bruises. Out before him, across the valley of the Rio Grande, rise enormous mesas, shouldering the night. He is the rhythm of his walking in the light and shadow of the now descending moon. What, exactly, has Lucy done but been good to him? He walks aware of the stillness. He walks unaware in the silence, through black shadow, over the silver-blue rock. He walks the winding, up-and-down trail all the while looking at the moon. Now he sees the faint lights of the resort and imagines Lucy hurt and alone on the edge of the bed. He walks and shivers. He was mean. The trail drops into a bowl of moonlight. Snakes and lizards sleep in the cool of their blood. He should have begged her pardon and stayed with her. He should have held her, kept her from her skinlessness.

The trail drops and Ethan makes out the resort buildings under the sinking moon. Understanding that Lucy is so vulnerable, how could he have hurt her so and just left her? He makes out their casita, and as he does, the moon drops below its roofline. What if she's killed herself? He starts to run down the path, running faster when he comes to the path lights until, breathless, he knocks on the casita door. No answer. But he still has the key. He opens the door and calls "Lucy?" No answer. He goes to the bedroom; her gown is on the bed, the bathroom door is shut. "Lucy?" No answer. He turns the door handle, afraid to find her dead under the blue, moonlit bath water. It's empty. She's gone out. She could be anywhere, dead or dying. He runs to the main building, is running to the desk when he turns back.

Lucy is sitting at the bar with someone, smiling. It's the man with the white moustache and edible mistress. Ethan walks up and touches her shoulder. He says, "Lucy, I was… I was…" He catches his breath. "I was worried. I saw the moon disappear behind the casita and thought you were, that you'd… Why are you laughing?"

She says, "That was Wordsworth's Lucy you were thinking of: the moon drops behind her cottage roof and he thinks: 'What if my Lucy is dead?'"

Ethan is on the verge of weeping or screaming. He says, "My god, I can't even experience *experience* except through someone else's version."

Lucy says, "I'm almost thinking of forgiving you: remember, Wordsworth says only others in love can understand these strange fits of passion."

For him, he thinks, it's more strange pits of fashion. The spoonerism is so awful, tears come to Ethan's eyes.

"Ethan," she says, "this is my friend Carlos Alvarado."

Alvarado stands. As tall as Ethan, he has sharp black eyes above a long, high-bridged nose. Ethan thinks of a hawk, an *hidalgo* hawk. Lucy excuses herself and leaves the two men shaking hands. Alvarado has the grip of a man in his prime.

He says, "Any friend of Lucy's is my friend."

Ethan nods.

"What will you have to drink?"

"Water," Ethan says. "A glass and a pitcher of water."

Alvarado orders in Spanish. When it comes. Ethan drinks a glass and pours a second before Alvarado speaks. He says, "I'm grateful for the chance to have a few words in private with you. As I said, any friend of Lucy's... True friend, naturally. Are you her true friend?"

"Look, I've just been running down a mountainside. I'm not going to discuss my relations to Lucy with a stranger."

"Ah," says Alvarado. He sips his drink. "As you wish, of course. What I wish to say is merely this: I am an old friend of Lucy and she's very dear to me. I hope you believe that my only concern is that she does not suffer. She has suffered enough in her relations with Dixon. And for what it's worth, off the record, I was not displeased about you hitting the man. He's a complete shit. Too bad about his firing you. Now, Lucy tells me you intend to stay here."

"Yes."

Alvarado says, "My hope, then, is that in you Lucy has found a truly loving and considerate friend."

Ethan is about to thank Alvarado, when he realizes that Lucy has been telling the man how badly he's treated her. He says, "Thank you," with what he hears as the requisite dryness.

Alvarado stands. "I'm glad we understand each other on this point. And who knows? Perhaps I may be of some future help to you. Now I have to return to work. You know what these weekend conferences are like."

He leaves, giving Ethan the same dazzling smile as when he wore tennis clothes, though he's now in a double-breasted linen suit, the same pale tan as his skin. Ethan finds him almost laughably elegant, finds he's not at all amused. He spends the next minutes considering how to make it up with Lucy. Tact, consideration, delicacy.

When she returns to the bar, he says, "Were you and Carlos lovers?"

"What does that question deserve, Ethan?"

He orders a margarita. Lucy says, "All I talked about with Carlos was you."

"So I gathered."

"About how much I liked you and how much you confused me."

He puts his hand on the back of her neck and says, "I'm crazy about you, too." Although he doesn't exactly feel like this, and she must sense it and feel cheated, he reasons that since Wordsworth has somehow suggested he say this, who is he to refuse?

Their bed has fresh linen. They fall asleep slightly drunk. He wakes on his side, his face between Lucy's legs, his half-tumescent penis on her ear, his feet under his pillow. Lost, topsy-turvy traveler. Flee-er. Returning from the bathroom, he sees out the window two bright stars. After a while, he's able to make out between these two stars the faint milk powder of ten thousand million others. He goes to the bed and puts the blanket over Lucy's bare shoulder. He draws the hair back from her face. He sits in an armchair and thinks this cannot really be him with this older, slightly insane, plain woman (all right, nice body) from Butte, Montana, gifted and insecure. Or is it just with him she's insecure? Isn't that how he wants it?

Lucy calls, "Are you awake?"

"I'm sitting, for a bit. On my Wordsworth walk I saw some wonderful mesas jutting out, across the valley to the north."

"Those would be Los Alamos. They found the most beautiful place out here and poisoned the world from it."

He says, "You sleep. I'll come to bed soon."

Ethan nods off in the chair, thinking of Oppenheimer and Fermi up on the beautiful mesas. When he wakes it's still dark and Lucy is talking from the bed. How long she's been talking, he can't tell. He hears, "...found out about your father in *Who's Who in Contemporary Philosophy*, not a very big book. There was something about him using an epistemological approach to linguistics through aesthetics. Or, no, an aesthetic approach to epistemology though linguistics. Or the other combination; any of them makes my head spin. I can't believe I'm saying this to you; you'll hate me. I wanted to say the titles of your father's works sound like poems. It doesn't matter whether I have or have not slept with Carlos. My father was a miner who became an engineer for Anaconda. He was a hard man who struggled to be fair. His most endearing trait was awkwardness. It had a moral quality."

Ethan waits for her to continue. Then he realizes she's asleep, somehow has been asleep while talking. This makes him wish for a picture book to look at in the dark. The most striking of the pictures would be of him sitting in this chair in the dark listening to Lucy talking in her sleep.

The next day, through play and laughter, certain moments spread poison, like Los Alamos. One of these is, indeed, standing among the aspens on the mountain behind Rancho Escondido looking across at the invisibly spoiled magnificence of the Los Alamos mesas. Small clouds fly in flat triangles, like showers of arrows. And on the drive up, daylight has revealed that the wild foothills of Ethan's moonlight walk are in fact filled with large houses, the hilltops flattened for the steel and glass and adobe displays of eight to twenty thousand square foot holiday houses (he cannot think "homes") sucking up the Rio Grande for lawns and gardens amid the high, dry plateau, the plateau showing as only one more designer feature between estates. It is also impossible for Ethan to forget the brunch brought to their casita on one, two, three trolleys, fifteen dishes he counted before giving up and remembering the dictum "less is more." Wondering about its attribution has helped him focus away from the nuclear and other disasters. But it isn't until they're back in the casita, late afternoon, that he remembers: Mies van der Rohe. Not politics nor environmentalism, it is as usual the shield of aesthetics behind which he hides and snipes.

They are slightly dehydrated, sitting, drinking water. He says, "Lucy, do you remember talking about my father and yours, last night?"

"What did I say?"

This is a bear-trap of a question that Ethan sidesteps by asking, "Do you know a book called *Who's Who in Contemporary Philosophy?*"

"Is there a book like that?"

He smiles to show that, should this be a joke, he gets it. "So you were awake," he says.

"You were lonely in the chair."

He strides past the safety of this offered tenderness to: "What did you mean by "moral awkwardness?"

Lucy finishes her glass of water and pours half a glass more.

"No, that wasn't it. You said your father's most endearing trait was his awkwardness. You said it had a moral quality." Ethan is pleased to have remembered her exact words.

Lucy takes a deep breath and says, "I wish you liked me more."

Ethan hears the bear trap shut.

On this last night of their weekend, the weather turns cool, too. He lights the fire laid in the kiva fireplace, and, kneeling by the growing flames, he tries to imagine Lucy's father being awkward in trying to be fair. He pictures a bony man in a plaid shirt stooping to pick up a small girl. The man struggles to smile. Suddenly, the man is in a tweed sports jacket and is Meyer. Ethan turns from the fire and his unhappy insight.

Later, they decide to drive out to the giant liquor store at the Pojoaque Pueblo. They buy a big bag of Fritos and a bottle of Krug. Back at the casita, they dine on the Fritos washed down with the warm champagne. When Lucy says she doesn't want to make love, Ethan takes her in his arms—this on the rug before the pungent, roaring piñon fire—and she wants to make love. Ethan has only the vaguest sensation that the meal and the sex may be the unhappy compromise between their visions for the weekend. As they go to sleep, he says, humbly, "I've had a wonderful time, despite my stupidity."

Again he wakes in the dark, his heart racing with the weight of lies he's told. He slips out of bed to the armchair. He still has not mentioned Meyer's illness. If it doesn't matter to Lucy whether she has or hasn't slept with Carlos, why won't she tell him? Why should he care?

From the bed, Lucy says, "In the main administration building at Los Alamos Labs there's a wall with a big quilt hanging on it. All around the border there are patches representing the different units and people working there, including all the local pueblos. And in the middle of the quilt is an enormous mushroom cloud—this fleecy, tenderly worked atomic bomb blast. It's unbelievable. They love it, they love that death. It's the AIDS quilt in reverse."

Under his breath, Ethan murmurs, "We were made for each other." He hears from the bed, where Lucy's asleep, "I know."

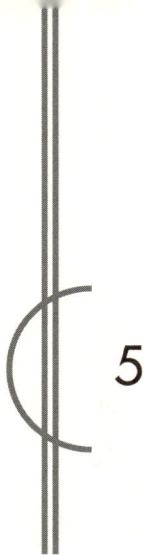

5

ETHAN STANDS AT HIS WINDOW looking down on mountain bikes being offloaded from a truck into the storage unit below his apartment. He's trying to understand what relation there is between the terrible weekend he's just returned from and his writer's block. Looking out the window keeps him from seeing the desk behind him with, dead center, its accusatory full pen and empty paper. Is he jealous of Lucy because she doesn't have writer's block? He knows other writers, writing writers, without being jealous of them. Is it because she's a woman? No, it's because she's, at least for now, his woman. Here, he pauses to applaud his honesty and urge himself on. And his woman is supposed to look after him and enable him to write. Yet Helen looked after no one but herself, and he'd written two books and started the third in those four years before the marriage went bad. But they were very young and newly wed and in love with their successes and energies. If he needs the emotional security of a relationship, he's too unsure about Lucy and him. About him. He's also disappointed that Lucy doesn't want to find out why he can't write. Has she no psychological curiosity?

Light flashes from the spokes of a bicycle wheel. What about his relations with men? He has never seriously discussed his block with a man. Is this because women are safer for him, because they're less likely to tell him—charming, handsome him—the truth? His father, for instance—

The phone rings. As he passes the desk to answer, Ethan jots down the words "men" and "father."

Lucy says, "Hi. I overreacted. You were mean but I could have had a sensible discussion rather than that ship launch."

WOLF TONES

"You didn't actually break the bottle on me."

"Anyway, I think we shouldn't see each other tonight because I want to give us a chance."

The call ends with an agreement to speak midweek. Ethan looks at the words "men" and "father" on the desk. He returns to the window to see the bicycle truck pull away down Copper Place. Men: why not Doc N? Because Doc is aloof and very busy and it would seem like asking for a free consultation. Stucic. He could reciprocate for that breakfast.

The next night, Ethan sits with Stucic at the sidewalk table of an Italian restaurant in the Nob Hill section of Central Ave. They give conventional signals: Ethan has had a very nice weekend; Stucic has had a relaxing weekend, when not reading student work. Ethan remembers to say, "I passed a sign about meetings of the New Mexican Bosnian Association. I thought you might be—" He stops at the wave of Stucic's hand.

"Thank you, Ethan, for this thought. You could not, however, imagine how dreadful these exile groups are: obsessively fixed in another place and another time, and forever full with the petty arguments of offended egos. Thank you, but no thank you very much."

The small talk exhausted over the antipasto, Ethan raises the subject with the main course. "Slava," he says, "you told me you've written plays. For whom, besides the audience, did you write them?"

"There are several possible answers. If I say why do you ask, it is that I may better respond."

Ethan says, "I'm trying to answer the question for myself because I haven't been able to write fiction for several years now, and my move out here hasn't, as I'd hoped, started me writing again."

"Ah," says Stucic, nodding. "I wrote, *au fond*, for my father, who was for me the model of culture and learning. He was…"

Stucic is speaking of his father, but Ethan hears only his pulse in his ears, boom boom. He wrote for Meyer's boom boom approval. Meyer never approved, so he stopped writing. Boom boom. "What?" asks Ethan, seeing Stucic's stare.

"What do you mean, Ethan, by 'boom boom'?"

"I said that?" This talk doesn't seem a good idea.

"You said that. Is it for you also your father?"

"No. No, I never presumed... My father is a philosopher. His interest is abstraction, not the messy details of fiction."

"Philosopher? Your father is Meyer Baum?"

"Yes."

"His *L'Esthétique des Questions* is wonderful! I am a great fan."

This is just what Ethan needs, another person who hasn't read his novels but who loves his father's writing, his father among them.

Stucic says, "There is some trouble here? Your father does not read your books?"

"He reads them," Ethan says. Meyer has admitted as much.

"So who, then?"

"Who then what?" Ethan asks, relieved Stucic hasn't asked if his father likes his novels.

"For whom at this deep level do you write?"

"I imagine I write for myself, projected into the concept of an ideal reader. Of course, when I think about it, this reader is intelligent, highly literate, and very critical. As a matter of fact, when I continue to think about it, this reader can't stand my writing, and I hate him."

For a moment, Ethan believes Stucic sees through this, but then Stucic laughs. "Very amusing. You have a fantastical irony not very American."

"That must be because when I was seven, I spent a year and a half in England, when my father was a visiting professor at Oxford. Though all I remember is getting my shins kicked black and blue at school soccer, which seemed to take place every day of every week. And there's a memory of holding my mother's hand as the Household Cavalry appeared out of the fog of the Mall and disappeared into the fog of Buckingham Palace."

"Great Britain," says Stucic. "I was there only once, but not to so august a place as Oxford or the royal palace. A weekend conference on the Bosnian conflict at Manchester University. Well meaning but, finally, meaningless."

Ethan is aware he has only to ask a question about that conference for the troubling topic of his novels and his father to leave the dinner table. He asks it, and the dinner becomes enjoyable and a failure.

Walking home on his own, Ethan works out that he's jealous of Lucy because at some level he expects her to do his writing for him. This means that he's always needed a relationship from which to write, though he became blocked before he and Helen literally split up. At the same time, his writing has obviously been his attempt to shake Meyer, the monkey, off his back. He therefore has become more and more resentful of Meyer's lack of real interest in his novels, because only Meyer's approval could remove that great gorilla, that sneering simian. Or, to be Oedipal, he wrote for his widowed father's attention, from a place of relative security with a woman. He, Ethan, had the wife, was part of the couple, so that Meyer was on his own as the son, and, hey presto, was *sin cojones*, impotent.

Ethan is pleased with his self-analysis until, back at Copper Place, he sees the blank paper on his desk. He makes no vow to write; he vows only not to waste time theorizing on why he can't write. As he goes to bed, he vows, for good measure, not to make any further vows.

The next morning, to Ethan's surprise, Alvarado phones him. "Ethan, I feel I may have seemed unfriendly the other night at Rancho Escondido."

"Not at all," says Ethan. Threatening would be more like it.

"Anyway, I mentioned that I might be of some use. I know you need work, and there are several projects I oversee as Director of the New Mexico Institute. Why don't you come over to my office to discuss the possibilities?"

"Thanks very much for the offer, Carlos. But my workshop looks to be shaping up well enough to support me while giving me time for my own writing."

"Good. Congratulations. But keep me in mind, just in case. I don't want you to think we're all like wicked Willy the whaler, over here."

After the call, Ethan knows that Alvarado is doing what Lucy has asked him to do. He can't thank Lucy, because she'll feel he resents her efforts to keep him here, to keep him. He wishes he were as confident of the workshop as he said he was. Fourteen have phoned to sign up so far, but that's not contract law. If all showed and he ran three a year, that would be—he stops to do the math—$12,600, which, with his savings, might give him two years. By then he might have a manuscript to sell. Or not. Or have one that nobody wanted to buy. The theoretical economics is depressing; he'll be practical and check the bookshops to see how many more phone number slips have been taken from his workshop fliers.

In the second bookshop he visits, Ethan has just found that six more phone slips have been taken when he happens to see into a room marked YOUNGER READERS. A girl, perhaps eleven or twelve, stands with her back to the shelves reading a book. A man faces the shelves some ten feet from the girl. What catches Ethan's attention is that the man's head keeps turning to the girl and that with each turn, he sidesteps closer. He could of course be her father, but it's clear he's not looking at the books, and when he's two feet from her he backs away from the shelves and with the same odd crab-walk moves directly in front of her, pauses, and continues to her other side. He could of course be her father, but he hasn't said a word to the girl. The man now sidles back in front of her. He says something inaudible. The girl glances up and moves away from him and continues to read. The man moves to the bookshelves where he again begins his head turns and sidesteps towards the girl. This time, the girl glances up, and as the man approaches she walks to the other side of the book table in the center of the room and turns her back on the man.

Something about this seems very literary to Ethan. Proust, of course: Charlus' little circling dance around Jupien. But they were consenting adults; this scene has a girl who does not look like a waiting, open orchid to the man buzzing around her. Now the man, across the room from the girl, is forced to turn his head enough for Ethan to see his face.

Ethan walks into the room and says to the girl, "Is that man bothering you?"

The girl looks at Ethan, thinks for a moment, and says, "Yes. I just want to read this book."

Ethan crosses the room. The man has taken a book from the shelf and is looking at it. Ethan sidesteps next to him. "Is *Fred's First Fishing Trip* any good?"

Dixon turns and steps back. The cast is off and his nose has a new, sharp bump, not an improvement. He says, "Leave me alone."

Ethan says, "This isn't your first fishing trip, is it?"

"Don't be stupid. I'm looking for a book for a nephew's birthday."

"That-eleven-year-old girl's not your nephew: for the past five minutes you've been trying to hit on her. I asked her. She said you were bothering her. You're a creep, Dixon. There are laws against creeps like you. Why don't you leave the store."

"Why don't you leave Albuquerque," says Dixon. "I can still press charges about this." He points to his bumpy nose.

"I don't think you'd want your child pornography brought into court, creep."

The girl has left the room. Ethan sees her buy the book and leave the store. Dixon walks into the main room and goes to the poetry section. Ethan follows him and says, "Leave the store, creep. I'll follow to make sure you go in the opposite direction of the girl."

"Do you think I'm afraid of you, Baum?"

Ethan is looking in the L section. The book before the poems of Lorca is *Lorikeets: All You Need to Know*. Ethan takes it from the shelf. He says, "Yes, I think you're afraid of me. Look at this: the book doesn't belong here. Nor do you. You're sick: go home, get help. Go now." He brings the book up to Dixon's face.

"You make this place unbearable," says Dixon.

Ethan puts the book down and follows him out of the store. The girl is walking down Central Ave. Ethan says, "Walk up there for a while."

Dixon says, "That I don't want public fistfights doesn't mean I won't find my time and place to repay you for this tenfold."

"Tenfold? Tenfold? Get walking, creep." Ethan watches Dixon walk two long blocks by which time the girl is out of sight.

In the perfect, arid sunlight, Ethan's sense of righteous triumph evaporates. The girl, it's true, is unharmed, but the creep walks free. Besides, there's Ethan's suspicion that vanquishing Dixon would mean more to him if Lucy did.

At his apartment, there's a message from Lucy to phone her office between two and three. That leaves two hours to sit down and break his writer's block. Write anything. Write a description of Dixon in the bookstore. A parody of Proust. He finds *Cities of the Plain* for a quick check.

Later, leaning against the bookshelves, he pulls himself out of Proust's two-page sentences on Charlus and Jupien and homosexuality and Dreyfus and Jews and Christ. It's almost one o'clock. He'll make a quick lunch and write.

As he finishes eating, he understands that making the salad niçoise wasn't so much the time waster as deciding to do it right and going out to buy the anchovies. He could start writing a notebook of evasions, beginning with Anchovies, a can of. But it's now time to call Lucy.

She answers, "Ethan? I've moved to one of the campus houses on Las Lomas, and Roberta and John are giving a little dinner party at seven tonight to celebrate the move, but I have to attend a faculty meeting and might be late so you could go on your own, I'll give you the address, and if you'd like to see the place, mine, not Roberta's, it's the last house on Las Lomas, opposite the Business School, and I can be there from four to five-thirty. Hello?"

"I'm here, smiling. It's wonderful and I'll see you at four."

He knows he can't mention seeing Dixon. Dixon and happiness are incompatible. In the time before he visits Lucy, Ethan works on outline notes for his workshop. He can do this because it isn't *writing*.

He arrives, bouquet in hand, to see a large, low 1940's adobe style house sitting back of a lawn and semi-circular drive. Lucy stands in the open door. "Very nice," he says, kissing her, as she takes the bouquet and shows him in. They tour in silence the simply furnished rooms, go out through a windowed porch to a large, weedy garden with a wilted orchard on one side and an empty swimming pool on the other. They stand by the pool looking back at the house.

Lucy says, "It's not real adobe, you know. Is it authentic enough for you?"

"*Mea maxima culpa* and I really like it. Can we fill the pool?"

"No, I asked. It's cracked. Anyhow, that would take away from the seedy charm. Come inside, there's something I want to show you." Ethan has a good idea of what this is even before she leads him into the main bedroom.

Afterwards, Lucy explains the swamp cooler system, and Ethan is touched by her clarity and happiness and the sense of the two of them on the bed in the big bare room in the afternoon. He says, "This is our brave new world and we can spend the entire weekend here."

"It is and we will," she says, "but not this weekend. Remember? I'm off to Vanderbilt tomorrow for a week. But it feels so good to be here, away from all that dreadful perfection with Willy. You'll meet Emmy here. I'll show you her photo."

She goes naked to her handbag on the dresser and brings back her wallet, opening it for him. "She was a lot younger then, but isn't she cute?"

Ethan looks at a ten-year old on a mountain, her hair blown wildly in the wind. "She's beautiful, Lucy."

Lucy gets into bed again and pulls the sheet over them. "I'm sure your workshop will go well. And something might come up in the English Department. There's an idea to start a separate department of creative writing." She turns on her side and rests on her elbow, looking down at him, stroking his hair. "You're really not going to leave Albuquerque? Of course you're not. You're my good news."

He takes her in his arms. He feels happy; comfortable and uncommitted. Then Lucy sees the time and kisses him and rushes to shower. Ethan dresses, puts his head in the shower and soaks himself kissing Lucy goodbye.

By the time he's walked back to Copper Place, he feels so good he decides to phone his father. He remembers that Wednesday is Meyer's day at Brandeis, his status at the university marked by a one day per week schedule, his personality marked by his compulsion to keep to this schedule even during the summer vacation. As he phones, Ethan feels magnanimous: never mind Meyer's not praising his novels (though his sudden fame caught his father's attention). The man is ill. As a philosopher, Meyer must be going through a hard time confronting this situation, an unadorned sentence of death as flat and ineluctable as the words from a gatekeeper in Kafka.

His call is answered by Gloria, his father's secretary who insists on this title. "Ethan, nice to hear your voice. Your father isn't here."

"What time will he be back?"

"He's on holiday in the West Indies. He left on Sunday."

"Ah. Good."

"St. Lucia and the Grenadines. He'll be back in a week and a half. Would you like the phone numbers of his hotels?"

"No, it's nothing important. Nice speaking to you, Gloria." There's no use in moaning to her that Meyer hasn't told him about the trip. If Gloria came across Meyer holding a bloody dagger over a corpse, she'd be annoyed with the corpse for disturbing the Professor. So much for his father's angst as he confronts his death. He's on a beach confronting a piña colada. But what should he do: sit alone in his dark living room sipping club soda? A Caribbean holiday is a good idea Ethan, proud of his understanding, prepares for the dinner party at Roberta's. It's Lucy's and his first social event as a couple, their coming out party.

His thoughts turn to Proust again. And why shouldn't he enjoy living through Proust's description of living, in that no one else, not even Tolstoy, can so perfectly put on paper the headiness of getting ready to go to a party? Dukes and duchesses, *haute bourgeoisie*, professionals of middle level, shopkeepers, tradesmen, servants, proletarians and peasants, all Proust's people enjoy this. With Ethan, it's the stiff vodka and tonic on the basin as he showers, a faint smell of fern from the Roget & Gallet Fougère soap out of the box he's brought from back East, the sound in French pleasing him as he draws tight the skin of his neck and cleanly draws the razor up in one long stroke, the sound of "air" in *fougère* echoing the fern-filled air, so that the forest mixes with an idea of perfume—some memory trace of his mother's perfume from his childhood: was it lily of the valley? Is that Nina Ricci's *L'Air du Temps?*—perfumes and greetings and meetings soon to come at the dinner party, and before he can say John Keats, he's thinking of the joys of anticipation and also of the darker essence of the ode on realized experience, and he ends by wondering at the closeness of the Latin *consummare*, to perfect, from which our "consummate," and *consumere*, to destroy, from which "consume." But then there's a good belt of the v & t between shave and shower, and all thought runs off in the feel of hot water on his skin and iced vodka inside it. Soon, standing back from the bedroom mirror, he checks out the denim shirt and black jeans under the camel hair sports jacket and declares himself a proper east-west mix.

But at the door of Roberta and Richard Palmer's house, he feels it's a mistake. He's going to feel isolated and patronized. Roberta teased him at the infamous party. Insulted, isolated and patronized. Once inside, he forgets all this; he's made very welcome. He puts this down to having passed their first test—he's stayed with Lucy. Richard Palmer is amusing, a lawyer with a background in rock and roll, and Doc N is here with Alice, a painter, a dark, pretty Navajo, and there's Roberta's friend from the party, whose name Ethan again doesn't catch, though he thinks it might be Sonya and he listens a while for it from others, then forgets to listen. He answers the door when Lucy arrives. As they look at a shelf of old kachina figures in the hall, Lucy takes his hand and brings it up under her skirt. She says, "I can't stop thinking about you." He likes this; he knows he can stop thinking about her, though not right now. Now she is his middle-aged Beatrice and this is his *vita* partly *nuova*. At dinner, around a big oak table on the back porch, Lucy's move is toasted as, later, is Ethan's workshop. After dinner, there's dancing in the back room on the saltillo tiles under the viga ceiling. He invites Lucy. She shakes her head.

He says, "But that's Big Joe Turner singing with the Basie band."
She says, "I don't dance."
"Anyone who can walk can dance."
"I don't."
"Right, then you stand still and I'll dance."
She follows him to the room. "Go ahead," she says.
"Sure, but you have to prove to me that you won't dance."
"I'm doing that now."
"No, to prove it you have to step on both my feet at once."
By this time, others are listening, dancing around them.
She says, "If I do that you'll stop asking me to dance?"
"Exactly."
"With or without my shoes?"
He sees they're not spiked heels. "Either way."
As she steps on his feet and puts an arm on his shoulder for support, he throws his arms about her and starts sliding his feet, singing along with Joe Turner: "Say that you love me, baby, Say that you really care."
She says, "Oh, no."
He says, "Don't you dare break your promise and move your feet."
On his feet in her heels, she's almost his height. Her pale blue eyes are flecked with sparks. "Do you know what you're doing?"
He whispers, "Abducting you to Kansas City."
"What?"
"This is not to be explained."
This gets to her. She says, "Fool."
"You bet."

Back at Copper Place, both undress and he tells her not to dance and she stands on his feet, and he slides her around the dark room with its French windows and books. Later, making love, the tops of his feet still tingle. He drives back with her to the campus house and, perhaps because she's off early in the morning, he tells her at the door of his father's illness and of not yet speaking to him. She tells him of an aunt of hers who's had ankylosis spondylitis for twenty years and is going strong. She says, "I'm telling you this to buck you up. When I'm at Vanderbilt, you're going to sit down and write, because you won't have anyone to dance around your room naked next week. You better not."

The next night, twenty people turn up for Ethan's workshop. It turns out that half of them have heard about it through the University. He doesn't ask, but he knows this has been through Lucy's efforts. The group is the usual mix from eighteen to fifty, with the usual mix of writing backgrounds. He'll get all of them involved. The session closes with five of them volunteering to bring copies of their writing in for the next time. When everyone leaves, Ethan does a quick calculation: he can make $6000 from each workshop if no one drops out. A student comes back in, re-introduces himself as Steve, and tells Ethan he thinks he should know that the four people who've come on bikes have had their tires slashed. "This is a pretty mixed area," Steve adds. Ethan promises to arrange that bikes can be brought into the entrance hall from now on, and Steve asks if it would be okay if people brought copies of Ethan's novels for him to sign. "Yes, certainly," Ethan says, and he takes up Steve's invitation and joins some of the group at Suds, a beer barn on Central, all plastic split rail and shaggy bark.

The usual questions come up around the table: what writers he likes, what about science fiction? As in class, much of the talking is done by Steve and Eileen Smith, a round-faced girl with a slight foreign accent. Ethan is charmed by Steve's answering, "No, I don't think so," to the question does he write science fiction, after Ethan explains why he so dislikes it. From time to time Ethan glances at the girl sitting next to Eileen. She doesn't say a word. She is terrible looking. The name she gave in class was April Gale, though she looks like a slight breeze might knock her down. Does she have an awful cancer? Is she a terminal junkie? She's five eight or nine and can't weigh more than seventy-five pounds. When she smiles, which she does often, her head under her lank pinkish hair, becomes a skull. And she pathetically, repulsively, tries to be sexy, crossing and re-crossing her pencil legs in her too short skirt. It's this behavior, as he listens to Steve explain why he likes James Ellroy, that gives Ethan the answer. He's witnessing full-blown anorexia nervosa, though "full" is a cruel word for this flirty, antaphrodisiac wraith. Nonetheless, they're a pleasant group, and after Ethan has his sandwich and stands another round of beers, he leaves and walks the long blocks to Copper Place feeling hopeful, even about his own writing.

Immediately after breakfast next morning, he sits at his desk. There's only one pad of yellow paper and two roller pens left. He also needs printer paper and inkjet cartridges. So he goes out to Central Ave. but decides the University bookstore will have the best stock of writing supplies. It turns out not to have the cartridges he needs, and by the time he gets back from the second stationers, it's nearly lunchtime, and it would be foolish to start writing only to stop so soon. He's so energized by the thought of writing that he has two beers with lunch and becomes sleepy. He goes out to walk this off and finds he's gone all the way down Central to the downtown area which he finds so hideous that he continues on to the old Spanish section of town, from where he decides to return home by a more interesting route than Central. This zigzags him slowly up the slopes onto the edge of the University campus. He is somehow amazed to find that it's half-past four by the time he's back at Copper Place, and now he has to strip off his sweaty clothes and shower. At five, Ethan sits barefoot in jeans and tee shirt, ready to, raring to, write. To write anything. He considers this. To write anything strikes him as very much the same as writing nothing very much. He might write someone a letter, but that wouldn't be *writing*. He means fiction. Fiction. It is already five-thirty. He laughs at himself. He's cowardly, he's lazy, he's an Oblomov of a writer. He gets up and finds the novel to see how easily Oblomov's indecisions, and unfinished and never-begun projects, could be translated to his writer's block. He reads on, impressed with Goncharov's detail—the sheer energy and work required to create the world of such inertia. Ethan stands reading the book until after seven. He finally shakes his head and puts on a Stan Getz CD. He likes the fast, cool, satisfyingly sad music. He has a vodka and tonic. At eight, he makes supper and sits eating, listening to the local NPR station, though not really hearing the voices and music. When he gets ready for bed, Ethan feels miserable. He pledges himself to go out in the morning and write his observations of the morning in the afternoon; he appends a subpledge never again to waste time reading about a time-waster.

On Saturday morning, Ethan walks around Nob Hill, vaguely

noting the vaguely Art Deco buildings. He browses some bookstores and finds a good second-hand copy of the Gregory translation of Catullus he's always meant to buy. After this, he sits at a sidewalk café and reads the *New York Times*. He watches a parade of cars from the 1940's, 50's and 60's roll past the street sign saying HISTORIC ROUTE 66. He goes home, sits at his desk and writes about what he has seen. He reads what he's written as he has lunch. The writing is very clear and depressingly irrelevant to anything that interests him.

He goes out again, to an art-movie house showing Hitchcock's *Notorious*, in which he sees as new some of the cars he's just seen on the streets. He also falls in Saturday-afternoon love again with Ingrid Bergman. Back at his apartment, he finds he's out of wine, so he drives out to Jubilation Liquors, the good store Lucy has shown him, and buys some Chablis for not too much more than he can afford. Driving back, he parks not far from the store and walks around a neighborhood of the same vintage as the film and the cars, a time when land was cheap and when big and low was beautiful. Many of the western style houses have fine landscaped gardens, some houses are of real architectural interest and a few of the horrors are hilarious. The daylight is down to one pink-blue gash at the bottom of the sky when, back near where he's parked, Ethan sees a spaceship hovering where a house should be. He crosses the road for a better look. Half flying saucer, half flying cigar, it appears to hang fifteen feet off the ground, but he then sees the staircase shaft designed as a docking tower. The windows are Buck Rogers portholes, and he can make out the galley kitchen in the spaceship nose. A car door opens behind him as he walks slowly along the grass verge by the sidewalk.

"Yes?" Ethan says to the tap on his shoulder. He turns and is struck in the stomach with what feels like a lead pipe. He doubles over sucking for breath, but he's pulled up from behind, his arms pulled back, his mouth stuffed with cloth. He sees only the close-up flurry of arms and fists, two men, maybe three, and at the edge of his vision, leaning against a tree, a giant of a man looking on. A long ponytail swings as the man turns his face away. Then the punches come to the side of Ethan's head; he's blacking out, trying to duck. Then he doesn't know if he's up or down; he's punched or kicked in the nose and red pain crosses in his eyes and he passes out. He comes to on the ground only to pass out on each of the further kicks—ribs, stomach and chest—as he writhes there.

He comes to. The men have disappeared like space aliens. He's on the grass at the curb seeing the space house shake as if ready to blast off. It makes a low O sound. He does. He can't stop. He gets to his hands and knees, all pain. The house settles back on its docking tower. Not one citizen is on the street to help him; all are safe in this dream neighborhood inside their domestic fantasies as he moans, limps and lurches towards his Jeep. When he slides his car keys past his wallet, he knows he hasn't been robbed.

He manages to drive back to Copper Place. He sits in the Jeep with his eyes streaming. He touches his face; the pain is so strong he can't feel his fingers. He pulls himself out of the Jeep and has to pee quickly. He goes at the foot of his stairs. They could be waiting in his apartment. He knows they're not, but knowing that if they were there would be nothing he could do to defend himself, he becomes terrified. He walks away from his apartment. He is bent with pain and homeless. He understands the poor Bosnians. He knows the police would be useless. His attackers could be waiting in any of these shadows along Copper Place. He turns off into a bigger, better-lit street and heads for the brightest light. It's an all-night launderette, and he's always thought of launderettes with some repugnance, places of transience and poverty: men's drooped grayed underpants, the child squirming on its mother's lap, snot hanging from its nose. Now it's the perfect haven, much better than a police station. Only a few people inside. They stare as he sits down. He stares back, checking they're not part of the gang. It has to be Dixon who's had him beaten up. Or Alvarado. The washing machines make a regular, comfortably churning sound. As his eyes close, he wonders where he's bought the red shirt.

Someone is calling in his sleep, "Mr. Baum. Ethan. Ethan." The light is too bright. Someone crouches in front of him. He squeezes his eyes shut to focus. "Ethan, please!" A round face comes close, he hopes not to beat him. "Ethan, it's Eileen, Eileen Smith from your workshop. You have had an accident. Can I help you? Should I call an ambulance?"

He shakes his head. It hurts.

"Should I take you to your home?"

He says, "Not there. Please." His eyes close, he feels her help him up. He walks on her arm, bent and squinting. What if they attack again? He aches and aches. He walks with her forever and then is helped up stairs. A door opens, she leads him across a room he takes to be his own at Copper Place, and he blacks out. Coolness, his jacket and shirt off. Wet cloth to his face and chest. He sees the flying saucer house take off, a giant with a ponytail at the controls. He opens his eyes. He's on a sofa in a place not his. He remembers Eileen and the launderette. He lies still. Through the wall beside his head a young woman's voice: "...getting so big you want to stick it into my tight little ass? My other hand's making my clit feel so good I think I'm going to let you. Mmm. Oooh, and no I don't want you to because it's so little but I know you'll shoot your big load into my ass. Oooh." It must be a porn film from the next apartment. He falls asleep. A cool cloth moves lightly over his sore face; something spoken softly in a foreign language. Someone calls, "Get in here quick for a lesbo."

Ethan wakes with Eileen on the edge of the sofa asking him to lift his head. A glass comes to his lips. He sips. A sort of liqueur that reminds him of something. He sleeps. He wakes and squints at his watch. Midnight. His arms hurt. Everything hurts. He feels sick to his stomach. It passes. The side of his head burns. He is helpless: from now on he'll be particularly vulnerable, a target for criminals. They'll smell his fear like dogs. Eileen's round face leans in. He says, "Thanks for helping." It hurts his ear and cheekbone to speak.

She says, "It was nothing. You feel better?"

"Yes. Was that slivovitz?"

"Yes. Would you like more?"

"No. I haven't had it in years, and now twice in two weeks. A Bosnian friend put it in an omelet. Stucic, his name is. A nice sad man."

"Do you want water?"

He nods. She brings some, he sips. He lies back, seeing he has on a large clean tee shirt. He falls asleep and hears through the wall the moaning and yelling of orgasm. He opens his eyes. Eileen sits on a chair beside the sofa drinking from a brandy glass. He says, "I'll be okay to leave soon, I think."

"Stay as long as you need. What happened to you?"

"I was attacked by three or four men. Out of nowhere. I don't know why: they didn't rob me."

She says, "If you can talk, what is your Bosnian friend's story?"

It hurts to talk but it's better than being alone. He speaks low to keep his head from breaking open. "Stucic is at the University, teaching languages. He was forced out of Bosnia by the war. He comes from Sarajevo, a playwright and diplomat. Because he only wanted to help and didn't side with any of the warring forces, they were all suspicious of him."

Eileen excuses herself. He dozes. She's back, giving him aspirin and water. He takes them and thanks her.

She says, "And when he told you his story, he used the expression 'impartial humanism'?"

"Yes. Is it a common expression?"

"No, only his, this Stucic friend of yours. My real name is Elena Stucic. I am unfortunately the daughter of Miroslav Stucic. He is a war criminal."

"What?"

"Murder, rape, torture, genocide."

The night is already nightmare enough. "That can't be true."

"I was there. There are witnesses."

"Eileen, Elena, I know you have some problems with your father, but what you say can't be. It must be the slander of his enemies, the ones, you know…"

"Who found him guilty of impartial humanism? Oh, my father is clever and charming, and so you believe his story, part of which is true. So you are sorry for this man who should be tried, convicted, and shot." She stands and walks to the closed window curtains. He's too stunned and beaten to defend Stucic.

Eileen returns and pulls her chair close. She drinks down the snifter. "My father's diplomacy, yes. He was a diplomat. We lived in Stockholm for five years. He was deputy ambassador and cultural attaché for Scandinavia. We returned to Yugoslavia when it began to break up in the early nineties, to Sarajevo. You have been there?"

He shakes his head.

"An old city. Pretty. Very mixed in religion, as he may have said to you. The story is my father always had the hots for a neighbor of ours, Kanita, a Moslem. She was beautiful, but happily married with two children. Not to speak of my mother and me. So my father went off on diplomatic missions as the war came to Sarajevo in ninety-two. He would return for a few days and go away for weeks. Supposedly he was negotiating with the Serbs who were shelling the city. We were good friends of Kanita and her family, so when they wished to leave, my father said he could arrange a safe conduct for them to join the rest of their family in a Moslem enclave. Kanita was not his mistress then or ever, you understand. On the way to this enclave, which it turns out was not safe, the van they were in was ambushed and Kanita's husband and brother and father were killed. She and her children and her mother weren't touched. And who should come along at that moment to rescue her but your friend, my father. What a lucky coincidence!" She stops and tips the empty glass to her mouth and licks her lips. "He tells her he will take them to their family in the enclave, in Gornji Vakuf. This is a beautiful old town in the middle of Bosnia, in forests and hills. Rolling hills, you say. What he also says to Kanita, a woman now without her family men, is that he alone can protect her and that he has loved and wanted her for years. She understands, of course, what he means, and she rejects him but is afraid of him. So she joins the rest of her family just as the terrible fighting there begins between Croats and Bosnian Moslems. Maybe this place you have heard about? The barrel bombs in Gornji Vakuf?"

Ethan shakes his head. Eileen/Elena is losing her English.

"This town is of hills for streets and is surrounded by more hills. Terrible fighting and then the Moslems all squashed back into the town and surrounded by Croats who make these bombs, are big barrels filled with explosive come rolling down the streets, so big even before explode could kill anyone. And so heavy they break what they hit and then they explode whole street blown up. Day after day, you see, they never know when come, kids, everyone trapped, day and night barrel bombs rolling down for weeks for months this horror on and on, and who comes then but wonderful Miroslav Stucic who was before with bastards Serb Chetniks and now your friend is with bastards Croat Ustasi. So this his big diplomacy for both sides."

She stops and hangs her head. Her face is covered in sweat. Ethan's breath is drawn in rasps; his exhalations end in a high piping sounds. She gets up and leaves the room. She returns with another snifter of slivovitz, sits down and drinks half of it. Ethan is unable to talk.

A twisted smile comes to her face. She says, "And then comes my father and rapes Kanita in front of children and old mother. Let me tell you: later in Gornji Vakuf they find name of Croat who makes these bombs from barrels but he is run away, so they find his wife and children and crucify them up like Christ and slice them open? But is my father who deserve this and nothing happen to him. Your friend so nice, playwright and diplomat who make you omelet with slivovica, he gets away because helped by Serb and Croat gangster bosses, also United Nations friends. He calls this omelet *diable de Bosnie*, but he is devil of Bosnia, butcher of Bosnia."

Ethan can't accept this but at the same time remembers how vehemently Stucic rejected meeting with other Bosnians. Was he afraid of being recognized? But there are lists of war criminals, and his pal Pete Walsall in Boston has a friend in a human rights organization who could find out. He feels awful. He reaches out to touch Elena's hand. She pulls it back and runs from the room. His eyes close. Women's voices argue on the other side of the wall. He sits up slowly, rocking with pain. He takes off the tee shirt and puts on his jacket and folds his bloody shirt over his arm. He starts to get up but falls back to sit on the sofa longer. His pains have joined up. He is one long ache from his left ear to his right knee.

He dozes, wakes, and pushes himself up. Elena's friend April comes into the room. Her hair is pulled back and, in tight tee shirt and long, tight skirt, she is at once the comic image of Popeye's girlfriend Olive Oil and a terrible semblance from the concentration camps. He says, "I'm sorry if I've woken you up. Please thank Eileen for me. Goodnight, April.

She smiles. He can make out her teeth through her cheek. She says, "You didn't wake me. I don't live here, I only work here."

"What do you do?" he asks. His hand is on the doorknob.

"We do telephone sex. I guess I should tell you my name isn't really April Gale. I use that for your class. I'm Emmy. My mother is Lucy Evans."

He says, leaving, "Don't be so silly," knowing everything she's said is true.

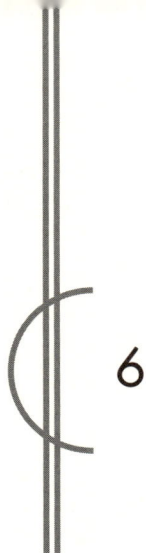

6

AT COPPER PLACE, no one waits inside his door to beat him. He swallows what painkillers he finds, takes off his clothes, and waits in bed for some numbing of his pain. At last, it moves from hammer beat to heavy throb, still too strong for sleep but enabling Ethan to establish his own emotional counter-rhythm: it's impossible that Eileen is Stucic's daughter; it's impossible that Stucic has done what she claims; it's impossible that April is Lucy's daughter, since it's impossible that Lucy would not refer to Emmy's illness. At this point, Ethan thinks it impossible that he's been beaten up, whereupon the architectonics of his denial implodes. Who had him beaten and Why are questions he saves for later in what he judges will be a long, sleepless night. Now he starts to argue against his original denials. How would Eileen know Stucic's phrasing and the name of his omelet unless she's Elena? Why did Stucic make a point of explaining why he was so disliked in Bosnia and why he so disliked Bosnian associations unless he's something of what Elena says? And why would Lucy show him a ten-year-old's photo of her eighteen year old unless she didn't want him to see Emmy as she really was? And the telephone sex? Why is everything deception?

As if in hermetic answer to these questions, he remembers the incident of the sudden stewardess, years before his split with Helen. He'd just told Meyer that the marriage had problems. Betty and Van, Helen's banal yet bananas parents, phone daily to say how much their daughter loves him, despite what she says, and how they, if he doesn't mind them saying so—the loons are always on the phone together— love him like a son, not a son-in-law, and they don't mind saying so. Meyer, on the other hand, speaks sensitively about the difficulties of two creative people being able to let go of their egos. So, on Meyer's return from a philosophy symposium in San Francisco, Ethan looks forward to more of what he thinks of as Zen and the Art of Marriage Maintenance. This takes place at McCarthy's Grill, at the corner of Beacon and Washington, in Brookline, a toofer night, though Meyer has changed his order from lobster to chicken. He asks, "Are you sure Helen doesn't mind not coming out with us?"

"She approves of the Baum Boys' night out, especially these days. You said you had to talk to me. I guessed it wasn't about the symposium."

"The symposium? The symposium was hijacked by a gang of semiotics birdbrains. They're to philosophy what plumbers are to chemistry. Let them go to a plumbers' symposium. No, I want to talk about something personal."

Ethan prepares for a sensible talk on trussing his herniated marriage. He has ample time for this preparation, since his father is off in who-knows-what far realms of a long, long pause. Finally, Meyer says, "They gave me a first class ticket, and on the way back the plane was two-thirds empty. And what can the airlines do for all that money but throw food and drink and their staff at you? So I get talking with my stewardess, a nice young woman. Mary Keegan."

Ethan is surprised that his father, in widowhood a celibate to the memory of his wife, should remember the name of a stewardess.

Meyer says, "It turns out she lives in Boston. So I say I'm from Boston. Of course, the plane is going to Boston, so there's no particular coincidence there. And when she asks, I tell her what I do, et cetera, and she turns out to be a bright Northeastern graduate who loves travel and has interesting business plans for the future. Also, this Mary Keegan is what my friend Jan Pavlick would call 'drrrop-dead beautyfull.' The greenest eyes and fairest skin and blackest hair."

Could his father, pillar of the faithful, be dating her? Years after his mother's death, Ethan had asked his father about seeing women. His father shook his head and said, "Well, no. There was Marion. And now that she's gone, I have to say there still is Marion, strangely and satisfyingly."

Ethan stays quiet.

Meyer says, "Well, in all this pleasant airplane chat, I took out my wallet and showed her your photo, you know, with Marion's. And she remarked how handsome you were, and I told her about you, at which she said she knew your name, had heard of *Jack at Bat*. Anyhow, one thing lead to another, and just before I left the plane she wrote her address and phone number and said maybe you'd like to call her. Only, you know, not in a tawdry way. Here."

Ethan is so shocked he can't ask if his father told the stewardess he was married. He recognizes the folded paper as a page torn from Meyer's green notebook for philosophical jottings, a piece of four by six graph paper. He has teased his father about not having a blue notebook out of respect for Wittgenstein, and this makes him even more ashamed of what's on the page. Ethan whisks it from the table and stuffs it into his pocket before it, or he, bursts into spontaneous combustion. He is also ashamed of being ashamed of his father.

Meyer says, "Look, call her, don't call her. I'm merely passing this on, as requested."

Ethan keeps looking at his two red lobsters. His father is now speaking about San Francisco as if the stewardess business were the most natural thing in the world. Ethan could not be more shocked had Meyer turned up in drag. Meyer the monogamous has just pimped for his married son by way of solving said son's marital problems. Ethan feels so bad that he's grateful when Meyer at last brings up the familiar syllogism: San Francisco is to Los Angeles as Boston is to New York, behind which lurks ancient "as Athens to Rome." He picks it up as something he can talk about, abandoning his actual belief that for at least the past century, all of Boston's culture could be dropped into New York's and disappear without trace. Which is what he wishes for the entire evening when, at its end, he feels he must raise and refute this stewardess madness. He says, "Good night, Meyer. About that stewardess..."

Meyer gives a dismissive flutter of his hand. "Oh, that. Amusing, but of course I couldn't give you her address."

With which Meyer walks up the path to his apartment house leaving Ethan in his car muttering, "What? What?" One of them has flipped out. Was there, after all, nothing written on the paper? He pulls it out, uncrumples it, and there in a hand not his father's is Mary Keegan's name, address and telephone number.

Ethan shifts on his bed of pain in Copper Place. Pale blue light comes through the curtains. Might that have been the first onset of

Meyer's illness? A deficiency of blood leading to some synaptic disconnect, the loss of memory about giving him the address? A worse idea arrives as Ethan tries to shift away from the drumming pain: Had the illness caused Meyer to forget his disguise and reveal the *real* Meyer Baum—mischievous, priapic?

Beneath his already aching stomach, the ibuprofen gives him a stomach ache. What happened then? What happened is that he phoned Mary Keegan to find out, so he supposed, what his father was up to. The minute he hears her voice, however, just her ordinary "Hello," something else takes hold, an idea thrilling in its craziness. What if Meyer is purposely demonstrating that his stated beliefs have nothing to do with his real beliefs? And what if his meaning is Do As I Do? Mary Keegan's laughter on the phone is long and ringing, the only laugh he's ever heard that fits the cliché "crystalline." She accepts his invitation to dinner the next night so they can talk about "my dad's strange behavior." He picks her up at her apartment off Mass. Ave. in Cambridge. When she answers the door, he nearly gasps. Mary is everything his father said. His heart races like a dog with a bone, with a boner, until, holding the door as she gets into the car, he notices what Meyer had not or had not minded—her heavy ankles. He almost yelps in disappointment, so critical is the ankle's in-turn to his turn-on. And so the beautiful but now unattractive Mary Keegan dines with him at a Lebanese restaurant on Brattle Street and tells him how good looking he is and says she knows he's had hundreds of women. He answers that he knows he's good looking because he keeps being told he's good looking, but that he's also shy with women and, being good looking, he is lazy with women so that, no, his behavior isn't at all like she suggests. They talk of her meeting with his father. He learns nothing new. Back at her apartment she asks him in for coffee and he accepts, a mark of how secure he is in the lack of his sexual interest. She says, as they primly sip, that what really interested her about him on the plane wasn't so much his photo as the way his father made him seem attractive.

He says, "My father did? How was that?"

"The way he made you seem so funny and bewildered in your marriage. Your wife's a well-known painter, isn't she?"

His father has picked up a stewardess by charming her with droll tales from his son's failing marriage! Has picked up a stewardess for whom? He says to Mary's question about Helen, "Yes, she is," rather than "Wife? My father must have meant his other son, Tannen Baum." And why does this make him forget Mary's ankles, her anklelessness, right to the point of naked penetration on her pretty, bird's-eye maple bed, when he wilts—not her ankles but his many residual guilts swelling up to deflate him and, emotionally, Mary? Is it competition with his father, or is Meyer merely the stalking horse behind which his own libido lopes? Poor Mary of the peach-and-cream complexion and so soft black hair and green eyes, the wild Irish rose indeed, deserves better than this unfunny son of a father who has, Ethan thinks at the point of rolling off her, in some way taken advantage of both the people naked here in bed.

Ethan leaves his bed in Albuquerque, turns on the light and swings open the closet door. Its inside full-length mirror shows a tall naked man with a three-foot red-purple bruise winding from mid thigh to right nipple. His left eye is blue-black, two-thirds closed, his nose is swollen, the nostrils full of clotted blood. His stomach, totally unmarked, hurts most. What does it mean that he hasn't remembered any of this stewardess story until now? And why now? It strikes him that quite often he can't tell if he's thinking about his father or himself.

At some time after dawn, Ethan drops into a sleep of sighs and winces. He wakes after nine, wincing, sighing "Ah, ah," as he coaxes and bullies himself from bed. Should he call the police? No. He realizes his distrust of police comes from Mexico, but the local police really would be of no help. In the bathroom mirror, he sees dark blue streaks running from the side of his nose across his cheek; between the blue run rills of scarlet. He looks like a mandrill.

By late morning, he's worried himself into the emergency room of University Hospital. He says he's had a bike accident on a mountain trail. "A mountain bike accident," he adds. The doctor inspects Ethan stripped to his underpants and orders X-rays and urine and stool tests. As he waits for the X-rays to be checked, he imagines his father sailing the Grenadines with Mary Keegan. She fusses over the ankylosis spondylitis of this poor man who will die of it one night in his ninety-seventh year. Ethan knows he's confusing anklelessness with ankylosis. He feels guilty about being beaten while he was avoiding writing, though the thugs would have caught him some other time. The doctor comes and tells him there's probably some slight cracking near the tip of two ribs, but it's not worth strapping. She gives him painkillers, writes a prescription for more and says he needn't come back unless he finds blood in his stool or urine. As he stands to go, she says, "And stay off that mountain bike for a while." He promises.

He thinks, The bike! His beating and the slashed tires at the workshop. When he gets to his apartment, he phones Doc N, and after apologizing for interrupting his weekend, to which Doc N says, "Huh, you must be joking," Ethan asks, "Do you know if there's much vandalism around the workshop building?"

Doc N says, "First year we used it there were a few broken windows, but since then, for the past four years, no. You having trouble?"

"It might not be anything. I'll let you know. Thanks." There's no point in telling Doc N of the beating until it's necessary, but now he's sure the tire slashing and his beating are connected.

It has to be Dixon, Dixon whom he's twice humiliated, who's vowed to repay him "tenfold." Dixon must have known about the workshop from seeing notices on campus or in the bookshops where he lurked. Dixon has covered his bets by having attacked the workshop and Ethan: stop work and leave town. And if he doesn't stop the workshop, the beatings could extend to the students.

So Ethan spends the afternoon contacting the students who left phone numbers or emails. He also prints out a notice and puts it up on the classroom door. It says that for personal reasons he's unable to continue the workshop. There's no need to mention refunds, since no one has yet paid. By the end of the day, Ethan is stunned with anger, disappointment and painkillers. He wakes in the middle of the night to take more pills.

On Monday morning, he wakes with his first positive thought for days: he can take up Alvarado's offer to discuss working for his Institute. No sooner does he think this than a terrible thought arises. Why must it be Dixon? Why can't it be Alvarado? Alvarado with his power and shady contacts and his dislike of how Ethan treated Lucy on that weekend at Rancho Rauncho. Ethan shuffles around his apartment all day, increasingly depressed with the dilemma of whether it is Dixon or Alvarado who has ruined him. Why not—despite Alvarado's stated contempt for Dixon—both working together? By the next day, Tuesday, Ethan has concluded that the only link between the two men and him is Lucy. Monday's depression seems a flowered hillside to the pit in which he now sits, or shuffles or lies down with painkillers.

By Wednesday—Lucy is due back in the evening—Ethan is terminally confused. What has Lucy said to Dixon? How could she bear even to talk to the creep? What has she asked Alvarado to do? Why should she want him beaten if she wants him to stay? What if he suggests to her he thinks she might be involved? Would she complain again to Alvarado and have him killed? What in the world is he thinking? Yet Alvarado is clearly some sort of father figure to her, a lover turned father figure. And how is it Lucy has shared the same house with slimy Willy all this time after the party? He remembers she hasn't, but it doesn't cheer him up.

Late in the afternoon, head in hands, he thinks what, really, is Lucy's story? She's never told him about Emmy; she's carried on as if her daughter were little Miss Normal. Ethan's head in his hands develops a headache. He takes two more painkillers two hours before he should and shuffles out to have dinner. This is the worst, he thinks.

As he walks onto Central Ave. from the restaurant parking lot, a car pulls up to the traffic light just beyond him. It's a sleek, black, open convertible, a Ferrari, he notices, after noticing the man at the wheel, a very large man with a long black ponytail. Him. Ethan steps into the shadow of the restaurant doorway to look at the man who oversaw his beating. The light changes and the man drives off.

Ethan sits at the restaurant bar and drinks a vodka martini. He'd thought it was the worst when he spent the day thinking about Lucy's involvement. Now he's seen the thug prince and knows it's not the worst while he can still say it's the worst. This seems to him good enough to jot down. He remembers it's from King Lear, which makes him feel even worse, proving the point and making him order a second martini. Over dinner at the bar, he envisions Lucy at the apartment when he returns. He works out his greeting. Hi. Hi, honey. Hi, honey, I'm home. Hi, honey, I'm home from the beating and intimidation and the loss of yet another job before I've begun it. Oh, and, honey? Your honey of a little girl has turned into an anorexic telephone whore. But his dinner cabaret doesn't please him. He finishes his wine and orders an after-dinner brandy with which to take his painkillers. He checks his watch: yes, it's now the right time to take them.

Lucy's white Jeep is parked tight to his apartment steps. Until he unlocks the door, Ethan doesn't realize how angry he is. Inside, Lucy stands at the windows in his bathrobe. She's just washed her hair; it hangs in a red wreath of curls. She says, "My darling man."

He steps into the light. Lucy says, "My God! What's happened?"

He's too drunk, drugged and angry to say. He steps out of his shoes, pulls off his polo shirt, takes off his pants and shorts and stands naked to show her what's happened, but Lucy misinterprets him and comes and throws her arms around him. He howls with pain.

"Sorry, I'm sorry," she says, backing and at the same time reaching out her hands to soothe him. This makes her bend so far forward that she totters into him, banging his chest with her shoulder. Ethan bites his lip.

Lucy says, "You've had an accident."

He finds his tongue: "Nothing accidental about it. An intentional beating, on Saturday. That wasn't the worst of it. The bikes of my workshop people were vandalized on Thursday. Not the worst of it. For my own safety and the safety of my students, I've had to cancel the workshop. Even that isn't the worst of it. After the beating, a workshop member found me bloody in an all-night launderette. I was afraid of coming back here, so she took me back to her place. Her name was Eileen. She cleaned me up and gave me aspirin and told me she was Elena Stucic, the daughter of Miroslav, at the University, and then she told me a terrible story about him being a war criminal. Still, not the worst of it. She and her friend April, also in the workshop, were running a telephone sex service from that apartment. April told me she was your daughter Emmy. April, that is, Emmy is a skeletally thin and maybe dying anorexic. You never told me: that's the worst of it."

Lucy, during his speech, has backed away until she falls into the sofa and covers her head with her arms.

"You spoke about her. Lucy, you told me about buying pots and pans for her apartment. What would she do with them? Pots and pans are for cooking food."

Lucy's head is still in her arms. She pulls her legs up under her.

"You showed me a picture of a healthy ten year old and said nothing except that she was now eighteen. What is going on?"

Lucy is curled tight onto her side. Her eyes are closed, but there are no tears.

Ethan says, "This is the worst, without even considering that it was either your husband or your old boyfriend who had me beaten up. I'm tired. I'm going to bed now. You can play dead at your own place." Minutes later, he hears the front door close and her Jeep drive off.

The next morning, he moves in slow motion, putting off for as long as possible having to think of Lucy, his workshop, his writing, and the rest of his life. Just after noon, the phone rings. It's Carlos Alvarado's office; the Vice President would very much like to speak to him. Even before he comes on the phone, Ethan knows that all this has been planned. Alvarado's first words are: "Ethan, Lucy has just told me everything that's happened." Ethan wonders if this included what he told her about Emmy, or that they were both naked, or that he kicked her, as it were, out of his bed. Alvarado says, "Awful. Shocking and horrible. Could you manage to come to my office at two-thirty?"

Ethan says, "Yes."

At two-thirty, he walks into a grand, semi-circular office whose wall has a mural with the sign PREHISTORIC NEW MEXICO. The office is staffed by the mistress from Rancho Escondito, the Administrative Assistant for Hanky Panky, Rita Sanchez, who ushers him into the still grander and completely circular office of Carlos Alvarado. Alvarado, seated two first downs away, rises and comes forward from his semi-circular desk, which sits under the focal point of this room's mural, HISTORICAL NEW MEXICO. Around the wall, Indian cultures meet European cultures; Pueblo people and conquistadors lead into farming and ranching, the building of cities, the mining and logging industries. The circle completes with diagrammatic atoms orbiting over Los Alamos and a sunburst which might be a nuclear blast, this ambiguous apotheosis of history taking place just over the distant desk, as if Alvarado were the embodied end towards which all these ages had evolved. He clasps Ethan's hand with both of his. "Good God, man, you've taken a beating. I'm so sorry. Sit down, sit down."

They go to an area of chairs and sofas along the room's great arc. "What happened? What do the police think?"

Ethan says: "I was beaten up but not robbed. I haven't gone to the police; there's not much point. I don't think it's going to happen again. The beating and the intimidation of my students has served its purpose: I have no work and Dixon has his revenge."

Alvarado strokes his moustache. "Maybe he wasn't behind it. Not that Willy is morally incapable of such behavior, but he doesn't stick his neck out like that. And I can't think of anyone else who'd want to buy such bad luck for you. Can you?"

"Yes. You. You admitted your behavior at Rancho Escondido was threatening."

Alvarado leans forward, smiling: "I said it was 'unfriendly,' not threatening. Don't be loco, Ethan. I don't want you out of work: I called last week to offer you work. And Lucy would never forgive me if I had you beaten up. Besides, I don't do things like that."

Ethan finds he has no counter arguments. He says, "I don't know what to think."

"Well, I do," Alvarado says. "I think I may have something for you, a text for you to write, describing various places in New Mexico. I'll be perfectly honest: Lucy was our first choice. She refused. Then we thought of several other leading New Mexican writers, but there were political problems. I won't name names, but some wanted the Hispano writer, some wanted the Anglo, and there were others interested in a Navajo or Pueblo Indian writer, and so on. But you, a complete outsider, wouldn't, it appears, raise these problems."

"Just like that, Carlos, the job's mine?"

"No. You know the work of Charles Lavery?"

"Yes, he's a fine photographer."

Alvarado nods. "You bet. The New Mexico Institute has landed a sizeable grant to produce a book based on Lavery's photos. It will show what would be at risk environmentally if all the impending government land deregulation were to go through."

Ethan says, "And I'd write the text for the pictures?"

"Maybe or maybe not for the pictures. That's Lavery's call. But I'm getting ahead of myself. No disrespect to your writing, Ethan, but Charlie Lavery is the big name here. We got the grant essentially because he agreed to do the photography. I've taken the liberty of sending him your books. Don't look so puzzled: Lucy suggested it a month ago. It comes down to this: if Lavery agrees to have you, I'm pretty sure I can persuade the Institute Board. If Lavery doesn't want you, that's it. Maybe an editing job will come up."

Ethan tries to smile but his face hurts. "I want it, but it's also true that I'm in no position to refuse work."

Alvarado says, "The rough idea is that the book should be ready in about six months. We've wasted time trying to find someone local to write it. Your fee—there's no advance, the grant is straight fees—would be fifty thousand dollars, and there's a good travel allowance, as well as the use of our research resources at the Institute."

"It sounds good, even the deadline."

Alvarado stands. "Set up a meeting with Lavery. Make him like you. I know Lucy's put in a good word."

Ethan is put in mind of the hole he's dug for himself with Lucy. He stands and takes Alvarado's hand. "I'm sorry for suggesting you could have been involved in—"

"Forget it, *hombre*. You're still in shock. I'm happy that whoever did this hasn't been able to run you out of town. I'll walk you out. I have to go now, myself."

As Ethan slowly walks down the stairs, he asks, "Do you know Doc N?"

"Of course. A good man."

"He told me I have to understand the land out here."

Alvarado says, "He's absolutely right. Of course, my people don't go as far back as his, here. Mine arrived only in the 1590's. Then my ancestor went back to Mexico City and returned with his family in 1610 and stayed. And despite all these centuries of my family here and studying it all my life, I still can't say I know this state. It's so layered with cultures. We New Mexicans have our own geology—strata, folds, uplifts, sinks. And the climate zones! We have golden eagles over Wheeler Peak and eyeless albino fish swimming under Carlsbad Caverns. This state is more like a separate country. Did you know Spain has a special Consul to New Mexico, and we have what amounts to our own foreign policy with Spain? And the Indian land is literally separate nations. Any ten-square mile Pueblo can issue its own passport. This state has three separate levels of law: ordinary US-New Mexican law, law applying only to Hispanos, and Indian law. Oh, yes, Doc N is right. The land rules here. *La terra grande*. We live on it, we live off it, we have to protect it. Hence the book. And here you are, set to get involved with it, too."

As they part, Alvarado asks, "What did you think of the murals in my office? Russel Ingersoll Leigh, late 1950's, the last gasp of the Taos School."

Ethan says, "It's sensational, especially how it ends over your desk."

Alvarado gives his grand mustached smile: "I like your tact about the pretty picture in my office—and in my assistant's."

Ethan's way home goes through the campus. No use confronting Dixon. He sits to rest on a bench by a pond. A duck quacks. He should confront himself. He's a quack, a fake writer with a fake anger at Lucy. He gets beaten up, so he turns and beats up Lucy. What, after all, is her crime: that she hasn't been able to tell him about her daughter's illness? She deserves his pity, not his anger. He stands. And what if Lucy knew nothing about Emmy's phone sex? And he just had to blurt that out. The duck goes, "Quack, quack."

"You're absolutely right," says Ethan.

He walks to the English Department building. Lucy's assistant says she's working at the library. He leaves a note: "Have just seen Carlos. A million apologies and a thousand thanks. Love from Ethan the duck. PS: Last night I must have been on quack."

When he gets to Copper Place, there's a phone message. Lucy says, "The last part of your note is incredibly silly."

By the end of the week, he's made it up with her and feels healed enough to suggest they celebrate his coming to his senses and maybe coming into a writing job by taking the tramway up to Sandia Peak. Ethan says that what he'd said was mean; he knows it must be difficult for Lucy to talk about Emmy's illness. Lucy has said nothing but—to Ethan's asking did she know about the phone sex job—"Yes. It's not because she needs the money. There's her trust fund."

They don't say much that Saturday afternoon on the half hour drive to the tramway station. He buys the tickets and they get into the back of the cabin. The only other passengers stand at the front, a middle aged man and women in Pittsburgh Pirate hats. Ethan remembers Sandy Milocic was a Pirates fan. This and Lucy's silence, and the grubby bareness of the tramway station depress him. What on earth is he doing here? Doing here with his life?

The car moves forward, tilts and, settling, starts off over the desert scrub. They look out the rear windows. Down below, the fenced buffalo on the Sandia Pueblo look like garden furniture.

They turn and lean against the rail and watch the mountain wall come on. Beneath is talus, rock outcrop, and hang-on, acrobatic pine.

Twice, as the car crosses the cable pylons, it slows and judders, and Ethan feels a nauseous glee at the thought the car could drop and they'd die.

Lucy says, "Sometimes I forget what Emmy looks like. Sometimes she gets locked up in this palace of a clinic. It's a cage. It costs fifteen thousand dollars a week. Eventually, after two months, she puts on weight, four or five pounds. She gets out and I catch her looking at herself in the mirror, pulling at her thin skin as if it were rolls of fat. Sometimes I see how she manipulates me and gets all my attention. But she's dying. I don't know how to stop her. So I stop thinking she's dying or even too thin. When I met you maybe I thought: He's younger and better looking than I am; he doesn't need to know I have such a terrifying daughter. Then I feel guilty and think, forgive me for thinking that, Emmy darling. Then I stop thinking."

Ethan puts his arm around her shoulder. The cable angle becomes steeper. They swing towards a straight-up, thousand foot rock face, and they swing back over ponderosa pine. They slow, and swing, and pull into the cable station.

Lucy tells him not to look back or out until she says to. He follows her outside. It's cool and windy and smells of damp pine. After a series of steps and ramps, she tells him to look out. He sees an airplane's view of Albuquerque: a beautiful desert covered by an ugly desert. He says, "It's high, here."

She says, "The city's awful in this light."

They walk to the mountaintop bar and restaurant and stand in its doorway: the place is a series of deep wooden seating wells, each beneath a massive stainless steel chandelier. The windows are tinted so that for all they can see they might be on the second floor in a flat Midwest town.

Ethan says, "Oh."

She says, "It's like a place in smoke. Let's go."

He says, "Anyway, it's wrong to celebrate: I may not get the job."

"You will. I know Charlie will like your writing and you."

"Oh, yes, you know him."

Lucy says, "Let's go for a walk. I want to show you something."

They go down a flight of concrete stairs. Below them are acres of blacktop parking lots. They walk along a concrete path. Above them, the mountain ridge bristles with electrical blockhouses, communication dishes, aerial masts. Ethan looks down at his shoes or at Lucy ahead of him, hands in her jean jacket. After a while, the path turns to earth. Rocks appear out of the pine needles. They're climbing. Finally they're in ungardened forest, but he has the treasonable suspicion her walk will end in a heated swimming pool complex.

They walk on, single file. His breathing comes harder. Lucy is waiting for him at a break in the trees. Behind her, pure air. A raven lifts off a cliff just north. Sleek, enormous, it gives three grunts and drops five hundred feet, spread-winged, to become a sparrow speck. Lucy says, "Another ten minutes." Ethan, interested, walks on behind her. The path gets rough. It plunges into tree shade and rises and falls over ridges of pine root. Winds suddenly roar out of the east and suddenly fall silent. They come to a series of breaks at the edge of the mountain wall where the land juts out. They can see along the ridge for miles. Lucy says, "Just there," pointing to the next promontory of rock. She goes on. He catches up to her where she stands at a side path leading toward the edge. They walk between small pine and juniper growing at wind-cocked angles. The path disappears. He follows her between brush and the odd tree that seem to grow without soil, the roots disappearing into fissures in the sandstone. The promontory drops and they go down thirty feet among rock and twists of root rope. The wind hits him in the back and nearly knocks him over. He moves by watching his feet, at times stepping heel-to-toe. Ahead of him, Lucy is crouched between two low junipers. She says, "It's okay here. There's no wind. Come and see."

He doesn't know what he expects, maybe an eagle's nest. He crouches and duckwalks to a juniper and grabs onto it to look over. Three feet below is a perfectly smooth slab of sandstone, five feet wide and ten feet long, sticking out from the mountain wall like a diving board. He pulls his head back and shuts his eyes. "Lucy," he says.

"Come here."

He opens his eyes. Lucy is down on the slab, smiling, holding her hand up to him.

He smiles back and takes her hand and makes it down by sitting on the edge, holding her hand and looking at her smile. When he's sitting beside her, his legs stop shaking. They're out past the wall of the mountain. The next thing solid is two thousand feet down. He's sure Lucy knows the exact distance, but he doesn't want to ask. After a while, with his arm on her shoulder, he feels the warmth of the rock slab and the heat of the sun. He wants wings here. His shoulders almost ache from the absence of wings, as if they'd been amputated.

Lucy puts her arm around his waist. "We used to call this 'Emmy's Ledge,' when she was little. She was amazing, a mountain goat child. We had to keep her on a harness, not for her safety but to calm us down. And Perry was a climber. She never even stumbled. Last time I brought her up was three years ago. She couldn't make it to the end of the concrete path." She stops for a while. She says, "People think it dumb I named her Embrace. But that was for me, not for her and *men*." Lucy drops her head and looks at her legs in jeans out before her. Her loafers hang over the edge. An orange butterfly appears up over their toes, flutters around them, and wafts away.

"It's true I do these stupid things like pots and pans, as if French copper would get her eating. What's amazing is her tact in asking for cheaper cookware rather than saying, 'Mom, who are we kidding?' If we go to a bookstore, I'll work our way over to the health food section and my diplomatic daughter nods and listens to me talking about food instead of doing what by now is her instinct—to throw up in disgust, throw up the nothing in her shrunken stomach." When she stops talking there is perfect silence. Air, he thinks, that is airless.

"And we have talked about everything, and we have been to the counselors and psychiatrists and psychologists and behaviorists. Don't you think I knew about this pathetic phone-sex thing she's doing? Don't I know she's dying? Doesn't she? She said she knows she's the baby in the bathwater. She actually said that. Willy, to do him justice, tried with her at first. Then he gave up. I know that breaking us up is what Emmy wanted, though that doesn't mean I didn't want it, too." She stops.

Out of the silence she says, "What should I do, force her back into the clinic? into college where she'll also die? Her joining your workshop is best thing she's done, and now that's over. Of course, she wouldn't tell me. I know she's been writing, but, given it's what I do, she can't share that with me. I think she also wanted to check you out. She'll flirt with you, but you're also her competition for me. Ethan, you should have seen her scamper here, right out here. Oh, you would have loved her. I love her more than anything."

They look out at the sky in the softening light. Lucy pushes back and turns towards him. She says, "Remember Kafka's 'The Hunger Artist,' how at the end when he's about to die, the cage sweeper finds him and asks why he's never eaten?"

He nods.

"And he says because he's never found anything he's *liked*. That's Emmy's secret. Emmy is an artist. That's why she never cries. She's perfecting her rejection and wanting to draw crowds. To her cage."

Lucy stands up, as if anticipating Ethan's urge to get her away from here. He gets up carefully. Lucy's foot buckles as if it's gone to sleep, and she reaches to hold him and misses and falls backwards on her side and goes over the edge.

"I'm all right, I'm all right," she says.

She's half on the ledge, propped on her forearms. He goes to his knees saying, 'Wait, wait," and she nods seeing he's going to slide his arms under her shoulders like a harness. Before he can, she tries to pull up and stretches an arm out. Everything inside him goes cold and everything outside goes slow: her other forearm slides back and he grabs her outstretched hand by the wrist but she's still sliding back. He falls forward, clawing down on her hand as she stops sliding back, only her head and shoulders now above the ledge. His head is just above hers. She hangs with her legs kicking to find purchase, but the ledge goes down only to her waist. She looks at him with an embarrassed smile as if she hates causing trouble or being clumsy. He's about to tell her to stop kicking when one of her loafers drops off. He watches it. She stops kicking. She stops smiling. Her shoe is still falling. He sees it shrink to a dot just to the side of her face. He says, "Okay now," and works his left hand to her wrist and, squatting, begins to pull back. He's disturbed by her expression. It isn't panic or despair. It's a cold serenity against which he can only shut his eyes and scream, "Come on, Lucy, help! Damn it, come on!" He pulls back knowing he can't keep her from going down, if that's what she wants. He looks into her eyes again and recognizes the look. In a nature park he'd been to once, outside Tucson, a place someone promised he'd love. It was terrible. Surrounded by real desert, it had artificial rocks and a net dome full of wild birds. Worst was a mountain lion in a cage. Trapped, gorgeous, crazed, it was a mountain lion out of Rilke, and Lucy has its pale blue eyes.

Ethan is terrified, crying, screaming, spitting in her face, and

Lucy wakes from whatever bright death she dreams and manages to get propped again, and he pulls and she pushes, and he feels her inching up, sliding and scraping onto the ledge. As she gets one knee over, he hooks his arm behind her shoulder and yanks her back. They tumble over, he down backwards and she heels over head, onto the ledge. He doesn't stop: he crouches up and drags her until she sits with her back propped against the rocks of the promontory. He sits propped between her and the rest of the ledge because he is too tired to move, and it keeps her from running back out and diving off to await her daughter. Woman, he keeps thinking: woman, man and woman.

He comes to his senses with Lucy rubbing his back, saying, "Shh, shh. It's all right, my darling, my Ethan." He's crying, as if instinctively choosing the one sure way to calm her—to be the child-man, to do his unwitting version of what Emmy can not do: weep in Lucy's arms.

The same rocks they've come down in five minutes take them half an hour to drag up through. There's little light left by the time they get off the promontory and back onto the ridge trail. They're all scraped up. They stop from time to time to ask if the other is all right. By the time they're back at the peak restaurant to clean up, they're able to smile at how they limp and at their torn clothing with its little trails of blood. Going down in the tramcar, they slump against each other and close their eyes. Then he drives them to University Hospital where, sitting in the cubicle while the intern dabs him with disinfectant, he notices the drag marks of Lucy's fingernails over his wrists and hands. If she'd gone over, she would have taken him down with her.

Later, in bed in her house, he understands that anything he might suggest to her about accident or suicide, about suicide or murder, would not only be superfluous—since Lucy knows all the possibilities—but wildly beside the point. The point is he's saved her. The point is the Chinese proverb about saving someone. Stinging and burning, still feeling the bruises from his beating, he pushes himself around under the blanket and rests his cheek at the top of Lucy's thigh. She's deep asleep. He says into her pubis, "Must I look after you forever?" But this, too, he senses, is beside the point.

II. LAND

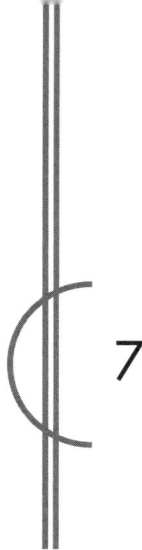

7

THE RADIO IN THE JEEP tells Ethan that at 3:35 P.M. this August Saturday, the temperature is 107. The radio reminds him to drink lots of fluids if he's out in the beautiful New Mexican sun. The radio reminds him that he's nervous; he turns it on only when he's nervous. He's driving out to meet Charles Lavery, and it's taken him weeks to set up the appointment. The support of Lucy and Alvarado seems to have failed. Each time that Ethan calls and leaves an answer-phone message, Lavery doesn't call back; each time he answers the phone, Lavery responds with something like, "Who? Oh, yeah. I don't know. Call in a day or two when I have my dates straight." Only after a dozen such messages and monosyllabic rejections does Lavery concede a meeting.

On the other hand, why should Lavery be impressed by a writer of three more or less mordantly droll East Coast novels, a writer who knows very little about the beauty of New Mexico? Nothing is beautiful now, as he follows Lavery's directions southeast of the airport, where the Sandias crumble to the cracked plateau. Dry yellow earth dusts the prefabs set behind chain fences; it dusts the chained dogs that lie on it and the scrawny chickens that peck in it. The prefabs give way to eroded outcroppings of stone in dun yellow and mud beige, as if, here, even nature were a slum.

Why wasn't Lavery friendly? Why, Ethan means, is it so difficult for him to make friends? Friends, male friends. It must be linked to how he spends his time. He had friends enough in school and college, in the middle of so many people. And teaching at Thoreau, there was a group of them whose friendship extended off campus—Pete and Aamer and Richard. But now he's in a new place where he spends all his time alone, writing at a desk; all right, avoiding writing at a desk. It means he doesn't meet anyone. Should he join a club? He's not aware of any except the N.M. Bosnian Association. When last week Lucy and he gave a dinner party, nice enough men were there—Robert Palmer, Doc N, Brian, the boyfriend of Lucy's assistant. But they're too busy with their lives. Ethan envies the ability of some men—a very American ability—to walk into a room unknown and instantly strike up what appears to be a real friendship: big laughs, taps on the back, and a date for lunch set up in the first ten minutes. Perhaps it's superficial, but it's a start. Is it that he's an only, lonely child? Or could that eighteen month stint in Oxford as a small boy have formed in him that British reserve which makes of friendship what it makes of port, something tasted only after long years of maturing? Yet of all the men he knows out here, the one with this most American ability to make friends is Stucic, though perhaps a Bosnian immigrant (especially one who may be a war criminal) must work hard and fast to make friends.

Ethan turns off Los Picaros onto an unpaved county road. He passes rock formations shaped like giant versions of those baroque sand constructions on the beaches of his childhood called "drip castles."

A mile along the road, he sees, as per directions, the tower rock with trees and shrubs at its base, and he turns into a track, swings behind the rock and sees the house. He has a strange feeling he's seen it before. That could be because he wants to make a friend of Lavery, who's standing at the door.

Lavery is thin and slightly stooped. His crew cut and close-cropped beard are shining white; so framed, his tanned face appears like brown leather. Ethan holds out his hand and says, "Ethan Baum." Lavery gives a touch of his fingers and says, "Mm."

Ethan says, "I feel I've seen this place, though I wouldn't know how."

Lavery says, "Could be a book I did when we built it: *A House in its Place*." He turns and goes in, leaving Ethan to stand outside or follow as if either choice meant about the same. Inside, Ethan sits at the end of a very long table facing the central stone core of the house. He says, "I remember this too, how the place looks more grown than built, with that stone solar collector and structural fulcrum." Lush plants hang from the stone, from the cantilevered stairs, from the joists for the floor above. Ethan says, "It's even nicer with all the plants mature and the walls of books and pictures."

Across the table, Lavery says, "There are some decent views through the narrow windows. This book project got screwed up, you know. I really wanted Lucy to do it. Then she couldn't. Then I thought of Tony, then of Rudy, then of John, even though he's not easy to work with."

"I know. Carlos Alvarado explained."

"Damned PC games," Lavery says from a scowl. He stares at Ethan. "Shit, you really are beautiful, aren't you?"

"What?"

"I mean in that dark, nervous, doe-eyed Jewish way."

Ethan can't tell if Lavery is making a joke, a racial slur, or a pass.

"What do you know about New Mexico?"

Ethan says, "Nothing. *Nada*. Should I go now?"

"Have a glass of water." Lavery stands. "It's 107 out there. You have to drink lots of fluids." He walks off.

Ethan gets up and looks through large windows opening to courtyards, through narrow windows framing wind-sculpted rocks, further rock formations, and, way off, the Bosque of the Rio Grande like a dropped green ribbon. It's better to look out the windows than to think of Lavery, the taciturn bastard.

The taciturn bastard returns with a pitcher of water and two glasses. They sit and drink at the table's living room end. Its other end, twenty feet away, is in the kitchen. Ethan will finish his water and leave.

Lavery says, "*A House in Its Place* was arrogant and vain. It has maybe three decent photos: it was subtitled 'One Hundred Photographs.' One hundred was spelled out. Shit, was everyone so pretentious in the Seventies? You're too young to know. How old are you?"

"Thirty-two."

"Thirty fucking two. About my age when I did that book. Are you working on something pretentious now?"

"I'm not writing anything now. I'm here, listening to you."

"Do you want to write this book?"

"Yes."

"You want to write this book on New Mexico and you admit you know nothing, *nada*, about New Mexico."

"That's right."

"That might be better than knowing everything or knowing something but wrong. I kept putting this meeting off because I couldn't get into your books. I told Lucy. She said I should read *Who's on Second*, stick with it. When I started it, I kept thinking you had to be related to Carlos because why else would he want you? I mean, urban angst isn't my thing. Then I came to where they stop at the apple stand, when Jack's brother takes him on that drive to discuss their business getting big, and Jack for the first time looks around him, and he walks past the stand and through the orchards with his brother chasing after him asking what the hell he's doing. And Jack keeps walking up into the hills and the woods. Then I thought maybe you could just work out." Lavery goes to the far end of the table and brings a cardboard box to Ethan. Then he turns and goes upstairs without a word.

Ethan tries to interpret "maybe could just work out," the most twisted, grudging compliment he's ever had. Maybe it's not a compliment; Lavery is too crazy surly for him to understand. He listens for sounds from upstairs. There are none. He puts his hand on the box top and thinks of that scene in the novel, and then of the memory behind that scene.

He and XHelen, unable to face an Indian summer Saturday at home with each other, go for a drive. XHelen drives, he's that enervated. As they start off, Ethan listens to her arguments for moving a few hundred feet onto a street identical to the one they're now on, into a house identical to the one they're now in, but which will cost something very different—approximately twice what they can get for their current, completely adequate home. From time to time he says yes and I see, to her bankrupting eloquence in support of their move to Cambridge, two streets from Somerville, as opposed to Somerville two streets from Cambridge. His attention wanders as they leave town. It goes out to the houses and telephone poles going by. By this time XHelen who doesn't smoke when she drives since, she says, there's then no possibility to give smoking the attention it deserves, she who lights her cigarettes as if torching a building, a house, for instance, in Somerville, is nonetheless constantly finding tobacco to spit, ptt-ptt, off her lips despite smoking, when she smokes, only filters. All her energy is going not into driving, which she does well, like riding, a car to her being a sort of horse that doesn't shit, but into talking and talking and into interrupting her own talking to talk, to say, "Ethan for god's sake you're not even listening." To which, without taking his eyes from the colorful, tired roadside trees, he replies, "I am, I am," and to her test question, "So what was I talking about?" he answers, "Cambridge," knowing that although he's lied about listening, he's aced the exam. And on and on the car goes, they go, she goes. He goes further, is out there seven hundred yards from the passenger seat, behind the houses and diners and barns and filling stations, thinking vaguely they may already be on the Old Mohawk Trail, the same road west they used to take during their fuck-like-bunnies courtship and early marriage, even that shorter time back when his first book came out and seemed to make both of them happy—one autumn, at least, of their own unmellow fruitfulness. He cannot now much think "them" because it scares him to know how little holds them to "them," how they have not even developed habit in common, do not even in some way *require* their mutual, deep dislike.

It must be past Fitchburg and Athol, somewhere near the Connecticut River, when XHelen brakes hard to make a turn, and he knocks his chin against the back of his hands and asks, "What?" and she says, "Covered bridge, the sign said, and at least in Cambridge I'd be happy, forget the reasons, what does your literary King Lear say: 'reason not the reasons?' or irrational or subjective, whatever you want, Ethan, but I'd be happy. Doesn't happy count?"

To which he nods and says, "Hmmm," which can, if she wishes, be taken for a "Certainly, my paramour, it's paramount," and by him as a "hmmm" meaning hum, as in ho-hum, so dumb, and he goes off imagining back out there in the yellow oak and red-orange maples on the Massachusetts hills. So much so that only at the slamming of the car door and XHelen's "Coming?" does he realize they've stopped, arrived somewhere. They're parked by a roadside apple stand. So he walks with her among larger and smaller baskets of redgreen McIntosh and stripey Northern Spies, and then XHelen is talking with the woman at the stand, by a display of painted woodcraft crap, and Ethan wanders out of and around behind the stand, and there are the veritable orchards. They rise up and fall over the rolling land in long waves, and he goes through a gate and walks in among the trees. The sky above is sleepy blue. The clouds stay still. He climbs the orchard hillside and sees the edge of the woods as he moves through the soft, high grass. He passes stacked baskets at the cross-lanes and comes to the woods, where a path leads in and on.

The woods are so clear and comforting: the trees, the leaf, the waist-high ferns October-edged brown. He walks among such sane simplicity. He isn't thinking as he normally does; that is, showing off to his own mind. He stops by a tree to consider this idea, to listen to the silence of the truth. What tree is this? Not an oak, not a maple, not elm, since they're gone to disease. Could this be ash? sycamore? Ashamed of knowing so few trees, he rubs the trunk in apology and walks on, feeling he's already been too cute. Ahead, the woods open to the right, so they must crest the hill. He can swing right and circle down again and wait in the car for Helen, and as they drive back tell her that, of course, they have to separate. He'll move out. He knows this now; he has the clarity of unencumbered thought; she couldn't critique his pure reasonableness. Out of the woods, he can't yet see the road, but he guesses at it and makes a wide downward circle and ends at an unrecalled landscape of fields of turned earth and cropped grass. Walking their edges, he makes out in the distance the orchards. He goes steadily towards them in his new, calm resolve. He comes to a low rail fence and walks along it. Soon he sees Helen on a bench beside a large mound of apples. Ethan feels sad for her and himself that their marriage hasn't worked. He feels deep understanding of her sadness and vows to tell her so. Now she sees him and stands and waves at him. As she does, something is at his feet, windfall from a tree. Again she waves. Something grazes his thigh. An apple hits his arm. He tries to catch the next one, misses, is hit on the forehead and the rotten apple splits piecemeal down his face.

Helen is yelling, "Two hours!" She is yelling as he comes closer. "—just leave me here to rot with these—" She has, he knows, said "apples," but he hasn't heard, as he's covered his head against her whirlwind arms from which the apples come at him like from a berserk tennis cannon. He's walking forward blind; an apple hits his crotch and stings his penis. Helen yells, "I am not here for you, I do not count in your sudden conversion to nature walks!" and she continues hurling apples at him from the pile. Then he attempts to hug her and share his insight that it is all over with them, this good news he brings down from the hill, and in his love of the truth which will make them free, he straightens up and opens his arms, and Helen backs to the high pile of rotten apples and throws five and seven at once, all of which hit him so that he is plastered and cidery. "You are," he calls through the barrage, "supposed to *comfort* me with apples," and he pushes her back onto the pile. She falls, clutching at him and punching him in the eye with an apple, thankfully rotten soft, as he falls to the pile, too. All of which, in memory, is the perfect time to tell her—lying with her, they their own cider press, the air drunk and buzzy with wasps—yet, not only does he not speak but sadly does not make love, although excited; XHelen, too, is much aroused by anger become applesauce. They stand up and away from each other without Solomonic singing, with tight smiles and drenched jeans, her nipples, he sees, still hard against her wet shirt. Then they take the two small baskets, one of McIntosh, her favorite, one of Northern Spy, his, and get into the car and drive silently, stickily home to spend a further year and a half immorally together.

Ethan's hand slides off the box onto Lavery's long table. He takes out a handful of eight-by-ten prints. Here's a black and white of flat land broken by a long, low plateau, a photo composed of two horizontal lines with, at the far right, two small squares. One square is a house, the other a truck beside it. Here's a close-up of a stream: white, shining, the white shining pebbles and white shining rock wall over which the band of white sky. The photo makes him blink from its brightness. Another has two ponderosa pines, shot down between them at a cliff edge. It's dizzying, it shakes in his hand. He sees Lucy's triumphal, suicidal eyes above the ledge, the loafer falling. He looks at the photo again: the angle is such he can't tell if the pines are growing up or straight out sideways. Here's a color photo: a wide landscape in pale colors—faint lemons and dust oranges and the lime greens of cottonwoods. Along a river valley, butte rises upon butte, narrow canyons cutting into them. The tiered buttes undulate back, mile after mile, to a thin band of flat white cloud stretched across a pale sky like pulled taffy. On the back of the print, in pencil, "Chama wilderness."

Ethan flips through a second batch. Most are black and white; a few are Lavery's strange color photos, pale colors that are nonetheless intense. Lavery is a wonderful photographer. But he already knows that. He flips back through the pile to what's caught his eye, but it can't be. Yes, a Harvard letter sweater. Here it is, a deep vee'd white tennis sweater with the big H. It's worn by Doc N. He stands in the middle of nowhere with six small Indian children, three on each side, all holding tennis rackets and smiling like Doc N but wearing scruffy tee-shirts and cut-off jeans. The net behind them stretches between two sticks banged into the ground. A few rocks prop the sticks. Behind and around the net is nothing but bare land: no tree, no cow, no tater, no lone ranger, not even a weed, only all the bare cracked earth in the world. The photo is almost colorless but for the white sweater with its crimson H. This is a holy terror of a picture, of having and not having in America. But it isn't what this book is going to be about.

He pours another glass of water from the jug and walks around, sipping. If he gets the job, is he supposed to describe Lavery's pictures? Is Lavery supposed to photograph places he writes about? Lavery has said he might just be able to do the writing: not much encouragement there. He looks at several abstract watercolors on the walls, all signed with the same oriental character. They relax him. He comes across a small, signed Max Beckmann ink drawing. He kneels on a sofa to get closer to a photo of neatly stacked boxes in front of storage sheds. Endless stacks in front of truly enormous sheds. One human figure, in military uniform, walks in profile before the stacks, five or six times his height.

Lavery comes downstairs. Ethan asks, "Is this Vietnam?"

Lavery grunt and sits on a sofa. "I was a kid, late getting over there. Other photographers were shooting the fighting, bombing and general murdering, so I went for US way-of-life stuff: I shot supply flights, unloadings, depots, the PX scene. The only photo of mine that had any distribution was when I happened to be around as VC rockets came into one of our supply dumps, and I got a shot of all these giant piles of American pride—refrigerators and air conditioners and TV's—blown to shit, sky high."

"Do you have that one here?"

"I don't show it. I keep this one around to warn me against getting pretty. Did you see the New Mexican stuff in the box?"

"Yes. I don't see how writing could add to those photos."

At last, Lavery smiles. "Not the idea. The writer looks around the state at various places on a list I've made and then writes some essays. I read them and shoot photos or put in existing unpublished photos."

Ethan says, "These would be places threatened by deregulation?"

"That sounds like pure Carlos, to end up with only pretty pictures. Some would be; others would be of land already turned to shit by mining or logging or over-grazing. I have a shot of hundreds of snowmobiles roaring down a slope in Kit Carson Forest near Las Truchas. You can smell the stink of exhaust off that one. Carlos will just have to take what I put in."

"I heard him described as satanic or angelic, depending."

"He supports environmental projects, but he's also in with fossil fuel and mining lobbies. Years ago he leased some of his gazillion acres to open cast coal mining. He's on record as admitting the error of his ways, but I wouldn't bet on it. Carlos has so far had things both ways, his ways."

Ethan can't go on like this. "Mr. Lavery," he says, "do you want me to write this book?"

"No, I don't, but time's running out and I want this project; I'm tired of putting together one retrospective after another. I want to shoot photographs. And it seems you're the best I can get. And do not call me Mr. Fucking Lavery. It's Charlie."

"Before I accept your grudging offer, Charlie, I'd like to know what else you have against me, other than my not being Lucy or Tony or Rudy or Emily fucking Dickinson?"

A smile creases around Lavery's eyes. "Since you ask, Ethan, your youth, your looks, but mostly that Lucy's fallen for you."

"Okay, I accept. I didn't know you were a disappointed suitor. Lucy hasn't said a word about you."

"No reason to. It was years ago. I'd been a widower for several years and Lucy was divorced. I sure as hell would have been better for her than Dixon."

"That's not complimenting yourself very much."

Lavery grunts.

"Can I ask you something?"

"Ask."

"Did Lucy have an affair with Carlos?"

After a pause, Lavery says, "If you ask me, which you haven't, it's never worth asking that sort of question. How about a drink? I have some good mescal."

"Vodka and tonic, if you have it." Ethan thinks no mescal, no Oaxaca, never.

Lavery sets up a tray with the drinks, and they go out to a courtyard. Ethan tells himself he has the job, he should be more pleased. The courtyard smells like gin from the crushed blue juniper berries underfoot. The view goes southeast along a natural rock wall that slants down to a plateau. The plateau runs to the horizon.

Lavery raises his glass to Ethan and they drink. Ethan says, "That was some photo, the one of Doc N and the kids at the heartbreak tennis court."

Lavery sips his mescal. Then, with more interest than he's shown all afternoon, he says, "Two things about Doc. One: what you see is what you get. Two: he might be a saint. If so, the miracle is he's not obnoxious. I say that because I once spent two afternoons trailing Mother Teresa around hospitals, clinics and meetings. I came away wanting to punch her out. My humble opinion is that she was great and good only if you were a beggar with leprosy, dying in the street."

Ethan says, "Meaning what?"

"Meaning she didn't give a damn about making *life* better. Meaning she was a soul hunter. Obnoxious."

Lavery pours more drink. A rabbit breaks from a sunlit corner of the courtyard and stops stiff. Its nose and ears twitch and it turns and scampers into the bush.

Ethan breaks the silence: "I like those watercolors, inside."

Lavery nods for a while. "They were painted by Min Hua, my wife. She's been dead twelve years now."

"I'm sorry."

"I had the good luck of living almost twenty years with Min. Here's to her. And to Lucy."

Ethan raises his glass. He wonders why he can experience jealousy over Lucy yet not love her. The two men watch the light soften into creams and yellows. The phone rings and Lavery goes to answer it.

He comes out with the phone. "It's Lucy. She suggests we have dinner here. Fine with me." He hands Ethan the phone and goes back inside.

"Hi," Ethan says.

Lucy says, "I told you he'd like your writing and you."

"Is that what he said?"

"Yes, in his way."

"In his crabby, negative way."

"So you like him, too."

He laughs, "I think so. It must be my inner masochist."

"Isn't it clever of me to suggest dinner? You're plastered and can't drive back."

"A bit plastered, thinking of a third drink, and I can drive just fine. Dandy. But it is clever of you, and you'll be surrounded by adoring men."

"Don't start that, like with Carlos."

"Did I say a word about sexual jealousy? Besides, it's the other way… No, not a word."

"Good. Tell Charlie I'll bring the bread he likes from the Co-op bakery. I'll be there in an hour and a half."

Ethan puts down the phone, smiling. It would be nice if his father could be here to sit sipping soda water with old Charlie and him and then to meet Lucy. Of course, Meyer doesn't know about Lucy. He goes in to give Charlie the message.

Lavery says, "I'll get a trout from the freezer, a five pounder I caught in the Big Blackfoot, in Montana. Ethan, this is a critical moment in the proceedings. Do we have another drink or sober up and prepare dinner until Lucy gets here?"

There's nothing grumpy now in Lavery's voice, and Ethan knows it's not just the drink. He answers, "Both. We drink our third drinks very slowly while we prepare dinner. It's not for nothing that I'm a philosopher's son."

In the kitchen, they drink water before making new drinks. Lavery says, "The toast is 'sobriety.' In moderation."

"And to philosophy."

Lavery takes a large plastic bag from the freezer. "So what's your father's philosophy—in one sentence?"

"One sentence. Here goes. My father's philosophy is that things are probably *what* they seem to be, but they may not be the *way* we think."

Lavery grunts.

Later, Ethan toasts, "To getting our act together before Lucy gets here."

By the time they hear Lucy drive up, the fire is burning in the courtyard grill, salad is made and the kitchen end of the table respectably covered with plates, napkins and cutlery. Charlie goes to the Jeep and kisses Lucy as she steps out. Ethan watches their long hug. Lucy says something in his ear and Charlie nods. When she kisses Ethan on the cheek, he says, "No whisper for me?"

She says, "All right: Wasn't I right about Ethan, Charlie? Now behave."

They sit in the courtyard, Lucy between the two men. The sun goes from dark gold to red. Lavery says, "Ethan explained his father's philosophy to me in one sentence, clear as mud."

Ethan says, "I was thinking how nice it would be if my father were here." He turns to Lucy. "He doesn't even know about my job adventures, let alone you."

She sips white wine. She says quietly, "He knows about me. We've spoken on the phone. He's a wonderful man, Charlie."

Ethan is astonished. "Meyer calls you?"

"I called him first, after that awful weekend. We spoke last week."

Ethan leans forward and says, "Charlie, this is news to me." And to Lucy: "But he's been in the Caribbean. How could you have called him?"

"I called his office and got his hotel number from his assistant."

Ethan remembers he didn't ask. "May I ask what you talked about?"

"You, me, books. He never mentioned his health. He's a charming, dear man, and he's Ethan's biggest fan, Charlie."

Charlie stands, "I'm not refereeing this tennis match anymore; I'm grilling a trout."

Ethan says, "Why on earth didn't you tell me?"

"Meyer thought it would be nice if we could get to know each other, first. He said that way we could perhaps assess each other more objectively."

"And, in addition to making you a philosophical exercise, has he suggested you fly out to Boston and spend an objective weekend together?"

"How can you talk like that about him?"

"You're right; I'm awful. Sometime I'll try to explain. You look lovely in that red, western skirt."

"You look lovely too, and your father has been nothing but nice."

They drink white wine with dinner. When Lucy turns up her shirtsleeves, Lavery says, "You told me how Ethan got banged up. What about you?"

Lucy looks at her scratches and says, "We were walking up on Sandia Peak and had a little scramble at a ledge It's fine now. Isn't it, Ethan?"

He says, "It only hurts when we laugh."

Later, they talk about places Ethan should visit. Lucy thinks he should also find places on his own; his unaccustomed eyes will be an advantage. She says, "I love his unaccustomed eyes." After dinner, Lavery lights a fire. They sit around the fireplace, eating sliced oranges, drinking wine spritzers and listening to the piñon snap. Lucy says she misses Min. Lavery nods and, to Ethan's surprise and pleasure, asks them to spend the night. They say yes, together, without looking at each other.

The bedroom is round, the top of a stone tower. Lucy comes out of the bathroom in only her shirt. Her legs, still scratched and bruised, are long and muscular. Ethan pulls her to him on the bed. She says, "No, I'm noisy and it wouldn't feel right with Charlie thinking of Min."

Ethan guesses Charlie is probably thinking of Lucy, but he does as she says, kisses her, and falls asleep. He dreams that he and Charlie are both making love to Lucy. He wakes up excited and whispers to her. He pushes her onto her back, but she remains asleep. He puts himself inside her and asks if she's awake. She makes an mmm sound. He moves on her and comes and groans. Lucy, eyes closed, mutters, "Shh, shh, Ethan will hear us." He puts his lips to her ear and asks if she's awake. She makes an mmm sound.

Ethan moves off her, gets up and steps to the open window. The night is cold and clear. Maybe he didn't hear her right. Or maybe she's a somnivocal tease. The stone formations against the starry sky look like ancient temples. He imagines Meyer as a Zapotec priest on Monte Alban, above Oaxaca. One of his gold-braceleted hands is on Lucy while his other hand digs into the open chest of the altar victim, Ethan, to tear out his beating heart. Hell, he thinks. Hell.

When they awake on Sunday morning, there's no sign of Lavery. They make coffee, write a thank you note and leave. Ethan will meet Lucy at her place in the afternoon. Back at his apartment, Ethan listens to the phone messages.

"Ethan, hello. This is Meyer. I'm back. Please call. Bye."

"Meyer again. Give me a call, please."

"Ethan, this is your father. I know it's early out there; two hours difference, is it? Are you asleep? I'd like to talk to you."

Just as this message ends, the phone rings. "Ethan?"

"Meyer, hi. How are you?"

"Better for hearing your voice, son. I miss you. I was in St. Lucia, vacationing. I fell in with a—you'll be interested to hear—a band of Derek Walcott worshippers. Women, mostly, all of them white. By day two, I was convinced he'd fucked them all."

"Jesus!" says Ethan, despite himself. He has never before heard Meyer say anything stronger than "damn."

"By day three, or was it still day two, who knows—it was a terrible time—I was convinced the sexuality was all fabulous, mass literary hallucination. I missed you. I went away to think because I learned I was ill. I know Haskell Perlmutter spoke with you. Ankylosis spondylitis. Not a Greek tennis player, a disease, as you now know. Though a disease that mimics entropy. Entropy, as I see it, was Newton's most philosophically challenging discovery. Imagine, Ethan, this genius dedicated to perpetual motion, to the alchemist's dream of the philosopher's stone, the—if you will—nuclear fusion of his day, and he comes across the fact that the great clockmaker's clock is invariably winding down; the rub, as the man says. But being Isaac Newton, he investigates and *publishes* the rub. There's the rub. There is a great philosophical tract to write about entropy. The latest biographical scholarship, I believe, has it that Newton, qua man, was one of the nastiest pieces of work ever to crawl on the planet. Nonetheless, this profoundly religious and paranoid alchemist does not suppress the entropy that flesh is heir to. Spirit, also, one might say."

His father is raving. He needs loving, calming words. Ethan can only say, "You went down to the islands on your own, to think."

"No, with a friend, a woman. Her name is Hannah Miller. She's forty years old and I have been seeing her for some time. However, things did not go well for us on St. Lucia. All my fault. And, at her insistence, the relationship is over, *terminé, finito, kaput.* She is, of all things, an anal architect, I mean a naval architect."

"Meyer, come visit me in Albuquerque. Visit Lucy and me. She told me you've been speaking on the phone, so you'll know what's been happening to me, bad news and good. Lucy thinks you're terrific. And you should come because I miss you and love you."

"Yes, I see. Thank you."

There is a strange noise on the line. It takes Ethan some time to understand that this sound, like the grating of rocks, is his father crying. When he stops, they talk more of his visiting Albuquerque. He'll try to come out by Labor Day, for a week or so.

After the call, Ethan looks around the apartment wondering if it will do for Meyer. He feels he's, once again, measuring himself by his father. The shock of Meyer's eventual death, he sees, will be in catching himself continuing to perform for his father's absent applause. As a sensational non sequitur, Ethan becomes certain that his father had been unfaithful to his mother. Those arguments between Marion and Meyer he's recalled from childhood, on which Meyer has assured him the marriage thrived, had to be about betrayals. Why doesn't this cause him more discomfort? Is his memory of Marion so dim? Or has he always suspected yet forgiven Meyer's infidelities out of a secret, rogue affinity? He really doesn't want to think of this or of Oaxaca or of any of that crap.

Instead, he phones Doc N. Though he's had to explain why the workshop was cancelled, it's only now, when he has a job and an income, that he feels secure enough to try to find out about his attackers. "Doc," he says, "would you happened to know who this could be? He's about six foot seven, a muscle man, thirty to forty years old, with a long black pony tail, and he drives a black Ferrari convertible."

"Bud Brandon. There are not thousands who fit that description."

"You know him?"

"Yes. The center I work at is called 'The John "Bud" Brandon Mental Health Center.' Brandon was the major contributor. Do you want to meet him?"

"No. We've already met, in a manner of speaking. He was supervising the gang who beat me up. I only caught a glimpse of him, but, like you say, he's memorable. Later, I saw him driving. A philanthropist?"

"That and a big businessman—major car franchises, a friend of the high and mighty and the low and mighty, some of whom, it's rumored, are in the drug trade. In other words, your news is shocking, but not completely surprising."

Ethan says, "I don't know what I'm going to do with the information, but let's keep this conversation to ourselves."

"Of course. And your instinct not to go to the police was absolutely right. Brandon gives generously to all sorts of police funds, including the legal ones."

"Thanks for your help. By the way, it looks like I'll be doing a book with Charlie Lavery on the environment of your fair and foul state. This is off the record until there's a contract."

"Yeah, but will it be more fun than getting beaten up and having your workshop destroyed? Congratulations. How are your bruises?"

"Much improved."

"And Lucy's?"

"Lucy's?"

"Someone I know at University Hospital saw the two of you in Emergency the other day."

"We took a fall on Sandia Peak. She's fine. We were scratched up, that's all." Ethan is tired of suppressing his worries about Lucy. "Doc," he says, "I need to ask you something about Lucy. For the past several weeks, I've known about Emmy's anorexia and the strain it puts on Lucy. Do you know if Lucy's had a mental breakdown?"

There is a silence during which Ethan imagines the worst. Then Doc N says, "I don't think so. Not to my knowledge. Lucy is high-strung and odd, and way better than normal, in both my professional and deeply personal opinions."

After this conversation, Ethan thinks of this odd thug Bud Brandon. Maybe not so odd, sort of an extreme version of many businessmen. Putting aside the fact that Brandon has hurt him and should be in jail, Ethan sees that nothing has been more American in his development, the very *zeitgeist* he's breathed, than romantic capitalism, the hero as freebooting adventurer, as anarchist pillager driven to scale the mountain of profit and status because there it is, the way out of the cramped lowlands on which the garbage drops, driven to hack and slash up to the clear blue heights.

He's always had a sneaking admiration for the slightly tough (forget Brandon and mere thugs), for those around whose hands and sidelong glances hovers some lawlessness.

He recalls his attraction at fifteen to a high school classmate, Crazy Stevie Levenson, a normal boy but for his addiction to stealing cars. "Hey, Stevie, bet you wouldn't dare clip that," one of them would say, nodding to the shiny Olds Cutlass Supreme someone had parked right in front of Joe and Miriam's Delicatessen at Coolidge Corner, with its slogan "The Fresser's Shangri-la," inside which one or two chubby policemen could usually be found, snacking on free pastrami sandwiches. And, if the fit was on him, Stevie wouldn't even let on that he'd heard the dare but would immediately, and always on his own, steal the car, so that Ethan and the others were his amazed, breathless audience as he worked open the door, hot-wired the car and sedately drove it away. But what he did was not joyriding: he drove exactly like their staid fathers did. Crazy Stevie respected the cars; the cars, he would say afterwards, were *property*. He showed them that property was to be taken. The only thing wild about him was his compulsion to amass at fifteen years of age a phantom museum of fatass Chrysler Imperials and foursquare Lincolns. What Ethan and his friends had a hardon for in Stevie Levenson was that though he let some madness show, he was not only one of them but a prefiguration of their then still-forming materialistic selves, selves they couldn't consciously acknowledge, because they were so square, so uncool. Stevie's rich father protected these escapades until the evening, no witnesses, Stevie stole a blue Coupe de Ville without noticing its MD plates, got caught by state troopers, and could only grin foolishly when they found the trunk full of big-time hospital drugs, the kind the car's owner himself had a hard time explaining. But the doctor was Pill Hill old Wasp and got away with it. Stevie went to reform school, and Ethan and the rest of them kept their heads down and went on, nice boys, to Dartmouth or Harvard or Wesleyan.

Thinking of these cars reminds Ethan of the research he'll be doing for the book, traveling around New Mexico, taking notes. He can begin with day trips. He remembers that Meyer decided to give up driving several years back. He'd cited his eyesight and reaction time. He said that since he didn't really have to drive, he wanted to quit before becoming one of those old man menaces of no turn-signals and slow turns. Ethan had thought the decision sensible. Now he feels what Meyer didn't want was the inelegance of bad driving. Perhaps the decision had also been a brave face on the impairments from the disease, which he might have felt for years before its diagnosis.

Touched, he phones Meyer, again, wanting to talk about the drives they can take together when he visits. Ethan automatically begins with "How are you?" Meyer replies: "Who I am would be more appropriate, don't you think, Ethan?"

"No."

"Haven't you believed all these years I was wholly thought, a holy thinker, in fact, a superannuated Søren Kierkegaard? And now you see me revealed as an innumerate Bertie Russell, dick-brained, sniffer of undergraduate underpants, the old dog, eh? The connoisseur of cooze?"

"Stop this, Meyer."

"No? Then you have been very wrong, sadly misguided by me. Once, years ago, I went to your upstairs bathroom in Somerville and opened the door on Helen stepping from the shower naked. I left at once, apologizing. But for months, afterwards—"

"Don't, Meyer."

"—years, perhaps, I masturbated thinking of her skimpy tits and slick black pubic hair. I can imagine them to this day, this minute."

"It's the spondylitis."

"It is not! Or if so, it is *in spondylitis veritas*. If I am sick, I am sick of pretending. That is my fear and trembling, and not my sickness unto death, to paraphrase your great Dane."

"Not mine. I never much liked Kierkegaard."

"Is that so? I though there was an aesthetic affinity. Didn't you direct me to the early expressionist writers as a way of understanding Kierkegaard in his *Zeitgeist*? Read Georg Buchner, you said."

"That wasn't me. Perhaps it was one of your grad students."

"Perhaps. You don't have to have my particular condition to lose your memory. So where was I? Yes, discussing how many graduate students I've slept with."

"Father."

"No, Bertie Russell the fucker at least gave his wives an honest, if hard, time. I am in no way trying to be funny."

Ethan takes a breath and says, "Is it that you feel guilty about Marion?"

"Of course I do. But then, I felt guilty while Marion was alive, yet that didn't keep me from screwing around left, right, and center. Do you mind me saying all this?"

Ethan really doesn't know whether to say yes or no. He says, weakly, "Meyer, I'm really looking forward to you being out here. There are wonderful places to go. I hear the Acoma Pueblo is spectacular."

"And there'll be Lucy. Isn't she too old for you?"

"We'll have a nice time. The three of us will see the sights."

"Her writing is elegant and depressing. Do you trust me not to make a pass at her?"

Ethan stays silent.

"Of course, of course. You were faithful to Helen."

"There was a stewardess, you might remember."

"I once knew a stewardess. A beautiful young woman: wonderful complexion, green eyes, drrrop-dead beautiful! I cannot remember her name. A fine fuck. An Irish girl."

Ethan can't stand any more of this. "Meyer, I need to get off the phone, to prepare for some trips."

"But are we going to be traveling together?"

"When you're here. This is for my work, a commissioned book on New Mexico."

"Ethan, you were in dreadful shape in Mexico City. You don't talk about it, but the truth is that if I hadn't behaved like a beast, that is, just like any middle-class Mexican father would have, you might still be rotting in a Oaxacan jail. So much for my supposed memory loss."

Ethan is outraged. He forces himself to say, "Take care of yourself. Is Hester still coming in twice a week?"

"Don't worry about me. Ethan, the girl wasn't Irish—some sort of Yugoslav, I think."

"Bye, Meyer," he says, ringing off before he shouts or whimpers. He thinks how different his father is from Brandon, what a different sort of thug.

8

THAT AFTERNOON, Ethan tells Lucy that he's had two disturbing conversations with his father, though he's not going to repeat them for her.

"What particularly disturbed you?" she asks.

"How can I count the ways? For one, he said he'd been unfaithful to my mother. He'd always said how faithful he was, faithful even after she died—celibate."

"Can you forgive him?"

"I don't know. It's been a life-long lie. It goes to the heart of our relationship. And then there was the crudeness of his language in telling me about it. My father never used such language to me before. It was as if a dam of propriety broke, and out poured all this filth. It throws my whole picture of my father out of kilter, not just his morals. He was a standard of calm and consistency for me. This morning on the phone, he became another person, a stranger with a split personality."

Lucy says, "Could it be the illness?"

"I suggested that to him. Meyer said if it was, it was only that it made him drop the pretense and tell the truth. What's just as discouraging for me is that for a long time I've had glimpses of this other father but I've kept denying it. After I was beaten up, I remembered that Meyer once fixed me up with a stewardess when I was married, and he then denied it."

"What happened?"

He tells Lucy the story of Mary Keegan. She finds it amusing and touching. "You knew you and Helen weren't getting on."

"Just beginning to know."

Lucy moves across the sofa and puts her arms around him. "You're faithful to me, aren't you?"

"I am." To point out that it's been a fidelity of only several months seems cruel. He says, "Meyer even suggested he might make a pass at you, when he visits."

"What did you say to that?"

"I changed the subject. I wasn't going to come down to his level."

Lucy says, "Good for you. Your reward is me making a pass at you."

Ethan would rather have Lucy really engage in the subject, but he resigns himself to the intense but short solace of making love. Later, they go for a walk, following the shade of the big trees around the University golf course. Ethan is struck by Lucy's complete lack of censure for Meyer's behavior. Is this, he wonders uncomfortably, her delicacy in not interfering, or is it more connected with Lucy's need to disconnect from emotional disturbance, as with Emmy?

He says, "I can understand Emmy not wanting to stay in that unhappy house with you and Willy, but why isn't she at the campus house with you, now?"

Lucy says, "I've asked her to, but she says she wants to live on her own. Maybe she picks up my unhappiness when I see her. Maybe she's being kind."

Lucy stops walking. He says, "I should have understood that." She doesn't take the hand he holds out. They walk on. In the evening they have supper at a small Hispano restaurant with yellow walls and blue chairs. They talk about some day trips he could take once he gets the job. In bed that night, neither one mentions the disappointment felt with the other that day, though Ethan feels it lie between them like another body.

For the next few days he busies himself buying basic hiking equipment, thinking, superstitiously, it can be used even if he doesn't get the job. Meyer doesn't call and Ethan doesn't call him. On Wednesday, Carlos calls to tell him the board has met and he has the job. His contract will be ready by the week's end, and by Monday, Ethan's first check will be cut. Carlos ends with, "Ethan, New Mexico is a magnificent place. We expect wonderful things from you." Ethan calls Lucy to tell her. He's going to celebrate by taking his first day trip the next day: the Old Turquoise Trail and then on north of Santa Fe.

She says, "A fair mix of the ugly and the beautiful. And what will you remember?"

"To drink water and drink water and drink more water."

"And take your cell phone."

"Charlie said they often don't work in the mountains."

"Charlie's not your woman. I'll feel better if Eastern city boy has his cell phone."

That night, he returns from Lucy's to Copper Place and lays out his clothes, maps and backpack. He goes to sleep early. The phone wakes him. It's still dark. He puts the phone to his ear and hears, "Remember that I do not like William James."

Ethan is so disoriented, he assumes he's fallen asleep in the middle of a conversation. He says, "The American Bentham."

"Good, you remember. From utilitarianism to pragmatism is nothing but the loss of ethics."

Ethan rubs his eyes. "Maybe Unitarianism was also a version of utilitarianism. The words—"

"Oh, no, no, no," says Meyer. "Puns are no substitute for scholarship. I abjure Derrida and his leaden, linguistic play. Bentham, at any rate, begins from ethics, though he's not much, philosophically. He was essentially a political and social reformer. Oh, my, I'm giving you an old undergraduate lecture, 'Adam Smith and the Ethics of Self-Interest.' Well, Ethan, this is the dying mind. It's terrible. Terrifying. What time is it?"

Ethan, terrified for and by his father, says, "Philosophy is the last all-male club. You're a philosopher for the same reason you're a philanderer." Does he mean a wanderer, a meanderer?

Meyer says, "What are you going on about?"

Ethan says, "I know I'm responsible for everything I've done, yet I see you were my model. Model, mode, my way."

"Please stop derridaing me, I mean deriding me. Now you have me doing it."

Ethan is emboldened by sleepiness. "Of course you want to play. But as you grow older, it becomes more difficult to separate the philanderer from the philosopher; his hand is in your pocket. But why me, Meyer? What so excites you about my women—projected incest?"

"Ha! You don't remember your mother, how she was with you?" The Yiddish syntax and inflection are rare for Meyer.

"How was she?"

"Marion never abused you, of course. But such smoochie-coochie smother love!"

"You were jealous."

"If anything, this aroused me for her, this carrying on with you so openly. Perhaps it might be that her total openness in loving you is what I yearned for but couldn't give. Remember, the ethical problem for philosophy is not how people should behave, but how *thinking* people should behave."

This seems such an indictment of thinking people that it shocks Ethan awake. He says, "I don't understand."

Meyer says, "No wonder. Here's my watch and it says a quarter past four. Another time, please call earlier. Or later. Good night."

"Good night, Meyer." Ethan puts down the phone knowing he'll wake up unsure of who called whom or even if there was a call.

Next morning, he sets off at ten and immediately takes a wrong turn so that he has to pull off Silver Avenue to go back. The turnoff is a short unpaved road, a few houses set back of trees. When he puts the Jeep into reverse, he sees the hand-painted sign on the tree in front of him: LADY HAS ALZHEIMERS PAY NO ATTENTION.

He goes up Central until it hits Route 14 north, behind the Sandias. He is, philosophically, a thinking person, and while his life isn't unexamined, it's as if he's looked at it only before a mirror, as if all he can bear are the surfaces. The land behind the Sandias becomes flat, so that the mountains have a stage-set quality; this image comes to him, he knows, from a Stephen Crane short story. Of course Meyer called him—to bully and tease. Pay no attention. He sees a gas station with a phone booth. He pulls in. Twelve-thirty in Boston. He tries his cell phone. Useless. He gets out and goes to the booth. The buildings are ugly, prefab log-cabin style. The lot looks raw, recently cleared of trees and bushes. He ducks and crouches under the plastic dome and calls.

"Meyer Baum," his father says loudly, so that it sounds like Meyer Bomb.

Ethan takes one from Meyer's book and starts with: "What you said about pragmatism."

"Ethan, is that you?"

"It seems, on reflection, bass-ackwards. Dewey and James made a profoundly radical critique of conventional philosophy—that all of its standards followed from living, and—"

"Where are you? I hear traffic noise."

"And that philosophers therefore could not remove themselves from life, as they pretended to. This was an impossible position—logically, ethically, or aesthetically."

"Ah, yes, you're out there in the brave new west, but there is history, even intellectual history, despite that."

"Meyer, do you really not believe that our lives justify our thoughts?"

"There is something far too *a priori* in that formulation. Have you been reading Richard Rorty? Rorty's a nice enough fellow, but though he uses philosophical methodology, he's not much more than a sensualist."

"No, I haven't been reading Rorty. And, yes, I believe life itself is the inevitable, the grand *a priori*."

"Very clever. But that's a writer's cleverness, and that's why Rorty is only a Whitmanesque commentator. Ethan, where are you?"

Ethan unwinds from the booth to look. Some cars and a pickup truck come over the crest of the road. Way up behind is the mountain Lucy almost dropped from. He turns: down the bare slope between the buildings is a long chain link run. There are wolves there. Of course not. They're German shepherds. He says, "At a kennels, Meyer, in Cedar Crest, just outside Albuquerque."

"Are you buying a dog?"

"No. I'm… Maybe. I'm just looking. I'm on the start of a day-trip."

"I see. The dog would protect you."

Ethan sees a very small boy walking down the slope towards the dog run. "Protect me from what? All the German shepherds, I mean wolves, were killed a long time ago down here." As the boy nears the fence, three dogs rush at him, barking. They leap at the fence and stay reared against it, twice the boy's height, barking madly, nipping at each other with teeth Ethan can see gleaming even from this distance. The boy goes right up to the fence and the dogs come down, muzzles at the chain link. The boy puts in his hand. Ethan waits for the scream, but the dogs are licking him, tongues through the fence, knocking each other sideways in a frenzy of affection for the small, grabbing hand. The boy is laughing and shouting at them.

"Ethan?"

"I'm here." A woman's voice calls, "Billy, Billy, Billeeee! Didn't I say no? Get up out of there, Billy!" The woman walks down the slope into the wind. Her long, pale dress blows back tight against her pregnant belly and breasts. Ethan wishes he were the husband watching from the house, wanting her to finish dealing with Billy so that he, wild about her pregnant, can be with her again. Ethan says, "I'm here, Meyer, philosophizing. Why, really, have you been calling Lucy?""

"To get to know her. Can you be jealous?"

"Yes. Why not?"

"It's true, she's attractive, a fine figure."

"How do you know that?"

"The book jackets. Besides, I asked her to send me a photo. It was here when I returned. Didn't she tell you about the photo? It doesn't matter. It means nothing to her."

Ethan doesn't like Lucy not telling him. He doesn't like his father telling him. Down by the dog-run, the woman has picked up the boy and holds him with one arm at her hip. The boy's face is on her stomach, as if listening. She's walking up the slope, smiling. "Meyer, what is it with you and women?"

"I like them. I feel comfortable and comforted. You know, you didn't get all your good looks from your mother. I'll give you a bit of advice, if I may, which I never did when you were with Helen."

"Not so," Ethan says, bitterly. "You were forever advising me in your ostensibly rational way, when it turns out you were masturbating to your memory of her naked in the shower. Good lord."

"Here's the advice: if Lucy should happen to enjoy a little flirting with me, allow it. Tolerate it. Enjoy it."

"At least you've dropped the veneer of rationality. What a gem of self-interested advice. Meyer, Lucy is too old for you, and, please understand, if I ever catch you touching her, I'll bite off your hand."

Meyer laughs: "What, the hand that fed you? Ethan, I am an old man. A bona fide geezer. Have no fear."

"I have to get back on the road now." Ethan is ashamed of the entire conversation.

"Right. Call again, soon. This has been one of our best phone calls ever: philosophy, dogs, women. Terrific! Lots of love, son."

Ethan hangs up. His hand is stiff from squeezing the receiver.

A bearded young man in jeans and greasy tee shirt comes from the back building. "Need gas?"

"No, I was just making a call. Do you breed those shepherds for sale?"

"Not as a business, but we sell some pups to friends. They're really good lines, AKC champions, the bitch and the dog. Want to see them?"

"Sure."

Behind the near building is a trailer. The other building might be a convenience store. As they come to the pen, the three dogs lope up, barking. They're longhairs, a mix of tan, black and orange.

"They want to come out and play. We have them out of the run for about four hours a day, and then most of the night. Jean, my wife, says they're our other children. That one, Sky, is the mother, and the big guy is Clovis, and this is their son Dash. See his paws: he'll be at least Clovis's size. Sorry, I should have introduced myself. Dave Brown."

He takes Dave's hand and introduces himself.

"There's a pup in the trailer, already sold, but you could see it, if you want."

He wants to see the puppy, the trailer, the family, the wife. They go up the slope and Dave opens the trailer door. "Jeanie? Here's someone to look at the pup." He holds open the door and Ethan goes in. His legs are trembling. Pay no attention. The inside is cramped but clean. There's a baby powder, milky smell. Books are stacked solidly from the floor along one wall. Ethan stands in this living-dining room trying to make out book titles. Billy runs in, shirtless, in blue shorts.

Dave says, "This is Billy. Billy, this is Ethan. Say hello."

Ethan puts his hand out. Billy touches it and jumps back behind Dave, hugging his jeans, looking out at Ethan.

"Don't let him fool you. He's not shy. Want coffee? I'm going to get one."

"Thanks. Just black." Ethan hears the wife come through the passageway. She stops. A low laugh. He's sure she and Dave have touched, kissed. She comes in holding a German shepherd puppy.

It's licking her hair. To keep from staring, Ethan decides that if she weren't pregnant, she wouldn't be so pretty.

Dave calls, "Jean, that's Ethan. Ethan, Jean. Jeanie, you want coffee?"

She seems to find this funny, some private joke. "No, thanks. Sorry about this mess," she says, offering the puppy to Ethan.

The puppy is all ears and paws and tongue that licks his hands, arms and, when he holds it up, his nose. "How old is she?"

"A month. Friends from Utah are stopping by next month to pick her up."

Ethan says, "She's very fine." He knows nothing about dogs.

Dave calls, "If you're interested, we could let you know when Sky breeds next."

Ethan says, "I think so. Yes, maybe." He speaks to the passageway space beside Jean. He sees her brown eyes and full lips. She leans back and turns her head; her neck is breathtaking, heartbreaking.

She says, "Billy, let your father go, and come out here. Here, let me take the pup before she slobbers all over you." He wants to slobber all over her. Jean's eyes are gold-flecked, large enough to jump into. He sits across from her at the chromed Formica table. She says, "If you'd like to wash your hands, it's back there, past the kitchen."

Billy comes in and leans onto her lap and puts his face into the puppy's.

Ethan stands and thanks her. He passes a stack of CD's on the sound system; the top one is Mendelssohn's *Songs Without Words*.

The bathroom is full of clothes—in baskets, folded on the washer-dryer, hanging on a rack. Her underwear. What is he doing? He's showing his father. He touches the elastic on a pair of her panties. He sees the slight pouching of its crotch. He runs the cold tap and goes into the laundry basket. His father's son. He comes up with a pair of Jean's black underpants. He closes his eyes and moves the underpants slowly over his nose until he picks up the musky, fishy smell. He draws them away, and with his eyes still closed slowly puts out his tongue. When he tastes the salt, his heart pounds. He smells where he's licked. The smell is stronger now; it dizzies him. What is he doing? Pay no attention. Meyer called himself "a sniffer of undergraduate underpants." Like father, like son. Meyer's fault. Bullshit. Pay no attention. He puts the pants back in among the laundry and washes his hands.

Dave is at the table when he gets back. A bell rings outside. Dave says, "Someone's pulled in. I'll get back."

Ethan sits. Out the trailer window, he sees Dave trotting around the log garage building. He lifts his coffee. "Have you just opened here?"

Jean says, "No, though it still looks so unfinished. We've been here two years. The idea was the gas station and in this other building a good quality general store and a deli, with tables where locals could take their lunch or whatever and sit around reading newspapers. But just after we moved in, someone opened that kind of place back in the village, off Route Fourteen. It's doing well. So now we have financing problems and have to rethink."

She's smiling at him. The boy is on her lap, the puppy is on the boy's lap. Ethan thinks the whole thing—the puppy, the coffee, the bell—could be a setup. She's just said they need money. Dave could be pimping for her. Worse, getting him in here and going outside so that when she gets her pants off in the trailer bedroom (also, he imagines, cluttered; a smell of fucking and baby powder in the sheets) and he's lifted her dress from behind, there's Dave nipping back and just as Ethan puts himself inside her, BLAM from Dave's .38 magnum, or whatever, and they take his money and bury him in that other building which is a big, covered graveyard—cement slabs and a car-repair hoist to lift the slabs and beneath are the quicklime pits where the bodies go. But he will die gladly to take down his pants and lift her dress. He says, "Are you thinking of trying this some place else?"

Billy slides off Jean's lap and dumps the puppy there. Billy comes around the table saying, "Puppy, puppy."

"How old is Billy?"

"Just two. No, we want out of this. We're thinking I'll go back to work as an educational psychologist. Dave is a great photographer, but he's also wonderful with dogs. Maybe he'll breed and sell shepherds while he works on his portfolio. Of course, there's also this." She pats her stomach, next to the puppy.

Ethan licks his lip. Her taste is still there. He says, "I'll give you my address, for when you get another puppy."

"Puppy," Billy says, coming to him. "Name Billy I'm two."

Ethan says, "He's a beautiful child." To Billy, he points at himself and says, "Ethan."

"Ian," Billy says.

Ethan says, "Very good." He drinks coffee. Jean asks if he can hold the puppy while she gets something to write with. When she leans to give him the puppy, her hair comes forward and brushes his hand. He's in love with them all: Jean, the puppy in his lap, Billy who mauls the puppy in adoration, Dave outside pumping gas and wanting to be a photographer. Ethan wants to be in their skins. In Jean's pants. Meyer is not wrong about the novelist as sensualist. Jean returns and Ethan writes his name, address and phone number. He says he'd better be going.

"What do you do, Ethan?" Billy has slid to the floor where he sits seriously reading a book.

He says, "I write. I'm on a research trip for a book."

"What kind of a book?"

"A book of photographs of New Mexico. I'm just doing the text."

"Who's the photographer?"

"Charles Lavery."

She seems to blush. "Are you kidding? No, of course you're not. Dave did a workshop with Lavery three years ago. He'll be thrilled. Lavery's his hero. You're serious."

"I'm serious." He laughs. She'd be beautiful without being pregnant.

"So are you a nature writer?"

"No, I sort of fell into this. I'm a novelist."

"Ethan Baum. I'm sorry; I don't know your writing. What kind of novels?"

He is about to give her his "the out-of-print kind," but he says, "Novels about setting out towards something and maybe getting there but getting lost."

"Would I like them?"

"Writers get spooked by that question. It begs too many others. One answer would be: of course I want you to like them, to goddamn adore them. But I honestly have no idea. I don't know you."

"I'm sorry. That wasn't very sensitive of me."

"No, I'm sorry I snapped. You were just being polite. You're… You have a lovely family."

She follows him to the door. He asks if the Old Turquoise Trail is interesting.

"If you like landscape ruined by mining and an old mining town cutesied up with window-boxes."

Ethan wants to kiss her cheek. He opens the door, steps down, and says goodbye. Jean, his height now, says, "Hey," leans, holds him and kisses his cheek. He jumps off the step and doesn't look back at her, or at the puppy in her arms, or at Billy at her legs. A car pulls away as he comes to the pumps. He stands with Dave and watches it go over the crest. "Jean tells me you're a photographer."

"When I can make the time."

He thinks of telling him about Lavery. He takes out his wallet. He has four hundred dollars. He hands three hundred and fifty to Dave. "This is not a down payment on a puppy nor because you and your family are nice folk. I'd like you to send me some of your photos. Jean has my address." He grabs Dave's hand, lets go of the bills and walks to the Jeep.

Dave says, "Wait!" and runs to him. Ethan is sure that Dave is going to thump him. Dave holds out his hand. "Thank you, Ethan. I'll send you the photos."

Ethan gets into the Jeep. What has he done? It's not just competition with Meyer. It's being unfaithful to Lucy, proving his lack of engagement. Right, he's not engaged to her. Not even going steady. He drives away and glances in the rearview mirror, but the whole place has disappeared behind the crest of the road.

He drives the Old Turquoise Trail in a stew of guilt. The landscape, as Jean said, becomes pockmarked. Crumbled hills fall into crumbled arroyos. Old coal mines and cave-ins and sinkholes, the land worked to death. He is his sick father's son. Suddenly, the startling white of a mission church up on a small rise. Some of the wrought iron crosses around it are stuck with plastic flowers whose reds and blues and yellows are unfadingly ugly. Later, he skirts Santa Fe, slowly driving the roads he recalls from the weekend with Lucy. What was he thinking in that Cedar Crest trailer? Does he know who he is other than his father's son? The landscape grows horrid in the sink of Espanola. The Indian Country map shows the town to be the crossroads of six pueblos; the windscreen shows a place of erosion and pawnshops and vacancy, of poor earth and the dirt poor. A broad valley opens to its north. He drives to the valley's north end, stops to get gas, and buys a takeaway lunch of green chile quesadilla and Mexican beer.

Then he branches off to the small road that follows the Rio Grande into a state park. He drives for a mile, parks, and walks along the river beach to sit under the shade of a tree. The river is wilder here; it rushes downhill in rills and short rapids, no more than sixty feet across. Ethan eats lunch watching a small bird diving into the river off a rock. A flycatcher? He doesn't know. He remembers to drink water, and then he remembers the cold Mexican beer. He takes the can and draws his finger around on its water beads. It makes an O. He begins to remember Oaxaca. He cannot stop himself. Everything comes back, every detail. He sits until he feels sick and throws up his lunch into the river. He drinks water and packs his lunch things away. He's been sitting remembering for two hours. He has no idea what he should do. He takes out his cell phone, but the river canyon walls give him no hope. The call goes through. "Lucy?"

"Hi. Where are you?"

"On the river, a park south of Taos."

"Your father called this morning. He asked if he'd told me the joke about Alzheimer's."

"And?"

"That's the joke. I thought it was funny. Philosophical."

"Yes, charming. I spoke to him too, this morning. Listen, I've just had a bad, bad memory come back to me. I don't know if I can see you tonight. I have to work something out, and until I do I can't even tell you what it is."

"Well, just promise to call me, tonight or tomorrow."

"Yes. Thanks for... Thanks."

Ethan clicks off the phone. He can no longer pay no attention. He clicks on the phone and calls Doc N, but the phone doesn't work. He drives back to the gas station outside the park and phones from the booth. When Doc N answers, Ethan says, "I'm sorry to... It's Ethan. I need to talk to someone. A bad memory has come back and I need to tell someone. Not Lucy or you. Someone I don't know."

"You sound shaky. Are you?"

"Yes."

"Are you at home?"

"No, at a phone booth south of Taos."

"Give me the number. I'll phone back as soon as possible, half an hour at most. Try to relax."

Ethan reads off the number and hangs up. He moves the Jeep near the booth, and sits with the window open and remembers to drink water. He needs to keep in touch with Lucy. He's completely out of touch with himself, yet everything about Oaxaca is in his mind: touch and texture, color and smell, the voice tones. He drinks water. He goes to the bathroom. When he comes out, the phone is ringing.

Doc N says, "Good, you're still there. I'm going to give you an address. It's my family home, just off the rez outside Crownpoint. I've arranged that at ten tomorrow morning you're going to see my grandfather, Hosteen Charlie Wauneka. He's a healer, and a good listener, but you have to do what he says. What he says now is not to have anything more to eat after your evening meal. Just water from then until you see him. Okay?"

"Yes." Ethan takes down the address. Doc N has him read it back. Then Ethan sits in the Jeep at the gas station with the piece of paper in his hand for an hour. Then he sees the piece of paper and drives slowly back down the road. He checks into an old motel with cabins, near the river, and lies on the bed for the rest of the afternoon. When it's dark, he gets into the Jeep and drives slowly back to Albuquerque. He starts to make supper but stops: he knows he won't eat any. He drinks water and lies on his bed with his eyes open until, at around four in the morning, he falls asleep. At five-thirty, Ethan wakes up and showers and shaves. He drinks water. At seven-thirty he leaves and slowly drives west on I-40 for several hours and turns north at the Crownpoint sign. Four miles past the town, Doc N waits at the roadside. Ethan parks inside the rail fence and gets out. Doc N points out his parents' house, his Airstream parked beside it, his brother's house and his grandparents' house. He says behind that are two hogans and the log corrals and sheep sheds. "My grandfather's up there waiting for you. He's famous for sand-painting healing rituals, but I don't know that he'll do that with you. I once asked him if Anglos could be healed that way, and he said, 'Sure, if they can see past the Indian hocus-pocus.' He's a funny man, in addition to being a mystic. Yuh, I'm running off at the mouth because you don't look so good. Go talk to him. I have to get back to town."

Ethan walks alone up the slope. Out behind the bungalow is a short old man. An orange Indian chow dog is with him. The man is in black jeans and a faded red shirt. He has turquoise bracelets on both wrists and his belt has a big turquoise and silver buckle. A small leather bag hangs from a chain around his neck

He says, "Hey, I'm Hosteen Charlie."

"Ethan Baum. I'm a friend of Doc N, of John."

Hosteen Charlie says, "I didn't want the damn dog out here. Usually it goes when I tell it to, but it's just been hanging around me this morning, moved off a little and then come back, so I figure it's a sign."

Ethan looks at the old man and the orange dog in the middle of nowhere. He feels he's an Anglo who won't be able to see past the Indian hocus-pocus. He says, "A sign of what?"

Hosteen Charlie looks at the dog. He says, "Sign of at least he wants to be here. Maybe your body self needs to be closer to your spirit self, though that's a good bet even without the dog." He motions Ethan, turns and walks. Ethan follows him. The dog follows Ethan. Hosteen Charlie turns his head and says, "John says you remembered something that's troubling you a lot and don't know how to deal with it. I thought about it but can't exactly figure what ceremony might work best."

They come to the door of the smaller of two stick and adobe hogans. Ethan says, "So what will you do?"

"Wing it, I guess," the old man says. "Now will you look at that dog looking at me? How much he wants to come in but knows he can't. Come on in. Dog'll stay right out here until we come out."

Inside, the circular hogan is cool and completely bare. Its packed earth floor is clean swept; its side ledges and few shelves are empty. Light comes in through the roof opening, making a bright circle on the left of the floor. Outside this circle, the light is dim. Hosteen Charlie points to the floor near the center. "Sit there," he says. Ethan sits. Hosteen Charlie sits down slowly, about eight feet away, cross-legged. Ethan crosses his legs, knowing his knees will hurt after five minutes. Hosteen Charlie leans forward, looking down at the earth floor. He places his hands on the earth, palms down, side by side, and makes slow, outward-sweeping motions until his arms swing out to his sides. Ethan guesses he's studying some pattern he sees. The old man straightens and wipes his hands across each other. He says, "I better begin on the level. When a Diné, a Navajo, comes to me, it's because we're deep into some same ways of thinking and feeling. We still, those of us who do this, I mean, live in the tradition enough to be very close. Something like family, though that's not really it. But you Anglos—and don't take that personal because I do know your background is Jewish and German and Polish—you Europeans have an idea you can speak openly to me because you *don't* know me. You can speak to strangers, but you lock your heart away from friends and family. Frankly, I think a lot of you are screwed up that way. Hey, but that's who you are and the world's a big place. So there it is. I needed to get that off my chest and ask if, knowing that, it's okay I keep going."

Ethan says, "It's okay with me," but Hosteen Charlie's words make him feel giddy, and he doubts he can talk to him.

Hosteen Charlie says, "Then okay. Go ahead."

Ethan says, "I need to tell somebody, you, somebody, about something I thought I could forget." He looks up at the hole in the ceiling, the flat bright blue. "But I can't forget. It's hard to tell it." He glances at the old man whose eyes are down to the earth he's smoothed with his palms. Ethan cannot go on. He feels stupid. This man is a total stranger. He may as well tell it to a rock or a cottonwood tree. He decides he'll count silently to fifty and begin. He counts to fifty and decides to extend to a hundred. He looks at the floor and keeps counting. At a hundred, he counts another hundred. His knees hurt. At six hundred, he glances again at Hosteen Charlie. He sits looking at the earth, unmoving. At one thousand, Ethan rubs his knees and shifts his hip. The hole in the roof is brighter. The circle of light has moved closer to the center. He'll be found here years from now, one of a pair of skeletons. People will try to decipher what was going on. Nothing. Some time later, Ethan is nearly asleep with the frustration and boredom and embarrassment. What keeps him awake is his throbbing knees.

"Okay," the old man finally says. "You remembered. Close your eyes and try to think of exactly where you were when you remembered."

Ethan is happy to close his eyes. He'll sleep. He sees the stones out in front of his feet and the edge of the flowing water. He sees the river flowing fast and the water eddying back of a big rock. He says, "Up south of Taos, beside the Rio Grande, in a state park, yesterday."

"And you remembered?"

"Yes."

"Keep your eyes closed. Imagine the place. What did you remember?"

Ethan says, "That I went to Mexico, to Oaxaca. I'd finished a book. I was feeling low. I knew my marriage was over." And with his eyes closed, Ethan begins to tell it. It comes like a river running from his mouth. Sometimes he opens his eyes and keeps telling it, and then he shuts his eyes and it runs on. He tells everything and then stops. His mouth has run dry with talking. His head is light. He feels empty. He sits cross-legged feeling no pain in his knees. It could be an hour, an hour and a half.

After a long silence, Hosteen Charlie says, "I'm going to do something native now. I'm a Diné *hatathli*, something between a priest and a shrink. I also get to sing. Don't worry if it doesn't mean anything to you. It gives me a chance to sort things out."

Hosteen Charlie begins a slow, rhythmic chant. Ethan closes his eyes. Sometimes the chant sounds like stressed poetry; sometimes the old voice breaks on a vowel and sounds like a cry or a plea. Sometimes the chant lifts like it's gliding over cliffs. It ends suddenly, making a deep silence in which Ethan can still hear its rhythm, an echo of silence.

Hosteen Charlie says, "That was the Mountain Way. It's sung for nervousness. You told a pretty bad story. You're not guilty of the worst of it. You can't go back, but in your life now you can make amends. You have to ask forgiveness of the spirit you offended. Then you have to forgive yourself. Your father has his own problems. We're going to sit quietly for a few more minutes, and then we'll walk around."

Ethan sits looking at the earth floor. It is no longer flat brown: something wonderful is happening. Thousands of points appear— red, blue, yellow and green. He says, "My god, Hosteen Charlie, I'm seeing the floor full of color, point after point of sparkling colors, like an omen. Like, I was keeping myself from seeing all the colors in my life, but by telling you… Do you understand how fantastic this is?"

"Wait,' Hosteen Charlie says. "The floor *is* full of colors. It's from the sand painting ceremonies. Can't get rid of the colored sand. You're seeing them now, I guess, because the sunlight's moved onto the floor right in front of you."

Ethan says, "I'm an idiot."

The old man gets up slowly. "Just cause the colors are no miracle don't mean it's not an omen. It could be true, what you said about yourself and telling that story."

Ethan stands. His knees are sore.

Hosteen Charlie says, "In this bag I'm wearing, got some buttons for the peyote ceremony. Of course it's going to give visions, of course it's the peyote that gets you going, but what you see in those visions is your own. What I'm saying here is ceremony is a way to understand."

They go into the bright sun and walk by the split rail fence. They look up the valley. It's broad and green, checked with small farm plots and grazing sheep. Hosteen Charlie says, "Notice anything?"

Ethan is not going mystical again. "No."

Hosteen Charlie says, "The dog wasn't waiting at the door. He's gone off. Maybe because you got something off your chest."

Ethan stretches his arms and bends backwards to relax his back.

Hosteen Charlie says, "There's no money involved in what happened this morning. Sand-painting ceremony, now that is damned expensive. You'll find the right thing to give, sometime. Maybe help John coach some sports with the kids.

They shake hands. Down the slope, Ethan turns to see Hosteen Charlie standing with the orange dog again. In the Jeep, Ethan feels so much better that he smiles. He isn't sure that he's told it accurately, but what he couldn't remember was drowned in the torrent of words or might have bobbed to the surface of the story downstream. The story is no longer monstrous because he's spoken it, or is monstrous in ways he can cope with. He laughs: he can even tell Lucy now, to bring the story back into the world he inhabits. Besides, he'll show that he's open with her. How open is his business.

He phones her from the Jeep. She's anxious for him. He's better now, thank you. He's talked to someone, told a therapist. He can be at her place in about three hours. Would she be willing to hear his story?

"Yes, of course," Lucy says. "Don't make it sound so terrible."

Ethan says, "But it is."

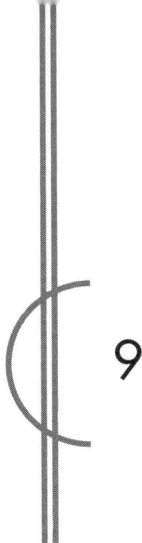

9

ETHAN IS SITTING IN THE ARMCHAIR. Across the coffee table, Lucy is on the living room sofa.

He says, "I was low. *Who's on Second* had been out for six months, and while the reviews were good, sales were nonexistent. My publisher's attitude, passed on by my editor Polly Ettinger, was, 'We love your writing, but your career would go much better if you were upbeat again. Your first two novels were so *funny!*' In addition to this damning support and the usual post-partum blues, I realized that my marriage had to end. Even Helen took pity and encouraged me to get away for a while. I was too depressed to decide where to go, so Meyer put it in the hands of his secretary, who handled all his travel. Or so I thought. It was actually Meyer who arranged it. You'll see why this became important. The holiday was a two-week trip to Oaxaca, a terrific bargain. It seems a guide in a charter group had cancelled, so I'd be lodged in an apartment owned by the linked Mexican travel company. Cut-rate was fine with me: much of my mediocre advance was spent, and I could foresee the divorce was going to be expensive.

"The charter group had done a Boston Museum of Fine Arts course in preparation for the trip. I think it was 'The Pleasures of Oaxaca, The Treasures of Monte Alban.' But I knew enough about the area's charms—the setting, the ancient and colonial remains, the town itself."

Ethan looks at Lucy. "I know it's long-winded, but it's important that you know my state of mind going into the trip."

"Of course," Lucy says. "Go on."

He says, "My luck, I had a cold when we flew down. But when we landed among the lush green mountains, I thought I'd done the right thing. As I walked to the bus, I even saw a hummingbird do its standstill-in-the-air act at the rim of a big red hibiscus."

Ethan is aware he hadn't mentioned the hummingbird to Hosteen Charlie Wauneka. He says, "But my cold had become worse on the flight. My eyes were streaming and my throat ached. And the closer the bus got to the town, the more the roadside was strewn with garbage. Maybe it was just that particular route, but Oaxaca, looked dark and nondescript. The bus stopped on a particularly dour, treeless street, and the guide who'd joined us at the airport told me the local agent would meet me here shortly and take me to my apartment. So I got off the bus and stood alone on the shadowed sidewalk by my suitcase. My nose was running and it hurt to swallow. The place was depressing: long gray buildings either side, four or five stories high—apartments or offices, I guessed—with deep inset windows. I was the only living thing on that narrow street. It was mid-afternoon, windless and silent. I could have been standing in a painting by de Chirico. Right behind me, a door opened, and I turned, a little startled, to see a woman, middle aged, in a severe gray skirt suit that looked way too heavy for the heat. She introduced herself as Estella Rosen, the tour company's agent in Oaxaca. She said the apartment was in the building she'd just come from. My heart sank, but I followed her in and up the stairs. She told me it had been her pleasure to have once met my 'illustrious father,' as she put it, in Mexico City."

Lucy says, "Ah, so you figured the trip was arranged by him."

"No, not then. I had nothing in mind then but lying down, I felt that sick. Then she said she was Jewish and told me that Jews had been in Oaxaca for a long time, but until the seventeen-nineties couldn't admit to being Jews. What did she expect me to do, ask where in Oaxaca I could get decent gefilte fish? It was a dark studio apartment on the second floor. When she opened the shutters, it didn't get much lighter: the windows looked across the street to similar windows. But it was adequate and clean: a kitchenette with a dining table, a sofa and large bed and bits of furniture, and a small bathroom with a stall shower. She said a girl would come to clean and bring fresh linen each day at ten in the morning. The girl's name was Carmen. 'Not really Carmen,' she said, something that sounded to me like Caxa Menje, which was her Indian name, but they called her Carmen."

Lucy says, "This story involves Carmen."

"Too right," Ethan says, pausing for whatever Lucy might say.

When she says, "Go on," he says, "The agent explained about the apartment: the only drawback was it had no phone, but there was a pay phone at the corner, and around the corner a good general store. It turned out to be only four blocks from the central square. She left her card and said I should visit or call the hotel if I wanted to tour with the charter group. When she left, I drank bottled water and lay down and slept.

"I woke in the early evening and went down to the store and bought beer, cheese and some rolls. Back in the apartment, I ate, took a hot shower, drank hot tea and went to sleep expecting I'd wake up feeling better. But in the morning, my cold was worse. I suppose I shouldn't have gone with the group to Monte Alban that day, but the thought of lying around the apartment on that bleak street was too depressing. Up on the mountain, my eyes swam and my head burned. I looked into the holes, the burial chambers. I saw the relief carvings, some of weird dancers, which our guide then told us were actually illustrations of various diseases, a Mixtec medical textbook, he said. But these turned out not to be the real carvings, nor were those in the museum on the site. The real ones were in the museum in Mexico City. I became very unhappy to find I'd been looking at copies of copies, and I walked away from the group and sat under a tree. I bought a peeled mango on a stick. I liked it because it was cut so it looked like a little pineapple. I ate it sweating like a pig. I felt I'd come down with something illustrated on the carvings."

Lucy laughs. Hosteen Charlie hadn't laughed, but Ethan hadn't said this to him.

He says, "For the rest of the afternoon, I sat on a stone and watched the group move around the ruins. On the bus back down to town, the guide who'd told us the carved dancers were really people with dropsy and goiters said that an excellent cure for my cold was to take a good glass of mescal with cups of hot tea and go to bed. That was a cure made for my mood. When I got back, I went to the general store. It had about twenty different kinds of mescal. I bought three bottles, more tea and some sugar. In the apartment, I drank a water glass of mescal, three cups of hot, sweet tea, and I passed out. When I woke up it must have been after ten in the morning, because the cleaning girl was washing the floor. I said hello, put my bathrobe on in bed, and went to the bathroom. I felt dizzy, awful. I must have looked awful when I came out and fell into bed, because the girl came over with a wet cloth and motioned I should put it on my forehead."

Lucy says, "She was only concerned with your health."

"With hindsight, I don't know. But then, yes. She had long narrow eyes and a hooked nose. Not what you'd call a beauty. Anyhow, she asked in Spanish if I wanted food, but I shook my head. She left tea by the bed. I slept all day, and when I woke in the evening, I found a roll and a tamale on a plate. I left some money for this under a vase of flowers on the table. I ate a bit and again tried the mescal and tea cure. This time, it seemed to be working: I slept better and woke less dizzy. After two days of this, I felt well enough to venture out for lunch on the square. Have you been to Oaxaca?"

"Once, years ago," Lucy says.

"Then you'll know how people kept coming to my table—kids selling gum, two Chiclets at a time, women with flowers, kids wanting to shine my shoes, lottery ticket sellers, and a man with a roll of paintings on tree bark. He was persistent. He spoke English and said, 'Wait, you see.' He unrolled the paintings and brought out his largest. It was of the square I was sitting in, with the band in the bandstand and the tourists and all the beggars and Chiclet kids and even someone he said was him showing a tourist a bark painting. I told him I liked it. He—"

"Ethan, is the picture seller important to the story?"

"Oh, yes. I promise. So he said, 'For an English, an American, I for you make a big painting special as you want. Good price, four hundred, three-fifty dollars US.'"

Lucy is smiling at his imitation. He keeps from smiling and says, "I said I'd think about it and see him there around the same time next day. He said, 'Okay, good, *bueno*, same tomorrow, good price maybe three hundred. Me Xavier.' I introduced myself and we shook hands. Then he carefully re-rolled the paintings, took them two tables away, and began his pitch again.

"I took it easy for the rest of the day. I stayed in the shade, drank mescal and tea, and napped. When I woke up next morning, I had no idea of the time. You know I sleep naked. But the apartment seemed empty, so I went to the bathroom without my robe. I opened the door, and Carmen walked past me with mop and pail as if I wasn't there.

My bathrobe, it turned out, was in there, so I put it on and went out and made breakfast as if nothing had happened. In that small place, I couldn't help seeing her as she cleaned. She looked like the Mixtecs on the Monte Alban carvings, a healthy one. When she was about to leave, she brought a small bark painting from her bag and unrolled it for me to see. I said, 'No, *gracias*,' but she shook her head and pointed to the signature. It said Xavier. She said, 'Xavier *su amigo*, me broder, broder.'"

"Oh-oh," says Lucy.

"I know, but wait. Nothing seemed odd about it, because when I saw him in the square that afternoon, he said, yes, she was his sister. When he told her of the tall American, she thought it could be me. We talked about the picture he'd do for me. I wanted the bandstand with a few musicians setting up, and me on a bench having my shoes shined, Indian women carrying bags or such on their heads—the usual. He said he could do it in five or six days, and we agreed on the price. I told him his sister was very kind; she'd helped me when I was ill. And that was true. I don't think anyone in my position would have seen anything calculating in the simple things she'd done."

"And you didn't find her attractive."

"Then? Far from it, with her ancient Indian face and head, and her height; she couldn't have been more than five foot tall. So for the next few days, I was a tourist. I took a bus back up to Monte Alban and slowly walked around with a guidebook. Another day I hired a cab and went out to the ruins at Mitla. When I ran into Xavier in the square, he gave me excited progress reports on the painting. He promised I'd have his best painting of all time for only three hundred US. I said I was sure of it; I was also sure we'd agreed two-fifty. He said of course, but when I saw it I'd want to give him three. I couldn't help liking him. He asked me to dinner at his home. He said, 'Very ordinary house, typical Oaxacan Indian on Sunday?' I thought it would be unfriendly to refuse. Besides, how many tourists got a chance to look into ordinary Mexican Indian life? We met in the square on Sunday. Xavier took me past the covered market and down the hill, to the open marketplace you might remember."

He sees Lucy shrug and he continues. "I stopped to buy flowers, an armful of those Diego Rivera lilies. We turned into a street of one-story whitewashed walls, a lot of them crumbling. Midway along,

Xavier opened a door in a wall and we entered a little yard covered in blue plastic hung on twine for shade, like at the market. Behind it was a low house. A plain wooden table and some chairs were out there. A little boy and girl looked out of the house door, smiling. Then Carmen came out in an Indian blouse and skirt, her black hair combed out long, an orange hibiscus over her ear. This suited her much better than what she wore to clean. Three more children came out; two little girls and an older boy, and then a woman Xavier introduced as his other sister. Then there was her husband, a thin *mestizo* with a long scar down his cheek and neck. I didn't see that as sinister: no one else looked like they could have been in a knife fight. And, finally came mama and papa. They looked in their nineties but were probably in their fifties, he on a stick, both half toothless. Everyone was smiling and nodding and shaking hands. They spoke mostly in their Mayan, sometimes in Spanish, a few words in English. I gave the flowers to the mother who thanked me with a bow."

Ethan stops. "This is important. It's the process I got involved with."

Lucy says, "I'm listening. I'm not going anywhere."

These are not the details he gave Hosteen Charlie. But this is Lucy he's telling it to. He says, "Then all the women went inside to prepare the meal. Carmen came out with glasses and a demijohn in woven straw. The men sat down at the table—the papa and Xavier and the brother-in-law and me. Xavier poured four glasses from the demijohn, and the sister appeared with a plate of halved limes, a jug of water, and bottles of orangeade. She went in, and we started to drink. It was mescal. Tremendous: a mule pleasantly kicking my head. We toasted one another and emptied the glasses. Xavier filled them again. We drank formally, seriously. We poured our hearts into drinking that mescal. Between drinks, I followed the others and drank a glass of cool water or warm, sweet orangeade. We sucked the limes. I could smell cooking from the house: tortillas and peppers and meat grilling on charcoal. The sheet of blue plastic was our own small sky. We each drank five of those triple shot glasses, and all of us stood steadily when it was time to go inside to eat. Flies crawled over the spilled soda on the table. When I walked, I felt I was on roller blades, but otherwise I felt fine.

"Inside, there was a dark, narrow hallway with a few doorless rooms off of it. We went into one packed with two tables and squeezed ourselves around and sat on plastic chairs that touched each other. More people had shown up — two aunts, I think, and a cousin. The room was jammed and the table was loaded with tortillas and roast jalapeños and wrapped tamales and grilled chicken and goat and chopped tomatoes and cilantro and three different *chilies picantes* and three jars full of the giant lilies I'd brought and water and orangeade and the demijohn of mescal. I apologized in Spanish for not bringing smaller flowers. Xavier translated my Spanish into Spanish and Mayan. My apology was found very funny. Xavier also translated into English for me, even if they spoke Spanish, much of which I understood. All of us ate a lot and the men, myself among them, kept drinking mescal. The scrawny papa was phenomenal: he looked as if he were putting away his own weight in food and drink. The chilies were going off on my tongue like firecrackers. I was having a great time. We all were. I left them US money, not that anyone asked, but because they were poor and generous and nice. I'm sure if you'd been there, you would have thought so, too."

Lucy nods.

Ethan says, "Carmen walked back with me. She had to prepare an apartment for the last minute arrival of three Americans. I thought that was pretty hard on her, but I was glad to have someone show me the way back. I told her I liked her Indian clothes better than the jeans and tee shirt she wore to clean. Markets were opening for the evening. The wind swung the light bulbs hanging over melons and carpets and cheap shoes. Carmen's posture was stately: she walked like a Mayan princess. I tried to copy it by pulling back my shoulders and concentrating on the swing of my thigh through my hip joint. After a while, I saw that Carmen was laughing when she glanced at me. I supposed it was my height and her shortness. At the square, I told her I could find my way, but she must have seen how drunk I was and stayed with me. By the time we reached my building, I was reeling. She helped me up the stairs, and unlocked the door. I walked fully clothed into the shower and let it run cold."

Lucy says, "She just let you do that."

"No, she was saying no, but she couldn't stop me. Somehow, I managed to get my clothes off, dry myself, and get into my bathrobe. I sat on the edge of the bed, and Carmen brought me tea. I thought that was nice of her, so I put the tea on the bedside table and opened my arms, and had her sit on my lap."

"You had her sit," Lucy says. "What does that mean?"

"That means I was incredibly drunk, and the idea came to me, and she was standing near me, and when I opened my arms and patted my thigh, she understood what I meant and sat on my lap."

"Didn't you think that was odd of her, to do that when you asked, out of a completely different relationship?"

"I didn't think that or anything. I wasn't capable of thinking."

"Go on, then," Lucy says,

It's the way she adds "then," the way it modifies not only the two words before it but everything that Ethan has so far said that makes him pause to consider where he's going—where he *should* be going next. He draws a long breath and says, "It gets sexual from here."

Lucy smiles. "I'm not surprised."

"There's no way I can leave all of that out. The problems, the story, would be incomprehensible without it."

Lucy is quiet; Ethan sees her thinking with her eyes, their pale blue shot through with fire. She says, "Tell me what you must, but skip as much detail as you dare."

He finds "dare" another significantly curious word, as if Lucy understands motives other than clarity, even motives other than he understands. "Yes," he begins, allowing her to understand his assent, if not its limits. "What she looked like naked. Carmen was a color like pale walnut. Her breasts were coffee-colored cones with chocolate tops. Her belly, hips, and buttocks were curved and heavy, and her skin was oily and smooth. Her hair was thick and black; under her arms and between her legs her hair was fine. She was very different looking from any other woman I'd been with. I can't explain why with so much mescal in me I was able to be sexually aroused. Some of it may have been the sounds she made: a moan when I kissed her breasts, a light ah-ah-ah sound when I licked her. She tasted of cilantro and mescal, though the mescal may well have been me. Something else: I was thrilled with the consciousness of the intense exploitation of what was taking place—the rich gringo tourist with the servant girl, *una india pobresita*. Perhaps the mescal allowed my guilt to heighten my arousal. Whatever, we did it on the bed she made so well each morning, and I liked the idea that she'd have to change the sheets.

Before she left to prepare this other place for the three Americans, she came over to me on the bed, where I was slowly passing out. She kissed me and said, 'Mi marido,' and I said, 'Whatever, Princess, just so I fuck you again.'"

Ethan looks at Lucy, but there's no way to tell her reaction. She might be listening to the weather. She is, at least, not telling the weather to stop. He says, "I awoke in daylight, sick to my stomach. And my cold, or flu, or whatever it was, had returned worse then before. I went to the bathroom and was sick. I went back to bed and woke in my own dirt and vomit, too weak to move. Carmen arrived and helped me to the bathroom. She propped me in the shower and washed me. She cleaned the bed and put on fresh linen as I sat shivering on a chair. Something strange came over me, a stoned feeling from the top of my skull to my toes. I told Carmen to take her clothes off; she did and I watched her go about her cleaning chores naked. What did I understand then about Carmen? Nothing. I wasn't considering that. I say I was stoned in my fever, but I felt a strangely weightless horniness. I made it to the bed and we had sex. No details, Lucy, but it was a sort of sex I'd never had nor wanted before. Afterwards, we both showered to clean up. Then, while she made tea, I brought the two remaining bottles of mescal to the bedside table and started to drink from one. I wanted to retch but held it down, drink after drink. Carmen held my head up and gave me tea. I was dripping with sweat again. She had to leave, but I wanted sex again. At the end of it, Carmen said, 'Mi marido.' This time I said, 'Someone else's *marido*, much good it does either of us.' She sponged and dried me in bed and I passed out.

"Then it was night. Carmen was there with a doctor, an Englishman named Radley, I now know contacted through Estella Rosen, the local agent. He wore a blue shirt with a starched white collar and starched white cuffs. He said, 'A touch of the you-know-whats.' I thought he might call me 'Old Boy.' He gave me paregoric and codeine, and delirious as I was, I thought it was fishy, his having prescription drugs to hand. He said, 'If your fever doesn't break in a day or so, our friend Carmen, good as gold, will bring me round again. Toodle-oo.' I didn't trust Radley, the over-dressed junkie. Two hundred bucks to hand me a bottle and pills. After the paregoric, I took the codeine, twice the amount he'd said, and washed it down with mescal."

Lucy says, "Didn't Carmen try to stop you from drinking?"

"Carmen, good as gold, didn't blink an eye. I woke in the early morning on the floor, sitting against the bed with the sheet around me. I guessed from the mess, I'd woken up being sick and rolled myself away from it off the bed. Carmen came with rings under her eyes and went straight to the bathroom. I supposed she was tired from the hard time I was giving her, being so sick. I hoisted myself up and drank mescal. I took more pills, I didn't count how many. I went to the bathroom door ready for more strange sex, but when I opened it, Carmen was douching and the peroxide smell gave me an instant, terrible headache, I mean the Trotsky special, the ice-pick-in-your-brain, sir, headache. I took the mescal bottle and made it to the table where there was cold tea. I poured the cup of tea back into the teapot, poured in mescal and drank the cup down. When Carmen came out she told me she was very tired because she had so much work to do for the three Americans."

"I'll bet," says Lucy.

"I had no idea she could be fucking them. She could have had more tricks then a porn film, but I wasn't thinking about her. I wasn't naïve, I was just in a parallel universe composed of mescal, codeine, testosterone and whatever virus or amoeba had decided to join the party."

Lucy says, "You weren't trying to kill yourself? No, you wouldn't do that."

Ethan considers Lucy on the Sandia mountain ledge. He says, "I wasn't looking for permanent oblivion, just local anesthetic. But it did then come to me that I'd taken for granted all the caring and feeding and nursing Carmen was doing for me. Not the sex: sick or healthy, stoned or sober, I could not conceive of paying for sex. While she was cleaning, I put five hundred dollars into her purse. Before she left, she put me to bed and kissed my forehead. I imagined it hissed. When the door closed, I groaned with the headache. The mescal was finished. I somehow got my clothes on and went to the store in the next block and bought two bottles of mescal, because two was all I could carry. It seemed to take me hours to get there and back. I was freezing. I lay in my clothes under all the blankets and drank mescal. It seemed to blunt the headache.

"By late afternoon when Carmen returned, I was full of mescal and codeine. She had soup and rolls for me, and I was suddenly starving. Out of bed, I felt the rush of cool air on my sweat-soaked clothes. The food was delicious. Then, of course, I was sick. I…"

He remembers Emmy and stops. "After Carmen cleaned me up, the sex shifted into sadomasochism."

Lucy says, "But you'll spare me the details."

"I'll give only enough for you to understand what followed. During sex, Carmen asked me to slap her ass. She kept asking for it to be harder. 'Muy fuerte,' she said, 'mas y muy fuerte.' We had a whole day of this. At some point she handed my belt to me and asked me to use it on her ass and the back of her thighs. 'Muy, muy fuerte y mas y mas.'"

Lucy says, "But you didn't want to: she was taking advantage of your condition. Is that what you think?"

"No, it was exciting. I was into it, though it hadn't been and isn't my thing, not like that. The most extreme of it — I need to say this — was welts on her ass, welts with drops of blood. That's it. It was just a part of this insane sex fest we got into — or, maybe that I got into and she faked. It ended with her leaving in the afternoon and me going to sleep.

"I woke in the dark, aching everywhere, but worst in my head. I drank cup after cup of sweet tea, interspersed with mescal. Then I took a double dose of paregoric and four codeine pills and went back to bed. I dreamt of traffic accidents, the screech of brakes, crashing metal, breaking glass, and sirens. I woke. It was still night. I stood under a hot shower, shivering. I thought of calling the doctor, but remembered I didn't have his number. Even if he was in the phonebook, I knew I couldn't make it down to the corner. I sat on the edge of the bed drinking mescal, trying to figure out what I should do. I couldn't. The more mescal I drank, the more panicky I became. At some point I went to the bathroom and passed out sitting on the toilet. I dreamt someone was knocking on the apartment door, calling my name.

"I woke up to loud knocking and heard people coming into the apartment. The bathroom door opened and a man in a suit pointed a gun at me He shook his head, put the gun in his shoulder holster, and helped me up and into my bathrobe. Then he led me into the room and sat me down at the table. The agent, Estella Rosen, was there. So were two other men, also in suits. One was taking photographs of the bedsheets. The other came to the table, and the one who'd helped me in the bathroom moved away. The man across the table was broad and heavy. He spoke good English and introduced himself as Detective Otero. He said there was a serious situation. The woman I knew as Carmen had been found terribly beaten and was in the hospital, in intensive care. There were indications, also, of sexual abuse. Did I wish to say anything? Did I require the services of a lawyer? The rule of law, he wanted me to know, was respected in the Republic of Mexico.

"I blacked out several times while he was speaking. Each time, Estella Rosen appeared and held a glass of water to my lips. She said my father was being contacted. She said she would arrange for a lawyer. She said I didn't have to say anything without a lawyer being present. Otero said certainly, I could wait for a lawyer. I said I didn't want to. I told him Carmen had left the apartment in the afternoon, and I hadn't seen her since. Otero asked what time she left. I said I only knew it was the afternoon, probably between three and five. I wasn't well, I said. I said he could see that. He could see I couldn't have taken Carmen anywhere because I was very ill. Otero said, 'And drunk?' 'Yes,' I said, 'unfortunately.' I said I was taking medicine prescribed by a Dr. Radley. Otero said, 'And you were having a sex relationship with this woman who might die of her beating?' He made it sound like necrophilia. Sick as I was, I understood that the other policeman was taking photographs of some blood on the sheets. I said, 'Yes, a sex relationship, but no violence.' I blacked out again. This time, Otero tipped back my head with his thumb under my chin and told me I would be helped to dress and then taken to the police station to be held for further questioning. I could bring my medicine. Estella Rosen asked in Spanish that my illness be taken into consideration and I be placed in a clinic, under guard. Otero replied out of my hearing. The first policeman helped me dress. When we left, the other one was putting linen in plastic bags. He was wearing plastic gloves. I was dazed. Halfway down the stairs, my legs went. Otero pushed me hard against the wall, propped me, and then half carried, half dragged me down. Estella Rosen stood at the bottom smiling tensely. I found that hateful.

"Then my head was pushed down and I was shoved into the back of the police car. It stank of cigarettes and the windows were closed.

I gagged and was sick on myself. The policeman sitting next to me swore. He said, 'Gringo chingado.' I was looking at the back of Otero's head: his dark hair, a bald spot.

"At the station, they took my passport and wallet and then took my fingerprints and put me into a cell on my own. I fell asleep on the hard bed. Later they gave me water and soup. Then they took me to a small room where Otero was at a table. I sat opposite. He asked if I wished to wait for my lawyer. I said I wanted to cooperate and could tell him everything I knew now. He gave me a funny look, like I was some sort of idiot. I was, of course, but I didn't know that, then. So then he said, 'Please tell me,' and I did. When I finished he asked me to repeat what I'd just said. After I told him again, he said, 'Once more, please, from when you first heard of the woman.' And then again. After four or five of my retellings, Otero said, 'Did you like to hit the woman for sex reasons?' I said, 'No, not like you told me she was hit.' Then I said, 'I would now like to wait for my lawyer before saying anything else.' I was about to pass out. I lay my head on the table. Otero leaned across and spoke over my ear. He said, 'If you think that less justice will be done because the victim is a poor Indian woman, you are making a big mistake, Señor Baum.' I couldn't lift my head, for fear of knocking into Otero's face, so I said out of the corner of my mouth that I didn't think that, I didn't want that. She was a nice woman. I wanted justice for her. He brought his mouth next to my ear and growled, 'You people imagine you can come here and do what you want, but here we have the rule of law even for poor Indians. Even for rich Americans. Señor Baum, we have taken your fingerprints: we have taken fingerprints from the victim's body and clothing. If yours should match, Señor, it would not go well for you.' I said my fingerprints might well be there, but not because I hurt Carmen. And Otero said, 'And after you had beaten her and broken her nose and gave her those terrible wounds, you did what, you had sex with her? You enjoy doing this?' I didn't answer. He said he was finished with me, for now. I asked Otero what I was supposed to do. As at the start of the interview, he looked at me with contempt. Then he motioned the guard to take me away."

"Ah," Lucy says, "you were supposed to be discussing money, not speaking about the crime."

"Exactly. But it was only after that interview that I began to put it together. For me, the cell was like the apartment without mescal. I mean, I slept, I woke, I crept to the toilet in the corner. Otero came by to tell me I had the best cell, the only single cell. He said, 'Because of your illness and the insistence of *Señora* Rosen.' I lay thinking of what a naïve fool I'd been. When, next day, I told the guard that I was running out of medicine, Radley turned up within two hours. He said the bill would be settled up through the police, with my credit card. He was wearing another fastidiously cuffed and collared shirt. He nodded to the seatless, stinking toilet and said, 'Bad show, this, but I dare say it'll all work out.' Weak as I was, if he said 'Toodle-oo' again, I was going to jump him. He didn't, nor did he mention Carmen, good as gold. This stage Englishman junky had to be part of the tourist sex business that Estella Rosen helped run. Now I understood that Xavier, the so-called brother, and, indeed, the whole extended, pretended family was on hire for the Sunday feast, that weekly farce.

"For four days in my windowless cell, I took my medicine, without mescal, in proper doses. Each afternoon, I was led down corridors to the small, windowless room where Ortero questioned me, but after that first time, I stayed quiet, waiting for the lawyer Estella Rosen had promised. Yet despite Otero's reminders of the rule of law in Mexico, no lawyer appeared, and when I asked about this, he gave me his look of contempt. Physically, anyway, I was getting better. I could hold down some soup and bread.

"Late in the afternoon of my fourth day in jail, my father turned up. One moment I was sitting on the edge of the bed. The next, there was Meyer with a guard on the other side of the bars. The guard set down a stool and told him he had ten minutes. He said, 'Ethan?' I went to the bars. He put his hand through and touched my face as if feeling who I might be. I must have looked pretty bad after the illness and still in the clothes I had when they arrested me. He sat on the stool and I sat on the end of the bed and he asked what happened. I told him the story, in outline. Once, he interrupted to say, 'Yes, the three other American men.' I asked why no lawyer had shown up. He said I had a good lawyer who didn't need to see me. That's how things were done here. He said I should do whatever was asked by the lawyer or Estella Rosen. When I asked how Carmen was doing, he gave me the same look Otero had when I asked what I should do. Then Meyer stood and said, 'That's not your business. Your business is to get out of jail and out of Mexico.' Then he signaled the guard and left. Only then did it come to me he hadn't even asked how I was. He seemed like a stranger. He gave me the creeps."

Lucy is shaking her head in sympathy. He continues: "A few hours later, I was taken from jail by the lawyer's assistant, a young man named Guzman. He drove me to a small hotel, in the hills outside of town. My wallet, passport and suitcase were waiting for me there. All my clothes were clean and ironed. I never saw the lawyer. Early the next morning, Guzman took me to the airport and accompanied me to Mexico City. On the flight, he told me I was to sit tight in the hotel I'd be put up in until I heard from him. I was not to leave the room. I was to use room service to eat. Did I understand? I asked him if this was part of the rule of law in Mexico. He was silent, obviously offended. I felt I should have stayed in Oaxaca, or not allowed this comfortable house arrest. But I was too weak and too frightened to complain.

"The next three days were surreal. I was put into the Grand Hotel on the Zocalo, in an enormous room with white, imitation baroque furniture. The room had four huge windows, two with small balconies overlooking the great city square. My health improved on fruit and steaks from room service, and I'd switched from mescal to Russian vodka. I ordered drink by the bottle, and up with it would come six glasses, a bucket of ice and plates of sliced limes, as if I were throwing a party. Without becoming sick drunk, I managed to stay unsober. In the evening, I ordered hors d'oeuvres and nibbled on them as I watched the giant Mexican flag come down in the middle of the square to the accompaniment of a military band. In the mornings, I put brandy into my coffee and watched the political rallies form: first a few people, a sound truck; then more people and banners being unfurled; then the crowds ordering into long files and marching, the white words waving on red banners. I watched the tour buses draw in by the cathedral and the soldiers march out from the Presidential Palace.

"On my third day there, drunk in the heat of noon, I decided to make an important political speech and stepped out onto one of my balconies. My subject was going to be the rule of law in the Republic of Mexico, with special reference to poor beaten Indian women and rich *gringos chingados*. I struck poses. I leaned forward like Lenin. I rocked back, hands on my hips, like Mussolini. Then I thought of Oaxaca and went back inside and made the speech to myself, drink in hand, in front of a mirror. I said: 'The rule of law here was Meyer and his Mexican lawyer busy laying on the bribes in the right places, for instance to papa and mama, to sister and her husband scarface, to Xavier the brother-pimp. And laying on even bigger bribes, *las mordidas*, with the bureaucrats who must be nameless and on El Señor Detective Ortega, he of the contempt for my *chingado* naïvety, a contempt equaled only by that of my father, Don Meyer. Ah, Don Meyer, *qué hombre*! a gentleman of the world and friend of the grand procuress La Doña Estella Rosen, who had met this pinnacle of patriarchs in this very same city where his pathetic, ridiculous, and unworthy son now languishes. *Ay Chihuahua! Ay chingado!*'

"The next morning, Meyer phoned and told me to be ready to leave at noon. No hello, no how are you, just the command. Guzman drove me to the airport, whisked me through customs and delivered me at the door of the plane to a waiting steward, who walked me down the aisle and sat me next to my waiting father.

"Neither of us said a word until the plane was racing down the runway on takeoff. I leaned to Meyer in the roar and asked what I owed him. He said, 'Nothing.' I said, 'Well, what did all this business cost you?' He said, 'Twelve thousand, five hundred dollars, cheap.' The nose of the plane tipped up and we left the ground. I said, 'Dirt cheap, considering.' I stood to get my checkbook from my jacket in the overhead. A stewardess shouted at me from in her safety harness. The steward lurched down the aisle toward me. I found the checkbook and sat down. I wrote out the check. It was several thousand more than I had, but the bank would cover it. I folded it and put it into the pocket of the jacket Meyer wore. He said, 'I don't want your money.' I said, 'Think of it as one more favor you're doing me.'

"When passengers were allowed to move around, I moved to an empty seat near the back and started to think of Meyer's role in the proceedings. He'd set up a little sex trip for his sad son with his old friend, not to say lover, Estella. Hadn't she said she'd had the pleasure of meeting him? Maybe he'd known Carmen. Maybe he'd been at the family bean feasts. Had he been Carmen's *marido*, too? I tried so hard not to think of it, I couldn't bear it. I fell asleep. The last Meyer spoke to me about it, before I suppressed all memory of these events, was as we walked from the customs hall at Logan Airport. He said, 'You hate how I've behaved. Well, if I hadn't behaved like a beast, that is, just like any middle class Mexican parent would have, you'd be rotting for years in a Mexican jail.'"

Lucy is looking at him with her face in her hands. He says, "It all came back to me yesterday, because, on the phone a few days ago, Meyer repeated this charming speech to me, word for word."

He waits to see what effect his story has on Lucy. He knows that's what he's told it for, this second time.

She runs her hand across her forehead and pushes back her hair. "Ethan, dear, being crazy about you doesn't mean I'm stupid about you."

10

"MEANING WHAT?" he asks.

She stands. "I need some water. Want some?"

He nods. He goes to the window and stretches. Outside are the old untended apple and peach trees. Small puckered leaves, brown edged, some branches bare, some cankered. The trees need water, too. What deception has Lucy picked up in his story? He'll water the trees. Does he want Lucy to tell him to have nothing more to do with his father? He feels he's deceived himself more than he has Lucy.

She returns with a jug of water and two glasses on a tray. Until Ethan drinks, he has no idea of how thirsty he is. He drinks a second glass and joins Lucy on the sofa. "Meaning?" he resumes.

"Meaning you phoned this morning assuring me you had a terrible story to tell. But as you told it, there was a big hole at the heart of the story—you. You weren't there."

He shakes his head. "I don't see that."

She says, "For example, what really was 'terrible' to you—that your father set up a sex holiday for you, or that you chose to make it a sex holiday? That your father bribed the police and officials, or that you were grateful to get out of there despite being morally offended? I could go on."

"I'm surprised that, like my father, you don't mention Carmen."

"Carmen?"

"Yes, how terrible it was for her; how little my father cared."

"But Ethan, from what you told me, I have no reason to believe that Carmen was beaten. Did you see her? Were you shown photos?"

He knows that saying yes could raise more inconsistencies. "No. I assumed she was beaten by those three Americans, the ones who obviously knew how to buy off the law right away."

"Don't you see," she says, "you're still missing the point? What was 'terrible' to you—that a poor prostitute was beaten, or that you'd been with a poor prostitute who then, a risk all poor prostitutes run, was beaten? The point is: where are you in any of this?"

"I needed to tell you."

"Why? You've told a therapist; you got it off your chest."

"I suppose I thought by sharing it I could come closer, we could."

"No, you wanted me to say poor you, poor nice Ethan. You told me because you wanted complete absolution."

"Not so," he says, his voice rising. "Complete absolution isn't enough. I want you to be not only the forgiving mother but the punishing father. I want, I want…" He stands, shouts, "I want to water the orchard!" and leaves the room.

Outside, in the late afternoon heat, he listens to the hiss and rustle of the water he directs at the base of the fruit trees. What made him shout was a longing for water, for the truth, he means, however confusing and contradictory. He thinks of the burning of the orchards at Canyon de Chelly. And there was the orchard episode in his novel and, oh, yes, his life. The horror is that his whoremonger father did save him, the whoremonger son, from more time in a Mexican jail. But if he'd had the courage to confront the police, they'd have had to let him go. They could bring no evidence to trial… Ethan moves to the last peach tree. "Drink," he tells it.

"Drink," says Lucy, behind him. "I've brought drinks."

She's smiling, a tray with two iced drinks in her hand. He says, "Thank you I apologize for shouting at you. I'll just finish watering this tree." He watches her go to the chairs under the big cottonwood.

When, ten minutes later, he sits there, Lucy raises her glass to him. "It took some work, but you finally got there, to the truth about what you wanted from me."

"Is that right?" he says, knowing it is. "And is that what you're giving me?"

"I can't give absolution or punishment for what happened back then. I can give my love now." The light catches Lucy's hair so that its red looks dusty, as if it needs watering.

They make love that night, and it seems to him that Lucy is especially passionate, as if stimulated by his story, as if her body were saying, Forget your Mexican whore; I'll be your Mexican whore. The deep disloyalty of his thought makes Ethan particularly tender with her.

He spends the following days preparing for a series of trips around the state. He confers with Lavery and Lucy; he goes into the woods on the eastern slopes of the Sandias to practice putting up his tent and using his water-purification pump. Much of his time is spent with his new toy, a digital camcorder. His idea is that this will be the sight-and-sound-notebook from which he'll write. To avoid sarcasm and scorn, he decides not to share his bright photographic idea with Lavery. He stops thinking about his father. He feels better for having remembered and told his story, yet he cannot explain to himself what he means by "better," even as the feeling recedes from his consciousness. When he passes the log-cabin gas station at Cedar Crest, as he must on the way to and from the woods, his heart beats faster and he wills himself not to slow down and look, but he thinks of them—of Jean and Dave and Billy, and the dogs. But who is he kidding, of Jean, with a sad pleasure.

On the afternoon before he leaves for the first of his trips, Emmy Evans turns up at his apartment. Ethan is checking on his driving routes when the bell rings. Emmy is at his door. He says, "Hi," thinking how ridiculous his casual tone, as if they met every day.

She's wearing a black baseball cap, dark glasses, a black tee shirt and black jeans. She looks like a burnt sapling. "Hi," she says. "Mom told me you were going on a trip tomorrow so I thought I'd give you this. I mean, do you think you could look at this?"

Ethan takes the padded envelope. On it is written: "Please do not open until you are out of town. Emmy." "Please" is underlined in red and green and red again. The envelope is sealed with packing tape. He says, "Come in out of the sun."

A heavy smell of sandalwood falls as she passes. She accepts a glass of water, and they sit on stools at the kitchen counter.

"So what's in this: something you've written?"

"A story. Look, you don't have to read it. I mean, you might not even have the time."

"And you don't want me to read it in Albuquerque because I'd be here and so would you."

"Something like that. Anyway, it's probably crap."

"But you'd like me to be the judge of that."

"Yeah, and I don't want Mom to influence you, like if you were here."

"Has she read it?"

"No, no! God, I couldn't show it to her."

"I understand, what with her being the famous writer."

A small smile comes to Emmy's face: "I thought you would, like with your father being the famous philosopher."

"But I'm not a philosopher."

"Whatever."

"Aside from not showing Lucy your writing, do you two get along?"

"Yes, sure. What kind of a question is that? We're best friends."

He says, "I asked because I never see you at the house on campus."

"I've been there. I don't want to hang around and, you know, be in your way."

"In my way?"

"In both of your… Look," she says, hitting the counter with the flat of her hand. Ethan can see every bone in every finger. "Do you… I mean, do you seriously like my mom? You're not, like, just fucking around with her, are you?"

"I like your mom. And what I meant about you not being around at Las Lomas was that it would be nice to get to know you." He puts his hand on the counter besides hers. Emmy pulls her hand back as if she'd touched a hot stove.

She says, "So you and Mom, who likes who more? Or what?"

He says, "Emmy, it isn't like that." But it is exactly like that: her mom likes him more.

Emmy tips up the visor of her cap. Her hair is a faded version of Lucy's red. He supposes it's the illness. She says, "It's just that we're close, and she's my mother and all that, but sometimes I have to look out for her. I don't want anyone to hurt her. Don't get me wrong, I'm glad she's left Willy. He's a fucking piece of shit. It's just that…" In her frown, her forehead draws so tight, the skin looks about to tear open.

"What?"

"A few weeks ago, that fall you and Mom had up on the Sandias: was it that, really?"

"Of course."

"Because Mom can get so sad. I know how my problems can get her down. She didn't try anything crazy?"

"No. She slipped, and I slipped trying to grab her, and we slid over rocks and roots until we stopped." He doesn't want her to know the truth. *He* doesn't want to know it.

She says, "Where were you?"

"Somewhere along the ridge."

"Did she take you to my ledge, Emmy's Ledge?"

"Your ledge?"

"You're just another bullshitter."

"I'm sorry. Here's a proposal: I won't bullshit on that if you won't on something *I* ask you about—that phone sex job."

Emmy looks at her thumb crossing over and under her next two fingers. She says, "Deal. You first."

"Lucy and I went up to Sandia Peak to celebrate my getting this book contract. We didn't like the restaurant up there so we went for a walk, and she took me out to that ledge and told me how you ran around the mountains when you were little, before you were anorexic."

"Anorexic-bulimic."

"Yes. So we sat on that ledge, and when Lucy got up she slipped and fell half off. I dragged her back up and that's how we got scratched and bruised."

"And she really didn't try to jump."

"No. Though I don't know what was going through her mind, hanging off that rock or hanging on to me. You didn't ask, Emmy, but you're number one for Lucy, and you always will be and you would be even if you weren't anorexic. Don't you know that?"

"Anorexic-bulimic."

"Now you're bullshitting me."

She says, "I heard. You're telling me I don't have to be screwed up to get Mom's love. I already knew that. Hasn't she told you how smart I am? How I'm way out there ahead of all the shrinkologists I go to?"

"What she's told me is that you've been to therapists and clinics. And she's said you're smart and good and kind. And she said you'd always be number one for her."

"And that I'm breaking her heart."

"This is way past my no-bullshit quota. It's your turn."

"Yeah, well. I've changed my mind."

Ethan stares at her. She stares back, enjoying herself. He picks up her story envelope. She says, "I know: you're not going to read it. I don't care."

He says, "Worse: if you don't keep your promise, I'm going to read it right now." He pulls at the wrapping tape.

She shouts, "Don't!" and grabs his arm. He pulls back, forgetting how slight she is, and she comes off her stool into his arms. Her face at his, she mouths: "Would you like to fuck me?"

"No, I wouldn't," he says, and she pulls back from him. Is she aware of what she's said? All he can do is hold the manuscript over his head and look up.

She says, "All right. Ask me, then."

He brings down the envelope and sits back on his stool. "You say you're concerned about me not hurting Lucy. But what about you hurting her by doing that phone sex?"

"It isn't about her. It has nothing to do with her."

"But you must know it hurts her. So why do you do it? No bullshit; why?"

"Lots of reasons."

After a silence, he says, "Tell me one."

"Okay. Like everyone thinks I'm such a dweeb, and here I'm doing something so much more ice cool than they'd dare to, even though they don't know I do."

"Another reason?"

"Because I'm not going to have real dates, am I? Well, look at me." Emmy sucks in her cheeks and pulses her lips so that she looks like a skeletal fish. He can't help smiling.

"And what else?"

"No, that's all."

"Just one more reason and I won't read the story here."

She closes her eyes. "Because it shows me what pigs men are. I mean, in case I forget."

"You don't think what they say on the phone are just fantasies?"

"It's what they want."

"How do you know?"

Her eyes open. "Truth game's over. Anyhow, how do you know I was telling the truth?"

"The same way you know I was."

"Right. The trust thing. I have to go now. Thanks for taking the manuscript to read."

Ethan holds out his hand. She walks past it and leaves. He puts the envelope in his briefcase. Poor Emmy, he thinks. Poor Emmy and poor Lucy. And how's poor him going to fit in? Poorly. But even as he asks if he really needs all this dysfunction, he feels how passionate Emmy is about her story. He can't mention it to Lucy unless it's good.

Next morning, just after dawn, Ethan drives off on the first of his research trips. He follows the main road north, then east, under the Santa Fe Mountains, and turns off to explore the Pecos River valley. The attraction, besides heading towards the source of the mythic western river, are the romantic names of hamlets on the map: Monastery Lake, Windy Bridge, Holy Ghost, and Bert Clancy, a name out of a stereotype dream. Lavery, when told of the planned visit had said, "Why not? As good a place to start as any." But now, as the road climbs up, Ethan understands the ambivalence of that "Why not?" Even mid-morning, the mountains loom so steeply on both sides of the narrow valley that little light comes through; the forests of pine are darkly monochrome. Their occasional clearings are for various fundamentalist Christian conference centers, each, behind its high steel fence, large, silent, and unforgiving. He imagines what they confer about behind their massive gates and tinted windows, tinted against so pitifully little light, may be topics such as ways of barbecuing those who are not fundamentalist Christians. Nor is his spirit lifted by the smaller clearings on which sit private houses with signs like KEEP OUT, NO TRESPASSING AND THIS MEANS YOU! and THIS PROPERTY PROTECTED BY SMITH AND WESSON, that old poisoned chestnut.

Up at the road's end, he walks up the trail and sits on a log, looking back down the valley through his camcorder. He turns it on and says, "Pecos River Valley, late August. Don't know if this is among the ruined or the already too saved. It drops down before me like a Doré lithograph of the Earth cracked open to reveal hell. It's full of religious centers and paranoid residents. A god-forsaken place."

From there, Ethan drives back to Santa Fe and turns north. He stops at the pass over the high plateau of the Rio Grande. To the northeast are the Sangre de Cristos, the mass of Taos Mountain to the front, and at its lower slope the outlines of the ancient Taos Pueblo with the town of Taos under that. Driving from the pass, Ethan recalls that seventy years earlier D.H. Lawrence called this the most beautiful approach to any place he'd ever seen. To make it such again is only a matter of wiping out eleven miles of roadside junk souvenir shops, gas stations, chain fast-food restaurants, motels and trailer parks. He has ample time to record this, stuck as he is in the eleven mile traffic jam, during which he has the good luck to catch a back corner of the Mission de Taos immortalized by Georgia O'Keeffe as it shows behind the tour buses parked right up to it. Just before Taos, his patience runs out and he turns east to drive up behind Taos Mountain. There is, it's true, less traffic, but what he drives through now is mile after mile of vertically stacked suburbs. The higher he climbs, the more rustic the houses become, yet they don't stop. Too much driving, he thinks, and too little worth saving. At last, as the road soars into the Wheeler Mountain range, the houses are stopped by the national forest. He drives through pines and aspens. Ahead, a woman on horseback disappears off the road onto a trail. Ethan parks at a clearing and walks in. The air is cool, the forest is green and gold in the late afternoon sun. After a few shots, he puts his camcorder away and just walks. The trail underfoot is hard and soft with pine needles. Wind soughs in the branches.

Then he drives across the top of the mountain range, past ranches, through woodlands. There's little traffic. In the sunset, an owl glides across the road before him. He's still thinking of it when the mines appear. Very neat, as close to camouflaged as possible, but a vast range of enormous dark green sheds stretching back into the rock walls of the mountain. He parks and records it on the camcorder. The sign on the fence says, simply, TRIROCK MINING, and the sheds give no more information than the numbers on each—1, 2, 3. The light fades out by number 7, perhaps a quarter of the buildings. Ethan tries to remember what's mined here; something dangerous to the miners, he seems to remember—molybdenum or vanadium? He speaks into the camcorder to check it out and gets in the Jeep again, disgusted by this mine blandly disguising itself for this so public place on public lands.

A near full moon comes up bright orange, like a dented pumpkin.

The map says he's crossing into the Cimarron Mountain range; somewhere close above him is the peak of Mount Wheeler. He is so tired of driving. As the road begins to go down, he opens the window and cold air slaps his face. The slope is steeper, the bends in the road are tighter; his wrists ache with the turning. He stops by a narrow bridge and gets out. He leans over and listens to the waterfall, makes out a lick of whitewater below. He gets slowly back in. What can he write about if he never leaves the Jeep: the imprint of the steering wheel on his palms? the cramp of his thigh against the seat? When the road runs along it, the river appears like the silken silver of a fairy tale. He comes out of the mountains onto the plateau just before eight-thirty. He feels he's been at the wheel for weeks.

Minutes later, he's at Cimarron and follows a sign to the St. Peter Hotel. He goes in to a high mahogany front desk in a big Victorian parlor stuffed with old furniture and hunting trophies—bear heads and elk antlers, whole mule deer, a mountain lion in frozen stride halfway up a wall. The man behind the desk tells Ethan most people stay in the new motel wing behind the restaurant, but he's done the right thing by booking into the historic old part. He's been put in the Governor Lew Wallace Room, but for a few dollars more he could stay in Miss Annie Oakley's Suite. Unfortunately, the Buffalo Bill Cody Suite has just been taken by a foreign tourist. That's where, the desk clerk continues in the same monotone, Miss Oakley was said to slip down the hall at night to visit.

Ethan sticks with the room where the Governor, the brochure says, wrote several chapters of *Ben Hur*. He leaves his bag at the desk and heads to the new wing to eat. The clerk calls after him not to miss seeing the bullet holes in the old barroom ceiling. Ethan starts his dinner starving and finds, halfway through, he's nodding off over the enchiladas. He gets his bag and goes up the polished stairs and along the polished hall past the slaughter mounted on the walls. He's never before been so aware of his dislike of hunting. His room, though he doesn't like *Ben Hur*, Christ, no, reminds him to review his camcorder impressions of the day. He showers, sits on the brass bed—original to its sagging mattress—and calls Lucy.

When he says hello, she says, "Ethan, Ethan."

He tells her that sounds nice. He says he could slip in between her words and sleep.

"Where are you?"

"On the edge of Lew Wallace's bed, having turned down an offer to share Annie Oakley's. Oakley and Cody, I was thinking: Jesus, they were a good-looking pair, and what I want to know is, What do you think of your blue-eyed couple now, Mr. Death?"

"What's that?"

"A parody of e.e. cummings; an early performance poem called 'Buffalo Bill's Defunct.'"

"Smarty. What did you think of the Pecos Valley?"

"Absolutely ghastly. Those fundamentalist conference centers are gloomy enough to give racist, sexist, fascist sects a bad name."

"And your hotel: Aren't all the dead animals awful? The poor bear made to stand like a beggar at the bottom of the stairs? But aren't the rooms good?"

"They are. I'm just moving across to a red velvet armchair. Next door is Jesse James' room. I think he's in there now, lying fully dressed on the bed, looking up at the ceiling, just about to have an idea about ceilings and life, but he's disturbed by a woman's footsteps in the hall. They stop at his door. Now they're going on to William Cody's. Jesse thinks he maybe would have liked to open his door when the footsteps paused there, but, then, Miss Oakley is very proud and is such a damned sure shot."

"I'm thinking of you, too. When are you going up into the old land reserve in the mountains?"

"Tomorrow. I'm looking forward to being on the land rather than in the Jeep. I'll miss you on this bad mattress tonight."

But when he lies down to sleep, it isn't Lucy who comes to mind but pregnant Jeanie Brown. He sees the faint blue veins in the milk translucency of her breasts. Sandy was like that. His last waking thought: Is it children he wants or just to be a mother's child himself, or to leave Lucy and her lunacy and her awful daughter?

Despite the mattress, he sleeps well, gets up just after dawn, and walks around Cimarron. The buildings stand oddly isolated from each other, and the long shadows of early morning emphasize the big distances between them, as if the town had originally been laid out for an in-filling expansion which hadn't happened. Now, walking past the one or two hundred yards of high wild grasses between buildings, the effect is of a place where neighbor is unable to reach neighbor, a peopled wilderness. Is this, he wonders, a decent metaphor for New Mexico, America, or just the inside of his head?

Three hours later, Ethan is happy, holding on to, leaning in to, a young pine tree to keep from falling back down a near vertical slope. Somewhere down the mountain, he's lost the trail. To get back to it would take at least an hour. He drinks water and has a chocolate bar with one arm wrapped around the tree. Even if he gets no further, he'll have seen his first elk. Still in the Jeep, he'd come into the second meadow on the rough track and, at its far end, seen the herd. Through binoculars he looked at the animals—high, pale rumps, the muscle humped behind their necks, the heavy longhaired necks of bulls and their antlers down or up, moving slowly as they grazed. He looks up through the trees. The slope appears to level out five or six hundred yards above. He puts the canteen away, leans forward, and begins sidestepping up the slope, grabbing saplings, branches, and roots that come to hand. Often he has to move sideways in four-inch lifts of each foot. His ankles stiffen. He should have worked out in a gym before doing anything like this. Several hundred yards up, his calves begin to cramp; his groin muscles burn. But not far above, the trees thin out. So he looks only down, step after small crab step, until he feels the slope ease off. Then he turns forward and strides between the trees into bright light.

He comes out to a mile-long meadow. The crags of a peak rise from its top end. The short grass is mixed with small wildflowers, white, yellow and blue. Rock outcrops stud the grass, their sides white and red-orange with lichen. He records it on the camcorder, knowing the electronic images will hold nothing of the life that makes the scene. He walks to a stream; the light flashes over its mica-flecked pebbles. The sun is warm. He goes to a large clump of rock, sets his pack at its base and sits. His legs still tremble from the climb, but he feels better to be in this place. He looks out at the panorama below. He must be at eleven thousand feet, seeing the Rockies sweep southeast into the Great Plains. He brings the camcorder up: this illusion of endlessness is worth saving.

After some minutes he stands and walks to the far side of the rocks to pee. Then he goes the few feet to the stream to wash his hands and face. The water is ice cold. He turns around and around, checking that each view, far and near, remains as perfect as it seems. Sitting against the rock, eating lunch, he can't see how even Lavery's photographs could capture this. As for himself, what is there to write but Oh, wow, wow! He eats two egg salad sandwiches and drinks liters of water. He spreads his jacket under him and lies down. He could write that the only way to keep this is to leave it be, is for no one to come here, is to *not have it* at all. And what about his being here? Hasn't "wilderness" always been a relative term? Way up above him hangs a shred of cloud. He hears the stream and the bees in the wildflowers. He dozes off and wakes. He'll wash his hands and face again and start back down. He checks the map: the trail he lost is at the other end of the meadow.

Ethan is crouched over the stream, about to put his hands in, when he smells it. Before he lifts his eyes to see it eight feet away from him across the stream, he smells it and realizes, in shock, that he must already have seen, without taking in, the brown bear.

The bear is not quite looking at him. This very large animal—a person, Ethan tries to think—sees Ethan but is trying not to catch his eye. Ethan is aware he's stopped breathing. It is as if the bear were thinking of ways to avoid embarrassing either of them. It is so close that Ethan can smell its breath and the thick, acrid reek off its body; it would be possible to count the flies around its big head. On the other hand, the smell, he understands, could be his own: everything his body can secrete, it does. He stands still and the bear stands still. The bear has a pointier snout than Ethan feels bears should have. It looks, in fact, like a long nose. And there's a noise, which, like the smell, comes either from the bear, whose head has begun to loll, or from himself. This is a complex noise from the back of one of their throats, a deep gargle with reedy overtones. Ethan forces himself to think of safety. All that comes to mind is that when swimming among sharks, you must give them your biggest outline rather than trying to stand or go vertical, since then they would see you as smaller-fish sized, bite sized. Is it the opposite for bears? Is he now to roll up into a ball? Play dead? How can he play dead while standing and perhaps making noise? Or is that the bear, whose dark head is lolling faster, as if trying to shake something off? It isn't, he hopes, a grizzly bear. Ethan urges himself to forget grizzly bear. It is definitely just a brown bear. Is that more or less aggressive than a black bear?

Ethan's throat is so sore he has to cough. He raises his arms to clear his throat and chest. It is difficult to believe that this roaring noise is coming from him. His hands, fisted over his head, shake with fear. The bear's head for the first time swings directly at him. This is a bear as big as a mountain, but its eyes are slightly crossed. Ethan's chest is about to split open. The bear shakes its head as if about to charge and then it runs away.

Away up the stream, up the meadow, it runs with long, bunched strides and pigeon-toed feet. Ethan sees that it's funny: the long-nosed bear fleeing gladly, the cross-eyed bear with pigeon toes. It is at the same time terrifying: that sheer bulk and raw stench. What is bewildering in all this is the animal's beauty.

Ethan stops roaring and drops his arms. He's been behaving like a badly frightened bear. The actual bear is a dark, loping lump in the distance. Ethan sits down. He's in the stream. The water flows in inch-high waves around his shoes. The cold soaks through his trousers and cools his buttocks. He douses his face with water and stands up. The bear is out of sight. Ethan pees, this time voluntarily. He collects his backpack and crosses the bottom of the meadow. The meadow is as before, quiet, perfect, unknowable. He is still frightened about but grateful for the bear.

At the hotel, he washes and puts on clean clothes, and drives out to the diner he's passed on the road. He eats chicken in green chili, biscuits and butter, hash brown potatoes, salad and apple pie. He drinks beer with his meal and iced tea with his pie. Afterwards, he can barely drag himself up the hotel staircase to fall onto his bed, though it's still before eight. Just as he falls asleep, he tries to imagine XHelen and his Boston life. He can't. He decides to call this progress. He sleeps and dreams he's climbing the mountain with the live bear across his back. He tries to control the bear's front and back legs with his arms, because he knows if the bear runs off on its own it would be in great danger. Lucy is somewhere cheering him on. Emmy leans against a rock, cursing.

He wakes as if he's slept for twelve hours, but it's only eleven at night. He decides to go for a walk before trying to sleep again. The town is quiet. A shuffling comes from a horse trailer parked down beside the motel wing. The moon is almost full; the Milky Way hangs like a mid-sky fog. He walks around the grassy streets and then to the highway. Not a car on the road. The lights are out in the store and the gas station and the diner. In the distance is some red and white neon from a roadside bar. He passes it and walks to the canyon turnoff, turns and starts to walk back. He walks on past the turn to the hotel and on until the town runs out, and then he walks a few miles more along the empty road until he stands looking up towards where he's been today, the peaks beneath Black Mountain and Valle Vidal. The mountains are massed shades of blue-black over green-black; the bare rock picked out in moonlight shows as streaks of cream. He concentrates on the sounds he's heard from up there and back behind him.

What he makes out first are dogs on an outlying ranch. The barking is fast, high and low, a hoarse panic in it. Then, behind him, he picks up the sporadic barking of dogs in town. As he turns and walks back, this barking quickens to a town-wide alarm which doesn't stop until he's standing in front of the St. Peter Hotel, when for some reason of echo and wind, the barking falls to a background, and from far in the mountains, but clearly, he hears what he's never heard before but is unmistakable, the long howl of a wolf.

Then he hears another. There is a long howling and a short double howling and then, he's certain now, a second wolf howling on its own. Wolf tones, he thinks. Down the street, a dog breaks into a coarse, longing howl. Then it whimpers. The first wolf howls again, and by the motel the horse starts kicking in its trailer. The horse neighs and whinnies. A cowboy comes from the motel and taps at the side of the trailer and talks quietly. The kicking stops, but the trailer trembles with the horse's nerves. Ethan stays to hear the wolves once more. Then, exhausted, he goes in to sleep.

The lobby parlor is pitch dark. He feels his way forward and stops. Gasps and a moan come from across the room. At first he thinks it's lovemaking. When he senses it isn't, he calls out, "Anyone there?" He hears rasping, gurgling sounds and moves in their direction with his hands out. He kicks over something like a stool and then trips over it and continues on his hands and knees, one arm sweeping before him to fend off the furniture. The noises now sound like small growls. He imagines a revenge of the stuffed animals or the ghost of Clay Allison dancing on the hotel bar. He calls, "Who's there?" and stands.

He takes two steps forwards and is pulled down. He won't let them beat him again without a fight: he hits out, hits a chair leg, throws another punch and hits someone, a cheek and chin. There's a groan and a hand weakly pushing back against him as he grabs down and finds his hands around a neck. Then he feels the rope. He pulls and loosens it, even before he understands it's a noose. The man is coughing, groaning. Ethan gets up and makes out the moonlit lace curtains and a lamp at the window. He turns it on.

The man on the floor has rolled onto his stomach to avoid being hit again. There's a deep rope burn at the side of his neck. Ethan looks up and sees a steel support rod stretching from wall to wall. He kneels down. The man stinks of whiskey. He's in white flannels, his white shirt stuck to his back with sweat. Ethan lifts the man's chin and slides off the noose. He pulls a spread from a sofa and covers the man, who now sobs and shivers on the carpet. Ethan sits on the edge of the sofa and finds himself telling the man that it's all right now. But he knows this can't be, since the man has failed to do what he wanted—to hang himself. The man turns onto his back, hands to his face against the light. He says something.

Ethan leans forward. "What?"

Between his hands, the man says, "Ho. Mo' hominy loops."

"What?"

"*Homo homine lupus.*"

Ethan says, "Man is a wolf to man. Horace?"

The man takes his hands from his face. "Hobbes," he says. It's Stucic.

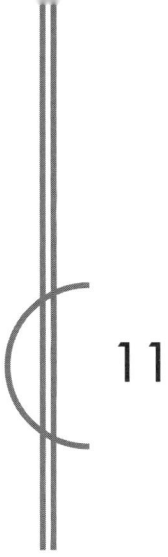

11

IT IS STUCIC, his face puffed purple and the rope burn on his neck, wrapped in an afghan spread, lying on the carpet by an overturned side table. Might this be an elaborate trick, Stucic having staged it to prove he's not a war criminal? No, this is more the behavior of a war criminal with a conscience. Ethan bends closer: "It's all right now, Miroslav."

Stucic stares at him through red eyes. "You? Ethan? This is you? Beyond comprehension. That of all people it should be you who…" He stops, choked with sobs. He says, "I wish you had not appeared. Not put in an appearance?"

"'Not appeared' was right." Would a genuine failed suicide worry about idiom?

Stucic sits up slowly and pulls the afghan over his head as a shawl. Ethan says, "I'm sorry I hit you. In the dark. I thought someone was attacking me."

A harsh laugh comes from under the shawl. "Your blows brought me to life. There is some comfort in so European an irony."

"Why did you want to kill yourself?"

"Why? You heard the wolves howling?"

"Yes. It was beautiful. I remembered the phrase 'wolf tones' from our first night in Albuquerque, at that party."

"The howling was to me infinitely sad. Cries of loneliness and torment and pain—the wounded and dying. You are a good man, Ethan, but…" Stucic is coughing. "But there is much one cannot understand about anyone else."

"Like your daughter Elena?"

"Ah, yes, I spoke to you of her uncommunicative independence."

"She was in my short-lived writing group. She used the name Eileen Smith."

"Eileen Smith. Ah."

"Miroslav, she told me a terrible story about you in the war, and there was a Moslem woman. And a town, Vakuf something or other? So I may have an idea of what's troubling you."

Stucic is rocking under the shawl. He looks like a roadside refugee from his war. He says, "Kanita." He coughs. "The woman's name was Kanita. The town is Gornji Vakuf."

"Is it true that you're accused of war crimes?"

"No, no, no. But this is connected with why I want to die. I would like to tell you. Perhaps you would be so kind as to help me to my room."

Ethan rights the table and kicks some broken pottery under the sofa. Quickly looping the rope over his arm, he helps Stucic to his feet and supports him across the gloomy parlor and up the stairs. He drops the rope outside the door. Inside, he gives Stucic a glass of water, and, at his direction, pours two whiskies from a bottle on a tripod table. They sit in old armchairs.

Stucic raises his glass without making a toast. He says, "I planned this, so to speak. I had heard of this hotel and found something appropriate in the folly of spending my last hours in the rooms of Mr. Buffalo Bill. I shall, my friend, keep to the point. Nothing is so tedious as the insistent eloquence of the polymath, as I clearly demonstrated when we met on the airplane."

Ethan, set to protest, returns Stucic's smile. His face has gone from purple to plate-white in minutes.

"Kanita and I had been lovers for ten years. The great love of my life. This is not to excuse the relationship. It was very hard on my wife Vera, who knew though she pretended not to. Our tacit understanding was that I would be discreet, and she would not allude to it. However, as the war grew worse, Kanita and I decided to part, to devote ourselves entirely to our families in such difficult times. Ah, the nobility of it, the futility of it. It was precisely the extremity of the wartime conditions that made our vow impossible to keep, and we came back together with, it must be said, a reckless intensity." Stucic pauses to sip whisky. "Kanita, as you said, was Moslem. She had relatives in Gornji Vakuf who needed help—a grandmother and aunts and uncles. There is, I should add in light of whatever my daughter has told you, no one in Bosnia who does not know the story of the barrel bombs of Gornji Vakuf. Kanita, you see, insisted on personally bringing medicines, food, and other aid to her family there. This was dangerous, but also the best guarantee for the safe arrival of such aid. She did this against my wishes, yet I was able, through my UN contacts, to get her out of Sarajevo under siege. I could do this, but it is truer to say that the war had made my style of diplomacy as irrelevant as if I were a courtier of Louis Quatorze. Nevertheless, I continued to try every contact I could. I was never, as I know Elena maintains, connected with Chetnick or Ustasi elements, though I met with anyone who might help in getting in the aid so that Kanita would not have to make these dangerous trips." Stucic stops to cough. He says, "I am not boring you?"

"No. I'm listening."

"So then the situation at Gornji Vakuf became critical and still Kanita went. But this time, she didn't return. I became crazy in my worry, and, crazed, I was indiscreet. This was humiliating for Vera. She became embittered and made Elena her confidante and ally against me. Perhaps this was not a good thing for her to do, but in these circumstances, I can understand. Everyone, you see, was under tremendous emotional strain during the Sarajevo siege. So. What I did then was make my way to terrible Gornji Vakuf. This was during the worst of the siege there, but through some miraculous luck and large bribery, I was able to arrange a safe-passage out for Kanita. We met in a ruined house in no-man's land. I pleaded with her to come out with me then, but she insisted she had to return to say goodbye to her family. I begged her not to. I told her I had little hope of arranging another safe-passage. She wouldn't agree. We spent that night together, as one might say, with doom as our blanket. At dawn, she returned to the town, and I returned to the besieging forces. I made them wild promises, I begged, I lied, but they knew I had nothing more to give them. I was forced to leave. I returned to Sarajevo. I learned only two weeks later that Kanita had been killed that same morning. I became mad with grief. Awake or asleep, I spoke only of Kanita. This, you can imagine, was very hard for my wife and daughter. Finally, I came to my senses, and through an old diplomatic contact, then in Dallas, I was in 1996 able to bring my family out to this country for a new start. A new start was impossible, of course. Vera despised me, and Elena, prompted perhaps by her mother, made a monstrous story of my love for Kanita. I had raped her, I had members of her family killed, et cetera. She told newspapers in Dallas that I was a war criminal. They had the sense to check, and, of course, finding it baseless, refused to print her lies. But my daughter had more success with local Bosnian, Croatian and Serbian associations, where, with suitable ethnic variations to her tale, she insured that I became their enemy. These pathetic places. This was why I had such a negative reaction to your well-intentioned information about such a group in Albuquerque. I imagine Elena has spread her poison there, also. And you can now understand my white lies about my wife trying to join me. She will not. She continues to despise me—and I trust you will understand this paradox—despite my always having loved her. And my darling only child wants nothing more than for me to hang for war crimes, crimes I have committed only in her unhappy imagination. I was, this night, attempting to give her what she wants. But my knot-making was weaker than my will to die."

Stucic drinks back the remainder of his whiskey. "I tell you all this because you have had the bad luck to find me. It is curious: until telling you, I did not know why I chose hanging." He gives Ethan a twisted smile and drops his head. The wind moves the lace curtain behind his chair. It's quiet now; no horse, nor dog, nor wolf.

"I'm very sorry, Miroslav."

"Slava. Please call me Slava." He pulls the afghan tight around him.

He looks to Ethan very ancient and fourteen years old, at once. "You mustn't kill yourself, Slava."

"Really? And why is that?"

"Because 'Slava' is a nice-sounding name. And for your irony. And because you're a good teacher. Not just what I hear about your courses. I mean, you carry all of your culture with you."

"One might say this of an infection."

"An antibody, Slava. Promise you won't try this again."

"I don't really know."

"Promise."

"Very well. I am not going to try. Having failed at tragedy, I shall not descend to farce. Ethan, I am very tired, but I am also terrified to sleep."

"I'll sit here. I'll go across to my room for something to read. Okay?"

"Okay, yes. This is kind of you." Stucic looks pathetic.

Unsure about Stucic keeping his promise, Ethan runs out to the hall, grabs the rope, unlocks the door to his room, throws the rope under his bed, grabs his briefcase and duffel bag and gets back to the Buffalo Bill Suite to find Stucic coming out of the bathroom. Ethan says, "Will you mind the light out here?"

"I want the light."

Ethan sits and watches Stucic get into Buffalo Bill's bed. He imagines ghostly Annie Oakley on tiptoes in the hall. The suite's furniture is nice looking and uncomfortable. No problem staying awake. Stucic's eyes immediately close. They open: he sees Ethan and they close again. His breathing steadies.

Ethan opens his briefcase and takes out Emmy's envelope. He pulls it open. Nothing says the daughter of a good writer has to be a good writer. The manuscript looks as if it's been typed on a fifty-year-old Smith Corona. He reads:

Vanishing Cream
By Embrace Evans

> She called herself Billee. Like the boy's name with a little shriek at the end. As a small child, when she was still Suzanne, her biggest thrill was finding herself in her parents' empty bedroom, on her mother's stool at the vanity table. In the triple mirror, the jars and bottles and brushes seemed to have depths much more real than the unreflected world.

Ethan looks up and checks Stucic. He's asleep. Even if the writing falls off, he can tell Emmy she can write. He can tell Lucy. His heart beats as if not Stucic but the wolf were in the bed. Why couldn't Stucic's story be as fabricated as Elena's? The suicide attempt could result from either version being true. He would rather believe Stucic. He can call the Dallas newspapers and check. He must email Pete in Boston. He goes back to reading Emmy's story by the light of the Wild West Show genuine electrified old oil lamp.

Later, he wakes. Light comes through the curtains. Stucic is asleep: grizzle-cheeked, slack-mouthed, the bags under his eyes large enough to carry a traveling omelet. Ethan is dozing off, thinking about how little he likes the artifice of Dostoyevsky putting Svidrigailov into a rented room next door to Sonya, yet how much the novel gains from having Svidrigailov listen through the wall. His cell phone rings in his briefcase. He fumbles for it and says, "What?"

His father says, "Ethan, good morning. I wanted to get you early, before you hit the trail."

He stands and walks around the sitting room. "Morning. Where'd you get this number?"

"From you. Don't you remember? Are you having memory loss, too? Maybe I got it from Lucy. Lucy's wonderful. Old as she is, you'd better marry her before I do."

Ethan says, "Please don't."

"I'm only joking. Have you lost your sense of humor as well as your memory? What I called about, Ethan, was this: Do you remember where I work?"

Ethan wonders if his father can't remember which university he's at. He asks, carefully, "Do you mean at which desk?"

"Of course."

"In your study. Not the big desk at the window, at the smaller one in the corner."

"I haven't worked there in years. I work out at Brandeis, at my office desk."

Ethan is sure his father has for years been at his university only one day a week, for his seminars. He looks through the door at Stucic sleeping.

"And do you know what I keep in the top drawer of that desk?"

"No, I don't." He's ready to hear anything: a loaded pistol, strawberry-flavored condoms, a false passport and two tickets for Tierra del Fuego.

His father says, "A Latin tag. How's your Latin, this morning?"

"Only so-so. I've already mixed up Horace and Hobbes."

"This is Cicero. '*Nihil tam absurde dici potest, quod non dicatur ab aliquo philosophorum.*' Well?"

"Only the gist, Meyer. I'll pass to you."

"It means: Nothing so absurd can be said that hasn't already been said by a philosopher."

"A nice way of staying modest. Is it apropos of anything to do with me?"

"You were speaking the other day about mainstream philosophy being out of touch with life. Cicero reminds me that's true."

In the bedroom, Stoic groans and snores. Ethan says, "Speaking of memory, later in the day that we spoke of dogs and philosophy, everything about Oaxaca came back to me."

"Really"

"Yes, and I owe you an apology. You acted like a beast only in setting me up for a sex vacation without informing me. But afterwards, as you said, you did what you had to for me. I was the one who didn't do what I should have—challenged that scam and found out what really happened to that poor woman, Carmen."

"If you say so."

"Do you remember Oaxaca, Meyer?"

"I believe so. Pretty much, yes."

"So who did it, the three other Americans?"

"I never knew. Those three obviously did for themselves what I did for you. But they did it immediately and were released after being questioned. I am sorry, given your depressed state at the time, that I set up a holiday for you that involved female company, if you wished it. At any rate, I had no idea of this racket that the police were running. Neither had my Oaxacan contact: she was shocked, but once the police involved you, there was nothing to do but pay up. Your insistence of innocence was irrelevant, an embarrassment for them. And that's the sum of what I know."

"You had no sleepless nights over it?"

"Once you were free, no. Your anger pained me, though."

"You never once said you knew I was innocent."

"There never seemed time to tell you. In Oaxaca, I had to concentrate on practicalities and details. And afterwards, well, you were angry and wouldn't speak to me about it. Then, after a time, you seemed to have put it behind you."

Ethan hears his father's reasoning with a sort of horror. Meyer's rational mind would have had to consider that his son might have been capable of brutally beating the woman. Carmen, the poor, lost thing, not being part of Meyer's personal or philosophical interest, meant nothing to him. Nor did how screwed up his son could become in repressing these memories.

Meyer says, "I suppose I am a somewhat strange man, after all. But I do love you. And, despite what you now know of me, I loved your mother very, very much."

Ethan is reminded by the snoring that Stucic has just said he loved his wife very much. He says, "I'm sure you loved her," with the makeshift conviction of someone on suicide watch.

Meyer says, "May I ask something personal?"

"Please do."

"Might you and Lucy want to have a child?"

"I think not. Lucy's daughter, as you know, isn't at all well. And Lucy, as you keep reminding me, is older."

"But if you wanted to, would Lucy be able to?"

"She still has her periods, if that's what you mean." Ethan is immediately unhappy he's said this. He can imagine Meyer imagining her periods.

"To have a grandchild would give me such, would be such—a blessing."

"Meyer, that's a sweet thought. I'm sorry I haven't given you a grandchild." He looks through the door to Stucic on the bed. He looks at Emmy's anorexic story on the table. "And you'll be out here pretty soon now."

"By mid-September. Is that still good?"

"Wonderful. You pack lots and stay long. We'll keep in touch about the details."

"I'm going to take you at your word and make a proper old pest of myself. Might there be anyone out there I'd like, beside yourselves? There's not a philosopher for a thousand miles. Well, Rasmussen at Austin, but I've never taken to him. A *schicker* from Duluth with a phony English accent, like someone at a party, as I once told him, doing a bad imitation of Freddy Ayer."

Ethan says, "There's someone here called Carlos Alvarado, a genuine American Spanish grandee. Meyer, sorry, I have to go now."

"Until later, Ethan. I love you."

The cell phone immediately rings again: "Ethan, I meant to say not 'blessing' but *nachas*. A grandchild would be such *nachas*."

Ethan has thought *nachas* meant blessing. Perhaps it means pleasure. He's never heard his father use so much Yiddish before. Lessons in Latin and Yiddish. What can he feel about his father but conflicted? He could have had this talk with his father five years ago, but it didn't seem right. It never seems the right time for so much that should be spoken. He looks at Emmy's manuscript. Emmy and Willy Dixon, for one good example.

He phones Lucy, says he's on his cell phone. She says she'll phone back in five minutes. Ethan looks in on Stucic and finds him sleeping. He goes back to the armchair in the sitting room, leaving the curtains closed.

Lucy rings back and says, "I was lying in bed, not really asleep. How are you?"

"Fine," he says, realizing he's beginning his new regime of honesty by not mentioning Stucic. "Just before I left town, Emmy showed up and gave me a short story to read, when I was on this trip. She was nervous about you knowing of it."

"I know she's been writing, but she won't mention it and I won't because it might make her more secretive. Yuck."

"Well, I've read it It's really good. Emmy can write." There is no reply. "Lucy?"

"Yes, sorry. I was thinking that if she's interested enough to finish something like a story, maybe writing could save her. Then I thought, what a stupid, simplistic idea. Because it doesn't work like that with her. But is her story really good? What time is it? Oh."

He says, "Poor you. I understand."

"I'm okay now. I miss you. What's her story about?"

"An anorexic. But it's a real story, not a memoir. Wait a second." He gets the story and reads Lucy the title and opening paragraph. Then he summarizes the story: "Billee is making up at her mirror thinking about being a little girl at her mother's vanity table mirror. She's getting ready to go out with her girlfriends. After some arguing about where to go, they decide on a carnival. First, Billee has a nice time with her friends. But then the other girls start flirting with some boys. They eat lots. Billee is alternately repelled and attracted by the food and boys. She likes to see the cotton candy, because, big as it is, it's mostly air, a trick. Her girlfriends eventually leave her to go off with the boys, and at the story's end, Billee is standing in front of the crazy mirrors, trying to see how long and thin she can make her image before it disappears.'

Lucy says, "That sounds good. I mean, god, it's terrible, but a good story idea. You really think it's good?"

"It is. Some of it is over-written, and the end gets rushed, but you have a talented daughter. I'll find the right time to tell her I've told you."

"I can't say anything about it until you do."

Ethan says, "If she asks if we've spoken, you can say I told you I came across my first bear, yesterday, and last night I heard wolves howling over Cimarron."

"Is this true?"

"I'll tell you about it when I get back. And yes, at least two wolves."

"They must be moving south from Colorado through the mountains. That's wonderful."

"Lucy, there's something else I learned from Emmy's visit—how much she dislikes Willy."

"That's not surprising, considering how much I dislike him."

"Did Willy ever try anything sexual with Emmy?"

"No," she says. "No, never. I wouldn't have let Emmy stay one minute, I wouldn't have stayed if I thought he… I've told you that in the beginning, Willy really tried to help. When we grew apart, he stopped. But then he ignored Emmy."

"The week before I was beaten up, I saw Willy trying to hit on an eleven-year-old girl in a bookstore. I confronted him and made him leave."

"Is that why you think it was Willy who arranged to have you beaten?"

"That's one reason, but it's not what I'm talking about. The reason I was suspicious of Willy's behavior in the bookstore goes back to the fight we had at the party. When you asked me about it, I left out the real cause: Willy kept forcing me to look at the child-pornography photos in his study. They were horrible, violent, and he was in some of them. I didn't tell you then, because I didn't want to be that involved, or involved in that."

Lucy says, "Oh."

Ethan waits. He then says, "To paraphrase, where are *you* in that 'Oh'?"

"I didn't know about the photographs. I never went into his study; he was very fussy about his space. But, yes, I knew about him. There was an incident at the University a few years ago. Things had already gone bad between us, and that made it worse. I tried to support him; I helped get him to see someone. I really didn't want to pull you into Willy's sickness."

Ethan says, "I understand. But now I've met Emmy. And she chooses to do phone-sex work, and there's Willy, and her anorexia began, didn't it, when she was living with you and Willy."

Lucy says, "You did the right thing to tell me. But, believe me, I have watched my daughter closely in her illness. Willy didn't dare abuse Emmy: he knew what I'd do to him."

Ethan grunts.

"And now I'm half afraid to thank you for your concern for Emmy because all this could drive you away from me."

"It doesn't. I'm not so easily driven off." Ethan says, believing more in his first assertion than his second.

"Good," Lucy says.

There is a silence in which they hear the other's breathing calm down.

Lucy says, "Oh, Carlos called last night and asked you to call him as soon as possible."

"Thanks. And to show you how committed and mature a fellow I am, I won't ask what else you and he talked about."

"I'm not thanking you for that. Carlos knows I'm spoken for, not that you've spoken to me about it. Do you miss me any, Mr. Baum?"

"I miss you any. I'll tell you exactly how much on the phone tonight."

Ethan goes back to sleep in the armchair. He wakes with a start and a sore neck. Stucic comes from the bathroom shaved and cleaned up. He says, "I am, you see, resolved not only to live but to have an excellent, slap-up breakfast with you, pardner!"

Ethan finds himself standing, laughing, and hugging Stucic.

Stucic says, "I impersonate an American, and you react like a Central European."

At breakfast, Stucic seems his old enthusiastic self. He eats sausages, eggs, and home fries, and cleans his plate with buttered toast. "There," he says, nodding back to the old hotel wing, "is actual history, the real McCoy and Wyatt Earp, so to speak. And yet, these little bullet holes, these over-polished floors and banisters, all these so brittle dead animals with their eyes of glass—the effect of all this reality is pure ersatz. My point is that between the real thing and, let us say, its Disney representation, there is so little to choose."

Ethan says, "That doesn't bode well for reality. Maybe the essential reality of the West is of a natural world so overawing as to make the manmade appear particularly artificial."

Stucic grabs Ethan's hands and covers him with praise and butter. This swing from suicidal depression to *joie de vivre* doesn't bode well for Stucic's emotional stability. Ethan, who has to sleep, makes Stucic promise to look in on him in the late morning.

Stucic comes to his room at eleven, saying, "I have spoiled your work day. Of course I can never thank you enough for sitting with me, last night. I am now able to accept that Vera and I must separate, as she wishes. I hope that time will bring Elena to her senses. Meanwhile, *'Il faut cultiver notre jardin.'*"

Ethan knows this quote, but Stucic doesn't ask. "Remember what you promised, Slava."

"Promised? Ah, yes, I shall live, my friend. Or, at least, I shall stay alive. I shall now drive carefully back to my life. By the way, one small question: Do you believe my story?"

Ethan, taken aback, actually tilts his shoulders away from Stucic. "Yes," he says. "Yes, of course."

Stucic nods. "Thank you. I know—as the airlines tell us—you have a choice of stories. Thank you for going with mine."

Ethan throws his arm around Stucic's shoulder and promises to see him soon. He watches Stucic walk down the corridor with his leather duffel bag and remembers that he must email Pete in Boston to check on Stucic the minute he gets back to his computer.

Before checking out, Ethan phones Carlos.

"My dear young friend," Carlos begins, with condescending magnanimity. "I hear you've been up at the delightful St. Peter's Hotel."

"Yes, I've had an interesting stay. I'm still there, about to leave. Yesterday I saw my first elk and first bear, and last night I heard my first wolves."

"Marvelous! It happens that I want to talk to you about elk. I asked Lucy if you did any hunting. She wasn't certain, but thought you didn't."

"That's right. I don't."

"Simply don't, or won't?"

"Simply don't and won't."

"I'll tell you what it is. Each year I give a small elk hunting party; three or four days for a few interesting people in different parts of the state, quite often on my own land. But this year—the beginning of October—I've been given sole use of Valles Caldera. It's probably the last year before it becomes a national park. Nothing else like it in the country, you know. So I thought what fun it would be, and how good it would be for the book, if you got to visit this gem of New Mexico in some depth, close-up, intimately. But I don't want you to feel you have to come."

Ethan says, "I'd like to come, Carlos, though I'll do my shooting with a camcorder."

"Wonderful, Ethan! That's just wonderful. It will be a small group, but very select."

"I feel honored to be asked."

"And I, *señor*, that you accept."

Ethan hears the exchange as out of a play by Calderón, or Pirandello.

Alvarado says, "Now that you're on the phone, there's something else, a somewhat delicate matter. I understand that you're friendly with a new professor, Miroslav Stucic."

"Yes," says Ethan, looking at his door and hoping Stucic won't, on a whim, come back.

"It's almost certainly a false alarm, but the University has received a tip that Stucic may be a Bosnian war criminal. We're checking that out. Meanwhile, if you know anything, it would be good of you to share it, as a way of helping him."

Ethan wonders if Stucic knew the accusation had reached the University; this would have contributed to his despair. He says, "I know his daughter doesn't get on with him. And he's spoken about family problems during the war. He also told me that a Dallas newspaper had been given the same false tip, and checked it and found it was baseless."

"I see. Of course I don't believe it. It's just that the University has had some damned bad press in recent years: a sex scandal or two never really laid to rest, and that notorious archeology affair. Perhaps that's no worse than any other university, but relative to the state population, we're very big and visible and politically vulnerable. Please don't mention this conversation to Miroslav. It would worry him. I'm sure we'll soon find out he's perfectly innocent."

"I'm sure he is," Ethan says, vowing to tell Stucic as soon as possible.

Alvarado says, "Thank you so much for your help and for agreeing to join us at Valles Caldera. I'll be sending you the particular dates and other information about the hunt in the next few weeks. And, Ethan, I want to tell you how convinced I am that in choosing you as the project writer we've made the absolutely best decision."

"Thanks."

"*Adios*, Ethan, and thank *you*."

Ethan thinks at least Carlos didn't say *"Vaya con dios."* He wonders how enthusiastic his *hidalgo patrón* might be about the visit he's making tomorrow to Los Alamos.

Ethan tours the Los Alamos National Laboratory with a friend of Lucy's, Dick Johnston, a former top lab technician there turned anti-nuclear activist. First, they drive around the dead ugly town set on the high, beautiful finger plateaus. Then they go into the labs, to the central administrative building, where Ethan gapes close-up at the nuclear quilt with its lovingly appliquéd cotton-puff mushroom cloud. Johnston then takes him on a tour of the unrestricted labs, and they end at lunch in the big lab cafeteria, where Johnston tells him that, despite practically every damned janitor in the place having a doctorate in physics, no original science has ever come out of the place. He bangs his fist down by his fruit salad, saying, "Not one damn paper, one page, not one jot, not one *atom!*" People stare from the surrounding tables, but they look away when Dick stares back.

Two days later Ethan is in the southwest of the state because this is the only date that P.T. Applegate has open to guide him in the Gila Wilderness, and Lavery has urged him to see it first with P.T. "And don't bother asking," Lavery had said, "what P.T. stands for." When Ethan meets the guide in Silver City, this is the first thing he asks. P.T., a tall, bony man with a long-brimmed cap, says, "Stands for P.T. Bet Charlie told you was no use askin'. Makes everyone ask." The next afternoon, walking with P.T. on a slope of the Mogollon Mountains in 115 degree heat, they round some big saguaro cactus and almost collide with two pronghorn antelope standing in their shade. For five or ten seconds, the antelopes freeze. Then they prance off as prettily as ballerinas. P.T. says in over thirty years guiding he's never walked up so close to them as this.

Next morning, Ethan calls Lucy while he's driving and tells her he'll be in Albuquerque in about two-and-a-half hours. She says she may still be in her office in a phone conference with her editor Vijay, but he should go to her place anyway. He spends much of the rest of the drive thinking he's not jealous of her. Is jealous of her. Thinking he would like to have a phone conference with his editor, would like to have an editor, would like to have something to edit. His current project doesn't count. He drives to Lucy's, showers, and lies on the bed under the swamp-cooler ceiling grate. He wishes Lucy were here. He puts on shorts and sits out on the back porch-room writing up some notes on the trip. Later, when he looks up, Lucy is in the doorway watching him. He asks, "Have you been there long?"

She shrugs and walks over. He puts an arm around her hips. He knows she's thinking how good it is to see him writing. Her other sick child. She kisses his head and says, "I like your hair." He says, "I just washed it." She says, "No, I mean how straight and dark it is always, like an Indian's." He asks how her conference went. She tells him Vijay has made some good suggestions about a story. He says she must have the world's last good editor. He tells her about the mountain meadow and the bear. He reads her some of the notes he's written up. She says the writing is very good. He says, "Well, it's okay," but is very pleased. They have dinner out on the sun porch and go to bed early. Ethan gets into bed first. He thinks to make love, but he's asleep before Lucy comes back into the room.

In the middle of the night, he wakes wanting to make love. Lucy is sleeping in underpants, a sign she has her period. He remembers telling Meyer she still has periods. Ethan has made love to Lucy in her period. Her flesh was tender. But she was willing, pleased that he'd desired her. Willy, she'd told him, had never touched her then, as if by religious ordinance. She said, "He put me aside." Ethan suddenly feels awful, the obscene father's obscene son who wants Lucy's blood.

At four in the morning he's drinking tea in the kitchen. Lucy joins him. Her tumbled red hair looks like a brush fire. He says, "Meyer is still keen on coming out here. How am I going to put up with him? It's clear to me he was constantly unfaithful to my mother. And he says I should marry you before he does."

She says, "We'll talk about that romantic proposal of yours later.

We'll both do fine with him here. He could use your apartment as an office. Or I could find him some place in the department. We could probably set up a lecture for him, if he wanted, with the philosophy department, or a seminar for the faculty. Whatever he's done, you can't turn your back on him. You're his whole family."

Ethan says, "I don't know where Meyer stops and I begin. I had my teenage rebellion, I separated from him. But these days, the more I find to dislike in my father, the more I find the same traits in myself. I don't mean that I've been with anyone else." As he says this he can smell Jeanie Brown in her trailer.

"Thank you for another passionate declaration to put with your proposal. I know you're faithful."

Before going back to bed, Ethan tells Lucy about Stucic's failed suicide at the hotel. He retells Stucic's story, which entails relating Elena's version. At the end, he says, "I don't want to keep all this to myself." In bed, as he turns to sleep, Lucy says, "Your father would like Stucic. And you asked me to remind you to email your friend in Boston."

He wakes at eight and leans over the sleeping Lucy. "Lucy, wake up."

"I'm awake," she says with closed eyes.

He says, "You never mention your family."

"I do. My dear, uptight father died nine years ago. And that aunt who gets on with her ankylosis spondulitis, she lives in Boseman. She's never married. My mother is eighty-five and healthy, and 'active' in her Baptist church in Butte. In over twenty years, she's been down here only twice and cannot stand the heat or the dryness. So I visit her once or twice a year. She prays for Emmy. Emmy hates that and won't see her. I have an older brother, Ernie, in San Diego. He's in hardware, a tough nut in hardware. He calls me a scribbler, as in 'My kid sister is some sort of scribbler!' If pushed, he'll say I'm a 'highbrow scribbler.' Ernie thinks Emmy's only problem is that she's a lazy, spoiled brat. I don't see a whole lot of Ernie."

At some point in this, Lucy's eyes have opened. They focus on Ethan. "And there was Betsy, the youngest of us, eight years younger than me. She died in a car crash when she was sixteen. There are supposed to be second cousins of my father in Oregon, but we've never met. That's about it. My family, except for Emmy."

"Does it anger you to talk about them?"

"Ernie's attitude towards Emmy angers me. My mother just makes me sad. A few weeks ago, I mentioned you, on the phone. Mother's response was a long pause and then a question about Emmy's weight. My mother believes I had no right to split up with my first husband; she therefore would never meet Willy. Of course, by the end, I thought she had the right idea, there."

Ethan says, "I'll charm her. I'll grow a long beard and put on a yarmulke and go up to her Baptist church in Butte and let her convert me."

"You're very wicked," Lucy says. "Now kiss me good morning."

Later that morning, back at Copper Place, Ethan gets a call from his father who tells him that he's started work on something, an idea he put aside years before. He's making notes and doesn't want to break the flow of his work, so he wonders if it would be all right if he puts the visit off until late September. Ethan insists so; he says the weather then won't be so hot. He says he's pleased about Meyer's project. He puts the phone down with only a little guilt at his sense of reprieve.

Early the next day, Ethan drives up to the Chama Valley in the north of the state. After supper, he meets with Doc N's friend Robert Running Horse in the run-down El Chama bar. Robert is a council leader of the Jicarilla Apaches. Ethan isn't sure what he expected an Apache to look like, but it wasn't like this darker, smaller-eared Clark Gable in light linen pants and a blue linen polo shirt drinking iced tea.

Robert says, "Doc N says you want to hear the story about our land. Doc's a good guy. Navajos could use people like him on their council, rather than the time-serving old sell-outs they have. Do you know about the Taos Pueblo winning a land suit against the US Government?"

"Wasn't that some years back, when they got a lake returned?"

"Yes. Though it was only a few acres, it was water, something the government doesn't like giving back to Indians. The other great thing was the potential legal precedent: they held the US to an old, broken treaty. It got a lot of attention, naturally, on and off the reservations. But our tribe doesn't operate that way. We don't want attention; we just want land. We had the luck to have gas and oil on our reservation up here, but we also had good leaders. They decided that the lease income, after improvements to health and education standards, should go to land acquisition. We started buying land adjoining our own. I was brought onto the council as a lawyer to head that program. Fifty acres here, a hundred there. Now and then, we've bought big chunks, too. Today, we have twice the land we started with. We like to say we've gone on our warpath with the white man's weapons: money and private property."

"What do you do with the land?"

"That's the best part. Nothing. No building, no rental, no extractive leases, no logging. We walk on it and ride and hunt and fish. No jet skis, no snowmobiles."

"Not like the public lands."

"America's public lands are run for private business. Even the recreational use is lobbied by the makers of the motorcycles and ATV's and jet skis and snowmobiles. Not to mention the NRA. But the worst are the logging and extractive industries."

"Like TriRock?"

"There you go: that's the biggest and baddest. They've been on to us for years for leases on our new lands, as well as on the rez. So far, no one's taken their bribes."

"But your oil and gas?"

"Yes, that's our compromise. At least it's all in a relatively small area. Another of my jobs is to write very tight anti-pollution and clean-up clauses in our oil and gas leases."

"What did Doc N tell you about my project?"

"Just you were doing a book with Lavery. He's a good photographer. But, no disrespect, if it's another pretty book about New Mexico, so what?"

"That isn't our idea."

"But I'll bet it's Alvarado's. He's useful to outfits like TriRock. He fronts some of the light green projects they fund to distract public attention from what's really going on. Like these upcoming State bills to deregulate a lot more land for logging and mining. You see those Federal signs: 'land of many uses.' We say: 'land of many abuses.' I wish you guys luck. It won't be easy."

After some small talk, Robert Running Horse leaves without inviting him onto the new Apache land. Ethan can't blame him. At any rate, he reasons, this project is just an interesting job, something to pay him and get him writing again. He's not an environmentalist. He's a sleepy writer who's walking back to his room at the Chama Steam Bed and Breakfast.

Next day, Ethan drives into the San Juan Mountains and hikes west along the Rio Chamanita, and then east under a fork of the Brazos. He's dog tired when he returns, but he thinks he's slowly getting into better shape. He changes and goes for an early supper to a café across the street from Chama's steam railroad station. As his food arrives, he looks out the window and sees a black limousine roll up. It's odd to see the limo among the pickups, four by fours, and occasional tourist RV. He turns back to his trout. After a few mouthfuls, he looks out the window again. The limo is gone. Standing on the sidewalk all in black is Emmy Evans. She looks like something drawn by Keith Haring. He gets up from the table and goes out.

"Emmy?"

"Hi. Oh my god, I shouldn't have done this, right? Will my bags be okay out here?"

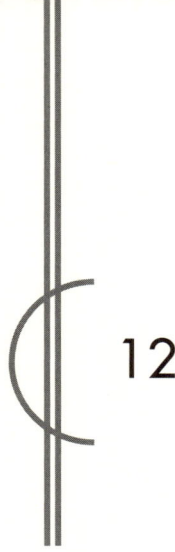

12

EMMY IS SITTING AT the restaurant table trying not to look disgusted by all the eating going on. Ethan says, "Do you want anything?"

"A diet Coke. Maybe soup. Do they have soup?"

He signals the waitress. She says they have homemade tomato-vegetable. Emmy nods.

He says, "So what brings you up here, other than the limo?"

"Oh, that's, I can't drive, my arms get too, you know. So Perry, my dad? I have this trust fund he left me and I go places in the limo. But I know you didn't ask that. I wanted to know what you thought of the story. You probably haven't even read it, yet."

"I have."

"And, anyhow, maybe work on it. It's nice to get out of town, in the summer. I won't be any trouble."

Her order comes. She sips Coke and moves her spoon slowly through the soup as if she were searching for mines.

"Does Lucy know you've come up here?"

"No, she'd be jealous."

"There'd be no reason, Emmy."

"I just meant Mom would like to be up here with you herself."

"Ten out of ten for manipulation. Emmy, you're trouble already," he says, but can't keep from smiling.

"No problem, I'll go. I can stay at that El Chama Hotel and go back tomorrow. I can even call the limo back." She pushes the soup away and picks up a cellophane packet of crackers.

"Wait a minute. Since you came all this way, the least I can do is tell you what I think of your story."

She opens the packet and crushes a cracker between her fingers into the soup.

"I like it. It's a good story. You write well."

She looks at him with such a dazzling smile that he laughs; it's Carlos Alvarado without the moustache. She says, "You mean it?"

"I mean it. 'Vanishing Cream' is a good story."

"You're not just saying it because of Mom and because I'm like this?"

"It's a good story by all the literary standards I know. It also needs some work, especially at the end. But if you can keep at it and get it better, there's a good chance you can be a writer, which is more than being just talented."

"So if I stayed here I could work on it and maybe discuss it with you?" She swallows a spoonful of soup.

She's eating for him; though she's eighteen, she's acting like a small child, taking one more spoon for Daddy. He says, "Yes, but two conditions: first, that I tell Lucy. Actually, you should call her first. I'll see if I can get you a room at my bed and breakfast. The El Chama is for beer and tequila, not a place you'd want to stay. Well?"

"Sure."

"And, second, I'm not going to tell you to eat. But if the food business gets to be a problem—I mean a problem for me—the deal is immediately off."

"Okay, you do the *in loco parentis* thing. I agree."

Ethan says, "Ha-ha," but he's pleased.

The first thing Emmy says to Vic and Tony, the gay couple who run the Chama Steam Bed and Breakfast, is, "The name of this place is like a bathhouse." And while Ethan cringes, they laugh and are charmed and give her the nicest first-floor room. When Tony takes Emmy's bag and shows her to the room, Vic says, "Poor baby. AIDS?" Ethan tells him it's anorexia; Vic says he'll use a technique he learned as a volunteer in a Cleveland hospice—leaving around lots of tiny portions of rich food.

Ethan is out on his porch upstairs, drowsing in a rocker, when Emmy knocks. He calls her out onto the porch. She sits in the other rocker and says, "The guys here are nice. They have these little bowls with slivers of Godiva chocolate in my room and all over the place."

"They're trying to trick you into eating."

"Yeah, well, maybe they will."

"We should work out a schedule for the week. I'm up and away at dawn, and I get back at five, or so, with just about enough energy left to manage an hour of writing up my notes, then get something to eat and then crash. How are we going to work in your story?"

"I could go out with you and we could talk on the drive out and back. In between, I could work at the story, you know, hang around the Jeep while you're out hiking with the bears."

Even in the thick sweater and the parka she wears against the cool night air, Emmy looks way too thin. He says, "Do you do much off-road travel?"

"No, I.... Oh, I see. But if I got some comforters and stuff to cushion me, I could do it. And if not, okay, like you say, the deal's off. Just give me a chance."

"That's what I'll do. We leave at six-thirty in the morning. I'm going to call it a night." Inside, he gives her the envelope with her story. "I've made some notes on it. We can start from there."

She says, "Thanks. And for tomorrow, too." She touches his hand with her cold, bony fingers and closes the door.

Ethan sits on the bed and phones Lucy. He says, "I miss you. Emmy turned up here, tonight, with her manuscript. I've found her a room at this B and B. I said she should call and tell you this first, but I don't care."

"Oh, Ethan. Should I call her?"

"No; she'll call, I'm pretty sure."

"What do you feel about it?"

"Charmed and exploited. Mostly charmed. She's worked everything out. She said you'd be jealous, not being up here with me. Or maybe she meant with us. Anyway, I'm pleased. She has the sweetest smile."

"She gets that from her father."

"How do you feel about me looking after her?"

"You might do better than I do. I am glad you'll spend some time together. Maybe you'll like me more for it. Or maybe less; maybe you won't want to let yourself in for having to deal with this, because, as hard as it gets, I'll never abandon her."

"It's going to be fine, but I'm getting too tired to talk."

Lucy says, "I'll do the talking: I love you," and hangs up.

Ethan wakes early and drives out to the gas station. He fills up the Jeep and stands around the convenience store trying to decide what to buy for lunch for a five-foot-ten girl who weighs maybe eighty pounds. Pay some attention. Finally, he thinks the hell with it and makes a choice he'll eat, if she doesn't. When he gets back to the B and B at six, Emmy is in the dining room actually eating off the end of a cruller she dunks in her *con leche*. Tony brings out waffles and eggs for Ethan. He says if Ethan would only be around for breakfast from seven-thirty, he'd see what the full breakfast was like. Ethan finishes and tells Emmy they'll leave in ten minutes.

When Ethan comes down, Tony and Vic are helping Emmy into a cocoon of pillows and comforters in the passenger seat. She's wearing a smart hiking jacket and trainers. At her feet, in a plastic folder, is her story. Tony hands a small bag to Ethan, saying, "Treats for our girl." Ethan nods to Emmy: "Ready?" She nods back with one of her brilliant smiles, and Ethan slowly pulls out of the graveled parking lot.

They're not yet out of town when Emmy asks to stop. He pulls over, she gets out, puts her head down and vomits up her coffee and half a cruller. Ethan comes around and helps rebuild her cushioning. Emmy says, "I'm sorry." She wipes her mouth with a scented tissue.

He says, "That's okay." He tries to imagine Lucy coping with this for eight years. Back in the Jeep, he picks up the scent of soured lilac and feels slightly nauseous, as if Emmy's anorexia were contagious. That could be their bond: they'll puke the upper Chama Valley together.

As he drives off, she says, "I'm fine, now. So what should we do with the story?"

Ethan is grateful to think of writing rather than vomit. "As I remember, all the writing that needs work comes to no more than a page. And most of it, except the end, is where you, one way or another, tell the reader what to feel or think. You don't have to. Enough's already there to get the reader thinking and feeling those things. And it keeps the reader from participating—which is the pleasure of reading: putting things together and having feelings come up as you read—wham—like that. So you can first see what you make of my comments in the first half of the story, and we can discuss it when I come back for lunch."

"You don't have to come back for my sake."

He improvises: "No, there's a short trail I want to check out this morning."

He turns onto the dirt road and goes half the speed he would alone. Still, he sees the bumps and scoops in the road throw Emmy around. She has no muscles to brace with. When he feels the snap of a stick under a tire, he thinks it could as likely be one of her bones. He slows down even more and pulls off the track to park under some cottonwoods at a stream. He gives Emmy his cell phone number and takes hers. He says, "The water and everything are back in the coolers, but you know that."

He walks off. The mountains and valleys here are majestic and delicate, at the same time. He sees this but he doesn't feel it. He keeps thinking of Emmy bent over her story, back at the Jeep. At a particularly fine vantage point, he sits looking into the mountains and begins to write down what it might look like with some opencast mining.

When he gets back just after noon, Emmy is sitting on her jacket under a cottonwood, reading her manuscript. He gets the cooler from the Jeep and carries it over. He takes out water and a sandwich for himself. He's not going to feed her. "Well, what do you make of my comments?"

She reads the first one and says, "So this means this here is crap. I know. So I throw it out. Right?"

"No, I want you to understand. And to understand you have to explain what's happening here. What you were trying to do and what you think my comment means in light of that."

Ten comments and forty minutes later, Emmy is still at the "so-it's-crap" stage. Ethan repeats, "No, you have to explain it to yourself by explaining it to me." He feels this is about all he can say to the ego of an eighteen year old, even an anorexic's inverted ego. Ethan takes another sandwich.

Emmy points to the third. "You going to eat that?" So far, she's sipped diet Coke and toyed with several Frito bits.

"No."

She lifts the top slice: "This tuna salad, lettuce and tomato?"

He nods. She takes the half slice of whole wheat bread and peels off a bit of lettuce and tomato, puts them on the bread, and nibbles. Ethan looks off at the hillside. He closes his eyes and leans back against the tree. "We're going back into town soon. Then I'm going up to a mixed-use forest south of town."

"Okay if I have this bit of chocolate?"

"I guess."

He half dozes off.

"Ethan? Do you like it here?"

"Yes."

"So do I. I'm really not getting this, am I, about what you mean?"

"You will. It can take time."

He packs up the food and then packs up Emmy into her seat. A few minutes down the track, he hears her choked groan. Then the sound changes; she's swallowing back her vomit. How can Lucy become used to this?

Tony is on the porch when they get back. He says, "How did it go?"

Emmy looks down. Ethan says, "It went well. I liked the chocolate."

Emmy says, "Yeah, the chocolate was good. I'm having a bath and a nap." She takes her jacket off. There are bruises on her upper right arm, where it's slammed against the door through the pillows.

Ethan spends the afternoon at the edge of a national forest where locals collect firewood from a logging plantation. The woods are bald-patched, stump-choked, spotty with rotting logs and the bases of trees left as too massive to mess with. Ethan tells himself it's at least ordinary people laying in winter fuel. But, of course, it's the big timber corporations cutting and cutting the forest reserves until what's assumed is real forest from up in an airplane is nothing but mountainsides of monocrop subsidized by public tax. What metaphor could explain this beauty gone to ugliness? Illness, he thinks.

When he returns, Emmy's on the porch, waiting for him. "Hi," she says. "Okay, how's this, for instance? Here, when I say the boys seemed big and pink and empty *like the cotton candy*, the cotton candy is already in the story. And if I leave it out, it's also more the way Billee herself would see it. She wouldn't make it so neat in words like that."

This is the nicest thing that's happened all day. He says, "That's right; you've got the idea." He sees a half-eaten chocolate bar on the table by her chair. She could have thrown away half, to impress him. She could have eaten it and thrown it up. He asks if she wants to go out for supper. She says okay, and they drive to a crowded roadhouse south of town. The place is smoky and noisy and full of drunks. She orders soup and vegetables and French fries and, he can't help noticing, eats some of everything. When they leave, she says, "That was nice." He doesn't want to get too hopeful about her, but it has been a good day.

Next morning, they drive further out of town, up into the Cruces Basin. Emmy walks a few hundred yards along the trail with him. The land south falls away to the jutting cliffs of Los Brazos, still in blue shadow; beyond that is a panorama of the entire upper Chama Valley. Emmy says, "I'll go back now." He watches her slow, spindly walk and keeps himself from asking her if she'll be all right.

Two hours later, through field glasses, he's following a bald eagle falling on prey. Then he loses it and is glassing back to find it when he catches some movement along a ledge. A mountain lion is on a rock the same pale mustard color as itself. For a moment, Ethan convinces himself it must be the rock formation that looks like a mountain lion, but then it jumps off the rock and disappears.

He gets back at three-thirty, and as he sees the Jeep he realizes he's forgotten to call and this is two hours later than he said he'd return. Emmy's on an air mattress in the back of the Jeep. For a terrible moment, he thinks she's died; "slipped away," he thinks. She opens her eyes and says, "I'm fine," without his asking. She must be used to these concerns. He has a sandwich and iced tea and tells her about his luck with the eagle and mountain lion. She's full of questions; she seems happy for him. When he packs up, he sees she's eaten half a sandwich, the cheese and tomato filling as well as the bread, though she might have thrown it away. He asks her if she wants to drive out a little further on the ridge before they go back. She says, "No, we shouldn't even walk here, with all these grasses and wildflowers: we're so heavy on the land." He hears anorexia in her environmental stance.

Driving back, he says, "Are you thinking about your story?"

"About notes I was making, not on my story. I can't just hang around thinking about it all the time. I was thinking about the land here, about what mining companies would do if they got the chance, and about how creepy it is that I'm connected to them."

"What do you mean?"

"My grandpa Bill, my dad's father, was in mining. Perry, my dad, never went into it, but that's where the money's from, TriRock Mining, how I get to amaze all two blocks of downtown Chama with the Lincoln limo. Anyhow, this younger partner of Grandpa Bill, Roly Everets, he runs TriRock now, he was around after Perry died, as a family friend, and he introduced Mom to Willy. Which is something else I have against the mining companies."

"The CEO of TriRock is your mother's friend?"

"Sort of. Not so much, anymore."

Ethan swallows against the sour burning in his gullet. Why hasn't Lucy told him? Why, considering the project, hasn't Lavery? He knows why Carlos hasn't. Carlos, Lavery, Willy, Roly Everets, the dead Perry who was divorced from her but to his death was Lucy's friend. What has he gotten into?

Emmy says, "I have this revision of the cotton candy section."

"Read it, please."

She reads it.

"That's good. Have you revised the end section?"

"Not yet. Give me a break; this was hard enough. But I will."

What should he say to his secretive lover: If your daughter lives, she could be a writer?

That night, when he calls Lucy, he says, "We seem to be getting along. Emmy comes out with me and while I'm hiking, she stays around the Jeep working. When I get back, we go over the revision she's done. Something like that."

"That's wonderful. She called to tell me she's there and liking it. She's not giving you too hard a time?"

"No. And she seems to be eating a bit more."

"What do you do to get her to eat?"

"Absolutely nothing. The food is around in the Jeep and where we stay. I don't ask or offer."

"Does she seem stronger?"

"I can't tell. She does a little walking, if the trail is level. A few hundred yards out and then back."

"That's good. Of course it's good. And she doesn't seem on edge, a little hyper?"

"No. We talk about this and that. What I've seen, what she knows about wildlife. And, of course, the writing. She's very bright." He doesn't mention the mining connections; he's going to let Lucy bring this up, herself.

Ethan and Emmy stay in Chama for two more days. Ethan notices how Emmy walks a little further and eats a little more. He thinks he even sees a change in her appearance; Tony and Vic agree. Ethan says they're like three fathers. "Mothers," Vic says. Ethan thinks of Meyer and also says, "Mothers." The night before they're to leave, Ethan calls Lucy and asks, "What do you think about my extending the trip for a few more days with Emmy? We'd come down the Chama Valley and stop at Abiquiu, then swing up around past Valles Caldera and stop at Jemez Springs, then go down to the Malpais, and come back to Albuquerque. Emmy seems keen on it."

"If you think she's up to it, yes. You get on well. I trust you."

"If I see it's too much, we'll come straight back from Jemez Springs."

"I'm happy you like her. You do like her, don't you?"

"I like her a lot." He thinks what is the point of saying that he loves her because he sees her fighting so hard against her illness? As if Lucy doesn't know that this draws him to collude with Emmy's version of herself.

Two days after this call, at sunset, Ethan and Emmy stand side by side before the green wire fence at eight thousand feet on State Route 4, looking at the vast meadow of Valle Grande, its back rim of crater tops, its volcano remnants lifted like gigantic folds of green cloth. The red-gold light that floods from the west becomes blue-violet shadow over the meadow's eastern slopes, and in the swathes of sunlight, the range is dotted with cattle the color of sandstone. After some silent minutes, Ethan feels Emmy take his hand. She says, still looking out, "It's even better than I expected. I don't mind the fence, because the owners are going to sell it to the government as a national park."

"I know," he says, "I'm coming up here in October to observe an elk hunt." Ethan lifts her hand: "And what's this?"

"I'm not coming on to you. And it's not the story. Well, it is that, some. It's just nice to like a man without all that—crap. Can I read you something I've worked on?"

"Yes, if you understand that holding your hand, which I like, is not going to have anything to do with what I say about the writing."

She says, "Oh, damn," and smiles and goes to the Jeep. She gets her manuscript and reads him the rewrite of the passage where her character Billee first notices her girlfriends noticing the boys.

Ethan says, "Very good. Not a word too much or too little."

"Really?"

"Yes, and, by the way, I think right from the start, from the name Billee, you have the boy-girl thing just right."

"You mean the sex. Well, I told you my phone job is educational."

"Your phone job is an endorsement of your anorexia."

"Say what?"

"It's a vindication."

"Far out."

He wonders whether this means "well put" or "dead wrong."

She says, "But the stuff that goes on could be good for a story."

"Thrillers don't have to be written by murderers. Besides, Raymond Carver already did a story with phone sex."

"Oh yeah, the couple with a baby, and then the husband flips out. But here's something interesting: why it's busy at weekends is because the guys could call any time, but they wait so that it's like dating. Eileen thinks it's about Friday paychecks going into their credit card accounts, but I told her that makes it even more like dating."

Ethan sees there's nowhere to go with this conversation: he's not going to tell Emmy how much her phone-sex job is hurting Lucy and have Emmy go into an anorexic reaction, whatever that might be. So they take last looks at the vista, get into the Jeep, and drive down the mountains to Jemez Springs. The inn he's booked at has no free single room for Emmy, but they're able to get a two-bedroom suite overlooking the river and the hot springs.

Next day, Emmy decides to stay in town while Ethan goes up to hike in the Jemez Mountains. He feels he should have taken Emmy back to Albuquerque. He's not her father, he's not Lucy's husband. He doesn't love Lucy. He wants Lucy for comfort. When that goes, so will he. Where? Where will he take his writer's block next? He returns in the late afternoon with no memory of his seven-hour hike except that it's exhausted him. He says hello to Emmy and goes up to the bathhouse, gets the massage he's booked and afterwards settles slowly into the old stone bath. The water is so hot it brings tears to his eyes. His toes burn. He drinks cold water and sinks down in the bath up to his chin. When he gets out, it feels as if his bones have gone to rubber.

Back at the inn, he makes himself a drink and sits in an armchair. Emmy's door opens and she comes into the room naked and says, "Oh, whoops," and goes back into her room. He tells himself it was an accident, could have been an accident. It wasn't, he knows. And he can't refer to it, because if she wants him to refer to it, it pulls him into her compulsive world. Has she gained weight? She still looks like a figure from the liberation of Belsen, all collarbone, sternum, and hipbone, with skin like rice paper. Hideous. Pay no attention. Does she imagine she's attractive? Yes. Does she know how repulsive she is, her corpse of a body? Yes. What is he doing with her? What is she to him? What is Lucy to him? Where on earth is his real life? His heart is racing. The glass drops from his hand and his drink spills over his shirt and trousers, and he says, "Oh, shit," and goes to his room to lie down.

They go out for dinner to a restaurant that smells of new wood and floral candles. He orders a bottle of good white wine and Emmy tells him she'd like half a glass. This is their longest conversation since yesterday. He pours her wine and says, "Cheers." It sounds stupid.

She drinks and says, "I'm sorry. I knew you were in the living room. I wanted to tease you, I guess."

"You embarrassed me. I was embarrassed for you, too."

"Yes? So what do you think, professor?"

"You feel you've been taken advantage of. So you want to take advantage of me. End of lecture."

Emmy lifts her fork to her mouth. There's a bit of trout on it. "See how good I am with eating?" She puts it into her mouth, chews, and swallows. She drinks wine.

He's not going to get sucked in to approving.

She says, "Okay, okay, no more fucking around. Let's be serious."

"Serious would be a pleasant change."

"Why did you hit Willy?"

As he hears the question, Ethan knows that, at least in part, she has been screwed up by Willy. He is going to go slow. "We were both drunk. I didn't know who he was, I mean, that he was Lucy's husband. He was getting obnoxious and I wanted to leave his study. He tried to stop me and pushed me and I swung out at him." Ethan feels sweat on his forehead and under his arms.

"Yeah? How was he obnoxious?"

Ethan drinks wine, trying to find a gentle way of telling her. There isn't any. "He was going on about young girls, child pornography. He was trying to show me photographs."

Emmy looks off across the room. "Oh, he's such an asshole."

"Did he ever do anything to you when you were a child, touch you or talk to you like that?"

"No, nothing like that. What difference does it make?" She's looking around the room as if searching for someone she knows.

He says, "Of course." He knows not to push her on this.

Emmy looks at him and nods her head and reaches across the table and pats his hand. He doesn't want to think this is an improvement, or a turning point, or a breakthrough, but these are the words that come to him. And she proceeds to eat a quarter of the trout and a bit of summer squash.

Next morning, he asks if she wants to go back to Albuquerque. She says, no, she wants to go on to the Malpais with him. She says she's sorry for all that in the restaurant last night; the wine went to her head. The drive from Jemez Springs towards Albuquerque is unpleasant; first the land gets ugly—depleted, congested, polluted. But when they swing west onto Interstate 40, they start looking for stretches of old Route 66. Emmy tells him that she first heard the song about it as rock and roll, but then someone played the King Cole Trio version. She says, "It was so cool and delicate, like chamber music."

Ethan nods to himself, impressed. He tells her his idea for this short trip, how he's read that the Malpais, the badlands to the Spaniards, was a good place for the Indians since they could hide there and also use it as a safe route between the Acoma and Zuni pueblos. He wants to try to find a possible trail through, or even a way in through the lava beds.

Around nine, they stop at a big convenience store and fill the Jeep with gas and buy their lunches. He helps Emmy with her bags, not commenting on all the junk food she's bought to take back to Albuquerque. Past the Acoma turnoff, they turn south and drive down the road a few miles and turn in to park by the sandstone overlook. The slope is gentle, and Emmy walks slowly in her big straw sunhat. They're moving twenty feet above the shallow black valley of lava. Heat waves shimmer up off the pocked and scalloped stone. Ethan traces the streaks of green in among the lava. He can see how the Spanish on horses chasing the Indians on foot would end up as steak tartare on the lava, a hundred square miles of knife blades. Twice he has to give Emmy a hand, but she's able to get to the end of the sandstone ridge, where the creamy, rounded stone curls and lifts forty feet over the lava. Looking out from here, he thinks he sees how the green brush grows in a zigzag pattern between the six to twelve-foot lava walls. They get back to the Jeep, parked in the vague shadow of a stand of tamarisk. Ethan tells Emmy he's going around the low end of the sandstone to look for a way into the lava beds. She covers herself in sun block and sits by the cooler. She waves goodbye with the manuscript in her hand.

In ten minutes, he finds the dip in the stone he's seen from the ledge. Tamarisk, low juniper and spear grass stick out from an eight-foot lava wall. He puts on work gloves and pushes through. It's cooler inside the narrow glade, maybe the mid 90's rather than the mid 120's of the lava. The going is hard but possible. Some fifty yards along, the gully ends in another lava wall. He backtracks and finds a dip in the western wall. Close up, he sees the lava is riddled with ankle-breaking holes. He pushes through and finds another gully glade about ten feet wide. He thinks in the old days the vegetation might have been sparser, without the imported tamarisk. And the Indians would have known the trail. He moves roughly parallel to the first gully. There should be an east-west drift to the zigzagging, if the gullies keep being linked like this. They don't: he comes to a wall and can't find another opening when he backtracks, so he returns to his starting point and walks south along the lava and tries the next green dip. He walks on rivulets of sand. When he stirs them with the tip of his boot, he gets to lava, not more than an inch down. Sometimes the lava has a metal blue to it, sometimes a coal-coke sheen of gray. This time, he finds a way through to a third gully and a dip in its wall which looks like a way through to a fourth. He figures he's proved enough of a point to himself for one morning. It's too hot to go on. He makes his way out and sits in the shade of the sandstone drinking his water. He's soaked through. He's sure that if he could see this landscape from the air, he could check if his gully theory held right across the lava beds.

Forty-five minutes later, in the helicopter, he has his chance. He's flying directly over the Malpais, but he doesn't look out. He doesn't even see the medical team he stares at as they work on Emmy with oxygen and injections. What he keeps seeing is the scene when he returned to the Jeep: Emmy thrashing under the tamarisk in a convulsive fit, her jerking, stick-puppet arms and legs, her eyes rolled back to their whites, and all around her a debris of cookie packets, candy wrappers, Frito bags and Coke cans. She's swallowed everything, like poison.

13

SITTING IN the hospital waiting room with Lucy, her head on his shoulder, Ethan thinks, inappropriately: Lucy on the ledge, Stucic in Cimarron, and now Emmy at El Malpais—there's an awful, artsy alliteration to all his suicides. "All his suicides," too, has an over-ripe literary taint, a whiff of Ted Hughes or Anne Sexton. Pay no attention. No, pay attention to poor Lucy, here, to Emmy's surgery, the attempt to stop internal bleeding and peritonitis, to save her life.

Her ruptured stomach. The uh-uh assonance of the phrase. So stupid to go on like this. Yet, he thinks "her stomach burst," and in rushes a folk tale: The Girl Who Ate Nothing. One day, the girl who ate nothing decided to eat everything, and her belly burst, piff-poof! And out popped a rabbit, a canary, and a marmalade cat. W-w-well, I n-never, stuttered the rabbit. Phew! whistled the canary. Nine lives, purred the cat.

He's playing with the language of pain to turn pain into mere language. But it's immoral and immature that he can't bear to pay attention while Lucy leans on him, Lucy whose pain is illiterate, innumerate, mute. Let alone Emmy's pain. What must she have felt like when she stuffed herself? He pictures an ostrich neck showing the outlines of apples, sandwiches, candy bars. He goes from folk tale to cartoon because when Jerry gives Tom the dynamite cigar and Tom blows up and comes down in smoking bits, next frame he's whole again and sleek. Or is Ethan clowning to keep from acknowledging that his talk with Emmy about Willy, last night in Jemez Springs, may have brought on her breakdown, her blowout? He hasn't said a word of this to Lucy. He thinks his worst: Emmy's had a blowout but has no spare tire.

Lucy lifts her head from his shoulder. She says, "If she dies, Ethan." She says it declaratively. Ethan doesn't know how to answer this non-question. Does she mean will she still have him? Does she, for that matter, assume she has him now? He says, "She won't die."

Lucy in the same flat voice says, "How dare you assume such knowledge."

"I don't dare say otherwise."

She says, "You're rocking back and forth."

"I wasn't aware of it."

She says, "Jews do that reciting prayers for the dead."

He isn't sure that Jews don't do that for all prayers. His father is due in just over two weeks. He should phone him. He says, "I'm going to the bathroom. I'll be right back." When he stands, he bends and kisses the top of Lucy's head. He sees white hairs among the red.

The hospital seems deserted. Along the corridor, his feet go clonk-clonk like an old clock. Emmy has been in surgery for over four hours. He's hungry. As he thinks "hungry" he loses his appetite: if decomposing food gets into Emmy's blood… He stands in the stainless steel men's room peeing. He washes and rewashes his hands. In the mirror, he sees himself as preparing for surgery. He finds an alcove off the corridor and sits in a low armchair. He turns on his cell phone, breaking hospital rules.

It shows a list of messages; Doc N, who he's called, has obviously called others. He stops at a Boston number and picks up the message. "For Ethan Baum, second name B-A-U-M. Please call Haskell Perlmutter as soon as possible." So his father has had a stroke or a choke. He calls. Someone answers: "Mass. General Consultancy. How may we help you?" He says, "Dr. Haskell Perlmutter, P-E-R—" The voice says, "Yes, Dr. Perlmutter. Please wait." He hears a click and music comes on. Ethan doesn't listen to phone music; he disapproves. But he can't believe this: he hears The Stones' "Sympathy for the Devil" on the Massachusetts General Hospital's telephone system. Is this a practical joke? He hears another click and then *Eine Kleine Nachtmusik*. He recalls his teenage version of this and says out loud, "I'm inclined to knock music."

"I'm sorry to hear it, whoever you are. Perlmutter here."

"Dr. Perlmutter, it's Ethan returning your call. What's happened to my father?"

"Call me Haskell, Ethan, boy. I've known you since you were born. Since before. Nothing is physically wrong with Meyer, although who is to say this isn't a—what would you say—manifestation? of your dad's condition."

"What is? Haskell."

"Perhaps I'm out of line here, and you already know, in which case, I apologize."

"Know what? Haskell."

"About Meyer's relationship, ah, liaison."

"Yes, with a naval architect named Hannah Miller. They broke up in the West Indies. She was much younger than him, forty years old."

"I don't know anything about that. Your dad is parading all over town with a Chinese-American, Yang Chou is her name, a physicist at M.I.T. I have nothing against her race. Wonderful people, invented everything: paper money, acupuncture, moo-shu pork. But she is *twenty-two* years old. Only one quarter of your father's age, about. Or to put it another way, he is nearly—"

"Let me guess: four times her age."

"Ethan, boy, they are writing about your father in the gossip columns! I didn't even know we had gossip columns in Boston. But Joseph—you remember my son Joseph, he's always asking about you, he would love it, really, if you would call—he rang and read me this piece which said something about the philosopher Meyer Baum's new-found interest in Eastern philosophy, Kama Sutra, all that, though isn't that Indian, not Chinese, you know how we tend to lump together—"

"Haskell, thank you. I have to ring off now. Bye."

He calls his father, the man who said he had to put off his visit because of his new philosophy project. It's just after nine in Brookline, and the phone is ringing. Of course, Meyer is out nightclubbing and eating oysters with Yin Yang, whoever.

"Hi," says Meyer, chuckling.

"It's Ethan. We have a crisis here. Emmy has had a bulimic episode. Her stomach is ruptured and they're afraid of peritonitis. She's in critical condition; she's still in surgery."

"Should I fly out? I can fly right out."

"No, no. Thank you. I wanted you to know. You'll have to postpone your visit until everything's better. Until Emmy is, I mean, if she pulls through."

"Of course she will. My love and best wishes to Lucy. Poor Lucy. Poor Emmy. Poor you."

"Thanks. I'll keep in touch. Bye."

"Ethan, I do have some sense of what you're going through. I suppose Emmy is the closest I'm going to get to having a grandchild."

He walks back down the corridor. It's silent as the tomb. Bad simile. But the black and gray and stainless steel, the paintings so frantically blanc. This is necropolis. Shut up, he tells himself. He sees Lucy standing with Dr. Osborne, the surgeon. Osborne's hand is on her arm.

Ethan comes to Lucy's other side and puts his arm around her. Osborne says, "I was telling Lucy the surgery was successful. We have Emmy cleared up and the bleeding stopped. Repairing the rupture was the relatively straightforward part. This is still a very critical time, watching for peritonitis and other infection, because Emmy's anorexia has seriously compromised her immune system. On the positive side, she has two things going for her: one, she'll be nourished intravenously. The second is her will to hang in there. I have to admit, I didn't think much of her chances to survive surgery, but, considering the trauma, her vital signs remained surprisingly high. She seems to have a strong will to live. A great deal depends upon it."

Osborne is a dark-faced, lantern-jawed man whose words would inspire confidence but for what's been happening around them while he's been speaking. Out of the seemingly empty hospital, a throng has materialized. First a doctor and then two nurses talking excitedly, walking fast. And an orderly pushing a trolley stacked high with clean linen. And a young couple holding hands, she very pregnant and red-faced; he, solicitous, confused. And two children running from parents who call them back. When neither responds, the wife says, "Get them, George." He says, "They'll be okay." She says, "Either you get them now or I will. This is a hospital. They could, you know... I cannot believe I have to explain this!" And George trots off, calling, "Kids, kids!" By the time Osborne finishes, he, Lucy, and Ethan are pushed together in a tête-à-tête-à-tête of seriousness in the midst of laughter, people rushing with flowers, noise, movement, and a bald man, seeing Osborne's white coat, interrupting them to ask: "Say, would you know where E36 is? Peterson Wing, E36. No, E5 36."

Osborne points the man down the hall and says, "Shall we move into an office?"

Lucy says, "No. Can I see Emmy?"

Osborne says, "Go home and get some sleep. Come in tomorrow morning, after seven." He pats both their arms as he leaves.

They go to the elevator and pack in with the others, squeezed around an attendant by a gurney. Through the crowd they can see someone on it, under a sheet. Bottles and tubes on the drip stand. Lucy looks at Ethan. He says, "It isn't," and pushes around someone to see an old man's head above the sheet. Open blue eyes, small bent nose, gray stubble on the jaws, dentures out, his mouth pinched over his gums as if they were a small lemon. The ignominy of this. Meyer on his deathbed. Why not the medical elevator? Probably this came along first. Probably the attendant doesn't think of what the patient might feel. Probably pays no attention, does not give a shit. When they leave behind the trolley, Ethan says, "See?" He sees the violet and yellow bruising on the old arms where the tubes go in. Lucy hangs her head on his shoulder in the crowded lobby, and, walking back to her house, she lurches against him as if he were a Zimmer frame.

They sit in the living room for an hour, silent, washed-out. Ethan goes to the kitchen and comes back with a tray of salsa and tostados, ice, lime, beer and tequila. They finish all the food and a good part of the drink. It's ten-thirty at night.

Lucy says, "This is the critical night. I'm going back. I can be there, even if I can't see her. If Emmy lives, I'm going to be more open with her: you've shown that's the only way."

Ethan says, "I have to tell you something." He moves closer on the sofa to Lucy. "Last night—it seems so long ago—at Jemez Springs, Emmy asked why I hit Willy at that party. First I gave her a general answer. But she knew there was more and kept asking *why* I found Willy so obnoxious that I had to get away from him. Let me stop here to add something: this conversation was at a restaurant. Before that, Emmy had come into the living room of our suite naked, said 'Oops,' and left. At dinner, she apologized for teasing me; I said I was just embarrassed."

Lucy says, "I've ducked out of anything awkward with her for too long." She rubs Ethan's hand.

He says, "But then Emmy asked why I thought she did that, and I said maybe she wanted to take advantage of me because she'd been taken advantage of. And *then* she asked me about Willy."

Lucy's hand comes off Ethan's. She squeezes half a lime into her tumbler and finishes the tequila.

He says, "So I told her, without details, about Willy's child pornography photos."

Lucy murmurs, "Jesus."

"Emmy's response was to call him an asshole and look away. I asked her if Willy had ever said or done anything to her, like that, when she was a child. And she said no and clearly wanted to change the subject. I don't know: maybe I went too far, maybe that set off feelings that led to her food binge."

Lucy's head sinks. Ethan bends his head to see if she's all right, and she smacks his jaw with her tumbler. As he falls back, he sees the tumbler fly off, bounce, and roll over the rug in one piece. He moans but doesn't even ask why; there is no arguing with such pain as Lucy's. Now she's dropped her head again and is panting like a trapped animal awaiting its second wind. He sits against the far side of the sofa rubbing his jaw. He'll live. He wants to touch her but is afraid.

From within her seated crouch, Lucy says, "It's one thing to be straight, another to play amateur shrink with my very sick daughter. You're an arrogant bastard."

He wonders if she's ever hit Emmy hard.

After a while, she says, "Aren't you going to say anything? Am I the crazy woman? Is this the silent reproach?" She looks at him with miserable red eyes.

"What I want to say you'd probably think was me playing amateur shrink, again."

"Say it. I won't hit you twice. I'm not violent, just desperate."

He knows they're both exhausted and drunk, but that doesn't make his thought less real. "You told me that Willy never came on to Emmy. Maybe you're not so sure."

"Now you're playing amateur shrink with me. Why?"

"Why? Because here I am."

"Really? Why do I feel that I'm only some temporary comfort station on your way to anyone else who might come along and interest you more?"

He moves across the sofa and puts his arm around her. She doesn't move to him, but she doesn't hit him. He says, "Let's call the hospital. Maybe they can arrange for you to sleep there."

"Those photos you saw with Willy in them; it wasn't...?"

"Emmy wasn't in them. I shouldn't have pushed you about Willy. I'm sorry."

Lucy stays quiet. Ethan calls the hospital and finds there's a staff room with a couch they're happy to have Lucy use; he keeps forgetting her celebrity. Then they wash and walk back across Las Lomas Boulevard to the hospital. They get to look at Emmy through the Intensive Care window; she's barely visible under the tubes and bottles and wires. The night nurse explains the monitors, and they stare at the green pulse wave crossing and re-crossing the screen. Ethan finds himself saying, "She's all right." Lucy says nothing and keeps watching the screen.

In the staff room, they sit on the couch and sleep against each other. Sometimes Ethan wakes to find Lucy gone back to the IC window, looking through at Emmy under her oxygen tent, under her plasma and liquid and nutritive drips. At seven in the morning they drink watery coffee from a machine. They're kept out of Emmy's room until ten-fifteen, when Osborne accompanies them to her bedside, saying Emmy's pulse and blood pressure are improved, but it may be several days before she's fully conscious. Ethan sees the dark sockets of her eyes, her cheeks sunk like when she sucked them in and made him laugh. No, now they are much worse. He cannot see how Emmy can survive. Lucy is smiling, whispering to her.

On their way home, waiting for the light to cross the boulevard, Lucy says, fairly shouting above the traffic noise, "They never got on. I never thought Willy did or said anything to Emmy like that. I see I should have left Willy after that business with his students, but it seemed disloyal when he was so down, even though it destroyed my feelings for him." Ethan wonders if that's what his mother had felt.

Next day, because she's improved, Emmy is moved into a private IC room. Her eyelids flutter when Lucy talks to her. Lucy turns smiling to Ethan and says, "See?"

Two days after this, at Lucy's, Ethan picks up the phone just after Lucy does, hears his father's voice, and listens.

"Lucy, dear, how's Emmy? How are you?"

"She's a little better, improving. I'm okay. How are you?"

"Fine. Is Emmy still in a critical condition?"

"Yes, but they hope to be upgrading her to 'serious' today or tomorrow. She recognizes me and Ethan. She says hi."

"Oh, Lucy. Poor you. This is something only a parent can understand."

"Meyer, Ethan has been wonderful."

"Of course. He's such… I was imagining how I would have felt had Ethan as a teenager gone through something like this. I can tell you, I wept just to imagine it."

"Oh, Meyer."

"I'm sorry I'm not there to do whatever, to share the hard times. Especially as it might help make up for certain times I feel I let Ethan down."

"Thank you. No one could be more supportive than Ethan. You can be proud of him."

"Of course. Lucy, I understand why this wouldn't be a good time for me to be there, not that I'd need any looking after, for heaven's sake; I've looked after myself for seventy-eight years now. No, something about me irritates Ethan, always has."

"Meyer, he's trying to pull himself up from a low point in his writing, and, well, there you are, famous philosopher. It's a difficult situation. Anyway, we both hope you'll be out here as soon as Emmy's better."

"That's good of you, Lucy. You're able to say things that, frankly, Ethan never can, with me. I feel close to you, dear, even over the phone. I know you're good for Ethan. And you know I wish what you do for your dear daughter."

"That's kind of you. Would you like to speak to Ethan?"

"No, no. That's all right. Give him my love."

"And ours to you, Meyer."

Ethan quietly puts the phone down. Two parents commiserating. It's apparent he can't understand because he's not a parent. He's only a freaky writer, disconnected. A writer at the bottom of his writing who really doesn't write. He leaves the house through the kitchen door and walks over to the hospital. The staff is used to Lucy and him; a nurse calls them "one of the family." What family is that, the staff? The sick? Maybe he's one family and Lucy and Meyer are another—the family of parents with children. Well, he can at least, he decides at Emmy's door, tell Lucy's child he loves her. How could that be bad for her?

But she's gone. The bed is bare and Elena Stucic is sitting by the window, crying. He thinks, No, no, and says, "Elena, what's happened?"

She says, "Please say Eileen. They take her to new room because she better. She's better. I helped to take some of her things and came here back, back here, to check nothing is left. And I start to think of what is happened to Emmy and how she looks and I start to cry and forget my English."

He goes and puts his hand on her shoulder. "But she's better, the worst danger is over."

"I know is true. But I think of how a father can take a life from the daughter. Her step-father and my terrible father."

"Elena—I'm calling you Elena because that's the name both your parents gave you. Your father told me about his affair during the war. I believe him. It must have been hard on your mother and you. But your war criminal story is being investigated by the University. If they find nothing to it, you have to let it go. Your father is heartbroken at losing you. He loves you very much. I know that."

She pushes her hair back from her eyes and smirks: "Oh, yes. I suppose you say same about William Dixon."

"No, I don't. What do you mean?"

She stands, looks out the window, and turns to him holding her finger up: "I mean, I show you, this I have proof, audio tapes of this man abuse her for long time. I can bring these, you hear this beast and father."

He says, "If you have these tapes, could you bring them to me at Copper Place, tomorrow?"

"I know address from workshop. At two in the afternoon I can?"

"Two o'clock, yes." He squats in front of her. "Elena, why don't you give up this phone sex business? You could convince Emmy to, when she's well enough. She'd listen to you."

"I think of it. But I see you first, tomorrow. Here, I show you to her new room." She shakes her head, and, speaking slowly, says, "No, I mean to say: I'll show you to her new room."

She leaves him at a door down the corridor. The room is still hi-tech, but has no monitor window. He moves a chair up to the bed, glances at the screens on the wall, and sits. A bubbly breathing comes from Emmy's nose; now only one of her nostrils has a tube in it. Her eyes are shut.

He says, "It's just me, Emmy, Ethan. I'm glad you're better, in a regular room, now. I love you. You have a good short story; it's getting better. It still needs some work at the end."

He closes his eyes and listens to his breathing over Emmy's. A cracked whisper comes: "I hear you."

He opens his eyes. Hers are still closed. He says, "You get that trick from your mom."

As usual, Lucy spends the next day at the hospital. Ethan gets to Copper Place at half-past one to check his answer phone. He finds a message from Meyer:

"Ethan, I'm calling here because I don't particularly want Lucy to hear this, given her worries. Not, I hasten to add, that this is a troubled call on my part. I want to tell you what I'm doing with this adorable woman young enough to be my granddaughter. And, no, that's not an allusion to an earlier conversation we had about the Baum line, or loins. It's really that I'm fighting for my life, here. Don't misunderstand, not physically. Although this Viagra—no wonder they make all the jokes. Have you heard this one? 'Goys buy Viagra; Jews buy Pfizer.' Haskell told me that one. Typical of Haskell to tell me a slightly anti-Semitic joke. And of me, I suppose, to pass it on with that comment about Haskell At any rate, *this* Jew has to buy Viagra through his Brandeis doctor. Haskell, the old prude, refused to prescribe it to me. Ethan, I haven't felt this way since I met your mother. I'm in love with Yang. She is, quite apart from the Viagra side of our relationship, so bright. A physicist, as you may know, but I'm getting her to read and discuss philosophy. She's a whiz! She read through the three H's—I mean Hegel, Husserl, and Heidegger—like they were comic books. And she's witty way beyond her years. Would it be too insane for us to come out there and have a double wedding atop some hot red mesa? I realize Lucy isn't yet formally divorced, but... Am I raving? Not raving, fighting for my life, here, against all the conventional wisdoms. You know, I like this sort of answer phone that takes long messages. A phone monologue is very relaxing. Conducive. And, Ethan, now that you seem to have a decent job out there, and I assume Lucy is financially independent, my marriage, if it came to that, would not be irresponsible vis-à-vis your prospects, as they used to be called, not that I have much to leave you, anyway. And, sign of my mental health, I've decided to stop musing about my funeral. I think I've decided, quite simply, to live forever. A joke, Ethan. Love to all of you, including dear Emmy who doesn't yet know me. Tell her I wish her a speedy recovery. Tell her she has a wannabe grandfather back East who's dying to meet her. Living to. Bye-bye."

Ethan finds the call has cheered him. He'll make tea for Elena, in glasses, with sugar and lemon. He believes it's eastern European. He hopes Meyer will like this place. Meyer and Yang.

When Elena arrives—she doesn't correct him calling her Elena—she welcomes the tea. There's even a faint smile for him when he brings it out on the dining bar in glasses. He tells her he remembers his mother calling it "tcha." She says, "Yes, cha."

They sip tea. She speaks good English. She says, "This is a nice, bright place." She seems reluctant to bring up the point of her visit. He nods to the carrier bag at her feet. "Is that what you were telling me about?"

"Yes, yes. I'll get it." She takes out a tape player. "I promised Emmy I wouldn't tell anyone. But I cannot watch her die. She's been very good to me. I was already doing this sex phone in a terrible one-room apartment when we met. Emmy got me a better place—you were there. She said it was for the business, but, really, it was a way of helping me out. Emmy said she wanted to do it because it was fun. We keep tapes of calls because sometimes we listen to learn new ideas or have fun, because they're funny. Then we erase them. These I did not erase; I kept and re-recorded them. This first conversation is from a few weeks after Emmy started, almost two years ago. Then there are two more, later. All the same customer. We talked about them, but Emmy doesn't know I have kept these."

The tape comes on. A man's muffled, nasal voice asks for the "little girl" he's spoken with. Emmy's voice comes on saying, "Hi. Is this that big, bad man?" and the man immediately describes a scene: the girl is back from school early. The door to her mother's room is partly open and she sees her giving fellatio to the man. He asks what the girl does, and Emmy describes her shock and fascination; she's unable to stop watching. The man says he sees her watching and the rest of the scene has him performing with the mother for the girl, who ends up masturbating in the now opened door. This is not the language of the tape.

All Ethan knows is the man is grammatical, educated. He says, "Elena, I can't identify the man's voice."

She says, "It's him, Dixon, but the recording is not good… This next one is later, last year."

The man's voice comes on, less muffled and disguised. It could be Dixon, but he isn't sure. The man sets a scene where the girl is taking a bath after they've been out on a picnic where he knows she's come across her mother and him having sex in the woods. He asks, "How are you going to get me into the bathroom, daughter?" Emmy answers that she may have picked up a tick on her back and, since mom's out shopping, could he please come in and check, "Please, Dad?" The scene is played out through fondling, fellatio, and anal sex. Its language is crude.

When Elena stops the tape, Ethan shrugs. He says, "I'm still not sure." Whoever the man is, it's sad how willing and glibly creative are Emmy's responses.

Elena says, "But here is one more. You will see. This one is last spring."

She puts it on. It's Dixon's voice. He sets a scene on an old pirate boat, where he's forcing his daughter to incest. He says her name is "Emerald" for the jewels he's looted, but he'll shorten it to "Emmy." The language, on his part, is particularly violent.

Ethan turns off the tape. It is Dixon's voice, Dixon's awful nautical jargon, Dixon calling her Emmy, knowing of her anorexia. Is this why Emmy has continued in the phone-sex business: the chance to act out all her fears and fantasies with her stepfather? Fantasies or experiences? He says, "I'd like to keep the tape for a day or so, to make a copy. This certainly is Dixon."

Elena says, "I don't want the tape." She rewinds it and gives him the cassette.

He says, "I'll take care of it."

She says, "What are you going to do?"

He repeats, "I'll take care of it." He has no idea; he knows only that he can't tell Lucy.

14

AFTER ELENA LEAVES, Ethan sits at his desk looking at the tape in its unmarked case. He goes from thinking why, oh cursed spite, he should be landed with setting this right, to worrying about losing the tape. This at least suggests something to do: he dubs two copies of the tape on his sound system. Then, without being clear why, he goes out and buys a portable cassette player like Elena's.

It's six o'clock when he gets back to Lucy. She's asleep on the living room sofa. He pulls the shawl over her shoulder. Even in sleep, she looks anxious. He sits on the floor by her head and thinks of what he hasn't told her, of Willy's sex conversations with Emmy, of the tapes, of learning about her links with the mining industry, an industry her novels denounce. Why should she want to tell him? Who is he to judge her? She opens her eyes, turns, and kisses him.

"It's after six," he says. "I thought I'd visit Emmy and then come back and make us supper."

"Mmm," goes Lucy and closes her eyes.

He's walking down the hospital corridor to Emmy's room when he sees Alvarado come out the door. Alvarado breaks into a big smile. He's dressed as for a state visit in a double breasted gray silk suit, and he's walking with a silver-topped ivory stick. He takes Ethan's hand and says, "Our patient is definitely improving. We've just had a conversation, though I did most of the talking. Still, that's typical of many of my conversations." Ethan nods. Alvarado's smile goes. He grips Ethan's shoulder. "*Hombre*, I can't ask Lucy. Tell me the truth: Do you think Emmy will make it?"

"Yes. The doctors think so, though they say there could be some permanent damage to her motor system."

"Yes," Alverado says, his hand dropping to his side. "I've known Emmy since she was born."

"Have you hurt yourself?" Ethan asks, nodding to the walking stick.

"An old trick knee. Nothing."

It comes to Ethan why he's bought the cassette player. "Carlos, could we sit and talk? I'm only looking in on Emmy for a few minutes."

"About the project?"

"No, about Emmy."

"Of course. But, please, not here. I don't like hospitals. Perhaps a superstition I've inherited from my ancestors. Can you come over to my office when you're through?"

Ethan says he'll be there soon and goes into Emmy's room. Emmy is asleep. She looks terrible. He sits down beside the bed and puts the side of his hand alongside her arm. Her breathing is shallow, near silent. Dr. Osborne has warned that her recovery won't be steady, but in stages, with plateaus. This looks like a ravine. He sees why Lucy, or anyone concerned with Emmy, would prefer her willful and manipulative—her ordinary anorexic state—to this life tottering on its high wire of feeds and monitors. When he leaves, he kisses Emmy's forehead. There is no talk out of her sleep, no flutter of an eyelid to please him.

At Alvarado's office, Ethan wonders if it's his mood, or the late light, or does he now see clearly the grand historic murals as somewhat dusty, the fading mythology of another time?

Alvarado ushers him in. "Welcome. How was she?"

"Asleep."

Alvarado sees him looking at his walking stick. "Early eighteenth century. The silverwork is from Seville."

He holds it out to Ethan who takes it and turns it slowly in his hand. The design is a ring of armored giants each with a foot on the back of a little crouched person.

"Conquistadors standing on subject Indians," says Alvarado. "The twisted shaft is said to be the horn of a unicorn. It's narwhal, of course. A drink, *hombre?*" He opens a door out of the wall mural to reveal a full bar with refrigerator.

"Vodka and tonic," says Ethan.

"This is," says Alvarado, fixing the drinks, "completely forbidden on campus. I won't be fired for it. In the last academic year, our esteemed President Klotz managed to lose us twelve million in state research funds. In the same period, I brought the University twenty-five million dollars from the Spanish government, the Endowment for Science and the Humanities, and various private foundations. It's a matter of simple math."

"Why aren't you president?"

Alvarado smiles: "The Board of Regents has asked me that for fifteen years. But I'm much better placed where I am: more freedom of maneuver to go for projects I like, most of which directly or indirectly benefit the University. There you are. We now have our drinks, and I've bragged enough to be able to listen to you."

They sit in armchairs. Ethan finds Alvarado's charm slightly preposterous. He says, "Carlos, I know you're fond of Emmy."

"More than fond," Alvarado says, raising his hand both as in oath and to stop Ethan from speaking. "I love Emmy very much. I told you I've known her all her life. The story is this: Celia, my wife, wasn't able to have children. We adopted a wonderful girl, Margarita, six years older than Emmy. We adore her and are very proud of her: she's the youngest full professor of Spanish literature at the University of Texas in Austin. But Emmy was like another daughter. Ah, Ethan, *hombre*, she was such a bright, wild, fearless child. A real tomboy. And then—this." He shrugs and drops his head.

Ethan wonders whether Alvarado will ever be able to listen to him. He says, "Maybe you already know what I'm going to tell you, but I'll go ahead."

"Certainly." Alvarado elegantly waves him on.

"For the past two years, Emmy has chosen to work at an awful job. She—"

"Yes, yes, the telephone sex. I wasn't able to convince Lucy to forbid it. Then again, there's no use forbidding Emmy anything she wants. She'll do it even if... Even if it kills her. I have someone watch that she comes to no harm in that sleaze she's into."

"You know of her work partner, Eileen Smith?"

"Of course."

"You know who she is?"

Alvarado shakes his head.

"She's Elena Stucic, the daughter of Miroslav Stucic and almost certainly the person spreading the war-criminal rumors about her father."

"*Dios en cielo!* Happily, I can tell you there seems to be no substance to her story."

"Good. I met Elena in the hospital. She was distraught over Emmy and accused Willy Dixon of causing Emmy's breakdown and, by inference, being a major cause of Emmy's condition. More to the point, she has proof. She kept tapes of sex line calls he made to Emmy over the past two years. Three calls. I have the tape, I've made copies."

"Is it Dixon?"

"No doubt of it, on the most recent call. But they all show personal knowledge of Emmy. In the most recent, he finds a way to call her Emmy and refers to her extreme thinness. They're terrible calls, sexual fantasies of humiliating and, finally, of killing a mother while arousing her daughter and having sadistic sex with her."

Alvarado says, "I need to hear the tape. The bastard!"

"Carlos, you should know that Emmy seems a willing participant in these telephone fantasies. Given her other worries, I haven't told Lucy about any of this."

Alvarado says, "Willing or not, it wouldn't make Dixon less guilty."

"But guilty of what: phone fantasies or a verbal continuation of things he may have physically done to her?"

Alvarado sets down his drink. "Good Christ, this has turned my best tequila to acid."

"I know that Dixon got in trouble with a student, and you protected him."

"A student? That's rich. Listen, *hombre*, I protected him for Lucy's sake. I never liked the man. I'll never understand how he took in Roly Everets, who introduced him to Lucy. Perhaps he could be charming, then. Well, the scandal. He was, it seems, having an affair with an eighteen-year-old freshman named Donna Gray. It turned out that the purpose of that affair for Dixon was to get into the pants of her thirteen-year-old sister, Sharon. The girls' parents found photos of the three of them. Miserable stuff. Luckily, the family was from New Mexico, so I was able to arrange an out-of-court settlement. I paid out most of the money myself. The Grays left the state, and I warned

Dixon that was the last time I'd help him. And now, he makes these calls to Emmy?" He pulls at his moustache and looks into his glass, as if down a well. "If I recognize his voice on the tape…" He pauses, looks up, and quietly says, "I'll have him killed."

The man has not said "I'd like to," he's said, "I'll have him killed." Ethan stands and says, "Seriously, Carlos."

Alvarado waves his hand dismissively: "Of course I would never do such a thing. It wouldn't be good for Lucy or Emmy. What do you think is best?"

"I want him to leave Albuquerque, to get out of both their lives. Lucy won't even make him leave her house. What if I confront Dixon with the tape and see how he reacts?"

Alvarado says, "One thing he'll do is call me, since I've looked after him in the past. But if it's him on your tape, I'll let him know he's finished here."

"I'll get the tape to you in the morning and try to see Dixon tomorrow afternoon."

"I'll be here all day. Ethan, you'll want to be careful. I've told you that Dixon is cautious, but if he felt cornered, I don't know. And to completely change the subject: I understand that your coming up to Valles Caldera in three weeks will depend on Emmy's condition. We'd miss you up there, but you have to…" He puts his hand on Ethan's shoulder. "Anyway, I'd understand. Listen, *hombre*, I'm a proud man; it's difficult for me to admit I've been wrong. When you turned up, I thought you were just an opportunist, taking advantage of Lucy because she could be of great use. But you're a good man. *Adios, hombre. Adios, amigo.*"

Ethan crosses the campus slightly embarrassed not only by Alvarado's operatic manners but by the accuracy of his first impression. Is he now less opportunistic? At least he's now sympathetic.

When he comes in, Lucy is still asleep on the sofa. As if to test himself, he wakes her and says, "Hi. Love you." It doesn't feel hypocritical.

She says, "Thank you."

Next morning, Ethan brings a copy of the tape to Alvarado, who fast-forwards to the third conversation, listens for a minute and shuts it off. He sits dark faced behind his great half-circle desk, pulling hard at his moustache. He says, "It's him. *Cabron!* He's a dead man." He smiles at Ethan, "Metaphorically, of course. Go see him, Ethan. But take care."

Ethan leaves the office and crosses the sunken quadrangle to the Honors Department. He squints to shut out all but the southwest-style buildings and imagines how pleasant it must have been when the entire faculty lived on campus, in houses pretty much like the one Lucy's in. How quaint, life in an adobe tower.

The assistant says Professor Dixon is in a department conference. When Ethan says it's an emergency, she asks if he means a medical emergency. He thinks of Emmy and says yes, and she picks up the phone, speaks low into it and hands him the receiver.

"This is Ethan Baum, but don't hang up. I meant it, about an emergency."

"Emmy's worse?"

"No, but this involves her. You and her. I have a tape you need to hear as soon as possible."

After a second's pause, Dixon says, "There's no reason I should humor you, but since we're both concerned about Emmy, very well. I can see you at my home, up on La Vista Drive, this afternoon. Half-past three."

Ethan says, "Right." When he hands the receiver back to the assistant, he's still grimacing over Dixon's "my home."

He leaves Copper Place at three, the cassette player with the tape in his briefcase on the seat beside him. He remembers the house and the way to it as clearly as if he's driven there every day for the past months. At the top of La Vista Drive, his throat goes dry. He feels as alone as on that first night in Albuquerque. And there it is: "Dixon's home."

He walks to the door, sees the note, and is certain that Dixon has changed his mind. But, no, it directs him to go around left and down to the swimming pool. He wonders what humiliation Dixon has set up. He feels the sweat off his hand on the briefcase handle. The path goes down steps through thickly planted pine. At a turn, he sees before him a sixty-foot slab of water set in a pinetum of dwarf evergreens, a few small saguaro cactuses placed among them for what the landscapers call "accent." Another dramatic element in the design is Dixon at the far end of the pool, in shorts and tee shirt, with a shotgun.

Ethan takes a half step back before he makes out the opened barrels and the swab stick. Dixon's little humiliation. Dixon waves: "Come on over and pull up a chair. I'm cleaning my shotgun."

Ethan goes over, unable to stop thinking that Dixon will finish cleaning it, load it, and shoot him dead for a trespasser. In the bright light, Ethan sees that Dixon must once have been good-looking with his sharp-sculpted features in his long, bony face. His forehead, cheekbones and chin look dented, but not unattractive, despite Ethan trying to see them as large pockmarks or the signs of a nasty, wasting disease. Even the famous broken nose now looks in rugged place.

Dixon keeps working with the gun. He says, "There's water or juice there in the pool house. No? Well, what's all this about a tape?"

Ethan says, "I'll play it." His voice is dry and cracked. He should have accepted the water. Ethan puts the tape player on the low table between them. The sun is hot on the back of his head. He should have worn a hat. A bulletproof vest. He says, "There are three phone conversations here, the first from about two years ago, the most recent from a few months ago, in late spring. I'll play them straight through."

Dixon says, "Whatever," and Ethan turns on the tape. He turns up the volume and watches Dixon. After a minute or so, Dixon shakes his head and shrugs. "Who is this supposed to be?" he asks in a loud voice, over the tape.

Ethan will not turn down the volume. He shouts, "You and Emmy, on a telephone-sex line."

"That's not me. It could be Emmy. If it had been up to me, I wouldn't have let her do it; I would have threatened reporting her to the police. And I would have. But Lucy... Well, I suppose by now you know how impossibly complicit she is in anything Emmy chooses."

Ethan shouts, "That's a nice parental speech, even better acting than on the tapes. But let me play them through." Dixon turns up his hands in mock politeness.

In the pause between the first and second taped conversation, Dixon says, "You say two years ago? If that was Emmy, she certainly was sexually precocious."

Ethan says, "Why might that be?" and the second conversation begins. Dixon closes his eyes. Ethan thinks maybe he's protesting overmuch. When it ends, Ethan says, "Here comes the clearest tape."

The voice on the tape says: "No, on a boat flying the jolly roger, and I'm starving you, water rations only, until you fuck me, which you don't want to do because, of course, that's incest, and you've witnessed me fuck your mommy and beat her to death and then fuck her corpse. So, thou'st become a very skinny wench in the brig; it's hot down there. We're sailing the Sargasso and we're in the doldrums. I'm drinking rum one night, and what's thy name going to be?"

Emmy's voice says, "My name is Carlotta. You call me Candy."

"No, child. It's Emerald, for the jewels I've looted, and what does Daddy call thee?"

"Hot little bitch?"

"Aye, that, too, that, too. But he calls thee Emmy, short for Emerald. So this night I be rum-drunk and have thee brought up from the brig. And what's this I spy, Emmy, around thy scrawny wrists and ankles?"

"My shackle marks."

"Aye, aye, and I ask thee once more will ye fuck me, Emmy, ye scrawny piss-stinking bitch?"

"I say, no, you murderer, you Bluebeard. I hate you like mommy did."

"Right, and this maddens me, and I sweep everything off the table—maps, sextant, decanters—and I say, right, me hungry one. And I grab thee and tie thee face down athwart the table and say, Now I have the weather gauge of thee. Now I'll show thee how the skipper-father will embrace thee, Emmy. And I open thy asshole and I tell thee, Why? Because it's the cleanest part of ye. It's unused. And ye say what?"

Ethan stops the tape. Dixon, who has listened with open eyes, says, "Yes, that was the clearest. It may be Emmy; I'm not certain. But it's certainly not me." He puts the gun-cleaning paraphernalia—swab stick and rags and small cans of cleaner and oil—back in their case.

Ethan says, "It's you because it's clearly your voice. Because all three scenes involve the same family relationship. Because, in the last one, not only do you insist on calling her Emmy—against her own suggestion—not only do you allude to her anorexia, but you speak in that awful yo-ho-ho jargon I remember from the party here, the one where you tried to force me to look at photographs of you anally raping little girls."

"None of it can be proven."

"There's Emmy's phone partner who recorded it: she'll go on record attesting it's you. Then, your credit card accounts could be checked. And, if necessary, there's Emmy."

"Emmy? The same Emmy who's such an eager, full-blooded participant in these taped conversations?"

"Yes. She has no stake in keeping her sex-phone work private. As a matter of fact, I have an idea she might enjoy going public, so notoriously. But this is beside the point, isn't it? I understand there's a great deal at stake for you, not the least of which is your job."

Dixon stares at Ethan. Ethan feels the sweat running off his hair down the sides of his neck. He now sees, beside the open shotgun case, an open box of shells, their brass ends bright in the sun.

"Speaking generally, do you imagine I'd involve myself in anything the least bit risky without first insuring I'd be—*all right*?"

"What if your insurance has run out?"

Dixon regards the shotgun on his lap then looks at Ethan. He says, "Excuse me while I make a phone call." He sets the shotgun on its case, takes the cell phone from the table and goes into the pool house.

Ethan hopes he's phoning Alvarado. What if it's someone else? For that matter, if Alvarado tells him it's all over, why shouldn't Dixon kill him? He should take the shotgun shells away, right now. Throw them into the pool or down the hillside. He should take the shotgun and load it, if he knew how. He doesn't want to do that. He has to leave the shells. He's counting on Dixon being too tidy a sybarite to risk prison. But he remembers Alvarado's warning about Dixon when cornered, and all Ethan knows for certain is that he's very afraid yet cannot touch the damned shotgun shells.

Dixon comes out of the pool house and sits down. He looks grim, cornered. "Right, Baum. What is it you want?"

He says, "I want you to have nothing to do with Emmy. No contact of any sort, ever. Or I'll do everything possible to land you in prison, where you'll learn, on the receiving end, the meaning of sexual abuse. And I want you to facilitate the divorce Lucy wants, without any disagreement. She gets this house and everything of hers in it. And you leave Albuquerque, the sooner the better."

Dixon says, "As to that, I've in the past few days received confirmation of a career move I've been pursuing, an offer from the University of British Columbia for its chair in American Literature, a step or two up from Honors Program Director at this backwater. And, yes, I agree about Emmy; it will be good to have done with the little... I'll leave it at that. About the property: the Anasazi pot collection is mine, though I mightn't have been able to afford them had Lucy not provided this house."

"Take your looted pots, Dixon, and leave soon as you can. You know Lucy doesn't want what's yours: the pots, the yo-ho-ho library, the collection of child pornography."

"Baum, you get to town, come to my party and break my nose, go off with my wife—yes, we were estranged, but it still feels like that—and, as you see it, force me to leave my job and this city. You must feel very satisfied."

"No, I'm sorry about everything but Lucy. In all these other things, you're just an obnoxious creep. But in what you've done to Emmy—even if you haven't literally sexually abused her since she was ten—you're despicable. You've nearly killed her. You still may."

Dixon shakes his head: "It isn't at all like you think, but there's no use speaking of it, now. However, here's something you should know. When—on Lucy's pleading, of course—Carlos was considering you for the Lavery book, it looked as if the success of your workshop might make you refuse. Carlos, shrewd man, suspected your character. I've been a senior editor for Carlos's Institute publications for years, and I gave him the idea that if you and your students were frightened off, you'd have to accept the offer. I even suggested you might be roughed up, a little. Carlos, who had multiple motives, liked the idea. He's always been very protective of Lucy. And why not? He's Emmy's father."

"I don't believe it."

"His paternity or his arranging your being beaten up at my suggestion? Ask him, ask your new good friend. Or don't, I really don't care. I'll be leaving this dreary little place in a few weeks. I think you should go now."

Ethan puts the tape player back into the briefcase, snaps it shut and hears himself say, "The shotgun display was pathetic. You wouldn't shoot me, you wouldn't do anything you think you'd be held responsible for." Why has he said this? He turns and walks off without looking at Dixon. Halfway along the pool, he hears the click of the shotgun being closed. Has he loaded it? Why was he such a fool as to goad Dixon into shooting him? He can't give him the satisfaction of looking back. As he rounds the corner of the pool, he feels the shaking in his legs. He will not look sideways at Dixon. He knows Dixon has pointed the gun at him, has him in his sights. This is the widest pool in the world. Before he reaches the path, he's soaked in sweat. He goes up the steps as fast as he can without running.

When he gets to the Jeep, he stops, as startled as if the shotgun had gone off. Alvarado's smile. Emmy's smile is Alvarado's smile. The photos of her before her anorexia show her looking more like Alvarado. Alvarado had his students threatened and him beaten up. Alvarado is Emmy's father. No wonder he loves her as much as he does his adopted daughter. Ethan can see right away why Alvarado couldn't marry Lucy: not so much his Catholicism as his Catholic, land-grant wife. And, yes, yes, that's why for all his dear friendship, Lucy never sees the Alvarados socially.

He drives slowly down the hills back into town. But why should Dixon risk not only his job but his *life* in abusing Carlos's daughter? The answer, he knows, is compulsion. Even the need to keep risking discovery. The hills give out onto the long ugly sprawl back into town. Why hasn't Lucy told him? He, too, feels for poor Emmy. Why hasn't Lucy told him? What should he say about *this* to Lucy? Nothing and nothing and nothing.

When he parks at Copper Place, Sam, from the bike shop, hands him a UPS package he's signed for. Ethan goes up, showers, changes into fresh clothes and sits drinking a vodka in his old Boston armchair. He opens the package. Who is Dave Brown? He reads the note about the photographs. Of course, Jeanie: Dave and Jeanie Brown, and Billy and the German shepherds. He looks through the photographs, black and white mattes. The gas station at Cedar Crest, the empty store, the trailer on its patch of sparse new grass, the fenced dog runs out the back. He finds them Walker Evans-like; the simple things in themselves given the dignity of composition. The last photograph is of Jeanie in the trailer, sitting at the table with her head tipped back, laughing as both Billy and the puppy lick her neck at the same time. She takes his breath away. He remembers her smell. She must be due now. She is gorgeous in her family.

It is not, he says to himself, his family. But who, besides his father, is his family? A twenty-two-year-old M.I.T. physicist he's never met? An eighteen-year-old compulsive in a hospital bed? No, a forty-six-year-old novelist who is so crazy about him she can't tell him the father of her child is his boss.

15

IN THE WEEKS THAT FOLLOW, Ethan stays with Lucy; he visits Emmy several times each day. He can't see any improvement, but Lucy is more sensitive to change in her daughter—her eyes, her speech, her weight, her breathing, her weight, her weight. And though Lucy each time qualifies the weight gain with "Of course, she's being fed through tubes, but…" it's obvious how pleased she is to announce each new ounce she adjudges to her daughter, as if it were more ballast tethering Emmy to earth.

But since this doesn't take up all of Ethan's time and since he can't leave town, he finds himself writing from his audio-video notes. When he finishes two pieces, one on the upper Pecos Valley and another on Cimarron and the surrounding mountains, he mails copies to Lavery, with a cover note saying he has no idea if this is what's wanted.

Three days later, he gets a phone message: "It's Charlie. Ring me about the stuff you sent." Ethan calls, trying to forget how discouraging the message sounded.

Lavery says, "Yeah, well, the pieces are so different. I didn't see how they could be in the same book. But I think the Cimarron piece could be one of several inserts, like boxes of first person experience and response. The one on the Pecos would be the standard text sort of thing. Does that work for you?"

"Yes," Ethan says. "What did you think of them, beside that?"

"Beside that, I'm going up the Pecos valley to take a look. I haven't been there in twenty years. I have some meadow shots that could do for the Cimarron piece, but I'll probably go up there for new shots."

Ethan tries for a direct response: "So you think they're okay?"

"That's what I'm saying. They're good. Stimulating. They get me going."

Ethan says, "Don't say 'thanks.'" and hears a croak which could be a laugh, a yes, a no, or a screw you. He puts down the phone smiling. Then he calls his father and leaves the message Lucy has been urging, that Emmy is now well enough for Meyer, hopefully for Meyer and Yang, to come out to New Mexico, any time after the tenth of October, when he'll be back from observing an elk hunt.

In the late afternoon, he visits Emmy on his own. She no longer speaks in a whisper, but her voice has some slurring and sibilance, which the neurologist says may not improve. Lucy doesn't refer to it, so Ethan feels he shouldn't, either. He's noticed that Lucy continues to speak very close to Emmy, as if still hearing the whisper.

To Emmy's "What's happening?" he relates the story of prising a compliment of sorts from Lavery. Then Emmy, not for the first time, asks him to promise he won't change his mind on the hunt and shoot an elk. He tells her that just because he's smiling doesn't mean this isn't a solemn promise. And when in return she smiles—a slightly lopsided smile, as if she's had a stroke, he raises the difficult subject.

"Does Elena visit a lot?" He's explained why he wants to call her "Elena."

"Every day. She's a good friend."

"What do you talk about?"

"Besides how I'm feeling. Pretty much everything."

"Is she still working? I mean, the telephone work?"

Emmy lies quietly, looking at the ceiling. "No," she says slipping back to her whisper.

He asks, "Has she found another job?" although it isn't the question he has in mind.

"She has another phone job, you know, a real one."

"Good," he says.

"I don't think," Emmy begins whispering but then stops.

Ethan waits, looking at get well cards and a stuffed toy bald eagle on the bedside table.

"I don't think I'm going to do that sex phone any more. It's dumb," she says in her new normal voice.

"Good idea," he says, continuing to look away, hearing he's

whispering. After his breathing steadies, he says, "Lucy would like to know that."

Emmy says, "Don't you tell her. I will, when she comes later."

"Okay," he says, as if it were something by the way.

When he gets up to leave, Emmy says, "I know you wanted me to tell her."

"I certainly did." When he kisses her cheek, it still feels like her cheekbone.

On the evening before he leaves for the hunt, Ethan and Lucy are driving back from dinner downtown with Augusto Chimayo, the old Hispano painter, and his wife Marisa. "Your friends are very nice," he says. "I think, with these two, that must make eight, new to me, we've seen in the past few weeks."

Lucy says, "They all want to know how I'm getting on during Emmy's recovery."

Ethan turns out of Old Town onto Lomas Boulevard. "We never see the Alvarado's, socially."

"No," Lucy says. "Carlos is always busy with social functions and trips for the University and the Institute."

"I see," he says, neutrally.

"Besides, Celia tends to socialize within the old Hispano families."

"Ah, an *hidalga* snob."

"I don't know about snob," she says, "but don't ever call Carlos an *hidalgo* to his face."

"Why, he doesn't strike me as modest."

Lucy laughs. "He's not. '*Hidalgo*' is a term for the *minor* Spanish aristocracy. Carlos claims his ancestors were related to the Dukes of Albuquerque, or Al*bur*querque, as he calls them."

Ethan smiles, but he sees Lucy won't say anything about Carlos and her and Emmy. Since he'll be leaving early from Copper Place, he doesn't stay long at the house. At the door, Lucy says, "Say something to make me feel happy."

He could tell her about his triumph over Dixon at the swimming pool, but that would involve so much editing that he wouldn't feel good. He says, "I'm feeling good about the inanity of Meyer's calls. His 'Ethan, I'm so happy with Yang.' Or, 'Hello, Ethan. You have no idea how happy I am with Yang. I had no idea I could be so happy.' Yesterday, I called him, determined to have a more adult conversation content. Yang Chou answered, and I found myself saying, 'I have to tell you, you make my father very happy.' And what I got for this was Yang saying, 'Meyer makes me very happy. I can't believe how happy he makes me.' And rather than making me feel slightly sick, all this made me feel happy." He feels foolish having said this, knowing what Lucy wanted was for him to say he loved her.

Lucy, meantime, smiles, squeezes his hand, and wishes him a safe trip.

As he drives to Valles Caldera next morning, he tries to maintain a neutral attitude to hunting elk, an animal he knows must these days be culled. The trouble is he also knows about the hunting of elk, having prepared for the trip by reading articles on how to get your elk in several hunting magazines that advertise the rifles and bullets and bugles and scents and clothing and field glasses and all-track vehicles with which to get him, and him it is, since what any respectable hunter wants is the rack of antlers. By the time Ethan turns through the open gate into the Valle Grande side of the caldera, he feels less a guest than a spy battling his revulsion.

He stops a few yards in, where a man in a cowboy hat, a wrangler, jumps out of an open Wrangler and asks his name. When Ethan gives it, the wrangler asks if Ethan would mind showing him a photo ID. Ethan hands him his driving license. The man hands it back with an embarrassed mutter about "havin' to look after security," as if being shot by someone of the wrong ilk would irk the elk.

He hands Ethan an envelope. "My name's Fred. Work for the outfit that owns this place and runs it as summer pasture. This here has your huntin' stamps and tag and a license for one mature bull elk."

"I'm only shooting video," says Ethan.

"Yes, sir. I'm just here to see everyone has what's needed. You'll want to go out there to the camp." He points towards several dots in the great distance. Ethan stares at the view of meadows, inner mountains, and, beyond, the scalloped rims of extinct volcanoes.

He drives the track remembering the last time he's seen this, standing outside the fence with Emmy, when everything seemed going so well for her.

Fifteen minutes later, he arrives at the camp. The summer cattle have been replaced by a herd of four-by-fours: pickup trucks, a cream-colored Land Rover with gold trim, and, the bull, a camouflage colored Hummer. Black ATV's nose among the larger stock like calves. Out beside the further end of the two split-log camp buildings are two barn-sized trucks, one refrigerated, the other an electricity generator from which cables run like lines of a milking machine. Ethan stands by his duffel bag, indulging the over-extension of his metaphor.

A voice behind him says, "Hey, you must be Ethan."

Ethan turns, smiling, and stops. It's the man with a black ponytail who beat him up.

"Bud Brandon," the man says, putting out his hand. "Nice to meet you."

Ethan wonders: fight or flight? He's doing neither. He's shaking the man's hand and rationalizing that he only supervised his beating.

Brandon says, "Anything wrong?"

"No," Ethan says, "just trying to place you. Haven't we met before?"

Brandon shakes his head. "No. I have a good memory for faces."

Before or after you remodel them? thinks Ethan. Suddenly, hands clamp down on his shoulders from behind. For a moment, Ethan thinks of jabbing back his elbows: he won't let Brandon direct another beating without a fight. The hands come off his shoulders and Alvarado comes around in a cowboy hat, checked shirt, boots and sunny smile.

"Ethan, you made it! Wonderful! A thousand welcomes to Valles Caldera. Have you met Bud? Bud is one of Albuquerque's big shakers and movers, as well as a major philanthropist, though he's too modest to speak of it."

"We've just met," Ethan says, the grin stuck to his face like a bug to a windshield. It is Alvarado, more than Brandon, who outrages him.

Alvarado says, "I'll show you to the bunkhouse."

Ethan nods to his new buddy, Bud. It doesn't matter that Alvarado couldn't know he remembers Brandon from the beating: Alvarado's cheerfulness in introducing him to Brandon is arrogant and sadistic. He says, "I was already aware of Bud's philanthropy."

"How's that?" Alvarado asks, giving away nothing.

"His name is on the mental health building where Doc N works."

"Of course," says Alvarado, holding the porch door open.

He shows Ethan his room, one of four small separate rooms with its own bathroom, the other half of the building still a bunkhouse.

The 'hunt wranglers,' as Alvarado calls them, sleep there. Alvarado says, "I'll leave you to settle in. Come over to the cookhouse when you're through. We'll have lunch and then go out on a little reconnaissance drive, a good way for you to see some of the caldera."

Ethan watches Alvarado go off in his cowboy gear. At least he said lunch, not "rustle us up some grub." Ethan has the urge to groan or laugh out loud at how unreal this seems: the wooded mountains out his window like a painted set from summer stock for Brandon and Alvarado, these caricatures.

Half an hour later, Ethan walks over to the cookhouse. It's one long room inside, with a kitchen at one end, a dining table in the middle and at the other end a sitting area. This is made up of a number of elk horn armchairs around a stone fireplace. The dining table is two smoothed split logs, and the kitchen is stainless steel, connected to the power lines from outside, professional looking, probably rented in. Two chefs are working, dressed in white, with chef's hats. As Ethan adjusts himself between antlers, another man in white appears, without a hat, and asks if he'd like anything to drink before lunch. Ethan asks for a vodka and tonic. A wrangler comes in and lights the already laid fire. The waiter, or kitchen hand, or sous-wrangler, brings him a large vodka and tonic and sets it and a dish of green olives on the antler side table. As he walks away, another man comes in through the main door. Of average height, with short hair in patchy beige and white, like blown snow on sand, he has small eyes and a snub nose and the walk of a young man, but as he comes up to Ethan, he appears to be older, even seventy, seventy going on fifty-one, Ethan decides. "Hey feller," he says. "Roly Everets. You must be Ethan."

Ethan stands and puts out his hand. Everets looks at the hand as if it were some quaint folkway he once knew, and as Ethan says, "Nice to meet you,' Everets touches his hand with his own, but first and middle finger only. He glances at Ethan and tips his head back with a small snort, as if he finds Ethan too tall, not up to some standard.

Ethan says, "I'm sure I've heard your name recently, and not from Carlos."

"Well, my name gets around some," Everets says with a small smile.

"What is it that you do, sir?"

"Roly will do fine. I run a little outfit called TriRock."

"Of course," Ethan says, feeling foolish and angry.

"I'm an old friend of Lucy Evans. A great gal. Sorry to hear about the little trouble with Emmy."

Little trouble? The man should have his mouth washed with soap. "I believe you knew Lucy's first husband."

"And his dad. Augie Walsh was a great man. Perry was a nice guy, of course, but a little unworldly."

Ethan picks up his drink. "Wasn't it you who introduced Lucy to Willy Dixon?"

"Carlos tells me you're not going to hunt. I hope you're not one of these anti-hunting jerks."

Ethan can give as good a non-sequitur as the next man. "I'm here to take audio-video notes for the text I'm writing for a book of Charlie Lavery's photos."

"Glass of water, no ice," Everets calls at the kitchen. "Charles Lavery is one surly son of a bitch. You going to write about my poor exploited miners?"

"I hadn't known that you exploited them. Thanks for the tip."

Everets peers at Ethan. "Ha!" he says, by way of a laugh.

Ethan sits. Everets takes the water from the server, the servant—Ethan decides they are surrounded by servants—and slowly drinks it down. He puts the glass on the table and sits. "I never drink until before dinner. It's okay for a young man like yourself or Brandon. I take it you've met Carlos's weird protégé? But at my age, no can do. Carlos shouldn't, either, but he does, damned show-off." He glances out a window: "Still, it should be fine hunting. Hope the rain front keeps off. That wouldn't matter to you; you're not hunting."

"I hope it keeps off, too. And I promise to keep out of everyone's way."

The door opens and Brandon and Alvarado come in laughing.

Alvarado calls out, "There you are. Good. Now you've met everyone."

Everets turns to Ethan. "My name for Carlos is '*Duque*'; that's duke in Spanish." Everets pronounces it dookey.

"After the Dukes baseball team?" Ethan asks.

"No," Alvarado says. "My friend Roly is fascinated by my coming from an old family."

Everets says, "The hell I am. I call him *Duque* to remind him that some of us have made it on our own."

Alvarado says, "And I say that making it as a family over the generations is in many ways more estimable. But now I want to say that you're all very welcome. We should have been six, but at the last moment Juan de Suarez and Bob Hildebrand had to pull out. Shall we sit down for lunch?"

Everets stands and says, "I'll tell you, Ethan, before he does, that Suarez is the Spanish Consul and Bob Hildebrand's the Lieutenant Governor."

During this conversation, Brandon has loomed in the background, but as Alvarado and Everets go to the table, he comes up to Ethan and says, "A couple of years ago, when Roly heard this place might be on the market, he made an offer of a hundred and twenty-five million dollars for it. Not TriRock, his own private offer. You hear what I'm saying?"

"Loud and clear," says Ethan.

The lunch is chili, cornbread, and pitchers of ale. "I'm sticking to water," Everets says, towards the end, when a large bowl of fruit appears. "It's only the Hummer I want gassed-up this afternoon." He turns his head and shouts, "Fine chili, cooky."

Ethan says, "It's the best I've ever eaten, Carlos. Do the cooks work for the ranch?"

Alvarado smiles. "No, *Dios*! The cowboys up here in the summer live on canned food and maybe some fruit and bread in from Los Alamos. No, I bring in the cooks, the kitchen, the whole works."

Brandon says, "And it's always the best."

Everets says, "I have to admit old *Duque* treats us damned well."

"*Señor*," says Alvarado, acknowledging the compliment with a bow of his head.

Ethan says, "I take it I'm the only one who hasn't been here before."

"That's right," Alvarado says.

Everets says, "You and the Pope. *Duque*, what was his excuse for not coming this year?"

Alvarados says, "Ethan, I'll explain the topography of the caldera to you in under two minutes."

Everets is chuckling: "The Pope's excuse," he says. "Not bad, is it? That nails you fairly, *Duque*. Not the mackerel-snapper business but the name-dropping."

Alvarado says, "It was you, I believe, who told Ethan who Suarez and Hildebrand were."

Everets says, "That's not the point. But forget it, *Duque*. We're here for the great American pursuit of elk and some fun. And you, Ethan? Baum, isn't it? A German name, so you're probably, what, Lutheran?"

"Jewish."

"Really," Everets nods. "Some of my best—stockholders are Jewish."

Ethan sees Everets laugh silently, his face creasing in bunched, fine lines. He looks two hundred years old.

Alvarado stands. "Half the oldest Catholic families in the state are Jewish *conversos*. Coffee, everyone?"

Everets pours half a glass of water and says to Ethan, "You know a joke when you hear one?"

"I do. When I hear one."

Brandon lights a big cigar.

Alvarado returns with coffee on a tray. "Right," he says, turning to Ethan, "the quick topography of Valles Caldera. Imagine a double ring of volcanic mountains. The outer one is a continuous volcanic rim with a diameter of ten miles. The inner one is a more irregular circle of rounded volcanic cores, with the highest, Redondo Peak, over eleven thousand feet. In between these inner mountains are meadows. Woods cover most of the mountains and go up high on the outer rim. The pattern is most obvious from the northeast to southeast half of the circle. We're sitting in Valle Grande, the biggest grassland valley in the caldera, on its southeast side. And I take it you know what 'caldera' means."

"A cauldron," Ethan says. He thinks it a fair description of the four of them, as well as the geology.

"One minute and forty seconds," says Brandon, "including your question to Ethan."

Alvarado says, "So much for the lecture. Now, the good part—the field trip."

Walking from the bunkhouse forty minutes later, Ethan is joined by Brandon. "See the guy by the Hummer? That's Russell, Roly's driver. He drove down from Denver. Roly came by helicopter."

Ethan refuses to ask if it was Everets' private helicopter. Everets might well have an option on the sky. Ethan is put in the front, since he's new to the place. Everets and Alvarado sit behind, and Brandon is in the next row back. There's room to spare; the vehicle could take, for instance, a squad of fully armed infantry, the instance for which it was originally designed.

They head northeast over the Valle Grande grasslands. Ethan works on steadying his camcorder. After a few minutes, he stops and simply looks at the sweep of meadows and hills, gold and green spurs of aspen slanting down off the mountains.

Brandon says, "Hey, Ethan, you can get better shots when your camera stays still and what's out in front of you is moving. I know from taking videos of my kids."

Everets says, "Bud, he might have figured that out all on his own."

Ethan says, "And all of this will be a national park?"

"Correct," Everets says, "and the tourists will ruin it."

Alvarado says, "Russell, take the left track up here. We'll cut across the Jemez East Fork and go over into Valle San Antonio. Don't you think, Roly?"

"That's good," Everets says.

Ethan turns on the audio recorder as Alvarado says, "Valle San Antonio is where bull elk are most likely. Do you know anything about hunting elk, Ethan?"

"No, nothing." There's no point in mentioning his research.

Brandon says, "Well, I've been hunting them fifteen years, and I know maybe one or two things more than nothing. You wouldn't think such big, dumb things could be so hard to get."

They cross the Jemez River at a deep ford; the water wings up on both sides of the Hummer. Ethan looks back at the long J of the river, perfectly smooth again, its surface all sky and cloud. They head uphill on a rougher track.

Alvarado says, "What Bud says is true. Here's a typical elk story, Ethan. Two years ago, December, I was hunting up out of Vernejo Park Ranch. I was out day after day following a big bull on foot, in clothing I kept dousing with elk cow piss. I smelt disgusting, except, hopefully, to bull elks. Finally, third day, I have a perfect seventy-yard broadside shot on the bull, the middle of its lungs on the crosshairs of my sight. And the perfect rifle, a Harris titanium rifle with a .300

Win. Magnum bullet. And just as I start squeezing the trigger, there's this tremendous Bang! And the bull was gone. I thought it must be another hunter. But no, I look up at the mountain and see the long white waterfall of an avalanche that had chosen that instant to crack off. Let alone not getting another shot in, I didn't get to *see* another decent bull that year."

Brandon says, "See what I mean?"

Everets says, "Carlos, you are full of elk shit. I've hunted elk all my life. Mostly, I come back with pretty good bull elk racks. No big deal."

Alvarado says, "I hope we'll be lucky."

"Lucky?" says Everets. "This place has a herd of six or seven thousand elk. I saw them all over the place from the helicopter, yesterday. What more luck do you need, except wanting to shoot them through the fence at a zoo?"

Ethan says, "Will we see elk this afternoon?"

"Of course," says Brandon. "Because we haven't got our guns."

Just after ten that night, cell phone in hand, Ethan sits on the edge of his bed about to call Lucy. It is difficult to choose what to tell her from all the images of the afternoon's drive and walks. It isn't made easier by his being drunk and queasy from too much good wine and food.

He pictures the old volcano rims blunt as molars, and driving the forty degree slopes up basalt and down into bogs. That was when Everets mentioned a project at Jemez Springs and Alvarado said, "No business this hunt. Remember, Roly?" Then they walked onto a ridge between two volcanic rims and saw down its back slope a huge herd of elk, a five hundred acre carpet of elk. Through his field glasses, if he kept to the right height, the antlers looked like a forest of slow-moving branches. He pictures Alvarado holding up a squeeze bottle, a puff of powder up from it to get the direction of a wind too faint to feel. And then they walked through woods and heard the trumpeting and looked down on two bull elk, one on the creek bank, head down....

Ethan puts his head down between his hands. He pictures looking at his video viewer. The elk on the creek bank moved his antlers into the antlers of the elk standing in the creek below him Their trumpeting changed to hoarse roars. Their heads twisted sideways as they fought, standing stock still, pushing with shoulder muscles thick and knotted.

He remembers whispering to Everets how enormous they were and Everets saying they were only young bulls still hot in rut; the mature bulls wouldn't let them near the cows. He could tell Lucy how elated he felt at the sight of these bulls and how depressed at the thought of their being shot. Or how he fell into exhausted sleep the minute he got back into the Hummer.

He could tell her about Alvarado at dinner replying to his question about the nearest villages to the north, Coyote and Arroyo del Aqua, a story about how Alvarado's mother took him up there sixty-five years ago to have him cured of whooping cough by a *bruja*, a witch. Everets asked if it worked and Alvarado answered, "Am I here?" Alvarado remembered the *bruja* in long red and yellow skirts and gold bangles, the cramped room stinking of incense; there was a stuffed black raven which frightened him, Santos and *retablos* on the walls, and large jars full of pink-gray meaty things. The *bruja* cast bones, probably chicken bones, but for years he believed they were the bones of children she didn't like. "*Jesu, Dios!*" he laughed. "And my mother, God bless her, with her doctorate in Spanish believing in the *bruja*." He said that's why he loved this place. "Where but in New Mexico?"

He could tell Lucy about this and the lobster dinner with all those wines and hunting stories, Brandon saying you could spook an elk with a silent fart at half a mile or with the sound of a drop of snot falling to your lip, Alvarado adding that after all this, if you didn't get a perfectly clean shot, you could forget elk for that day, and Everets laughing at them tight-lipped, calling them two world class bullshitters.

Ethan lies back on the bed and lets go the cell phone as he falls asleep. He dreams of the click-click of antlers hitting. Above him, the tree sways; across the street is the spaceship house. Brandon, with Lucy behind him, watches. The tree is falling on him.

Ethan opens his eyes and hears Brandon's steady snoring through the wall. After dinner, Brandon showed him wallet photos of his wife and children. How many people has Brandon killed himself? Not as many as Alvarado has, second-hand, and this is a number insignificant to all that Everets has killed third-hand. Yet they do not love their loved ones less than he does his Meyer and Lucy and Emmy. Perhaps more. All of us men, he thinks, are so discontinuous, are such fractured animals. He stumbles to the bathroom to be sick.

At five the next morning, in the dark, in the light rain, Ethan collapses into the back of the Hummer, his head back over the seat top, his feet resting on the piled cargo of rifle cases, bullet boxes, canteens, food packs, field glasses and cartons of who-knows-what elk-kill esoterica. He hasn't called Lucy. He hasn't wanted to call Lucy. He feels better admitting it. He feels terrible. He watches the others direct the loading of the Jeep Wrangler and four ATV's. What more could they be lugging out for the hunt—rocket launchers? He pats the camcorder at his side and the field glasses hanging on his blaze vest. He's done his research and is proud of his blaze vest: no one could mistake him for an elk. Even at a distance, even if they called in an air strike with F-16's.

Alvarado gets in front. "You don't need the blaze vest. We're the only hunters on these hundred square miles."

Russell gets in behind the wheel, the other two in the seat behind, and they start off, followed by the five other vehicles. "Beaters" is the word Ethan has been searching for. Why shouldn't they have hundreds of locals beating the elk towards them? Or a *punk wallah*? No, that's the guy in India who works the giant fan. It's too cold up here for a *punk wallah*.

Everets says, "Am I the only one hung over? There's a drum beating inside my head."

Ethan says, "I'm inside that drum."

"Here," Everets says, passing back a tube.

Ethan says, "It looks like black grease."

Everets says, "It's black grease. Put it on your hands and face and on any shiny part of your camera. And if we're near elk and you have to pee, turn away. We don't want them spooked by our little white peckers."

Alvarado says, "Little? White? Speak for yourself, *hombre*."

Oh yes, three days of dirty boy-talk, too. Ethan blacks the back of his hand and braces against the track bumps.

Minutes later, Alvarado hands back coffee. Brandy wafts from the metal cup.

Alvarado asks, "What ammo are you using, Bud?"

"A .338 magnum bullet, hand packed cartridge."

Everets says, "We should get closer than to have to use that."

"My hunch is my hunch," says Brandon.

The sweet, heavily laced coffee is soothing. Everets, who never drinks before evening, drinks it, too. They bump along under the mountains of San Antonio Creek. At last, they pull up at the side of a bog. Pale, milky light comes up as the three hunters kit themselves from the back of the Hummer. The ATV's roar off. Rain billows from the ridge. The ranch wrangler, Fred, walks away, and then the four of them start trekking to the ridge. Soon after they reach the trees, Fred appears and says he's made out some cow elk over to the northeast. Everets thinks the big bulls will be further east, up the side canyon towards Cerro Toledo. They sit on wet, fallen trees and have coffee and then trek on.

Ethan practices using his camcorder as they move east and higher. They stop for coffee and sandwiches before reaching the ridge. The north wind picks up and the rain comes down steadily. Fred leaves to return to the vehicles. No one says anything about the rain. The views through the breaks in the trees are of clouds lying below them on both sides of the ridge. They walk through green and yellow leaves of aspen in the rain, through lichen-covered pine, their lower branches patchy, bare, dripping. They stop for lunch. Ethan assumes it's around nine. His watch says noon. Six hours of viewless plod.

Alvarado passes a flask of brandy. Everets and Ethan give it a pass. There's coffee and water, and they eat their sandwiches, rolling back the paper as they bite to keep them dry. They finish, get up off the wet tree trunks and continue going east, into a side canyon.

They reach its upper end after three o'clock. Everets, in the lead, puts up his hand, and they come up carefully behind him and set the field glasses at where Everets is glassing. Ethan looks at trees and below that, clouds. Alvarado whispers, "A big bull, about a thousand yards to the right, in the trees just off the ridge." Ethan still can't find it. Everets begins to bugle. Ethan remembers that bugles make the sound of a young bull, so that a mature bull in the area will respond to the challenge. Everets continues to bugle. The other three squat in the rain. Drip, spatter. Drip, drip, spatter. Everets signals to move on. There's no use getting more video of tree trunks in the rain.

Alvarado steps beside Ethan and whispers, "He should have used an estrus cow call. I'm sure the rut is still on more than Roly thinks. But it's his elk, his call." Ethan nods at the pun and moves on. Ahead, Everets moves faster and loses them. Then Alvarado signals Brandon and Ethan to stop. The three sit on a fallen pine. As he glasses, Alvarado points. Ethan glasses: trees, branches, branches. He glasses back. A tree is moving sideways. Its antlers the size of a small tree. He can see Everets standing beside a pine, a few hundred yards past the bull elk. Then Everets moves and Ethan loses sight of him and the bull. A few minutes later, Everets bugles. The three have another coffee. Ethan doesn't lace his. Brandon and Alvarado drink straight from the flask.

Half an hour later, Everets appears and sits on the fallen pine. "He was in my sights but head on. A Boone and Crockett trophy monster. But that bad angle and at a hundred and seventy five yards, forget it. When I started to work around him, he bolted off. I didn't hear or see a thing in the rain. Just bad luck."

Brandon says, "No, he just acted like a bull elk, thought of something better to do—get laid or pick a fight with a smaller bull he remembered was someplace else."

Alvarado says, "I think you should have used an estrus cow call. But he still might have bolted. No predicting with *señor* elk."

Everets twists the thinnest smile. "Give me a break. Of course there's predicting. Ninety-nine out of a hundred times I would have worked around and got that elk. Now there's not enough daylight left to track him down and up the other side of the canyon."

Alvarado opens his map and points. "We're about here."

"No," Everets says, leaning, knocking the map with his knuckle, "we're exactly here. Or are you going to tell me there's no way of knowing with *señor* map?"

"No," says Alvarado.

"Or maybe we should cast chicken bones to find out where we are?"

Ethan reads Alvarado's smile as saying, What can you do with such an ill-bred Anglo?

Brandon says, "Okay, Roly, we get the point. You can read a fucking map." He gets up and stretches, big as a ponderosa.

"Too bad, Roly," Alvarado says. "Better luck tomorrow."

Everets says, "Sure. Let's call the Hummer to come around the bottom of Cerro Toledo Canyon." He turns to Ethan. "Well, feller, not much of a day for your camera, but you'll have fun tomorrow when you're covered in estrus elk-cow piss."

Ethan smiles. This is Everets lightening up, apologizing to Alvarado. As they walk off after the call for the vehicle, Everets mutters, "Damned rain."

Back at camp, Ethan takes a long, hot shower. Then he goes to the cookhouse and returns with a whiskey. He stretches on the bed and recalls Everets talking about elk piss. The cold, flat voice. Perhaps Everets was Lucy's lover. Why not? Everets and Alvarado, two powerful old men. Does Lucy look for father figures? For that matter, does he? What these two have in common with Meyer is achievement, self-confidence, vanity, and, different as they are, a way of putting him down. If he thinks of it as being attracted to overpowering father figures, it sounds lunatic. He doesn't want to call Lucy. Did Everets introduce her to nice, "unworldly" Perry? Perry Walsh. Emmy calls herself Evans. Did Lucy leave Perry because he wasn't strong enough? Did Perry leave Lucy when he learned Emmy was Carlos's?

He sits up and calls Lucy, feeling he must, unhappy feeling it. "It's me," is all he can say when she answers the phone.

Lucy says. "You didn't call last night, so I took it you were having a fine time with the boys."

"Boys?" he says, knowing she's making an effort to please. "Last night it was more the fine wine than fine time. Today has been solid rain, so it's been long drives, long walks, and no views. The only good news is that it's also been no elk. And now I'm back in camp Mucho Macho."

Lucy laughs. "Who's there?"

"Besides me and Carlos, a big bruiser called Bud Brandon, and someone who knows you — Roly Everets."

"Oh, Roly," she says. "What do you think of him?"

Now he knows she's making an effort, one she often makes, to hide. "So far, I think he's awful, a walking sneer. But I'm sure I can get to like him less."

"He's not that bad, is he?"

Ethan sips whiskey. "He said he knew your late ex. Remind me again why you split up?"

There is a slight pause. Yes, there should be a slight pause here, he thinks.

"There's no 'remind' and no 'again' about it, Ethan," Lucy says with what he hears as a metallic ring to her voice. "I've never discussed it with you. We grew away from each other. I became more involved with writing, and Perry wanted to continue the life of a rich outdoorsman, jetting from one mountain range to another. That's a way of putting it."

"What way?"

"The way of putting it to an angry idiot on his cell phone!"

He says, "My love to—" But she hangs up before he can say "Emmy." He's pleased with this. It justifies his anger. It proves... But what it proves, he doesn't know, other than he succeeded in provoking it.

The next day, in a misty dawn, Alvarado and Everets decide to split in pairs, to have Ethan go off with Carlos, leaving the other two to split up as they will. As they start walking from the same place as the day before, Alvarado says, "There are two more days, but it would be wonderful if we got three great bull elk today and had tomorrow just for bragging and drinking. *Hombres*, good hunting."

But only the elk have it good, and perhaps Ethan, who becomes proficient with his camcorder. As the light comes through the mist, Alvarado picks up the pace, moving up the northeast side of Cerro Toledo Canyon. An hour later, when he stops for a five-minute coffee break, Ethan is soaked with sweat. Alvarado says, "Not bad, is it, for seventy-one?" Ethan says, "No," thinking it's even better for the seventy-five that Alvarado is. When they start out again, Alvarado flashes the grand smile: "This is the day. I can feel it."

He walks even faster. What is to Ethan a breakneck hour or so later, he catches up to Alvarado, who whispers that he's spotted a big bull down to the west, marking a tree at the edge of a clearing. He doubts if Ethan's field glasses will pick up what his 10x50 Leica will. They walk on. Alvarado stops and bugles. The bull immediately bugles back. Alvarado says that because they're doused in a solution of estrus elk-cow urine, he doesn't want to risk the bull getting the scent and being confused about the bugling, so they move south on the slope to keep downwind. At the lower elevation, Alvarado loses sight of the bull and bugles. Two bulls bugle back.

Alvarado now decides to go higher, change to a cow call, and hope the bulls catch the scent. The mist begins to burn off. They climb for thirty minutes. Alvarado is by now half jogging. He topples over a log. Ethan rushes up, but Alvarado impatiently waves him away. "Damn right knee went on me there. I'm fine." He stands, rubs the knee and walks on with a slight limp. He stops at a tree to glass. "Good," he whispers, "one of them is backing off." He blows the cow bugle. A bull answers. He says, "Walk down in that direction. I'm getting there fast."

Ethan videos him running down the northern slope. Then Ethan walks down. Ten minutes later, he spots Alvarado down behind a log. Ethan crouches and comes up carefully behind him until he can make out that Alvarado isn't aiming the rifle. He's sitting with his back against the log, grimacing. "Damn," he says, seeing Ethan, "damned old man's vanity, thinking I could sprint on this terrain. The knee went and I fell hard. The knee feels like shit. There's some good spray for it back at camp, but no more chasing the great American elk today. Damn, and look at this beautiful weather come in. I've already called. Fred's bringing the Land Rover in about a mile down there on San Antonio Creek. Give me a hand, *hombre*." Ethan helps him up.

"I hope you haven't videoed me in my damned dotage out here."

"The last shot I have of you is running off through the trees like — like an elk."

"Not the trophy I wanted," says Alvarado, pleased. Then he concentrates on getting down to the creek, arm over Ethan's shoulder.

The two of them eat their packed lunch mid-afternoon on the cookhouse porch. The sky is a dense cobalt blue. Alvarado has sprayed his knee; Fred has strapped it. "The others have to do better," says Alvarado. "At least I spotted a good bull. Sometimes you know the elk are all around, but you just can't see or hear one. It's like an enchantment, as if elk were mythical beasts from a golden age." He pulls at his moustache. "Let's say there are six or seven thousand on the place now. We know they're in the northeastern section of the caldera, on maybe ten thousand acres. But half of that is rocks, cliffs, and outcrop. Of course they're not spread evenly, but that makes one elk per acre. Have we seen one per acre? In two days hunting we've seen two over three or four thousand acres. Two! See what I mean, Ethan, I love it, hunting dumb, brute beasts who are much smarter at this business than we are."

Ethan says, "It's what they do, isn't it? I mean, do everything to stay alive."

"Certainly. But not tomorrow, *hombre*, not if the others come back without elk."

The others come back without elk. They come into the cookhouse at six-thirty, as Ethan and Alvarado are having their first pre-dinner scotch. Everets goes to the fireplace and looks at the fire with his hands in his pockets. He says, still with his back to the others, "I've figured out what's happening, though I hate to admit it because it's way too smart for elk." He turns. He looks as if he's sucked lemons all afternoon. "You tell them, Bud. It would get me too pissed."

Brandon pours a large whiskey and sits. "We made good time this morning, got up to the northern boundary fence and followed it west, and I shit you not, gentlemen, all the elk we saw, and we saw lots, cows and bulls, too, were out of the open gate areas. I mean off the property, on posted land. I swear we did not see elk on this side of the fence."

Everets turns from the drinks table and drops an ice cube into his whiskey. He says, "We made it to five—one-two-three-four-five—open gate areas and saw the same scene at each. The elk must have been drifting up that way since we arrived. And now, wouldn't you know, they're on Harrison James's twenty-five thousand posted acres. Not just posted but patrolled. That old fart seriously dislikes hunting on his land, as you'll remember, Carlos."

Alvarado says, "I'll tell you what we're going to do about that, my friend. We'll have some drinks and then have a first class dinner and drink the Montrachet I was saving to celebrate our trophy elk, and that will inspire us in planning and executing tomorrow's completely successful hunt."

Ethan leaves the other three toasting death to elk. He sits with his whiskey out on the porch, on a rocking chair. The air is clear and cold. The sky is dark enough to show the stars; to the west, the last reflected sunlight is deep greenish-purple. A large low quarter-moon sits over the mountains to the south. He takes out his cell phone and calls Lucy. She says, "Hello," very quietly.

"Greetings from the happily still elkless hunt. I'm outside, for better reception and to avoid some of the battle execution planning for tomorrow. I'll be back the day after. Will you want to see me?"

"Grow up, Ethan; of course I will."

Wary of the direction the conversation is going, he uses a surefire diversion: "How's Emmy doing?"

"She's doing pretty well. She asked—no prompting from me—about having her feed tubes removed so she could do it herself. She said she promised the doctor they could watch her eat."

"That's a relief," he says. The rest of their conversation is easy, a relief. When it ends, he considers what it meant. It meant keeping his options open.

He goes inside and joins the others at the table. Alvarado is saying to Everets, "Of course, if your helicopter did nudge some bulls back into the caldera, I wouldn't shoo them away."

He doesn't sit around drinking after dinner. He goes to bed trying to think of something to put all the how-to-kill-an-elk talk from his mind. Before he can, Ethan falls asleep.

Next morning, as they drive off before dawn doused in a solution of pine and estrus elk cow urine, Brandon booms out from the back of the Hummer, "The only thing we haven't done is dress up in elk cow costumes."

Alvarado says, "We don't have to. We're already getting fucked by the bulls."

"Good one, *Duque*," says Everets. "Pretty good."

The hummer is moving too fast over the grasslands; everyone has to use both hands to brace.

Everets says to Alvarado, "The helicopter's coming in from the north. By the time it reaches the caldera, the ATV's will be in place along the fence line."

Brandon says, "You better hush up, Roly, or you'll get Ethan crying up there over the elk."

Sticks and stones, Ethan thinks. But Brandon has already had a good crack at his bones.

They drive as high up San Antonio Creek as the Hummer can go. Ethan gets out and videos the line of dark red dawn come up over the rim of the Sierra de los Valles like a cut in the sky. When Everets and Brandon go off, Alvarado says, "My friend, you are going to get some great shots of a man getting a first-class bull elk."

"That's what I'm here for," says Ethan. He sets out after Alvarado, who walks off fast, without a limp.

The weather is perfect. Ethan records the shallow amphitheater of mountainside they walk to in the early, milk-blue light. He shoots Alvarado stopping to phone, offering the brandy flask, telling him most of the elk have been reported back inside the perimeter fence, testing the wind with a puff of talc and pronouncing it "Perfect, light from the south. Our scent will drive them wild, right into us." Ethan swings the camcorder up the slope and catches the sun bursting over the rim from a cloudless, high blue sky. Later, in an upland of small hills and hollows, he turns the lens on his own smeared, smiling face.

Time after time in the next two hours, Alvarado motions Ethan down, takes a stand, and bugles. Then he glasses. He alternates cow calls with young bull bugles. Nothing answers. But just before eleven, his bugling brings a high answering bugle that breaks into a heavy roar, and Ethan shoots Alvarado running up to a stand of ponderosa and bugling again. The answering call comes from further away. When Ethan reaches him, Alvarado is on his cell phone. He says, "*Merda*, don't tell me that. Stay there, we're on our way." He looks at Ethan. "The fucking animals are walking out of Valles Caldera through the open gates."

"I don't understand," says Ethan.

Turning in his near jog, Alvarado calls back, "Neither do I, but evidently the elk understand the grass to be greener on the other side of the fence." Alvarado moves quickly out of sight.

Half an hour later, he catches up with Alvarado at an ATV on which brush and branches have been heaped as camouflage. Fred, the ranch wrangler, appears and leads them up a steep slope to the edge of a clearing at an open, thirty-foot wide gate. And there, on the other side, are the elk. Ethan changes cassettes and keeps recording. Alvarado, behind his field glasses, says, "I want one. Just one bull from those hundreds of elk making fun of me out there. *Madre de Dios!*"

They go back down to the ATV and have lunch with Fred. Alvarado drinks two coffees half-filled with brandy. He makes a phone call and then tells Ethan that Everets and Brandon are two gates east, watching an enormous bull disappear down the wrong side of the fence. Five minutes later, he phones again and reports that Everets says Brandon is on to a good bull just this side of the fence. Alvarado walks up the slope to the clearing and returns and says, "Fred, why don't you drive the ATV through the gate and herd a couple hundred elk back this side?"

Fred does not find this funny. He puts down his bar of chocolate and says, "Sir. I'd lose my job. My boss is good friends with Mr. James, the owner of the land over there. We shouldn't even think of goin' beyond the fence."

Alvarado smiles. "I'm only kidding. Fred, take the ATV back down the ridge, west about a mile, just to keep the elk from moving back past us."

Ethan shoots the ATV crashing away as Alvarado says, "That should keep friend Fred off our backs. I'm going through the gate and down the hill to get some elk to move back up and in here." He phones Everets and turns to Ethan. "Ha, the others are already over there doing the same."

Alvarado goes off with Ethan walking behind. Alvarado walks through the gates, passes the posted signs, crosses the clearing and goes down into the woods. Hundreds of trees there have posted signs. Alvarado keeps walking north down the slope. He turns to Ethan and says, "James's house is at least two miles from here. You know, our plan may have backfired. I'm thinking we might have spooked the elk with all the noise of the hummer and Jeep and ATV's and the damned helicopter. It seemed a good idea last night. I'm responsible, *hombre*, it's my hunt. Now we need more silence and patience. You cannot hurry a big bull elk."

Half an hour later, when Alvarado stops, they hear distant bugling from bulls. Alvarado bugles, but the direction of the elk bugling isn't clear. "Lots of bulls around," Alvarado whispers. Ethan doesn't understand how the bugling will move the elk back through the gate. Alvarado bugles again, and the returning bugle comes from directly down before them, from trees across a meadow. Ethan pans the camcorder to take in the sweep of the slope and the pink-orange cliffs in the distance. Alvarado taps Ethan's shoulder and points. Through his field glasses, Ethan sees the elk just out before the trees, close enough to video.

It lifts its head and bugles up at them, the bottom of its muzzle jutted forward. The bull is huge: high, heavy muscled, thick humped. Under its big antler rack, a dark brown head, neck and forelegs; its back and flanks red gold. It moves forward into the meadow brush so that only its antlers are visible. Alvarado is raising his rifle to shoot, Ethan assumes, when the elk is passing to the side, so as to frighten it to running up to the open gate.

The bull comes out of the brush into a small clearing, looking up in their direction. It bugles, moves up some. It's now about two hundred yards away. Ethan, behind Alvarado, fixes his viewfinder along the line of the rifle. He can see Alvarado's hand around the trigger, tendons tight. When the shot comes, Ethan swings the camera to the side, hoping to catch the bull running up behind them. He sees nothing and asks, "Did you move it in the right direction?"

Alvarado says, "Are you loco? I shot it, got him right in the heart-lung area and he jumped back and out of there too fast for me to get another shot in. But he's not going far. Come on."

Alvarado runs off and immediately falls. Ethan comes to help him, astounded at what Alvarado has done and at his own naïvety in not understanding he'd always intended to do it. Alvarado says, "No, thanks. I'm okay, just excited." He looks up at Ethan. "Hey, *hombre*, I saw my chance and took it." He stands and crashes on through the meadow brush. Ethan follows at a walk. He catches up on a wooded rise, where Alvarado signals to move quietly. Up here, Ethan sees the line of a logging road about half a mile north, down the slope. Alvarado points. "*Christo!* There he goes, loping across that meadow. How can he do that with the bullet I put into him?" Behind and just to the side of Alvarado's head is a posted sign on a tree. Alvarado turns and rushes down the slope, stops, and listens to bugling. Ethan comes down. "That's him or maybe another bull," Alvarado says, and he rushes on.

Ten minutes later, Ethan finds Alvarado taking a stand at a ponderosa. His rifle comes up pointing at the bull elk. It isn't wounded. It isn't the same elk. It's the same size, but it has a smoother, light brown coat. The bull's front half is in a shaft of sunlight down through the trees, about sixty yards before them, fully side-on. The bull stands still—sniffing, looking, listening, but not figuring them out. Ethan thinks he can smell it, like rich piss and rotten straw. Alvarado shoots; Ethan sees the ruffling in the bull's flank. It goes down kneeling on its front legs. It totters up and turns. A second shot flurries its rump, but it's running off. Ethan videos the third shot shredding the bark under a posted sign. Alvarado runs downhill, pauses to reload and runs again between the trees. Ethan changes cassettes and runs after him. Alvarado squats on the pine needles, rubbing blood between his thumb and forefinger. "This bull is not going far," he says, his face red and sweaty. He stands, takes a step, and falls down. He allows Ethan to give him a hand up. "I'm fine. I fell before you came up." He rubs his bad knee and points to the blood on the ground. "Bull heaven, right here and now on Harrison James's pristine acres. We'll put the elk onto the ATV's and have them back in the caldera before anyone is wiser. But now, less haste, more speed."

Now Alvarado keeps stopping and pointing to blood on the ground, and it's easy for Ethan to keep up. Ethan walks slowly. Five minutes later, he sees Alvarado fall again.

When he gets down the hill to him, Alvarado has the stock of his rifle planted on the ground and is pulling himself up, hands on the barrel. He stands, takes two unsteady steps, and lets himself down with his back against a tree. He pulls at his moustache, making it scowl. "I don't get it," he says. "You were there. That first shot should have ripped a crater in its second lung as the bullet peeled open." Ethan remembers the shot being further back on the flank. Alvarado says, "It should have dropped him where he stood. And all he did was give me that sarcastic fucking bow. He should have at least dropped by here. Do me a favor, Ethan. Go along down and see how far we are from the logging road. I need to rest this damned knee. And if you come across my four-footed friend, hurry back with the good news."

After a few minutes of walking and sliding down the slope, Ethan sees the logging road. He hears shooting, faint to the east. When he gets to the road he sees a valley running north. Through his field glasses he makes out smoke rising from a chimney on a big house perhaps a mile away. Then he climbs back to Alvarado and tells him the only good news is the closerness of the logging road. Alvarado points down his leg. "My bad old tennis knee is swollen up. *Merda y mas merda!* No more hunting for me. Let's hope those shots meant good bulls for Roly and Bud. Ayee! What a fucking miserable beautiful day!" Ethan rests against the tree as Alvarado makes his phone calls.

Forty minutes later, he gets Alvarado down to the road, and fifteen minutes after that, the Hummer roars up. Everets and Brandon get out frowning, and with Ethan and Russell they get Alvarado stretched out on the rear seat, a rolled up towel under his bad knee. Out across the valley, bronze light streams from the low sun, and, far off, Ethan makes out the Chama Valley as dusty bands of red, orange and gold. Then he gets into the front seat and hears Everets and Brandon's sorry tales, the sum of which, with Alvarado's, amounts to four bull elk wounded on a private wildlife preserve, the three shooters hoping the elk die quickly so they won't reach where they're more likely to be found, closer to that big stone house.

On the drive back, a slow drive for Alvarado's hurt knee, they can't stop talking about it. Alvarado says, "My first shot was stupid, a head shot at two hundred yards. I probably got its shoulder, and the bull went downhill fast and I was not prepared to follow it down onto Harrison James's front porch." Brandon says, "It was fucking *raining* bull elk where we were. My problem was deciding which rack to go for. I think the one I had in my sights heard one of your shots, Carlos, and turned just as I squeezed. I put two into him, back of his side and top of his back haunch. And I would have caught up with the bastard, but he made for a bog and I was stopped a foot deep into the fucking mud." And Everets says, "I wounded a Boone and Crockett trophy, an enormous bull. And, fellers, I sincerely hope he's already met up with a bear or lion, because I do not want another lawsuit with James. The man loves nothing better than to bring San Francisco faggot lawyers out here from the Sierra Club."

And on it goes, Ethan looking out the windows at the beautiful day in the beautiful land, wishing he was anywhere else. He has recorded everything and never wants to see or hear it again.

That night, with the others, he drinks far too much. As he falls into bed, the room going liquid around him, he thinks of Everets, Alvarado and Dixon. Lucy falls only for shits. And she's fallen for him.

# III. THE PURSUIT

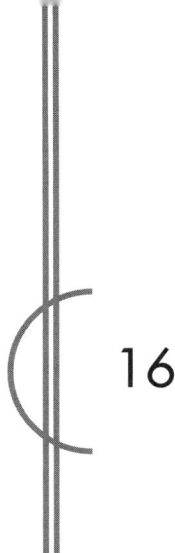

16

NEXT MORNING, ETHAN WAKES to the sound of Everets' helicopter lifting off. He's relieved to be spared a false farewell. It's ten o'clock by the time he gets to the cookhouse. Only Alvarado remains to host breakfast. The meal is quiet. From time to time, Alvarado goes over to the kitchen area to confer with the moving crew come to strike camp. As Ethan thanks Alvarado for his hospitality, Alvarado grabs his arm and says, "We acted a little wildly, foolishly, yesterday. Not the best of sportsmen. I'd appreciate you not speaking of it, my friend."

"Carlos, the less I think of it, the happier I'll be."

Ethan remembers this exchange in the afternoon, back at Copper Place, as he puts the video cassettes from the hunt in the back of his filing cabinet. Then he sits down and works on a piece from his notes on the Gila Wilderness. He stops at six, has a drink, and considers what he's going to say to Lucy; that is, what he's not going to say—that ever growing no-go zone.

As he walks up to her door, he hears the hose going along the orchard side. He walks around. Lucy, in the last light, is watering around the base of an old, raddled peach tree. She sees him and they hug.

He says, "It's good to see you."

"Do you mean that?"

"I do. I enjoy meaning it."

She squeezes him. Water from the nozzle drips onto the back of his shirt.

"You didn't have a good time up there."

"What was natural was beautiful. The rest was too fancy and

crude and awful. When I left, Carlos apologized, in his way, for how they carried on. I said I just wanted to forget it."

Ethan forgets it by making supper with Lucy—chicken with *molé*, rice and beans, and a salad. It is a pleasure to drink a decent, non-great, non-vintage wine. Ethan forgets it by making a fire in the living room and sitting peacefully before it with Lucy. He forgets it, afterwards, by making love.

Early next morning, Lucy wakes him with coffee. "I've had good news," she says, getting back into bed. "I received a letter from Willy saying he'd be out of the house and out of Albuquerque in two weeks. He's taking a job in British Columbia."

"Good."

"And he's not making a fuss about the property. He just wants his books and pots. I didn't think it would be so easy."

"Good and good riddance."

Lucy moves closer to him. She sips coffee. "What I said about Perry and me when you called the other night was only partly true. It was only partly true that the Alvarado's don't socialize with me because Celia sticks to old Hispano families. Carlos is Emmy's father. I felt I had to tell Perry. He stayed with me until Emmy was about one year old. But it became too hard for Perry and he left. He stayed friendly, though, and was always a good father to Emmy. I've never told Emmy. I've meant to, but then Perry died, and then, later, she got sick. About Carlos and me—"

"You don't have to tell me."

"I do. Carlos dazzled me. That confidence and sophistication, and there I was Miss Gawky Butte Montana. Mrs. Gawky. After Emmy was born, I couldn't continue with Carlos. I made him tell Celia about Emmy. Her response was to adopt a child and never see me again."

He says, "Thank you for—"

"As for Roly Everets: you're right. He's awful and TriRock is awful, one of the worst polluters in the country. I've thought about your impression of him and my response—that he couldn't be so bad. My double standards are tied to my love for my father. I told you he was a mining engineer for Anaconda. The engineers were company men. They were completely loyal to the bosses even while knowing, scientifically, that Butte was one huge mine-waste dump, even if, like ours, your house was nice. I was loyal to his loyalty. And there I was with Perry, the son of Augustus Walsh, the friend of Roland Everets. My father would have regarded them as royalty. And I still carry a trace of that, I'm sorry to say, from when I was young and dumb.'

"You do better with it than I do," Ethan says. "I'm still struggling with what to take and what to reject of Meyer. Besides, you have the entire American establishment behind your 'dumb' view: education, religion, politics, and the media, all dedicated to the proposition that everyone should strive to be a Roly Everets, the fifth horseman of the apocalypse become the American Dream. Damn, and I was doing so well forgetting the elk hunt." He puts his arm around her.

"Last night was lovely," she says.

"Ah, that."

"No, not just 'that.' Making dinner and sitting by the fire."

"And that"

She smiles. "And that."

Ethan spends the next days working on the Gila piece. He thinks about a piece on White Sands. His notes say, "the fine, contaminated sand," and "dunes—the hair of Jean Harlow or Marilyn Monroe." Each day he thinks of calling Meyer to ask when he's coming; each day he finds a reason not to call. It may be that he's writing and doesn't want to disturb his rhythm. But thinking this is to admit that Meyer disturbs him, is close to a superstitious sense that if he speaks to Meyer, he'll stop writing. Bleak as this is, it's better than thinking he doesn't call his father because he hates him.

So he writes, visits Emmy, and spends quiet evenings with Lucy. His calm comes from writing and from Lucy having told him about Carlos. He thinks of these as good days. They end with a call from Lavery.

"Have I interrupted your work?" Lavery asks.

He has, but since it's Lavery's book he's working on, he can hardly complain. "That's okay. What's up?"

"I take it you haven't seen yesterday's *Aguila*, the undergrad University paper?"

"No."

"The headline story is about Carlos and his hunting guests, Bud Brandon and Roly Everets, trespassing on posted land to shoot elk, and leaving four of them to die wounded. That's triple bad behavior out here. The paper says Harrison James, the landowner, gave them the story. Were you with them when it happened?"

"With Carlos. Yes, that's what happened."

"How would James have the names?"

"I suppose because he's friends with the owner of Valles Caldera, and the owner's ranch wrangler Fred was up there managing the place."

"The paper said the three were unavailable for comment."

"So?"

"If they actually deny it, especially Everets, it could make the mining lobby look bad and maybe help defeat the land bill."

Ethan says, "My bet is that they'll own up and apologize. Everets and Carlos are too smart to get caught out, and Brandon will do what Carlos does."

Lavery says, "You're probably right." After some talk about what Ethan's working on, the call ends. But now Ethan can't forget the hunt. He loses focus and can't work well.

Next day, he gets to the apartment at seven in the morning, and though it takes several hours, he's at last able to get into his writing again. When the phone rings, he looks at his watch. He could let it go onto the answerphone in two more rings. He picks up the phone after the first. "Yes?"

"Ethan boy, Haskell Perlmutter."

"What's happened, Haskell?"

"It's your father."

"Is he dead?"

"Without letting me speak, the first thing you think is he's dead?"

"He isn't?"

"Isn't dead?"

"Yes, Haskell. No. You tell me. I'm listening."

"Ethan boy, Meyer died early this morning. Try to control yourself. Sixty-nine years I knew the man. Oh!" Perlmutter makes a strange whimpering noise.

"What happened?"

"His heart stopped beating."

"That isn't funny."

"Funny I don't mean it to be."

"Haskell, everyone's heart stops beating at death."

"You're trying to tell me my profession?"

"Haskell, please. What was the cause of Meyer's death, the spondylitis?"

"No. One minute he's sitting up in bed this morning—this is Yang Chou telling me this when I got over to the apartment, and, by the way, this young woman made your father's last days very happy, he told me. So he's having his coffee, saying something, and he puts his coffee back on his bedside table and he pauses—she tells me she was used to his pauses, he was talking about philosophy, she says—and I remember those pauses. I used to imagine the thinking going on in those pauses. Ah, If I could write, could I write a book about those pauses! So she's next to him in bed having her coffee, waiting for him to express his thought, but the pause is, even for Meyer, a little too long, and she looks over at him, and that's it. He's sitting there dead with his head slumped to one side. I saw, Ethan. He didn't die in pain. His heart just gave out. No sign of a stroke. At least, without an autopsy… If you wanted, I could have one done, but I don't believe it would show… Be strong, Ethan." Perlmutter makes the whimpering noise again.

Ethan listens. Perlmutter was at Boston Latin with his father, all those years ago. He won't ask for an autopsy, but he suspects the Viagra. Perlmutter obviously doesn't know about the compliant Brandeis doctor. Meyer having coffee, my foot. Meyer having nookie. Meyer chemically erect, yinning his Yang, drawn one too many times to the petite palace of pleasure, well of the sorrows. Yang must have pulled him out, pried him off, propped him up and re-pyjama'd him before calling Perlmutter. An autopsy of Meyer would show nookie on the brain. He says, "Haskell, he told me, too, that he was very happy."

Perlmutter sniffles. "We should all go so peacefully."

Ethan hears "piece-fully." A Viagra scenario: Viagra rises and Viagra falls. He chuckles.

"This is funny, Ethan?"

"I was thinking his last days were like a honeymoon. Meyer spoke about marrying Yang Chou. Haskell, I'll try to get to Boston by tomorrow. I'll call Meyer's secretary."

"Yes, she's arranging the funeral details. This is so terrible. We have to bear up, Ethan boy." Perlmutter hangs up whimpering.

Ethan thinks he should pour himself a drink. He doesn't want a drink. He goes to his father's books on his shelves. He doesn't want to look at them. He walks back to Lucy's and stops to sit on a bench at the desert garden beside the University library. The plants are spiky and encourage him. So much life from so little support. Meyer gave him so little support. He leaves the cactus in peace.

Lucy is writing on the sun porch. He is truly sorry to disturb her. "What is it?" she says, standing up, frowning.

"Meyer died this morning. The doctor said his heart stopped. Just like that." He hugs her. It seems artificial.

"I'm so sorry."

He pats her back and says, "That's all right. That's all right. I couldn't help loving him. I hated him."

She says, "He was difficult. He should have praised your writing. But you loved him and he loved you."

Ethan looks over Lucy's shoulder at the big cottonwood tree, its leaves curled and pale yellow. "Not love, I think. I think I had a crush on him. That glamour, the way I felt like adolescents feel, continually pierced. I'd like some tea."

"I'll get it."

He follows her to the kitchen. "I'd like to get to Boston tomorrow."

"I have lots of air miles," she says.

He says, "Tomorrow's Friday, and I suppose the funeral will be on Sunday. I'd like it if you were there."

"Of course," she says. "I'm sure Emmy will want me to go. I'll go over to the hospital soon and talk to her."

"I don't want tea, thanks," he says. "Water will be fine. I'll call Boston about the arrangements."

He takes the glass from Lucy and stares into it. He says, "If you're wondering whether I want to cry or let out my emotions some other way, no. This is it, uptight puzzlement, learned from my father, but without his logic to work it out, to at least *think* about feeling." He kisses Lucy's cheek."

"Of course you have feeling," she says. "You're in shock."

"I know," he says. "You go over to Emmy. I'll be okay here."

In the early evening, he visits Emmy.

"Mom told me about your father. I'm sorry."

"Thank you," he says and pats her hand. "I'm going to Boston tomorrow. I hope Lucy can come out there on Saturday."

"She'll be there. I'll be okay here. Ethan, I wanted to ask you. Elena told me she gave those tapes to you. Now Willy's leaving town. Are those two things connected?"

"Sooner or later, Willy was going to get into trouble. Yes, the tapes were used against him. I assume you're glad he's going?"

"Yes, sure. Only…" She looks at her hands. "Only he didn't force me to have those conversations. Though they were like, gross and made me sick afterwards."

"I see."

"And the day before I ate all that stuff and got sick, when you asked me if he'd touched me and I got really mad? Well, he did, like brushing against me when we passed in the hall. When I was eleven. After a couple of times I knew it was no accident and I stayed out of his way. But even with that, it was sort of interesting."

"Well, it's good that you've told me. Have you told Lucy?"

Emmy says, "I will, before she goes to Boston. Have you told her about the tapes?"

"No. I don't think she needs to know those details."

"I think you're right."

When he leaves, he pats her hair and then bends and awkwardly kisses it. Today, he's grateful that Emmy is self-centered.

Lucy's air miles and travel agent get Ethan a first-class ticket to Boston the next morning. Just before he leaves Lucy's house, Alvarado calls to say he's read of his father's death in the morning paper. "My deepest sympathies," he says. "*Embracos. Via con Dios.*" Ethan is relieved that Alvarado hasn't mentioned the hunt.

In the luxury of his first-class seat, Ethan remembers his cheap flight out. He drinks a pre-take-off champagne and orange juice and reads Meyer's obituary in the *New York Times*. Meyer would have been pleased by the space he's been given, large photo and all, but he would have given the obit no more than a B minus. It comes down squarely on a philosophy of aesthetics-linguistics, quoting his *An Aesthetics of Questions*, and on what in his work is naturalism (what Meyer called his *sine Quine non* side) and what is Platonism under a veneer of linguistics. Ethan gives the obit an A minus. He misses

Meyer not being around to discuss his obituary. Meyer could be generous in his self-absorption. Though his life was the life of the mind, he hadn't assumed his mind was universal. Odd, how clearly he can think of Meyer now. Ethan catches his breath: Meyer is gone and he's still trying to gain his approval.

He falls asleep until Chicago. Then he deplanes, boards the Boston connection, and thinks of his morning call to Meyer's secretary. Gloria gave him his hotel reservation—he didn't want to sleep in the apartment—and then said Meyer (said "Professor Baum") had been a wonderful boss and fun to work with. Meyer as "fun" is a new idea for Ethan. Despite their "twofer" nights out or rooting together for the Sox or Bruins, he can't imagine either of them thinking the other was "fun." Gloria said, finally, "You meant a lot to your father. Hardly a day went by that he wouldn't mention you with love." This angers Ethan. Perhaps Meyer could show so little of this love to him because he was showing it off to so many other audiences.

At Logan Airport, Ethan is met by his father's lawyer, Vidal Sharoy, a big, bearded man with a big Mercedes. He drives and talks. He tells Ethan that though Meyer was not a big client, he'd been important to him as someone he could confide in. Meyer had helped save his marriage. After the reconciliation, his wife developed breast cancer and died, but they had those three wonderful years. Sharoy wipes his eyes with a linen handkerchief the size of a tablecloth. Ethan feels outraged: Meyer is reaching from beyond life with this sentimental blackmail. He doesn't want to hear about wonderful Meyer, he wants to hear what a shit he was.

Ethan says, "Out West, I lost all track of the Sox. Did they have a good season?"

"They had a good season, if there hadn't been the Yankees."

"If there were no Yankees, how could we know the Red Sox existed?"

Sharoy says, "Ah, a Manichean."

Ethan feels this is more like it. Good talk and, outside, a lovely late October day along Storrow Drive. Some eights row on the Charles, water flashing off the oar blades. When Sharoy drops Ethan at the Aspinwall Hotel, he hands him a letter he's held from Meyer.

A padded envelope is handed to him at the hotel desk, from Gloria. It contains the apartment keys, funeral information and phone numbers. Up in his room, Ethan stands by the sunny window and reads Meyer's letter. It's essentially an apologia for not having much to bequeath him. The reasons given are: A, renting an apartment an easier option than owning one; B, spending too much money; C, the belief that Ethan isn't interested in material things. Ethan looks up from the letter with burning eyes. The ABC of selfishness. The letter goes on to say that the old carpets might be worth something, and it ends with a postscript that Ethan keeps rereading: "To, for once, leave myself out of the calculation, I love you more than anyone except your mother."

Ethan regards the bright autumn out on leafy Beacon Street in Brookline, Massachusetts. Leave it to Meyer to put the carpets in the text and the love in the postscript. A casual reader might take the PS to mean that Meyer loves him very much, but to know Meyer at all is to understand it as a minor masterpiece of ironic ambiguity. Does it mean Meyer loves him more than anyone except his mother loved him? Does it mean that Meyer loves him more than Meyer loves anyone except his mother? Does Meyer leaving himself out of the calculation mean discounting Meyer's self-love, or does Meyer leaving himself out nullify all following statements about his love for Ethan?

Only now does Ethan notice the date at the top of the letter: it was written five years ago in the spring, just after they'd flown back from Mexico City. It's nothing but guilt. Worse, it's the guilt Meyer could never own up to. As to the love... It's sick. Goddamn the man to hell. Ethan wishes he believed in hell. But there are phone calls to make and arrangements to check. He sits in the armchair, staring out the window.

The phone rings. It's Yang Chou, in the lobby. He says he'll be right down. He decides to be polite but distant. So Meyer decided he wasn't materialistic? Let's see her try to claim any of the estate. There is no estate. She's only Meyer's final fling, the last shoot-up of a testosterone junkie.

Downstairs, Yang Chou comes forward from the desk. She's five ten or eleven, Meyer's height. Her soft black hair is clipped to half an inch from her head. She has large round eyes, and she's wearing a gray sweater and gray jeans under a black leather jacket. What can a young girl have seen in that mean old man? He shakes hands without returning her smile, looking somewhere over her shoulder. She says,

"Gloria told me when you were due in, so I thought... I wanted to see you. Thanks for coming down. You must be tired from your trip and everything."

He says, "Everything. Let's go to the bar."

They sit in armchairs. She orders coffee, he orders a large vodka on the rocks. He doesn't speak. It satisfies him to make this difficult for Yang Chou. Finally, she says, "I don't want anything of Meyer's, from his estate, if that's what your silence means." Her skin is the color of cream with a drop of coffee in it. Her eyes glisten. "Won't you talk to me?"

Their order arrives. He says, "I'm sorry. It's nothing personal. There have been a number of women in my father's life. You were the last. And that was for several months."

Yang Chou says, "You mean, if Meyer had lived longer, I wouldn't have been the last? I hope not, but it might have been like that. I know he had other lovers before me. But I know he mentioned me to you. We spoke on the phone last month. Remember?"

"I do." He drinks vodka. "He said you made him very happy. That was the catch phrase from Boston to Albuquerque. I said that on the phone to you. And that's all very nice. I swear, that's how I felt about it. But I had problems with Meyer, and it's only since leaving Boston that I've realized how deep they were. Now, since he's dead, I guess I'm stuck with them."

She says, "I met Meyer at an MIT party. I fell for him, not the other way round. I practically stalked him for weeks, until he agreed to meet me for lunch. It wasn't like I'd been attracted to older men. Until then, I dated men my own age. So then it happened between us. He was afraid it couldn't work. He tried Viagra a few times but stopped. It made him premature, he said, like a sixteen year old. Your father told me a lot about himself in the three months we spent together."

"His unfaithfulness to my mother?"

"Yes."

Yang Chou speaks quietly. Ethan looks across at her. She is really beautiful. What if he asked her to go up to his room and fuck? No, that's what Meyer would have wanted to do in this situation. Ethan says, "What sort of physics to you do?"

"Weak field."

"Wheat field? Physics has some wonderful language. Isn't there an electron-trace instrument called a cloud chamber?"

"Gravity."

"You think I should be more serious?"

"My work is in gravity: weak field physics. You remind me of Meyer. He'd get the wrong end of a stick and reshape it to something delightful."

He says, "I didn't want to like you—a way of getting back at my father—but I do."

She says, "I was lucky being with him when I was. He told me about his illness, but he didn't feel that was going to get him. He lived very intensely and openly. He told me about once sending you to Oaxaca on a sex holiday, when you were depressed. He said it was the worst thing he'd ever done. He knew he hadn't been able to apologize adequately, and he hoped he could somehow make it up to you out west, with me and your new family. He was the most stunningly articulate person I've ever met, but he was tongue-tied when it came to talking about you."

"Even my memories of my father are tongue-tied."

She says, "He knew he wasn't a great father. He said that was an irony of how well he'd raised you to be like him."

"That hurts, too: how he used his failings with me to intrigue and charm others. But I miss him. He intrigued and charmed me, too."

They sit quietly. He says, "I'd better get back to checking the arrangements."

"If I can be of any help."

"Thanks. It will be good that you're at the funeral." They hug lightly.

In his room, Ethan looks at Gloria's list and phones Davidson's Funeral Chapel and gets put through to Davidson himself, whose voice sounds like cough syrup. Davidson assures him of a perfect service, and of the honor of being chosen for the funeral of so renowned a thinker as his late father. He then informs Ethan that a Rabbi Weissman, from Brandeis University, has asked about officiating. When Ethan says his father had not been religious, Davidson replies, without irony, "That's all right; he's a Reform rabbi." Ethan's laughter confuses Davidson, but he gives him the rabbi's phone number, in Concord. Ethan imagines the non-religious rabbi comfortable among the shades of Alcotts and other Unitarians of that old town. A young boy's voice answers his call; it turns out to be Rabbi Weissman. "Steph," he asks that Ethan call him.

Steph says he hasn't really known Ethan's dad, has only met him at university functions and, of course, known him by reputation. Nevertheless, Steph understands what a loss it must be for Ethan, and, indeed, for humankind. Ethan repeats, "Humankind." Steph says he would be honored to say a few words about Ethan's dad and "our tradition's beliefs."

"That presents a problem, Steph. Even a few words about our tradition's belief stuff would be more than my father ever said."

Steph says, "Pardon me, Ethan, but isn't the very basis of philosophy the search for how it is we believe what we believe?"

"No, it's more the how we know what we know stuff. Not believe stuff, know stuff, Steph."

"Would you mind if I attended?"

Ethan says, "Not at all. You'd be very welcome." He notes that his good will has arrived via his sadism. That Meyer would have approved might be the hallmark of that sadism.

When Lucy calls, minutes later, he's simply happy to hear her say, "How are you doing?"

"The flight was good, thanks to you. I'm getting on, in a conflicted sort of way. I've met Yang Chou, who I wanted to dislike. She's really nice. And I've spoken with a university rabbi who's aggressively nice. I've received a strange and typically worrying letter Meyer wrote five years ago, and I'm about to go over to the apartment to—I don't know, just to be there."

"You're doing well. I get to Boston tomorrow afternoon. Should I come straight to the hotel?"

"Do. I'll let the desk know you're coming."

"See you," she says. "Love you." She rings off.

Ethan takes the apartment keys and walks the few blocks up Beacon St., turns south for one block and then west for one block. The trees and buildings are, as usual, too known, an assumption, a second nature. He enters the apartment and opens the curtains and blinds. The place is neat and clean. Meyer has died as he lived, in physical tidiness. All his messes were emotional. Ethan imagines himself as one of the carpets under which Meyer swept them. He regards the actual

Persian carpets. They're nice, but over-elaborate for him. Looking objectively, if that's what he's now able to do, he sees the apartment is really very large. Maybe he should keep the Louis Tiffany lamp from his father's Brandeis office, the one he was told his mother found in a junk shop after the war for thirty dollars. He goes to the photos on the sofa table. He wants these, he supposes. What he really wants is to know who his father was. He goes to the main bedroom and sits on the edge of the bed. Had Meyer lived to one hundred and six, Ethan would know nothing more than he does now.

He hasn't been in this bedroom for years. Does Yang Chou have the keys for the apartment? He's glad he didn't ask her. He's always thought of this as his mother's bedroom, with its pretty mahogany furniture, the slim, tapered bedposts a Grand Rapids daydream of Queen Anne. He opens the drawer of the bedside table. Box of tissues, bottle of ibuprofen, a nasal spray, *Selected Shorter Poems of W.H. Auden*, a spiral-bound notepad with a single pencil entry in Meyer's neat hand: "Make list to somewhat refute Sayyed Nasr re western phil. ignoring eastern." At the very back is a leather-bound notebook, six inches by four, an inch and a half thick. Nearly full, all in Meyer's tiniest, regular hand, written, Ethan can tell, with the fine-nibbed Mont Blanc. A woman's name underlined at the top of the page, below which are indented dates, comments. Chronological. His father's sexual diary. Ethan turns near the end and finds under *Hannah Miller*:

> Remarkable confession from H in bed, at last telling what she's hinted, that once, on a sea trial of a large ketch she'd designed, she had two men in her ass at once, which, true or invented, she told to excite me, which it certainly did, for later that is where I singly went, though imagined another cock sliding along mine, H pulling open her buttocks so much that the story seemed possible, great crater, H magnificently heedless of ass/cunt/mouth hygiene, my anal architect

.

Disgusted, getting an erection, Ethan thumbs through the top corner of the diary, as if it were one of those old children's books where he might see moving pictures of Meyer in the act. Who is he to judge his father? He's his son: of course he judges him. He moves several years back in the diary and finds Mary Keegan, the stewardess. The first two entries are merely statistical. The third is what he's looking for.

> What is most thrilling—the softness of her skin remarkable, but man cannot dwell on softness alone—is the idea that I've stolen her from E. I suppose it makes me feel young. An illusion, but how well I know the imprecision of the border between illusion and reality, those two dark fairy kingdoms. This must have been at the back of my mind when I told E about M, confusing myself as well as him.

Ethan skims the diary. A cold feeling comes over him, and he looks through the end of the book. There it is: *Lucy Evans*.

> Wonderful! She's met him and he's fallen for her. It will be no time until I'm in New Mexico and back with my adorable cocksucker.

Ethan flips back through the pages. No other entries for Lucy. He continues reading through his father's graphic, flat pornography. Meyer gives Lucy the wrong color pubic hair and too much of it. Ethan understands even before coming to this:

> Ethan, if you read this, I'm only teasing. Well, not teasing as much as jerking off. But you'll have already figured out this is fantasy because of the physical details and absence of prior entries. Pathetic, I know. And mean, for which, apologies.
>
> Postscript: This book is yours to destroy. Yang has read it. She says I don't have to write it anymore. She's right. Her statement has the clarity of natural life. The sky, a tree. Peace.

Ethan takes the diary into the kitchen, rips out all the pages and with a scissors cuts them in small pieces into a paper bag. He puts the bag and the leather binding into a plastic bin liner, ties it, and takes it out the back door and puts it into the big garbage hopper, where the dented trashcans used to be. Meyer has left him a message of peace in a time bomb.

Inside, he pours a large snifter of brandy, and sits on the sofa across from the armchair where Meyer will not sit again, and tries to think. All he comes up with is that his father was a shit and now he's dead and the world seems empty. Later, he thinks of a parody of Cicero: Nothing so absurd can be done that has not already been done by fathers and sons. Light from the streetlamp falls in stripes through the Venetian blinds. Should he phone Helen? Funny, now that Meyer's gone, he has no urge to think of her as XHelen. She's Helen van Leyden, and he has no particular interest in speaking to her.

He rinses the snifter, draws the curtains, locks the apartment and walks back to the Aspinwall Hotel with a brandy headache. He has a light supper in his room, undresses, takes two aspirin, and falls into a dark, dreamless sleep.

After breakfast next morning, he returns to the apartment to see if Hester is readying the place for the reception tomorrow, after the funeral. Hester Smith has been coming to clean twice a week since before his mother died, seventeen years ago. When he lets himself in, he finds Hester sitting on the sofa in her usual cleaning outfit, a loose, orange jumpsuit.

"Ethan, how you doing?" She stands and he kisses her cheek. The jumpsuit smells of furniture polish.

They go into the kitchen for coffee. Hester says, "I hoped you'd be round before tomorrow. This is the first time I've been in since the day Meyer passed. I been coming here such a long time. Your mother was a nice lady. Then she passed and I got to know your father."

"Yes."

"You like it strong?"

He nods. She pours him a mug and says, "You ready for this? I got to know him not like someone comes in to clean gets to know. We been lovers all that time. Not regular-like, but on and off. Good lovers when we needed."

He is not ready for this. He thinks: exploitation, sexual harassment. He thinks: Meyer, the Sultan of Twat. He says, "Yesterday, I found a record of his love affairs. I don't remember seeing your name in there."

"It wasn't. I know that book. He took that out after the first time, maybe two years after your mother passed, and he said, Hes, how you want me to describe you in this? And I told him you put one word about me in there, you gonna wake up next day without nothing to keep writing about."

They look at each other and laugh. Ethan wishes she'd done what she threatened.

Hester says, "I just want to tell you he was kind, and he didn't make the running any more than I did."

Ethan says, "Funny, I always thought he was slightly racist."

"Who says he wasn't? Man was sleeping with me, not marching down Selma."

"Hester, you should take what you want from here. I'd really like you to."

"Just that photo of Meyer on the sofa table. Not the frame, just the photo."

"You have to have the frame. I'm not taking it from its frame." He goes to the living room telling himself to give Hester a bequest from the estate, if Meyer hasn't. He picks up the photo in its silver frame. It's of Meyer about fifteen years ago, the time he started his affair with Hester. Meyer is very handsome, a Semitic Cary Grant. He folds down the frame stand. He's putting his father's affairs in order. He gives Hester the photograph and leaves her at work, cleaning the spotless apartment. His smug father. His tombstone should be a six-foot penis, saying, "Here lies Meyer Baum, the prick."

He walks to Davidson's Funeral Chapel to look at Meyer Baum the philosopher who fucked his Black cleaning lady but did not march to Selma. Ethan wants to look him in his dead face and spit on it. The chapel door is locked. Of course, Saturday, the Sabbath. He walks around back to the mortuary building. The façade might be closed for *shabbas*, but decomposing flesh makes no such observance. He enters through a door marked Private. At the end of a hall a door is open.

"Yeah?" A kid in a tee shirt and yarmulke, a half-eaten hot dog in his hand, comes to the door. The kid looks Irish. The dog smells good.

"I'd like to see my father, Meyer Baum. His funeral's tomorrow."

"Oh, yeah, Baum. Newspapers been callin' about him. Sorry for your loss. Hey, I ain't supposed to, but seein' he's your dad. Down around that corner, second on the right. Officially, the viewin's only from six, after sunset. I guess you know that."

"Thanks."

"Yeah, well, Jesus, bein' your dad and all."

Ethan goes down the corridor, turns into another and opens the second door on the right. He turns on the light and goes to the open casket and stares. What the morticians have done is grotesque. His handsome father. Had his face been so contorted as to need this? Haskell Perlmutter said it was a peaceful death. Ethan tries to find his father's features under the heavy makeup. Blue eyelids beneath the high arches of eyebrow pencil, the mouth hidden behind lip rouge. And why has his neck puffed up so much? His chin doubled? The top of his head is covered in a cloth which Ethan slides back. Gold ringlets snake down. His slim, elegant father has in death become a fatso in drag. Ethan grips the edge of the coffin to keep from screaming. Something touches his shoulder and he screams.

"Jesus, it's okay! It's me, Kevin, from the office. Take it easy. That's Mrs. Seigelman. Your dad's next door." Kevin swallows the last of his frank. He holds the door open and switches off the light. "I knew I shouldna let you in. If Mr. D finds out, I'm gonna catch shit, an I was only tryin' to do you a favor, for Chrissakes."

"I know, I know. I just got scared. I won't say a word. Thanks, Kevin." Ethan enters the next room. The light is on.

This certainly is Meyer, though something has happened to his face—rictus, rigor mortis. The right side of his mouth is lifted in a silly grin that the mortician, perhaps an apprentice, perhaps Kevin the *shabbas goy* himself, has tried to correct by rouging the unlifted half for emphasis. But the effect... Ethan says out loud, "Oh, Meyer, that smile—as if von Aschenbach, just having left the Venetian hairdresser's, had bumped into his mother."

Ethan's rage is gone. Death itself has spat on his father's face. He bends and kisses the twisted lips. Cold. He straightens and sees that Meyer is either in a bad imitation of a good suit, shirt and tie, or in a good imitation of an awful suit, shirt and tie. He says, "You're not going to look like this. Wait right here, Meyer." He goes back to the office.

"Kevin, hi. My name's Ethan, by the way. Kevin, I want my father dressed in clothes he liked. If I brought you his clothes, especially if I could knot the tie like he liked..." He puts three hundred dollars into Kevin's hand.

Kevin says, "I know what ya mean, Ethan. Like my dad always has to have my motha make this same friggin' Windsor knot for him for mass on Sunday."

Ethan says, "I'll be back in twenty minutes. It's only at Coolidge Corner."

He runs back to the apartment. Hester stops vacuuming to listen to what he's doing in the bedroom. He's in his father's closet choosing one of Meyer's favorite suits, a light brown herringbone tweed from Brooks Brothers, and a plain brown leather belt, and one of the white, long-staple cotton shirts Meyer had made in London, on Jermyn Street, and the white boxer shorts and white tee shirt he always wore. And long, dark brown socks, and his good cordovan shoes. He doesn't want to consider how much of the underclothes Kevin will undertake to put on. But when Ethan swings out the tie racks, he goes into despair. There must be over a hundred neckties, many similar. Looking at them, he sees how little he knows about his father.

He's aware of Hester staring at him from the doorway. She shakes her head and says, "No, you mustn't." She goes to the bed and picks up the suit he's laid out. Hester is crying. He puts his hand on her shoulder and takes the suit from her. He says, "Help me choose a tie."

She says, "I don't know. I just do not know. He would buy them and then give them away after wearing them once, or not at all. I could never figure out why he bought one or gave away another. The goddamned vain man."

Ethan goes to hug her, but she pushes him away. "Get your hands off me. Just don't touch me. You choose his damn tie! It's no business of mine."

She leaves the room. Ethan thinks to follow, but the vacuum cleaner comes on. He chooses a tie, a foulard paisley print that he imagines Meyer didn't wear much but couldn't part with because it was so gorgeous. He gathers up the clothes and says goodbye to Hester. She keeps her head down into the vacuuming.

He returns to Davidson's and gives Kevin the clothing. He knots the tie on himself; it takes three tries before he gets it just right. He asks Kevin to take off the lip rouge. "Right, gotcha," says Kevin. "Leave it to me, Ethan." Ethan asks Kevin where he got the hot dog. "Gene's, right down Beacon."

Ethan goes to Gene's, sits at the counter and waits, starving, for his dog. He knows it will be perfect: a high-smelling frank in the softest white-bread hot dog roll, with the mildest deep yellow mustard flopped onto it. No relish, no onion, no Yankees New York sauerkraut. He eats one quickly, orders another, and between that and his third, he asks, "What's the secret?"

The counterman says, "Authentically bad ingredients." He's clearly a wit working his way through college. And clearly correct: two bites into his third hot dog, Ethan makes it to the men's room to be sick. Back at the counter, he drinks sweet tea to calm his stomach. He has seen his father's corpse awaiting its funeral, the funeral Meyer so intricately, repeatedly rehearsed. What, in his Derrida phase, would Meyer have made of "re-hearsed"? The funeral is shaping up to be unpredictable, an impromptu, or, in the words of the sage behind the counter, full of authentically bad ingredients.

Ethan goes for a walk. He keeps well away from Thoreau and other places where he'd be more likely to run into someone he knows. He vaguely thinks he should call Pete Walsall. Probably Helen, too. He walks down Beacon to Kenmore Square and around to closed Fenway Park. He crosses the street to the franchise store and notes with distaste some pro football clothing among the baseball shirts and caps. He regards the store-window-size photo of Ted Williams connecting with a pitch. The shift is on and the ball is heading into it, but he can see the ball has been drilled with such perfect eyes and wrists, it will be bouncing off the right field wall before the first and second basemen finish leaping for it. He remembers how his courtesy uncle Phil Friedman, as true a political lefty as Williams was a batting one, glorified Williams as "the only major league player who can stand up to an owner." Uncle Phil said, "'The Red Sox, Mr. Yawkey?' Williams says. 'You're not the Red Sox, I am.' Get it, kid? The players own the team. The workers own the means of production!" Ethan walks into the Fenway yearning for Uncle Phil to be alive, to come to the funeral. If only Meyer were around to remind him of when Phil died.

He sits on a bench looking over the bulrushes of Muddy River and knows that Phil is now truly dead because his father is. Alive, Meyer had held back his generation's ghosts from Ethan. Now they swarm him like bees of an Indian summer. Among them, his mother's absence stings most: he can recall her face only because he's just seen her photo in the apartment. He has been Meyer's rival and buddy, and, as such, disloyal to Marion's memory; as such, as unfaithful as his father. He thinks: Hypocrite lecturer, my dissembler, my père. He forgives himself the shield of parody.

He walks out of the park and crosses to Commonwealth Ave. He walks past Boston University. Somewhere in there, in a library within a library, lie his manuscripts and notes and letters, part of a contemporary writers' collection. He's seen it once, each sheet of his paper separated by a sheet of acid-free paper, in among drawer after labeled drawer that rolls out silently in the air-conditioned, humidity controlled, silent room. A manuscript morgue. Ethan crosses the street. He'll never write again, not anything of his own. And that particular smile on Meyer's dead face: Was he cheering or jeering?

Ethan walks back to his hotel via Amory Street, the street, park and playground of his childhood, once so dense with memories. Now it seems some other person's experience, a childhood he's only read about.

17

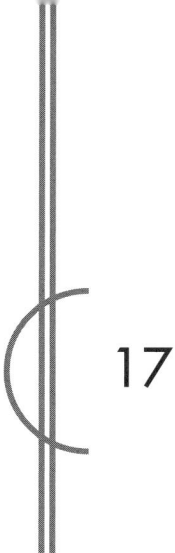

WHEN THE DESK CLERK SAYS, "Your wife has arrived, Mr. Baum," Ethan for a moment imagines it's Helen. He'll open the door to the reek of cigarettes and find her by the window, in mohair, her legs crossed, her top foot going round and round, her fingers drumming the sill. He smiles as he remembers it will be Lucy, Lucy who's good to him. As he opens the door, Lucy comes out of the bathroom in a white towel robe. Steam follows her out like a cloud. She looks like an ageing angel, he thinks, subversively.

"Welcome to Brookline." He kisses her.

"How has it been since we spoke?"

"Awful, funny, strange. Mostly strange. Let's lie down and talk. Maybe I'll have the energy to nap."

In bed, he tells her of finding the sex diary, with Meyer's awful entry about her. He tells her about mistaking Mrs. Seigelman for Meyer. He tells her of Hester's revelation and of the scene with Meyer's clothing. Then he asks, "And you?"

"Nothing, except Carlos called last night to say he had to talk to me in person. When I said I was off to Boston early in the morning, and couldn't we talk on the phone, he said in his grandest way, no, that was impossible. He'd drive me to the airport. I said I was driving myself to leave the Jeep at the airport. So he said he'd drive to the house, ride with me, and get a cab back from the airport. He was pleading, and Carlos, as you've noticed, is not a pleading sort of man. So I agreed, but still he wouldn't give me a hint of what it was about. It turned out all he wanted was to give me a message for you—that he felt as your host and friend he'd let you down at the hunt. And he hadn't made it clear to you how badly he felt and didn't want that to add to your worries at so sad a time. You know how he can go all courtly on you. So that's the message. I've read the *Aguila* article. What went on there?"

"Like it said, they shot elk on posted land and left them to die wounded. Do you think Carlos meant all that about letting me know how sorry he was?"

"Oh, yes. On matters of macho honor, Carlos feels strongly."

"Fine," he says. "Would you mind if I closed my eyes?"

"There," she says, kissing his eyelids.

He thanks her for coming to Boston, hearing her reply as a faint sound in his sleep.

When he wakes, Lucy is in the chair, reading the newspaper. He says, "I have no idea what I'm supposed to say about my father, tomorrow."

"You will. I was just reading his obituary in the *Globe*. Not as good as the *Times*."

He sees the time. "No," he says. "I'm going to dress and go over to the chapel to see Meyer. To see his body. Will you come with me?"

"Of course."

Davidson himself shows them into the viewing room. He is a dark man with white, wiry hair and a manner struggling, but losing, to keep from unctuousness. In their short walk, he manages to mention three times the number of reporters who've called about "your celebrated parent, may he rest in peace."

The viewing room is a far, hushed cry from the morning's manufactory. When Davidson leaves, Ethan tells Lucy what an improvement has been made by Kevin re-dressing and de-greasing his father. "It's him, except for the little smirk. Meyer's ironies were always delivered deadpan. Now his deadpan is smiling."

Lucy says, "I'm sure he wasn't always ironic with you."

"True, but always when he tried to show affection. Except, these last months, he had no irony: he was solipsistic and violently literal."

After some time, Lucy says, "It's better to be the one in love than the one who's loved."

"No," he says, "it's better if both are in love and loved."

"That's best," she says, "but not so usual."

Ethan stares at his father's corpse. "From where I stand, it doesn't feel so good."

"No, but at least you *feel*."

He wonders if Meyer never felt. He wonders if he himself never feels, is always the beloved of the woman, Helen excepted; with Helen, there was an equality of unfeeling. With Lucy—well, in her own terms, she's the better off. He stands for some minutes more, runs a finger along his father's pretty necktie, and says he'd like to leave.

Lucy asks if there's anyone he wants to see, relatives or friends. No, he supposes some friends will turn up at the funeral.

At dinner in the hotel restaurant, he tells Lucy stories from Meyer's sexual diary. "Please," she says, stopping him several times. "No," he says, "that was his legacy to me."

She shakes her head. He goes silent. They drink too much. Later, they lie in bed looking at a film until Lucy says she can't hear the dialogue for the creaking of the plot. Then they lie still in the dark. When Lucy's hand come onto his stomach, something breaks in Ethan—bonds of love, respect, propriety—and something else breaks out. He leaps onto her and makes love, makes hate, makes sex as if possessed by what, even in the act, he senses is the dybbuk of Meyer's libido. Ethan cries out in his orgasm and finds he can't stop crying. Lucy, holding him, means more in pain than pleasure.

Next morning, sore and tender with each other, without a word about the night before, they dress and walk the few blocks to the funeral chapel. From the start, Ethan notes how the funeral goes off with military precision. Why not, he thinks, since the military goes off with funereal precision. He's with Lucy in the reception room to the side of the chapel. The small wall clock shows ten-fifteen. From ten-thirty to ten fifty-five, he will head the family receiving line. In his pocket is the note given him as he came in, a message from Hester saying she's too busy supervising the reception caterers to attend. He understands. At ten twenty-two, Davidson pins a bit of black cloth to Ethan's lapel, explaining that its ragged edge, neatly machined raggedness, represents the traditional rending of garments in mourning. Ethan has done his reading in bed last night, so at ten twenty-four, he removes the bit of cloth. "Please stay right beside me," he says. Lucy kisses his cheek. It's ten-thirty, sharp, and in walk the dreadful Jacobs.

The Jacobs are Meyer's cousins. The brains they have are all business: they're so successful in banking and plumbing, that they live on the North Shore in extremely large houses with names out of Daphne Du Maurier. The remainder of their brains is taken up with snobbery and good looks. The Jacobs are tall and blond and pale blue-eyed. They are the sort of Jews whom the sort of Jews ashamed of anything Jewish-looking will cite as an example of how meaningless it is to speak of Jewish looks. The Jacobs are themselves such Jews. They've had to acknowledge Meyer because of his fame: they are incapable of understanding his ideas. They have even noticed Ethan during his spurt of repute, before his blip went off the literary radar. The long, blond line of them are led into the receiving room by their doyen Geoffrey (never Geoff) Jacobs, very tall and tired and pale, who limply takes Ethan's hand and says, "Your father, my cousin, was an ornament on our family tree." He says this slowly, his eyes on the back of his own slim hand, as if the words were written there to prompt him.

Meyer had never liked Geoffrey, and Ethan, honoring his father's memory and his own aversion, says in a most Yiddish singsong, "My father was an ornament on your family tree? Is this the same tree, Geoff, that grew from the acorn of your great-grandfather Moishe Jacobinsky, the baker from Vilna?"

Jacobs turns from Ethan to Lucy and says, "I'm Meyer's cousin, Geoffrey Jacobs. Meyer was an ornament on our family tree." Before Lucy can reply, Jacobs assumes a place beside her as one of the significant bereaved. Ethan is now shaking hands and pecking cheeks of various long, blond Jacobs, each of whom moves on to join the receiving line. Now Ethan's friend Pete Walsall is squeezing his hand and arm, saying "Sorry about your father. You're missed at Thoreau," which for him is near bathos. And here's Helen, whom Ethan introduces to Lucy.

Helen says, "My parents adored Meyer." She turns to Ethan. "Betty and Van are in Europe. They called from Athens to have me send their sympathy. How are you?"

"I feel weird, devastated. What's up with you?"

Helen is in a smart black suit, her face a bit more lined and twitchy than when he last saw her, two years ago. She says, "I'm with the Maureen Falla Gallery in New York."

"That's terrific."

"I'm also with Maureen Falla."

"What's that like?"

"It's funny; it's still like me. Maureen wants to get pregnant."

"What's that like?'

"Better than me," says Helen, "but I'm not thrilled. I want to be the only child."

Ethan waits for her to say, "Just like you," but she doesn't. He says, "Did Meyer ever make a pass at you?"

"Yes. About the third or fourth time he tried, I told him off."

"I wish I'd known about it. I guess we never spoke ill about our parents or in-laws."

"No," Helen says, "we saved all our ill for each other. Nice meeting you, Lucy."

A steady line of people forms. Between his father's academic colleagues and some of his own friends comes Haskell Perlmutter, led by his shambling son Joe, king of old people's battery homes. Whimpering, Perlmutter tells Ethan to bear up and be a man. Son Joe rolls his eyes as if to say, What can you do with these old parents except pay me to coop them up?

The line moves thicker and faster, a blur of hugs, handshakes, kisses, tears, slaps on the back and many That's the Way it Goes, What Can You Do's and other expressions of praise, sorrow and befuddlement, equally sincere and unmemorable. When Yang Chou arrives, Lucy insists she stand between her and Ethan.

At exactly eleven, Ethan walks into the chapel, followed by Lucy. He keeps his eyes down. He sits on the middle aisle of the front row, under the lectern. He looks up at Meyer's closed coffin. Red roses are strewn on it. He sees the tracks it will move on, back through closed curtains. He tries to imagines the point behind the curtains where it moves into the oven. No, what is he thinking? It will stay in a back room and later be taken to the crematorium. They wouldn't cremate it in the middle of the town. Who, what Jew, especially, would want to see up from a chimney the smoke of burning bodies? Davidson appears, nods to Ethan, and disappears.

Ethan goes to the lectern, looks out, and has nothing to say. The chapel is packed with hundreds of people, people standing in the side aisles and four-deep at the back. Was Meyer that well known, or has every philosophy department in New England turned up in the hope that some philosophy superstars will appear?

Ethan begins, "I think my father would have been embarrassed by the mix of friends, family and colleagues he typically kept apart, but he would have been pleased by the large numbers. I was raised by a philosopher, but not to a fault. When I said 'Good morning,' Meyer did *not* say, 'Define your terms.'"

Ethan then speaks of Meyer's frequent change of plans for this funeral and suggests that if *he'd* found it so difficult to see himself whole, how much harder for the rest of us. Or was it easier? This leads him to speak of *The Ambiguity of Opposites* and some possible relations between his father's philosophical work and his life. This doesn't make for good oratory: he hears himself rambling. Each time he heads towards a conclusive statement about the work and the character, he arrives only at another question, itself having at least two different true answers, each of which appears to lead to another mirage conclusion that turns out to be yet another branching, mirrored question, so that as Ethan winds up, or unwinds, or, to be honest, cuts through the tangle, he says all of this goes to prove the link between his father and ambiguity.

Ethan ends by saying, "What gave my father the greatest pleasure was reading, thinking and writing, and baseball, with particular reference to the possibility of the Red Sox beating the Yankees." He stops, takes a breath, and goes on. "And women, with particular reference to the certainty of sexuality leading to orgasm."

He looks out into a silence heightened by a few nervous laughs. Then he catches sight of Yang Chou's sad face and abruptly adds, "Meyer finally had the good fortune to find someone who meant much more. I'd like to ask Yang Chou to speak." Yang Chou, embarrassed, speaks quickly and quietly. Her halts and her breathlessness convey her loss. In awful contrast, Geoffrey Jacobs speaks next, offering the same eight-second sound byte about the tree ornament with which he'd earlier offended.

Next, Gloria Greene, Meyer's secretary, reads messages from those who can't be here. The first is from Willard Van Orman Quine, excusing his absence because of a bad cold. He neither wants to give it to anyone else nor, at his great age, steal the limelight by dying at the funeral. He goes on to say that Meyer will be remembered as an independent philosopher in an age of increasing conformity, and that *The Ambiguity of Opposites* and *An Aesthetic of Questions* are original contributions to philosophy which still had the power to get one rethinking. And finally, he'll miss Meyer as one of the funniest and friendliest of colleagues. Gloria next reads a fax from Peter Strawson at Oxford, slightly less enthusiastic than Quine, but, then, more English. She then reads an email from Donald Davidson at Berkeley. Ethan doesn't hear much of this because he's whispering to Lucy how pleased Meyer would be for the recognition by those he considered philosophy's big three, which, if it doesn't put Meyer into the Philosophy Hall of Fame, sets the seal on his having been a major league player.

Ethan returns to the lectern and asks if anyone else wishes to say something. Up pops Rabbi Steph Weissman. Ethan sits down prepared to cringe, but the rabbi never mentions the G word, and when he reads Emerson's poem "Brahma," the G word is there so ambiguous that Meyer might have approved. Then Meyer's biographer, Jerry Mossler, speaks. It is the best speech of all, since it is about Meyer's life's work, and it reminds Ethan he's not going to understand Meyer torn from that context. Mossler makes the distinction nicely between ambiguity and ambivalence, the former being inclusive, the latter exclusive, and says that Meyer was inclusive in the Whitmanesque sense of "embracing multitudes." Someone behind Ethan says in a stage whisper, "Well, he certainly *fucked* multitudes." In the local laughter, Lucy clamps her hand on Ethan's arm, but she needn't. Ethan imagines Meyer would have enjoyed the indecorousness.

After Mossler finishes, Ethan goes to the lectern and invites anyone else to speak. After a long pause, a woman comes up from the back of the chapel, a plain woman in black, with thick glasses and her gray hair in a bun. She stands quietly before the lectern microphone and then says, "Knowing Meyer Baum intimately was one of the very great pleasures of my life." And she walks back to her seat and sits down, leaving "Who was *that's*?" and "Who *was* that's?" buzzing about the chapel. Ethan has no idea. He half fears, half hopes, that now thirty women from the sex diary will rush the lectern at once, all grabbing at the mike to denounce Meyer as a filthy, fickle fuck. It doesn't happen, and Ethan announces that the memorial will end with the playing of two short pieces of music Meyer had asked for, after which everyone is invited to Meyer's apartment for refreshments.

Ethan sits down and listens. The first piece, Glenn Gould playing the twenty-fifth of the Goldberg Variations from his second recording of it, is expected. Meyer had loved it, had called it "Bach's bright darkness." The second piece surprises Ethan. It's a Scott Joplin piano rag. As he listens and watches the coffin move back on its tracks through the slightly parted curtains, he hears how the *boulevardier* jauntiness of its opening and closing sections enclose the sweet, sad central section which provides an ironic commentary on the other two. He feels this could be Meyer's parting statement that he had known something, at least, about himself. The coffin gives a small, awful lurch at the last, and the curtains close. Ethan quickly takes Lucy out the side exit to get to the apartment. Outside there's a brilliant blue sky and leaf smoke in the air. He says, "I didn't like the coffin going off like that." Lucy holds him.

At the apartment, Ethan introduces Lucy to Hester. Despite the caterers, Hester wears an apron over her smart black dress, symbol of looking after "her" apartment this one last time. All those nights of passion with Meyer have not confused her. She knows nothing here is hers, never was. Meyer knew this and exploited her, no matter how well he satisfied her sexuality. That sexuality—you only have to look at her—is not separate from the whole woman. Ethan says this in a low voice to Lucy as he shows her around the apartment.

There are two bars set up in the living room. A catering staff of five moves between there and the buffet in the dining room and the kitchen, where Hester stands making supervisory sounds, though there is no need. No need, no need; Ethan feels such anger against Meyer. He drinks two strong Bloody Marys before anyone turns up. And who should turn up first but Richard Apther, Meyer's most hostile critic. Apther is a corporate lawyer who once did a philosophy degree and, though he didn't do the obit, is the *Boston Globe's* perpetual philosophy man, and, alas, occasional reviewer for the *New York Times*, his approach being over-elaborated witticisms in generally wild pot-shots at any or all books of philosophy. Among his many *bête noires*, Meyer is lion king. When plump, jolly-looking Apther comes up to Ethan and Lucy and says, "I'm going to miss your father," Ethan says, "You always did."

Apther, one eye appraising Lucy, says, "I wish I'd said that remark Alan George made about *The Ambiguity of Opposites*: 'After this, semiotics will always be the same.'"

Ethan says, "I remember it—and Meyer's reply that George could just as well have *praised* him by saying, 'After this, semiotics will never be different.' That, Richard, was not only making a nice point about his book, it was my father being generous. Please help yourself to food and drink."

Lucy squeezes Ethan's hand and beams at him as if he were her knight of the burning epistle. But Ethan is confused at swinging from hatred of Meyer to his fierce defense. The place quickly fills with people. Ethan crouches in front of Haskell Perlmutter who sits on a couch tearfully saying how happy he is that "at last you boys are meeting up,' nodding at Ethan and hulking Joe Perlmutter sitting beside him. "But that it should take such an occasion, ah." He puts his handkerchief to his eyes. Ethan pats his knee and stands to talk with other guests.

Twenty minutes later, when Ethan is at the buffet trying to decide between chopped liver or chopped herring and opting for neither, Haskell Perlmutter pulls his jacket sleeve and says, "Your dad was one elegant guy. You know how far we go back?"

"Boston Latin School."

Perlmutter says, "To the Boston Latin School. You know how long ago?"

"Seventy years."

Perlmutter says, "I'll tell you, almost seventy years ago. I'll tell you something else, in private. Come here." He takes Ethan's arm and leads down the hallway to the door by the back bedroom. And since there are many people here, too, Perlmutter motions Ethan to bend his head and puts his wet lips to Ethan's ear and says, in a voice loud enough to be heard back at the buffet, "I don't think it was the Chinese girl. I am saying, in my professional opinion she didn't shtuhp him to death."

Ethan says, "Thank you, Haskell. Even if she had, I wouldn't press charges."

Perlmutter shouts in Ethan's ear: "Point taken, Ethan, boy. Meyer, may he rest in peace, had all the luck. We would go out to dinner, just the two of us, and, bim-bam, a woman would be at our table. Always elegant, often a knockout. And I would end up leaving on my own, odd one out. So I wish your father was still around to make me jealous."

Later, Ethan is talking and drinking by the bar with his friends from Thoreau, Pete Walsall and Mahmood Hussein, when a woman motions to him. He excuses himself and makes his way to her.

"You're Ethan. I'm Hannah Miller." She is short and handsome with white-streaked black hair.

Thinking only of what he must not say, Ethan says, "Oh, yes, the anal architect."

"What?"

"Aren't you a naval architect?"

"Yes, I am. You're much taller than your father, but you have the same looks. Not so much your features as your expression."

Ethan says, "Meyer was unhappy that you left him, in St. Lucia."

"He told you *I* left *him*? How droll. That young woman, Yang Chou, is exquisite. I believe you've moved to New Mexico?"

"Yes."

"Then, since we won't meet, it's quite true. He did call me his anal architect. Something else—the woman who spoke at the service, her little eulogy to pleasure? For the record, Meyer was charming and boyish. He was also enormously mean and selfish, incapable of a close relationship."

She nods and moves away, leaving Ethan, who has been yearning for such corroboration of the worst, feeling saddened to have received it.

Several Bloody Marys later, another woman, tall and matronly, stands in front of him waiting to be recognized. "Do you remember me, Mary Riordan, Mary Keegan?"

"Mary," Ethan says, "how are you?"

"Fine, fat-assed and happy, a wonderful husband and two kids. That's Bill, the big guy at the bar. I'm really sorry about Meyer. I thought he'd go on forever. He seemed so young."

"Did you and my father…"

"Sure," she says, "a little fling. I was a bit nutsy about both the Baums, the philosopher and the novelist. I was the stewardess who thought she was way too cultured for the job. Anyway, I wanted to see you and give you my sympathy and best wishes."

Ethan kisses Mary's cheek and walks off convinced that if the reception goes on long enough, everyone will turn up: the one-night-stands and the mistresses, his mother's ghost, the Mexican procuress, even the Derek Walcott groupies he now knows Meyer had left Hannah Miller for.

This has turned into a roaring party. He's drunk. Lucy is a big hit. The place is packed with arguing philosophers, friends in anecdotal groups, and the food flowing out of the kitchen on trays. Ethan stands out from and over it all. He has a sozzled insight: for all his bookish intellectuality, Meyer knew that real life is always potentially more fun, since the nice ass you find yourself standing next to at a gathering can actually be fondled and all hell or heaven might break loose, or you can laugh in someone's face and feel great or live to regret it, with the proviso that the more outrageously you act, the more dues you'll have had to pay. In other words, if you are, say, a pretty well-known philosopher, good looking, witty and well-dressed, you probably, why not, get away with the whole fucking bag, have a great American time pursuing your happiness.

The party is beginning to slow. Space appears between bodies. A tall, white haired man on a cane comes up to Ethan. "I was a friend of your parents. Parents, plural. Marion and Meyer. She was a wonderful woman. They were a nice couple. You wouldn't remember me. Phil Friedman. We went to Red Sox games when you were a kid."

"Uncle Phil?" Ethan is about to hug this miracle, this resurrection, when a heavy arm drops onto his shoulder. Uncle Phil backs off.

Ethan turns, smiling. He's immediately crushed in a bear hug so close he's not sure who's embracing him. He hears, "I was out here on business and heard, so I wanted to pay my respects." Black suit, black shoulders, and against his cheek, the long black ponytail. Bud Brandon's sympathy has its intended effect. Ethan is terrified.

18

BY THE TIME ETHAN EMERGES from his hangover late the next morning, the idea of Brandon being sent to threaten him seems slightly hysterical. Threaten about what, records of a hunt he himself wants to forget? It makes more sense to take Brandon at his own word, almost. He was in Boston, or near enough, and Alvarado asked him to look in on the funeral so that he, Ethan, would know how seriously Alvarado meant his apology. This strikes Ethan as correct, partially. Say, one part in ten. The other nine was to show how seriously Alvarado and Everets dislike the idea of the videos being made public. Such reasoning of course brings Ethan back to Brandon's appearance as a big, ponytailed threat. Should Alvarado ask him directly, Ethan will tell him not to worry about the videos. Having worked this out, he decides he too needn't worry about them, and he pours another cup of coffee and continues to pack.

Late that afternoon, he and Lucy fly back to Albuquerque. They drive directly to the hospital, but Emmy's already asleep. So they sit by her bed for a while. At one point, Lucy has one hand on Emmy's arm, the other on Ethan's. Lucy's poor children, he thinks.

Next morning, he begins work on the piece about White Sands. "Damned Beauty" is his working title. The mail at Copper Place brings notes of sympathy from Lavery, Roberta and Dick Palmer, Doc N, and Alvarado. Alvarado's makes no mention of the video.

When he visits the hospital on Wednesday evening, Emmy shows Ethan the revision of the end of her story, "Vanishing Cream," in a small notebook of lined paper. It's written in pencil, in an awkward, spidery hand.

"That's it," he says.

"So it's okay?"

"That's it means it's right, all right, as good as it can get."

"Yeah, but how good is that?"

She is so earnest and hollow-cheeked. "It's a good story. It should be published. You should send it out to literary magazines. That should be your project when you get out of here."

"And you won't mind me living with you and mom?"

"No. There's plenty of room. I work at Copper Place and Lucy often works in her office at the university. It will be nice to have you there, Emmy dear."

"Thank you, dear Ethan. We sound like people in Jane Austen."

By the end of the week, Ethan finishes the White Sands piece and sends it to Lavery. On Saturday morning, he's well into a piece on Shiprock and the Navajo Reservation when, as he imagines the black basalt rising from the high plateau, it comes to him how easily he's written since his father died. For a moment, this stops him. Then he shrugs, considering it's not a novel, and continues to write.

They bring Emmy home on Sunday. He shouldn't think of it as "bring;" bring is for babies and old people who can't walk. Emmy can get around pretty well on her cane, even though Ethan keeps looking at how, each step, her right foot drags along the floor a bit before it lifts. It reminds him of striking a match. Her foot catches fire, her paper thin legs go up in flames. He feels bad about his jealous fantasy and is especially solicitous. Would she like a desk in her room? The living room? The sun porch? He could go out to a mall and pick up a desk now. She says, "I'll work it out, thanks. I'll think about it."

When they sit down for lunch, Lucy brings out a bottle of cold champagne to celebrate. They toast Emmy and drink the champagne with the pasta and roast vegetables Emmy's asked for. He notices she eats some of everything, though he doesn't stare. No one makes a fuss about the fact that Emmy's eating. There's champagne sorbet for dessert, her favorite. After lunch, the three of them walk around the back garden three times. Emmy goes in for a nap, and Lucy and Ethan sit on the stone garden bench. She leans her head on his shoulder and says how wonderful it is. "It is," he says, and draws her close. It isn't and it isn't anyone's fault, and thank goodness for his apartment.

He's there the next morning when Lavery calls. Lavery gives his sympathies, Ethan thanks him for his note, and Lavery asks Ethan what he's working on.

"Shiprock, the town and the rock. I think I'll work in some landscape south of Farmington."

"The Bisti Wilderness?"

"That and the oil field. Maybe Chaco."

"I'll go up there," Lavery says. "The light gets better this time of year. I have your piece on White Sands. It's morbid and sexy."

"Gothic," Ethan says.

"Whatever. I liked it. I'm going to go down there. Do you remember where those particular dunes were?"

"I think just north of Heart of the Dunes, at the end of the road. I can check my video notes."

"No, that's close enough. You seem pretty stuck in to the project. I remember how important work was for me after Min died."

"Yes, thanks," says Ethan. After the call, he thinks of Lavery working to keep at bay the loss of his beloved and his own work that keeps away the rage of love and hate.

Ethan also works hard because he has to go to Boston in a few weeks to deal with Meyer's estate, such as it is. Some of his work is taking trips. He goes east to the plains between Fort Sumner, Roswell and Clovis—a land of Air Force bases and bombing ranges, memorials to Buddy Holly and Billy the Kid, and an endless flat aridity in which it's easy to imagine the Navajos and Apaches broken and starving in the Fort Sumner concentration camp set up to teach them how to act white. And he goes south, past Socorro, to a place of lush nature reserves along the border of the vast, forbidden White Sands Missile Range, where the older land features seem to have been prophetically named, like Massacre Gap, Poison Hills, and Jornada del Muerto, though even here there are sudden green mountains rising from the long, scarred lines of lava beds.

Lucy all this time is happy to have Emmy home. Emmy all this time keeps up her physio at the hospital and her diet at the house. And Ethan all this time spends all his time taking trips away and coming back late from Copper Place for a drink before dinner and then an opera video—Emmy has taken to opera after being given a CD of *Cosi Fan Tutti* in the hospital—halfway through which he wakes up to excuse himself and go to bed so that he can get up early and go back to work at Copper Place.

Three days before his trip to Boston, he returns to the house to hear Lucy calling him to the living room to watch the evening news. He comes in to a shot of Valle Grande on the screen and the voice-over saying it's from here that the alleged trespass took place into the posted land where four elk were shot and left to a lingering death from their wounds. And there's Alvarado very serious and soft spoken, saying if Mr. James found elk shot on his land they were not shot by himself or anyone in his party at Valles Caldera. Then there's a shot of Everets coming out of the TriRock building in Denver, in an important hurry, slowing to say no, he didn't shoot an elk on Mr. James's posted land nor, darn it, where he was hunting, on the private land of Valles Caldera. When Brandon comes on to say the same, Lucy says, "He was at the funeral reception, wasn't he?" Ethan says, "Yes, he was in Boston and I suppose Carlos called him and suggested he pay his respects." The TV reporter ends with, "Despite the denials, Mr. James and other state conservationists insist that the allegations are true. State political pundits are already saying the story is being used by those in opposition to the land-use bill currently being debated at the state capitol in Santa Fe."

Lucy clicks off the TV.

"What do you think?" Ethan asks.

"Kiss me hello." He does this. Lucy says, "I wish Carlos would own up to it and have done with it. I don't care about the others. And you?"

"I wish they'd all own up to it," he says. He goes back to kissing her, changing the subject.

That night, Emmy helps Ethan and Lucy prepare supper. When they sit down to eat, Ethan says, "I don't care whether I'm supposed to say this to you or not: Well done, Emmy."

Emmy grins, looks away and says, "Don't say it until you taste the food."

This night, the video is *The Magic Flute*. When Ethan stands to excuse himself, Emmy says, "But you weren't even asleep yet."

"I love the music," he says, "but not the Masonry. Goodnight."

He lies in bed listening, wondering if Emmy will figure out what he meant. He immediately catches himself being comfortable with the set-up, the two of them, the three of them, the family. He says the word "family" to himself once more and laughs. He wakes when Lucy comes into the bedroom.

"Good," she says, "you're awake."

He says, "Not only awake, I'm up. Come here, Queen of the Night. Come here."

At the apartment next morning, there's a message from Lavery to call him as soon as possible.

"Good morning," Ethan says.

"Did you catch the news last night or this morning?"

"About the great white hunters? Yes."

"Remember when I asked you about White Sands, you said something about video notes?"

"Yes." Ethan sees where this is going, is sorry he let slip he had videos, and at the same time wonders if he unconsciously meant Lavery to know.

"So you've been shooting videos as you've gone around the state."

"With a Sony C150. But don't worry, Charlie, they're not up to your standard."

"Did you shoot videos on the elk hunt?"

"Yes."

"Damn, you're making me work at this. Did you get shots of the trespass and illegal shooting?"

"I did."

"You did. You did and you know what this could mean to the environmentalists if Everets and Alvarado keep denying it."

"That's right. I don't want to use the videos against Carlos."

"Could you explain that to me, please."

"Personally, Charlie, I don't like it. I don't even like legal hunting. But I'm not going to rat on my host—he also happens to be my boss—over four elk, no matter how unsportsmanlike their death was."

"That's all you see in it, ratting on someone?"

"I don't want to get into this."

Charlie says, "Right. So long."

Then Ethan tries to focus on his writing, but the argument continues in his head. He wins it by considering that even if the videos caught out Everets and Alvarado, they'd merely be caught lying about four elk, not anything that could swing the vote against the land-use bill.

Ethan is just back into his writing when the phone rings. He lets it ring, hears Lavery on the answer-phone, and picks it up.

"Ethan, will you have lunch with me today, at least hear me out?"

Ethan thinks of himself as reasonable. "All right," he says. "That sounds reasonable."

It's a downtown restaurant he hasn't been to. Doc N is with Lavery at a window table when Ethan arrives. It's two against one, but Ethan keeps it friendly, reasonable. He lets Lavery order for him. Ethan keeps looking out the window across three parking lots to a corner of a large mural. He's seen the mural before. It shows the Spanish colonial style hotel and railroad station that were torn down to create the parking lots, exposing the bleak wall for the mural. He nods to it: "What is the matter with this city?"

Lavery says, "Cars, the 1950's and 60's, the myth of endless land, and Route 66. It's lucky the factory survived."

The factory is the Sanitary Tortilla Factory, the restaurant they're in. Its walls are covered with naïve religious paintings. It serves simple New Mexican food and endless pitchers of iced tea.

Doc N says, "All the good downtown Indians come here. There's no booze, and they get to mix with Anglo businessmen and Hispano power brokers."

Lavery says, "And what are we?"

"We're..." Doc N looks around and leans forward. "We're a fucking war council, which is the only reason I showed up. My lunch is usually a Taco Bell burrito and ale out of a brown bag with the bad downtown Indians and barrio boys, my blood brothers, compadres, and clients."

The table is strewn with various green chile enchiladas, red chile salsa, baskets of tostados, baskets of sopapillas and two large pitchers of iced tea.

"I'm not at war with anyone," says Ethan, reasonably.

Doc N says, "Man, you had the luck to be out on a hunting party with Roly Everets and Carlos. You know what bad shit goes down at hunts like these?" Doc N's expression is angry.

Ethan says, "Cussing? Drinking? Playing cards?"

"Go on," Doc N says, "mock the native. I'm talking about power—whole countrysides bought and sold, legislation decided, prices fixed. Yuh. And all in a setting of billionaire rusticity."

Ethan says, "'Billionaire rusticity' is good. What language is that, Harvard Diné?"

Doc N says, "'Diné' is good, too, white boy."

Lavery says, "Okay, you've had your jokes. Now, let's get serious."

"See?" Doc N says. "First he feeds you, then he makes you pay."

Ethan says, "That's life. Or maybe life is like these sopapillas: fresh, they're full of sweet promise. But after a while, they're soggy and heavy as lead."

Doc N says, "Ah, a simile of the thoroughly well-fed."

Lavery says, "Brecht said, 'Grub first, then ethics.'"

"Brecht never ate an old sopapilla," says Ethan.

Lavery says, "So what is it with you, really, Ethan, misguided loyalty to Carlos or the fear of losing your job?"

Ethan sits up. "Are you doing the New Mexico book for the money?"

"No."

"Well I am. I'm writing it the best I can, but I'm doing it for the money. You live in a ten-million-dollar home, so you get to quote Brecht on ethics. Brecht is right, but I'm more at the 'grub first' stage of the aphorism."

Doc N brings his large arm across the table between Lavery and Ethan. "Loathe as I am to break up a fight between white men, both of you have strayed from the point. Charlie's point and my point is to convince you to put your videos to good use, you know, the greater good, and all that."

Ethan says, "And you really think my videos will get all the undecided in Santa Fe saying, 'Illegally shot elk! Of course we don't want more logging and mining and ranching on state land!'"

"It won't be like that," Doc N says. "If it happens, it will be because they're damned politicians and don't want to be associated with the disgraced, by which I mean the suddenly unpopular and their causes. Second, with respect, Ethan, you have no idea how much stock most people out here put in what they call "fair" hunting. We don't do a lot of theatre and concert halls out here, we do outdoors. And Carlos is known and respected for his gentlemanly ways. It's not just Everets who counts, but noble old Alvarado. A lot of Santa Fe legislators won't hold on to him when he falls."

Lavery says. "I guess I deserved what you said about my lecturing you from the superior height of my bank balance. But our book deal is secure now, with or without Carlos, because, and I don't say this for vanity or to put you down, it's a book of Charles Lavery photographs. The Institute wants it, and there's no way Carlos can undo the grant or contract."

Doc N says, "Ethan, a few minutes ago you were moaning about the destruction of this city for parking lots. Don't tell me you don't care."

"Me neither," Lavery says. "I've read your pieces about the Pecos Valley and the Cimarron Range and White Sands. Or are you going to tell me you invented those feelings for the paycheck?"

"I wrote what I felt. Okay, gentlemen, I've had enough iced tea and antipathy for one lunch. I'm off to Boston for a few days. I'll think this over and give you an answer when I come back. But I'd better let you know that among my considerations will be that Carlos has sent me a health warning about this through Bud Brandon. Thanks for lunch, Charlie. I have to go now. Doc will fill you in on my history with little Bud."

Two days later, Ethan flies into a colorless, cold Boston. As he lands, the water in the harbor looks like broken gray slate. He rents a car, stops off for dinner, and arrives at the apartment to do what has to be done. He sleeps on the single bed in his old room. The room has long been redecorated. Nothing remains, he sees in the morning, but the views out the windows to the bare spindly trees that line the service road between this and the next block of apartments. As he spends the day making an inventory of the apartment contents, Ethan almost mourns the lack of ghosts.

The next day, he's about to set out to see Sharoy, his father's lawyer, when the phone rings. It's someone from the *Albuquerque Journal* wanting to know if he's the Ethan Baum who was on the elk hunt with Dr. Carlos Alvarado. He says yes. And did he witness any of the alleged trespass and shooting? Ethan says he did no hunting and can't comment one way or the other. For some reason, the reporter accepts this. But Ethan can't. It feels awful, having to lie for Alvarado.

Then he goes to the lawyer and reads the will. There's just over fifty thousand in cash and bonds, after a one thousand dollar bequest to Hester. Ethan asks if he can give twenty-five thousand to Hester and have it appear to come from Meyer. "Yes," Sharoy says, "though it will cost you a few thousand in tax." Ethan says, "Done." As he leaves, Sharoy gives him a letter. "Your ex dropped this off," he says. "She said she'd like you to read it before you left Boston."

Sharoy holds the door open. "So long, Ethan. I miss Meyer. I could always count on his good advice."

"And I on his being, as the man says, consistently inconsistent."

"What man?"

"Aristotle, I think talking of character."

It's mid afternoon when he parks in the lot behind the apartment house. He spends the rest of that day and much of the next organizing the turnover of the apartment lease at the end of the year, the last day, he notes, of the millennium, and putting red stickers on the books, furniture and pictures he wants to keep. As Meyer wished, most of the books will go to the philosophy collection at the Brandeis library. By late afternoon, he's sick of deciding what he does and does not want. He turns on the table lamps in the living room and pours himself a large whiskey. He sits in Meyer's armchair, which he does not want. He looks at the legal documents and decides to read the letter from Helen.

> Dear Ethan,
> Sorry we didn't have a chance to speak more at Meyer's funeral. He was one of a kind. My parents really were sorry to have missed the funeral, especially Van. You know how he admired him.
> I know you'll be busy settling family business when you're here, but if you don't intend on keeping the two old carpets in Meyer's living room, Van, who always liked them, wanted me to tell you he'd give you $8000 for the two of them. He says this is a good price considering he doesn't want them cleaned; he says cleaning these could run into thousands. Please give me a call on this when you decide. My number is below.
> It was nice to meet Lucy.
> Best wishes,
> Helen

He looks at the carpets. He hasn't yet put a red sticker on them. No, he doesn't think he wants to take them out west. He kicks off his loafers, pulls off his socks, and pushes his feet familiarly out over the carpet. He checks the soles of his feet. They're not dirty. The carpet doesn't look dirty. What was all that business about buying them uncleaned? Could cleaning them be as expensive as Van said?

Ethan finds the Yellow Pages and looks up Carpets, Carpet Cleaning. There's a small add at the top of the page: "A. Kiljanian and Company. Specialists in the Cleaning and Repair of Fine Oriental Carpets." He writes down the number and decides to call them in the morning.

Just after six, he turns on the news and there's the story, gone national. Alvarado sits at his grand office desk saying, "I don't think there's a problem. Fred Wilson, Mr. Gray's wrangler, was not with us at the time, and it's simply incorrect of Mr. James's lawyers to suggest Fred Wilson witnessed the alleged trespass. Mr. Gray has let me hunt at Valles Caldera for years and knows I'd never abuse his hospitality by carrying on in the way alleged by Mr. James." The newscaster comes on and says, "Despite continued allegations by Mr. James and the environmental lobby, it appears that Mr. Gray's support of Dr. Alvarado and the absence of a witness will be insurmountable obstacles to bringing a case against Dr. Alvarado, Mr. Brandon, and Mr. Everets, CEO of the giant multi-national TriRock mining group."

Ethan turns off the television and pours another drink. He can imagine Alvarado telling Everets not to worry, that Ethan will never use the videos against them. Or maybe Alvarado's confidence comes from Brandon and his associates having already broken into the Copper Place apartment and taken the videos. He sees he could sit around all night thinking about the videos. Instead, he phones Pete Walsall and is immediately invited to have dinner with Janet and him.

When he gets back, he calls Lucy. The talk is warm and flirtatious; it isn't the time to mention the altered bequest to Hester, the letter from Helen, nor the decision he's reached about the videos.

Next morning, he calls the carpet cleaning company and asks if he could get an estimate on cleaning two carpets. The man on the line, who has introduced himself as Aram Kiljanian, asks what kind of carpets, how old, and what size? Ethan says he only knows them as the old Persian carpets, though they may not be very old or very

Persian. But they're large, about twelve by eighteen feet, he'd guess. And they have different tree-of-life designs. When Ethan gives the address, Kiljanian says he could make it between six to six-thirty, on his way home to Wellesley. Ethan decides that if the cleaning estimate comes to over a thousand dollars, he'll accept Van's offer.

Just after six, Ethan opens the door to Aram Kiljanian, an elegant man with a nose like a broken crag of rock. Kiljanian doesn't take off his coat; he says it won't take long. Ethan brings him from the hall into the living room, where Kiljanian stands in the middle of each carpet, walks around in circles, and gets down on each and lifts an edge. Kiljanian says, "What you said on the phone is all you know about them?"

"Yes."

"Well, they are going to be expensive to properly clean."

"Over a thousand dollars?"

"Perhaps ten thousand."

Ethan is satisfied that Van can have them, and have them cleaned.

Kiljanian says, "But, though I'd like the work, we couldn't do it. It would tie up our workshop too long. You should contact David Kermani, in New York. David has cleaned some of the carpets at the Metropolitan Museum. Thank you for letting me see your carpets, sir. They're fine old Shiraz."

Ethan shows him out and stands at the door after closing it. He goes back to the living room and re-reads Helen's letter, frowning. He's confused by Van spending ten thousand dollars to clean carpets worth eight. Are carpets like yachts, more expensive to keep than to buy used? Maybe, but who would know? He sees Helen's signature on the letter and knows who: her landlords from Haemotics, the Goulatis brothers. They not only collected Helen's paintings but also old carpets. Ethan looks in the Boston residential pages. One of them, Alex Goulatis, is listed. Unless it's another Alex Goulatis. He calls and gets an answer-phone greeting in the high, edgy voice he remembers as Alex. Ethan leaves a message and goes out for an early supper.

A short time after he returns, Goulatis calls back. He says it's good to hear from Ethan. He's sorry about the death of his father. He remembers Helen used to call him and his brother "the haemogoblins." Ethan starts to say "What?" but says he remembers it, too. Then he speaks of Van's offer and the visit from Aram Kiljanian and asks what Alex thinks. He says he'd like to see the carpets, and they arrange that he'll come over at eight the next morning.

Before going to bed, Ethan phones Lucy. Without mentioning the carpets, he tells her about sorting through the contents of the apartment and Meyer's office. He says he's like to give Emmy Meyer's Tiffany lamp. A real one, he adds.

Lucy says, "I'm touched that you'd think to offer it. You know, if the nights are too gloomy there, you could stay in the hotel we were at."

"No, I'd only look out the hotel window and think I should be here. Actually, I'm not gloomy."

"Does that bother you?"

"Yes."

"You could try not to be."

Does she mean not to be bothered? Not to be not gloomy? He says, "There's a double or maybe triple negative in there, but I want to stay in the apartment and work it out. Goodnight, smart lady."

"Will you come back to me?"

"I will."

"Sleep well," she says.

In the middle of the night Ethan wakes up weeping. He can remember no dream, only the sense of sadness growing until it beats on his body like waves. That, of course, is the weeping out loud. He goes to the kitchen sink and drinks water from his cupped hands, as Meyer used to. He looks into Meyer's bedroom and realizes it is not the absence of his father that makes him lonely, but the absence that keeps him from pretending he's not. Before returning to bed, Ethan writes this in his notebook. He knows he won't look at it again.

By ten past eight the next morning, five-foot-two Alex Goulatis, jacket off, in wide red suspenders with white polka dots, white dress shirt and turquoise silk tie, is on his hands and knees on the carpet nearest the windows. The curtains are opened and, as Goulatis has requested, the Venetian blinds are pulled up to maximize the light. Goulatis crawls around touching and staring. He turns the carpet over and studies the underside. Then he repeats the process on the other carpet. He doesn't speak. When he finishes, he joins Ethan on the sofa and asks for a glass of water. Ethan offers coffee, but Goulatis says no, he'd like water. Ethan gets it and returns with a mug of coffee for himself. He sits.

When Goulatis finishes the water, he says, "You say Van offered you eight thousand dollars for these carpets?"

"Yes."

"Well, he was a shark in commercial real estate; no reason he wouldn't be a shark in other business. Aram was right, Ethan, as far as he went. These are fine old silk Shiraz. I don't think he saw how fine. I drank that glass of water to keep from passing out with excitement. I believe the carpet on the fireplace side is late seventeenth century, and this one is maybe a little later, early to mid eighteenth century. They are in as good shape as I've ever seen for their age. But it's their size: this quality at this age and this size is very, very rare."

"So eight thousand is too low?"

Goulatis laughs. "I wasn't saying anything about price. But since you ask…. Ethan, I sit on the board of the Museum of Fine Arts and I'm an advisor to the Textile Department on Middle-Eastern carpets. I know the Museum would love these. Of course, the Director of Textiles and a few others would have to inspect them. As to the price, you'd probably get more by putting them into auction in New York, at Sotheby's or Christie's. But by the time you paid their hefty commissions and charges—let's say the carpets made a million, close to a million for the pair—what you'd end up with wouldn't be that much more than what the Museum could come up with, maybe three-quarters of a million. This isn't, you understand, a formal offer."

"You've said a million at auction. Three-quarters of a million from the Museum."

Goulatis says, "Your father did well for you."

Ethan thinks about that. He says, "I'd like to sell them to the Museum, so that anyone who wanted could see them."

Goulatis tells him that's wonderful. He takes Ethan's phone and email, gives him a card and says he'll be in touch very soon. At the door he says, "Oh, about security. The best thing is to do nothing, the same security you had before you knew the carpets' value. You must be thrilled."

"At this point, I'm still shocked."

Ethan thinks about the carpets all day, as he sorts out the contents of the apartment and the office. At one point, out at Brandeis, Gloria Greene looks in and says, "Please don't offer me anything. I have the photos of your father and me that I want. I'm staying on for some months to help whoever they get to replace Professor Baum. To replace the professor is a figure of speech. Then I'll retire."

By the evening, Ethan knows what he's going to do with the money he gets for the carpets. When Lucy calls at eleven, he tells her the story: the offer in the letter, Kiljanian estimating the cleaning bill and, of course, Alex Goulatis.

She says, "It's like a fairy tale, with your father as the wise wizard posing as a roadside beggar, befriended only by the passing, poor young man."

Ethan says, "No. In this story, the wizard leaves his gift so that the poor young man will overlook it. Meyer left a letter for me when he died mentioning only that the carpets might be worth something. Those were his words, 'might be worth something.' Meyer had to know their value. And if Van, in his greed, hadn't mentioned the expense of having them cleaned, I would have gladly given them to him for eight thousand dollars. Meyer was counting on my ignorance. If the story is a fairy tale, my father is the ogre."

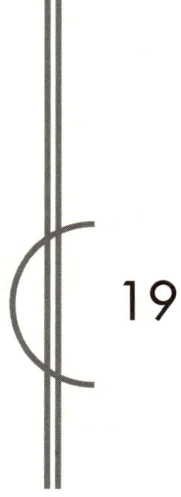

19

LUCY SAYS, "Maybe he didn't really know what they were worth. Did he have the carpets for long?"

"From his parents."

"You see?" she says, as if that proved her point. "Besides, he couldn't know about the offer Helen's father would make."

That, for Lucy, is the clincher. No use explaining Meyer's canny worldliness. She'd always defend the father figures, and every man in her life, except her first husband and himself, had been one. He gives her the details of his return, knowing she won't refer again to their contention.

On the flight back to Albuquerque, Ethan thinks of the writing still to do for the book. Several pieces will be on beautiful, threatened land; the Carson National Forest north of Abiquiu, for one; one or two on land already destroyed, like the erosion from poverty around Española, and the overgrazed mismanagement of grasslands in south Cibola and north Catron counties. He looks forward to the work, but what's going to happen when it ends and he has to face writing a novel? Face not being able to.

He gets back after noon and goes to Copper Place. The box of videos is still at the back of the filing cabinet. But his answer-phone is full of messages from newspapers, radio and TV stations asking about the hunt. He erases them, wraps the video box in packing tape and phones Dick Palmer's law office. When Palmer comes on, he says, "Dick, you told me you did some environmental work."

"*Pro bono*, yes. I must have been showing off."

"Could I give you a small package to hold for me, definitely *pro bono publico*, without telling you what it was, and with complete discretion?"

"First, for the record, I have no idea of what you could be referring to. Second, yes, as long as you give me your word the contents aren't stolen or otherwise illegal, and won't hatch."

"You have it."

"Bring it over. My assistant will give you a numbered receipt and take your instructions if anyone else is to have access, et cetera."

Ethan brings the box to the office, gets the receipt and names Lavery and Doc N as people to be granted access. Then he works at Copper Place for the rest of the day and goes over to the house.

He's sitting in the near dark with a drink when Lucy gets back. She turns on the hall light and calls his name. When he answers, she comes in to the living room and kisses him. She says she's missed him. Him too, he says, and does she want a drink? Where's Emmy? She does and Emmy's gone out with friends to an early movie. Lucy follows him through the dining room into the kitchen. He keeps the lights off, fixing her drink by the light of the open refrigerator. He says it's good about Emmy going out. Lucy says, yes, with three or four others. Steve, someone from his shut-down workshop is one. Yes, he remembers Steve, a nice kid. He follows her back to the living room. No, he doesn't want much light. She turns on a table lamp to its low setting. She's so careful not to disturb him, or anything. Would she like a fire? No, she says this is good. After some time, when he feels the silence has grown heavy, he says, "What news from the elk front?"

"Oh lord," she shakes her head, "Carlos said in an interview that unless James retracts, he's going to sue him for libel or defamation."

"One or the other is harder to prove," he says. "I never remember which. Or is libel defamation in print?"

She laughs at him being cute. What did Everets call her, a great gal? She says, "Poor Carlos has gone off the rails on this."

"That or he's very sure of himself."

She doesn't say anything.

"Or sure of me." The great gal continues not to say anything. He says, "The press and TV are on to me. The *Journal* called me at Meyer's apartment. I double-talked them, but, really, I lied and made them think I witnessed nothing. It didn't feel very good. But even before that I decided to release the videos."

"No."

"Don't worry, I'll give Carlos the chance to own up, first."

"No, you can't, you can't. Carlos I know is being very stupid about this. He's too proud, I know. But you mustn't...." She drinks her whiskey staring at him.

"Why not?"

"It's so..." Her free hand hovers in the air before her.

"You want to say 'disloyal,' but you find it hard, because that would be disloyal to your idea of me."

"Yes, disloyal. Yes, I can't stand having to tell you what you should know yourself. Disloyal to Carlos for giving you that job, and disloyal to me because he helped me when I first got here."

"And why not disloyal to Emmy? After all, Carlos was good enough to give her life? Wouldn't Emmy... You have told Emmy about Carlos, haven't you?"

"Not yet."

"Oh, well, we can rule out disloyalty to Emmy. So it would be disloyal to Carlos and you and to what else, a sense of fair play?"

"That too."

Ethan goes to the window. The peach tree is a smudge in the dusk. "I owe the job to you and Lavery. It never depended on Carlos. It was Lavery, by the way, who first wanted me to use the videos against Carlos and Everets. I said I'd think it over in Boston. I did. My head cleared up in Boston about fathers and father figures. Remember that huge guy Brandon, from the funeral, one of the elk hunters?"

"Yes."

"Carlos sent him there as a threat against using the videos. Carlos and fair play. Remember me beaten up? It was Brandon. I glimpsed him supervising the beating before I passed out. It was poor old Carlos who ordered the beating. Poor old, elegant old Carlos, father figure of fair play. If I left town after the beating, it would show I was the hustler he took me to be with you. If not, well, you'd already spoken to him about finding me a job, and he was making sure I'd need such a job."

"I find that hard to believe."

"It wouldn't be, if you let go of your adolescent notion of men. You met Carlos, you were unsure of your marriage, you had an affair with Carlos and bore his child. He neither had to acknowledge her or pay for her in any other way. That was nineteen years ago. He didn't write your books for you or teach your courses or help you raise

Emmy. You owe him nothing. I owe him less. Carlos may be charming, but he's essentially like Everets, one of the rapacious rich. And it's time you stopped being loyal to such a shit just because he wears trousers."

"Aren't you lucky," Lucy says, rising, tears in her eyes, "that I'm so loyal to men. Maybe that's why you think you can get away with anything. You do! And maybe you're right about me being too loyal. Get out."

"You're pathetic," he says.

"Pathetic, yes." She turns on the overhead lights, turns on all the table lamps, and comes up to him. "I'm pathetic. A pathetic old woman. Look at these lines, this hair! See?" She points to her eyes; she brings her hands to her forehead and spreads back her hair so the white roots show. "See? See?"

"Lucy, don't."

"Seen enough? Good. Get out!"

Ethan wants to hold her and doesn't want to hold her. He says, "You're better than your false loyalties."

"Get out, you sanctimonious bastard. Get out!"

Because he doesn't hold her, he thinks. At the hall, he turns back: "What do you imagine Emmy would say about this?"

"It's none of her business. Get out!"

"Of course it's her business. All of this is her business."

Outside the front door, Ethan feels sorry for Lucy. He doesn't like her less because she's on the wrong side of the argument. Her weakness, he thinks, brings her to his level—at which he can narcissistically empathize.

At the apartment, Ethan calls Lavery and tells him his decision. For once, Lavery is openly enthusiastic. Then Ethan tells him what he's done with the tapes and suggests he makes copies. Lavery says he'll do better: he'll edit the tapes and make computer disc copies of the edits. Ethan says this should be done quickly, since he wants to get to Carlos as soon as possible and offer him twenty-four hours in which to retract. Lavery says he can do it all and return the originals to Palmer tomorrow. He adds, "How's Lucy taking this?"

"Not well. But that's not your problem, is it Charlie?"

"No, of course not," Lavery says, making Ethan smile.

He spends the night at the apartment. He supposes Lucy will call, but when she doesn't, he doesn't mind. She's forty-six and loyal to her men; this one is thirty-two.

Next morning, Ethan calls Dick Palmer's law office and informs them Lavery will be picking up the box, returning it later that day or, latest, the day after. Then he phones Alvarado's office and is put through to the New Mexico Institute.

"Good to hear from you, Ethan. How are you coping?"

Ethan chooses to take this as referring to his father's death. "Well. And you?"

"Not at all bad, considering the harassment I'm getting from Harrison James and his witch hunt. And Lucy and Emmy?"

"Fine. Emmy's settling in well. Carlos, I'd like to talk with you. Today's not good. How's tomorrow afternoon?"

"I'm busy with the Institute, but here's my diary. Yes, just after four. Come over to the Institute, you know, through the library. What do you want to discuss?"

"Well, it was thoughtful of you to have Bud come to pay condolences and represent you at my father's funeral."

"*Por nada*, Ethan."

"I think we should talk about the extent of your thoughtfulness."

"Ah, yes. Very diplomatic of you. Yes, best done in private. Good. *Hasta mañana.*"

Ethan puts down the phone feeling almost satisfied. He's doing everything but what he should be doing, writing a novel. He goes back to writing what he can.

At noon the next day, he calls Dick Palmer's office; Lavery has returned the box. An hour later, Lavery calls. "Dynamite tapes, Ethan. I've made edits of various media-friendly lengths, every one an indictment."

"Can you have them ready to get to the media at five, tomorrow afternoon?"

"Deadline time. Yes. If I don't see or hear a penitent Carlos before, out it goes in time for the six o'clock news. Have you seen Carlos?"

"I'm seeing him in a few hours."

"What do you think?"

"I really don't know what he'll do. I hope he'll keep us from using the videos."

Lavery says, "Good luck," but Ethan realizes there's no luck involved, anymore, except to hope Alvarado won't have him—what? What is the worst? Killed. Yes, that's the word he was looking for, hoping not to find. He writes for a few hours more rather than sit around scaring himself.

He gets to the University library just after four. Alvarado is waiting at the entrance to the Institute.

"Ethan, *hombre*. I didn't know if you'd been here before, so I thought I'd take you up to the office myself. This is the gallery, you must have seen it. This current exhibition is '*Conmemorativos*,' you know, those roadside crosses marking an accidental death. A good young photographer, Jésus Fernandez. Our poor Hispanos have made a ceremonial cult of it. Look, the procession with the memorial cross, some carrying flowers, dolls, literal memorabilia of the deceased, all walking along the edge of the road to the accident spot, some sort of miracle they don't cause more accidental deaths. This one, look, this is a carving of the victim's dog. Pathetic, terrific folk art. And here, the simplest cross of wood with, what are they, decals of hearts stuck all around it. No, it's really worth spending some time. Good photos, very moving but not sentimental. So this way we document the culture, at all levels, and support artists, craftsmen, historians, every sort of academic discipline. Here, let me get the door; the elevator's through here. This is one of our archive rooms. Spanish and English land documents going back to the early seventeenth century: titles, deeds, maps, building plans, even drawings, some beautiful watercolors. And through there are the artifact archives. Blankets, rugs, pottery, tools, saddlery. One day I'll give you the tour. We have—Here's the elevator; after you. We have the sixteenth-century spurs and stirrups of a conquistador. The office is on the third floor. You know the Institute takes up this whole wing of the library. We're going up through stacks of books, research papers and the archives of the Institute's Proceedings and other publications, from a three-page monograph to twenty-volume book series. And also the seminar rooms and study centers for our research fellows. This is what I'm proudest of creating. This research and cultural legacy. Here we are. A bit different from my somewhat overblown University offices. And don't tell me you don't think they are. But this is nice, neat Western Deco. The right size, efficient, but comfortable. Please, have a seat. This is more like it; I've been running around all day.

"Before you say a word, I want to tell you how much I appreciate you being here. About this business, I mean. Ethan, in life there are times when things go well and times when everything turns to shit, and it's then, I've found, that friendships are really made. We fucked up royally, Roly, Bud and me, and you have been a brick. No, please, no embarrassment, let me say this. For Bud and Roly maybe it's just that—your loyalty and discretion. But for me it's more. It's that you have not even mentioned it! In this, you have behaved not only as a friend but as a man of honor. I know, I know how Roly finds me foolishly old-fashioned. '*Duque*' he calls me, and means no compliment. Well, maybe I am old-fashioned, but without honor, without grace— for that, too, is what you've shown—I say what is life? And I knew this about you. Between you and me, Roly and Bud have their doubts about you in this situation. But not me. I've kept telling them, 'Ethan may not be an outdoorsman but he's a gentleman.' And a friend; for what's at the heart of friendship but loyalty? First, last and always loyalty. Which of course works both ways. You have in me, and I daresay now in Roly and Bud, a real friend. I know you've had some problems settling in here, but now that you've proven yourself such a man, such a friend, you needn't worry about work problems. There will always be something interesting, worthwhile, and highly remunerative for you—a fellowship at the Institute, an academic position at the University, or something among the dozens of consultancies that Roly controls. We New Mexicans may not be the easiest to make friends, but when we do, it is deep and everlasting. And I know, Ethan, I see you smiling and know I'm a talkative and sentimental character, but there it is. That's me and I mean every word I say."

"I'm sure you do. It's just that I don't know what it is you mean. For example, I was smiling now trying to work out whether it was honor or whether it was grace that made you beat me up."

"Now you're confusing me. What are you talking about?"

"Oh no. No, it wasn't only Willy Dixon, though he's the one who told me. If it were only Willy, you'd say he was just trying to get even with you. No, it's your boy, wee Buddy Brandon. Just before I passed out in that beating, I caught a glimpse of him watching his thugs at their efficient work. You have to agree it isn't easy to mistake a six-foot eight-inch muscleman with a two-foot ponytail for anyone else. So, yes, I realize the extent of your thoughtfulness in sending Brandon to my father's funeral."

"I'm not denying it."

"Only because you can't. Willy explained your honor and grace. You have me beaten up: if I leave town, I'm the exploitative boyfriend of Lucy you take me to be; if I stay, I might not be so bad and you reward me with the crumbs off your table."

"I'd hardly call the book commission a crumb."

"No, but it's not off your table. Lucy got me the commission by interesting Charlie Lavery. It was his call, and you're trying to take the credit."

"I'm sorry, Ethan. I didn't want Bud to have you so roughed up. Yes, I sometimes act in a harsh way, but not for bad reasons. I was worried that Lucy had gone from one disaster—Willy—to another, in you. As I said when we first met, this is a different place; we are in many ways old fashioned."

"That's what you call it? Carlos, do you know what someone who hires thugs is called?"

"What?"

"A thug."

"Is that what Lucy thinks of me?"

"That has no bearing on why I'm here. Nor does the fact that you're Emmy's father. Nor, really, does the fact that you had me beaten up. You're criminally abusing public trust, and I'm not going to be complicit by my silence. My grace and honor, as you put it, are satisfied to give you until five tomorrow afternoon to publicly admit the truth about the elk hunt, in which case the videos won't appear. If you don't, the videos will be released."

Alvarado leans back in his chair and pulls at his moustache, smiling. Ethan smiles back to see him so shaken.

"Very moral and very touching, Ethan. But not very intelligent. Or perhaps you don't remember Willy making that call to me when you confronted him?"

"I remember."

"Then you've seen what I can do in one short call. Don't you imagine I can do that again? Now?"

"I imagine you can call and have me beaten up again. As to you having my apartment or Lucy's house broken into, I've already imagined it, so I've put the tapes beyond your reach."

"Do you think there's much beyond my reach here, young man?"

"Technology. It's a new millennium in six weeks. The videos are on computer discs. At the touch of a button, they can go out to every television and radio station and every newspaper in the country, Carlos, old man."

Alvarado's face goes dark red. "Lavery," he says.

"You know, he's not that much younger than you, Carlos, but he knows the technology."

"I hadn't thought you were so brave. Oh, I wouldn't think of touching you. It's Bud I'm worried about. He's very fond of me, and he can be something of a loose cannon."

"I'm not brave. I don't want to be beaten up, but that's up to you. You have twenty-four hours to do the right thing. For what it's worth, I think in the not-so-long run, coming clean could even be good for your reputation."

"Do you seriously think that having not only publicly denied this but challenged James and the environmentalists on this that I would now say to everyone in this city and state and country, 'Whoops, I've been lying. I'm not only an awful liar and awful sportsman, I'm an awful coward'?"

"I don't see it like that." Ethan stands. "Until tomorrow at five."

"You're not loyal and you're no friend."

"Funny how your ideas of loyalty and friendship sound like patronage and servitude, based on fear."

Alvarado leans further back into his chair. "Ethan, this old man still believes you won't do it."

"You have until five tomorrow to find out." He closes the office door on Alvarado shaking his head, smiling, pulling at his fine moustache.

When he leaves the library, Ethan goes to the bench facing the desert garden. He feels as if he's been talking to Meyer as well as to Alvarado. It feels good. So, he thinks, does walking out on Lucy.

Nevertheless, half an hour later, Ethan calls Doc N and, after listening to much praise for using the videos, he tells the story of the carpets.

Doc N says, "Wow. As we say in my anger management group, thank you for sharing."

"Doc, could you do me a favor? Could you ask around or keep an eye out for a property out your way, obviously off the rez, with some land and a house, maybe with a barn or such?"

"Sure, yuh. What kind of price?"

"Around the price of two old Persian carpets."

20

THE PHONE IS RINGING. Ethan puts the light on. Just after five. For a moment, he doesn't know whether morning or afternoon. It's morning and that must be Lucy about to blame him for her sleepless night. He pulls the blankets over his shoulder and closes his eyes. Then he props himself on an elbow and picks up the phone.

"You bastard. You smug, self-centered bastard."

"Who's calling, please?"

"What?"

"A little joke. You know, which among the hundreds who think me a smug, self-centered bastard are you? Not a good joke, I see, if I have to explain it."

"Do you know what time it is?"

"Five past five. Wait, did we have a date to meet at four for an early breakfast, or late supper?"

"You find it amusing that I've been up all night, miserable?"

"Not at all. It's too bad. But there's nothing I said or did that makes me feel guilty."

"Maybe you'll find it amusing that I called Carlos yesterday and begged him to retract and tell the truth."

"Not amusing, admirable. I did the same at four in the afternoon. Did you have any luck?"

"No. We spoke at about one. He was awful. I don't really want to talk about it."

"Neither did he. He didn't mention your call, when I saw him. Want to come over here for breakfast?"

"So you threatened him with the tapes?"

"Yes, if he didn't retract by five this afternoon. Want me to come over there for breakfast?"

"You know I can't stand fighting with you. You know how vulnerable I am."

"I know."

"You shouldn't use it."

"I try not to."

"Which doesn't mean I can't be wrong. My attitude towards Carlos. That call yesterday: I not only saw his feet of clay, I got kicked by them. And then I told Emmy about Carlos being her father. I shouldn't have told her like that, when I was angry, as some stupid way to get back at Carlos. I was a mess."

"And Emmy?"

"She said she knew, but I'm not so sure. She was crying by then, too. She said she'd always suspected it, she said she was crying because of all the time I suffered keeping it from her. That got me, you can imagine, that set me off even worse. But I think she's going to cope with it. After she went to bed, I got thinking it was all your fault."

"And now?"

"Just the timing."

"That's understandable. I could get up to the Co-op bakery by six, around the back like you showed me, and get some warm muffins."

"Okay. And some breakfast rolls."

"Right. See you soon."

"Ethan?"

"What?"

"You won't even say it, will you? I suppose I'll always have to pursue you, be the one to make it up, won't I?"

"No, not always. See you soon. Love you."

He swings his feet out of bed. He's pleased to know she'll always make it up. He has his feet on the ground.

That evening, at five to six, here he sits on the sofa, Lucy beside him, Emmy beside her, and in front of them the TV set already on to the news channel, the set on mute, but ready to speak to them at the click of a button. What an American scene, him and his family before the oracle, his wife who is not his wife but his girlfriend though that's hardly it either who, when he'll be only forty-six will be sixty, who has already forced him to stare at the white creeping up her red hair like a fungus on an autumn maple, stare also at the lines and creases edging her eyes like twin sunbursts of erosion; his daughter next to her who is not his daughter nor either of her two fathers' daughter but the daughter of the man she cheerfully waits to see ruined on the evening news, the daughter of the forty-six-year-old beside her, though at eighteen she looks older than her mother, forget how, he has described how to himself over and over. So here she sits with her drugs and vitamin supplements on the coffee table before her, and mom with her tumbler of gin on the rocks, and boyfriend him with his hefty vodka martini, yum yum, who is becoming aware of how the sex between ma and him has tailed down from its initial frenzy to a sort of wholesome, dull and wholesome and occasional business which is just as well, since his famous limber member won't stand for much more. His arm around Lucy's shoulder, he gives her a pull and a pat of recognition. She's holding Emmy's hand. Lucy's the bosom in the bosom.

What American days of revelation! What with Emmy being born again, though to the beast Alvarado, and Lucy forced to swallow her false loyalties, that is, to spit them out, and what with Ethan secure and aloof as an archangel. And the mid-day news on radio (they were in the kitchen, pottering with soups of blenderized vegetables, half of which he knew only as words but cheering Emmy in her brave new world of arcane nourishment) that Roland Everets, Chief Executive Officer of mining giant TriRock, had just released a short statement apologizing for his earlier denial and admitting that he had trespassed onto posted land where he left a wounded elk, and in addition to paying what fines were his due, he would be making substantial contributions to the Sierra Club and the New Mexico Wildlife Fund, organizations for which he had the highest regard (Emmy interrupted here with "fucking liar," and Lucy whispered that Emmy worked with the NMWF) and as he had not been with either Dr. Alvarado nor Mr. Brandon at the time, his statement should in no way be construed to contradict those of the other two men. To which Ethan: "That rat's just left the ship." And Lucy said, smiling, "Too late." And Ethan thought it was certainly a great gal who knew what side her bed was buttered.

So that now, about to click off the muting from the fourth consecutive commercial for a product beginning with C (cosmetic, car, car, cosmetic) Ethan wonders if he is a true believer in these sudden conversions, including his own into amused paterfamilias.

On comes the sound, on comes the news, and on comes the pre-news headlines. Secret video reveals shocking truth of Valles Caldera elk hunt. Ethan says, "Carlos held out to the end." Emmy says, "So did you." Lucy smiles at both of them. The actual news segment shows a video edit of the Hummer as it returns from the hunt. There are the posted signs out the window, the view down Harrison James's hillside, and the faces and clear-enough voices of Alvarado, Everets and Brandon talking of their wounded elk and the danger of James finding them. The newsreader says that the videos were taken by the writer Ethan Baum, a guest of Dr. Alvarado at the hunt. A "Yay!" from Emmy and "Our hero," from Lucy, our hero not reminding her that two days before he had been her villain. Dr. Alvarado, the news says, cannot be reached for comment, but leading environmentalists see the videos and earlier retraction by Roland Everets as decisive in the fight for votes against the land-use bill. And there, one after a nice, green other, they come, one of them naming Ethan the "best friend our environment's had for some time." Emmy says, "Right on, best friend!" At the end of the segment, Emmy switches off the TV and asks, "What happens now?"

Lucy says, "We toast Ethan and the likely defeat of the land misuse bill." Ethan joins them. Emmy uses the toast to take some pills.

"What actually happens," he says, "is that in about five or ten minutes, the media will find the phone number here and ask questions. Right now, since everything seems to be happening at once, I want to talk about us moving. Your house is on the market and the University wants this place back by next summer. I suggest we consider moving out into the country. What do you think?"

He looks at Lucy. She looks at Emmy. Emmy looks from one to the other and says, "Hey, if that's what you guys want, that's great."

He says, "It's us three guys who have to want it. We could still have apartments and/or offices in town. But I was thinking of someplace where you could have your own space, a wing of a house, or your own cottage, maybe a converted stables. I don't know what's out there."

"Where?" asks Lucy.

"Anywhere, but, for starters, I asked Doc N to look around east of Crownpoint. That's not impossibly far from town."

"It might be okay," Emmy says.

Lucy says, "And I'll have the money from the sale of the house."

"No," Ethan says. "No, I'm thinking of the place as 'Two Carpet Ranch.'"

The phone starts ringing while Lucy's hugging him. What comes to his mind is: "for I,/ Except you enthrall me, never shall be free." He knows he's traducing Donne's Holy Sonnet to understand from this that the more he commits to Lucy, the less dependent on her he'll be.

The phone call is the *Albuquerque Journal*. The next is from a stringer for *USA Today*, and it is solid for five days with this and radio and TV interviews, which he thinks he will enjoy, having done some of this on publicity tours for his novels. Wrong. They ask trick, aggressive questions, questions stunningly non-sequitur. "Why didn't you immediately agree with Charles Lavery?" "If you weren't really a friend of Dr. Alvarado, why would he invite you to his famous elk hunt?" "What exactly is your relation to Lucy Evans and her recent estrangement from Professor William Dixon?" To which Ethan's first responses are, "I'm not sure," "Huh?" and "What?" When he gets to read and hear and see these interviews, he's in the presence of a new persona, Ethan the Inarticulate. Lucy, doing her best, comes up with, "You look so good on television."

Despite his ineptness, he's asked to send a copy of the videos to Santa Fe and to appear there to testify at a Land-Use Bill Committee Hearing. This interests him. Two days later, he's informed his presence will not be required. A week after the videos are first shown, media interest in Ethan pretty much stops. The videos, however, continue, as does a complete silence from Alvarado and Brandon, rumored to be somewhere in New or old Mexico. Then ABC does a longer interview with Ethan, puts it together with the best of the videos and presents Ethan as the reluctant hero of green politics. This twenty-minute segment seems to him an improbable fiction; a series of cleverly edited statements he's made, he must have made, over images of Alvarado shooting an elk by the posted signs, of mountains of rock rubble leached with cyanide by TriRock to get gold, of leach reservoir spills into western rivers and the dead birds on their banks as the belly-up fish drift by, of Alvarado's grand haciendas in Otero and San Miguel counties, of Everets' thirty room house, "Getaway," at Jackson Hole, followed by footage of a demonstration outside his Denver headquarters protesting his last year's salary bonus of fifty-seven million dollars.

This program brings Ethan so much publicity that, after years of silence, it elicits a call from his agent, Sonny Legman. "Jesus, Ethan, you have like five million bucks of publicity here, so if you had something to sell, anything—notes, an idea, even—we could do very well with it right now. But right now!" This is enough for Ethan to say, "No, nothing," and hang up angry and desolate about his writing, his own writing, not the New Mexico book which is essentially overblown caption writing for photography.

Yet it is this he works on, sometimes conferring with Lavery, into early December, when he has to go to Boston to finally close up the apartment. In all this time, nothing is heard from Alvarado, though much is heard about him. The University Board of Regents is meeting to discuss his future, as is the Board of the New Mexico Institute. There's an unspoken understanding between Ethan and Lucy not to speak of this. If she has given in, he mustn't rub it in. Lavery, on the other hand, is lavish with background: both the Regents and the Institute Board have been looking for years for a suitable pretext to dump old Carlos. Why? Because he sails too close to the wind for these starchy arch conservatives; because his arrogance has made bad enemies among both boards, and because his pride is keeping him from doing the one thing that might still save him—begging their forgiveness, getting down and kissing each august, uptight ass.

Lavery is right. Two days after the Regents ask for Alvarado's resignation as Vice President, the Institute Board announces that while fully appreciating the magnificent contribution Dr. Alvarado has made, it is time the Institute looked to the future with a new, possibly younger Director. On both these occasions, Lucy and Ethan say, "It's too bad," and "The whole thing's too bad," respectively. Emmy twice says, "Good. He got what he deserved."

Then he goes to Boston to close the apartment. Close that life, he thinks. Thirty-two years since birth, good-bye. No regrets, that is, no regrets about leaving. The other regrets accompany him back on the plane to Albuquerque, where new regrets arise as he lands: he was too hasty in committing all his money to buying a place for them, a home. He regrets choosing this plain-looking, successful writer *who keeps right on writing*; he regrets opting for a home life with an eighteen-year-old, seventy-pound *memento mori*, a jealous, fractious, self-obsessed… He leaves it as poor Emmy. Poor Lucy, poor Emmy, poor him.

It's surprising that, given these regrets, when he comes into the airport's central hall and doesn't find Lucy waiting for him as promised, he feels so let down. Instead of Lucy, there is Stucic, Stucic waving and nodding and practically jumping up and down to get his attention, and Stucic coming his way.

"Ethan, I am so happy to... That is, your father's death is so very sad, but not, of course, for me to see you. How are you? How are you? Miserable, of course. I am so sorry, but that even in your misery it is for me a delight to be able... That is, it seemed under the circumstances of your bereavement and your heroic fight against the forces of land despoliation, not to mention your book deadline, that there would be little time for you to see me, so that learning from your dear Lucy that she was to meet you, I suggested myself, not as a substitute, naturally, for there could be no substitute for—"

"Where are you parked?"

"Yes, yes, of course, your bags. I had thought they would be less, smaller, since you were away, I learned, only a few days. But never mind. All will fit. My car, which you do well to remind me of, since I would not want any infraction to cause you delay, is parked directly at the entrance. This way, right down here."

Ethan says, "I brought the big suitcase to bring back some personal items from my father's apartment."

Stucic turns to look back up the escalator: "Yes, I will continue reading through your father's *oeuvre*, of course."

Ethan says, "Of course."

Outside, Stucic says, "*Merde, alors!*" What he curses towards is an old two-tone VW Beetle by which a New Mexican State Trooper stands, pen poised above a ticket pad.

Stucic waves and says, "Officer, my good fellow, please, wait."

The trooper, tall and lean as a whip, looks up: "Are you the driver of this vehicle?"

Stucic says, "Yes, yes, driver and owner. The papers...." He fishes in his pocket. Ethan sets his small bag and his briefcase down beside his big suitcase.

The trooper says, "This is a pick-up zone only. No parking, no waiting. It's painted all over the road. There are signs every ten feet. Didn't you think they applied to you?"

Stucic says, "Of course, certainly I knew. But you see, I was picking up—"

"May I see your license, please," says the trooper.

Stucic says, "Yes, here, here it is, all in order." Ethan hopes Stucic will now be quiet, get the ticket, and take him home.

Stucic says, "I was picking up this man, this local hero, as you say. You perhaps recognize him from television? Mr. Ethan Baum?"

The trooper continues looking at the driving license. Ethan says, "That's all right, Miroslav, Slava, please."

Stucic says, "This is the man who took the video of, who videoed the men who illegally shot those elk and left the poor beasts to die miserably and who denied it."

The trooper looks up from the license at Ethan. He says, "Oh, yeah. You're that guy?"

Ethan gives a small nod and a modest shrug.

The trooper says, "You're the guy was this friend of these other guys?"

Ethan says, "Well, not exactly a—"

"Was their guest up there? The one who doesn't hunt?" says the trooper.

Ethan says, "Well, that doesn't really—"

"And then you rat on your friends?" says the trooper.

Ethan says, "I—"

"And you're from where, New York? Boston?"

Ethan says, "Boston."

"Boston," says the trooper. He looks down at his boots and repeats, "Boston," as if it were something he's stepped in.

Ethan glances at the trooper's boots. Stucic watches a plane fly away from the airport.

The trooper holds the license out to Stucic. "I don't want anything to do with you. Take this and your friend and get that piece of shit car away from this airport right now." He turns to his motorcycle.

Stucic says, "Yes, officer. Thank you so—"

"Don't thank me. Don't thank me, just get out of here!" The trooper puts his helmet on, starts his motorcycle and slowly moves off.

Stucic says, "You see it was, one way or another, a good idea of me to mention you."

The kind of good an idea that makes headlines like Trooper Shoots Local Hero at Airport, thinks Ethan. He says, "How are we going to get this into the car?"

Stucic says, "Leave it to me, my friend. It will be a simplicity itself."

The trunk is simply full. Ethan's luggage is simply thrown into the back seat, a corner of the big suitcase protruding between the front bucket seats. Never has "bucket" seemed so literal, as in the little plastic bucket in the hand of a small child at the beach. Ethan's left knee is splayed to the stick shift, his right to the door; both knees jammed against the dashboard. His left shoulder is bent forward by the protruding suitcase so that his torso is twisted right, forcing his bent, twisted head to look up and out the side window. His head he understands only in its denotative sense, since he's totally without one to accept this ride.

Stucic says, "Ready?" To which Ethan can say only, "Go."

There follows a whirring, clicking sound, as if a group of large grasshoppers were in the back, or, perhaps, as if a VW starter motor were defective. Again, a whirring and a clicking, like thoughts of a dry brain in a dry season.

Stucic says, "It is nothing. Don't worry."

Ethan says, "It is nothing is why I'm worried."

Stucic says, "Very witty, my friend," and makes the car produce the rustling noises, again, though somewhat quieter.

Ethan is about to suggest he put himself and his luggage into a taxi, when he thinks he hears the car start. No, it is only the sound of a motorcycle drawing up behind them, a sound impossible to verify by sight, since Ethan cannot turn his head back. Stucic keeps turning the dying starter motor, and now Ethan, from his Quasimodan viewpoint, is looking up and out into the dark blue crotch of someone he bets is his friend the state trooper and NRA *gaulieter*. Stucic has reduced the starter to a click or two, a noise not much louder than, say, that made when the safety is snapped off a police handgun. The lowest crag of the trooper's chin appears in Ethan's window, the hard line of his mouth—Ethan knows he's seen salmon with softer mouths—and here's the black-gloved index finger coming onto the glass and tapping, tapping, in time with the clicking, clicking of the car. The car clicks, clicks and bangs, the banging continues until each one is almost connected to the next; there is a roar of bangs, the shift slams into Ethan's left knee, and they're moving away from the trooper at the curb.

Ethan is so relieved that for several seconds he doesn't feel the pain. Stucic says, "You are probably wondering why I so much wanted to talk with you."

Ethan has never before felt a pain like this. It is an arrow which begins inside the back of his left knee, goes to the top of the thigh and in through his groin to the base of his spine, slants up the right side of his back and ends, that is, has its arrow point, in a vertebrae he's not until now known he possesses, a few inches up into the back of his head. Ethan says, "Ah, ah. Why?"

Stucic says, "Many, many wonderful things have happened and continue to happen, for which I know you are, if not the cause, then, at least, the reason I have survived to, as it were, experience them."

Stucic begins to explain the happy reverse of his fortune as Ethan sees the top of an airport hotel down off the airport road. The roof is flat, tarred and graveled. There is good news about Stucic and his daughter Elena. Ethan, unable to nod, says, "Good." Stucic goes on to explain how the rapprochement began. The airport hotels out the VW side window come thick and fast. There is further good news about proof of Stucic's not being a war criminal. The car stops, Ethan guesses, at a red light. The hotel outside the window has a Spanish look, as mass-produced in pre-cast concrete. A man comes out of the hotel door and turns back, as if waiting for another person to follow. Ethan sees the side of the man's mouth working. The side of the mouth looks annoyed. Stucic is finishing up with Elena and going on to Vera. Who? Yes, his wife. Even there, things are better. Ethan says, "Good." Things are not yet good with Vera, but they are better. "Good," Ethan says. The hotels switch to motels. Lower and cheaper motels, as the VW window goes down Yale Avenue. Stucic is now onto the gossip about Carlos and the Institute and University. Ethan has not followed this closely enough to judge when to interject a "good," or is it a "thank you" that's now called for? It isn't just the physical discomfort he's in, and he is happy enough for Stucic: but what, he wonders, is one to do, listening to an unbroken tale of glad tidings? The dungaree factory and retail outlet goes by. Ethan wonders what the dungarees are like. He means, Stucic is like a salesman giving you his upbeat pitch. You're really not expected to discuss anything; you're there essentially to be worn down by the patter and, at its close, to buy whatever it is he's trying to sell. Now they're passing the old cemetery he first walked with Doc N. What had Doc said? What is Stucic saying? Oh, thanking him for saving his life. "I didn't, really," Ethan says. Not much longer now until they're at Las Lomas. Maybe Stucic and Lucy will, working together, manage to extrude him from the car. And now they're driving into the campus, and, by counting, Ethan can hang on. They pull into the small semi-circular drive. Ethan sees the blessed fake adobe. Stucic is saying, "and for so much of this, you are, my good friend, so to speak, so to thank." The car stops. Stucic's hand comes across to shake Ethan's. Ethan's hand cannot cross over to the left. He hears something clicking that is not the car but something simultaneously in his neck and in his left knee. He manages to further squinch his left shoulder and move certain parts of his body in response to Stucic's profered hand. Ethan says, "You're very welcome, Slava. I wonder if you could get this door opened from the outside?"

The house is empty. Lucy, freed by Stucic, is not there to greet him, him the orphan. Good, he can do some thinking. He decides to stretch his legs, walk across the campus, walk over to Copper Place, do some thinking in *his* place.

At the apartment, he pours a vodka and sits at his desk. It's nice how it's turned out, here. All his books, his paintings, the two rugs—Lucy's old Two Gray Hills and his newer but still not too new Ganado. But this place isn't his. Navajo rugs, carpets, the old Persian carpets that he caught notice of, just in time. There was some link, old Hubbell at his trading post showing Persian carpets to the Navajo a hundred years ago, or more. What on earth difference does it make, since he can't write a novel at Las Lomas, can't write a novel here, can't anywhere. What is he getting himself into? Why buy a ranch? To saddle himself.

He looks in the kitchen cupboard to see if there's soup for lunch. The phone rings. Lucy, for sure. "Hello?"

"Is this Ethan?"

He recognizes Jean Brown. Jeanie; her voice, her hair, her eyes, breasts, belly, the smell of her. He's breathless, says, "Yes. Who's this?"

"Jean Brown, from Cedar Crest? You wouldn't remember me. You stopped at the gas station last summer and we showed you a German shepherd puppy."

He says, "Oh, yes, of course. Your little boy, and you... Weren't you expecting a puppy?"

"A baby."

"A baby, of course, a baby."

"Yes, Lee. She's three months old."

"Congratulations, that's wonderful. Your husband sent me his photographs Dave, that's right. They're good. I've been meaning to show them to Charlie Lavery."

"Dave's photographs, yes. I was wondering—a friend is looking after the children this afternoon. Would it be possible to see you? I mean, I don't want to impose. I know you've recently lost your father. I'm sorry. You probably won't, this is such short notice, but—"

"Have you had lunch?"

"No."

He says, "What about Blue Heaven, in Corales, at one o'clock?" There's no one he knows out there.

"Corales?"

"It's that I have to be out that way."

"Sure, of course. This is really good of you."

"Not at all. It'll be nice to catch up. Blue Heaven is about halfway up Corales Road."

"I know. I really appreciate this."

He says, "I'll see you there at one."

He calls the restaurant and reserves a table. Blue Heaven, he thinks, showering. Blue as in blue movie. Not sad like the blues or learned like blue-stocking. Blue stockings, Jeanie's underpants. He puts on fresh clothes and goes down to the Jeep. There are traffic jams from Alameda. There's nothing wrong with agreeing to see someone who's asked to see him. So what if she happens to be younger than him, much younger than Lucy? What could she want to see him about? He resists honking his horn at the idiot in front of him who's gone too slow to make the traffic light. He's merely someone who's shown an interest in her, her husband, child, dogs. For heaven's sake, a patron, in a small way, of Dave Brown's photography. The light turns green. Ethan smiles at the shallowness of his rationale and steps on the gas.

In the Blue Heaven parking lot just before one, the afternoon turns gray and cold. In through the window, he sees the restaurant is half empty; Jean's not there yet, and there's no one he recognizes.

He goes in and sits at a table where he can see the door. If someone recognized him, how could they read his thoughts? The bar waiter comes. He orders a vodka martini. He thinks of Corales, a farming village with maybe one farm left, where the newer settlers keep llamas and Lamborghinis. The martini comes and isn't cold enough. His waitress comes over, wearing what looks like a cowgirl dirndl. She says, "Hi, I'm Tamsin, your server. What's your name?"

He wants to say, "Hi, I'm your customer Mr. Customer, but you can call me Sir." He says, "I'm waiting for someone to join me."

"Sure, no problem."

To her back, to himself, he says he hasn't in any way said there was a problem. He drinks his uncold martini quickly, before it can get tepid. Is he at thirty-two an old fart? He looks around. No offense registers on these chewing, talking faces. He's certain he isn't a sort of fuddy-duddy Miniver Cheevy. He signals the bar waiter and keeps on drinking.

The second martini is properly cold. She isn't coming. Okay, he'll have lunch and try to understand why he wants to buy a home to settle down with Lucy. With Lucy and Emmy. Not to settle down, to settle up. Gratefulness and guilt. He's high, at the end of the second martini when at one-thirty in comes Jeanie Brown.

He tries to frown at her lateness, but he stands and smiles. She's wonderful looking. She shines. He kisses her cheek; it's damp.

"Hi," she says. "Hi. I'm sorry I'm late. I..."

"Have you been running?" He's still standing close to her, unwilling to move from the smell of her sweat.

She shakes her head. "No."

He pulls back a chair for her. She sits. He sits. His chair seems to be floating towards hers. He says, "Would you like a drink?"

She says, "No, I've been here, sitting in my car in the parking lot for twenty minutes afraid to come in. Thinking I couldn't: you wouldn't be here or you would and this was, you know, you don't even know me." She pushes her fingers across her forehead. "Oh, I'm dripping wet. Excuse me." She stands. "I'll have whatever—Is that a martini?"

"A vodka martini."

"Yes, a vodka martini, thank you."

He orders and pours a glass of ice water for himself. He can smell her on his fingers. He thinks of the nobleman in Saint-Simon's memoirs who, smelling the handkerchief of a young woman who's used it to wipe her perspiration from dancing, asks an attendant whose it is, and then returns to the ballroom to find her and marry her. And does. And what, dear reader, would Jane Austen have thought of that? Ethan sips ice water. What cools him down, just as Jean returns, is the certainty that she's nervous because she's here to ask him for money, a loan for Dave and her and the failing business. He stands, smiling to think what a lucky time for her to ask.

But first he must listen to Tamsin's recital of the day's specials, the usual specials of a country so sick rich it is devouring the planet in recipes with two too many ingredients: mandarin orange in the curry sauce, balsamic duckling dusted in crushed almond, the elk loin on truffled arugula. They choose salads. Ethan expects they'll be of gilded lilies. Tamsin says, "Why not? Good choice."

Before Ethan can think of a toast, Jean begins to drink her martini. He says. "How are Dave and Billy, and the dogs?"

She says, "The dogs. Billy's good. He's very sweet with his new sister. Dave's fine. Well, he's well. I mean, we're breaking up." Her hands fold around the stem of the martini glass on the table. "Not that that's what I wanted to talk to you about, though it is at the back of what I'm trying to work out." She looks at her hands and repeats, "Work out."

He says, "I'm sorry." He is strangely sorry that his image of her family intimacy is broken.

She says, "Don't bother. Dave is just stuck into that gas station. He's set on making a bad deal with the owner of the Cedar Crest Deli to run their operation at the gas station, too. Look, this isn't what I… Something I didn't tell you when we first met: I write. It used to be a private thing, but for a few years now it's been more. Anyway, God, I don't know how I can look at you and say this. I've just read your novels. *Jack at Bat*, *Jack off First*, and *Who's on Second*. They're wonderful. You're just a wonderful writer."

Ethan says, "Thank you." She's just told him he can have her but also that he can't write fiction anymore. He can't imagine how he wrote those novels.

She says, "*Who's on Second* made me weep. It's very sad and very funny. But it's not corny, not sentimental."

He feels like weeping. Tamsin brings the salad. He concentrates on the production she makes with the tree-length pepper mill. They neither of them want pepper. Ethan thinks of the baseball metaphor in *Jack at Bat* of "a little pepper," the call for teamwork, energy, enthusiasm. He wants a little pepper. He calls Tamsin back and says he's sorry but, yes, he'd like her to mill some pepper on his salad and also bring them or ask the drinks waiter to bring them a bottle of the Cordon Rouge. "Is that all right, Jeanie?"

"Champagne? Yes."

Tamsin says, "Good choice."

"Is 'Jeanie' all right, or do you prefer Jean?"

"Jeanie's good. I like it."

They sit quietly, not looking at each other while looking at each other. She finishes her martini. Ethan drinks two ice waters. The bar waiter brings an ice-bucket stand and opens the champagne. When he leaves, Ethan raises his glass: "To you, to your writing." Jean shakes her head, smiles, and drinks. The side of her neck below her ear glistens. He looks from her neck to her eyes and back to her shining neck. He wonders if her beauty will louse up her writing. He can taste the salt of her cunt in his champagne. That old Frenchman was no fool. Of course he was. They're looking at each other now. He'd better stop this drunken foolishness. He says, "Look—"

"May I ask you something, Ethan?"

"Of course."

"You were something like twenty-three when you wrote your first novel. I'm twenty-eight and just beginning. Is that too old?"

"Too old? That's eighteen years younger than.... You're four years younger than I am. Of course you're not too old. Writing isn't like gymnastics or ballet."

"Right. Okay, thank you." She pushes her salad around. She begins eating. Sometimes her hair swings forward and she pushes it back, fork in her hand. She catches him watching her and smiles at him. The best thing he could do for her writing career would be to convince her she was a plain Jane. Plane Jean. Jeanie with the light brown hair and those eyes. Chaucer, of course: *Your eyen two wol sle me sodenly,/ I may the beaute of hem not sustene...* He says, "So are you still out at Cedar Crest?"

"No. My friend, the one looking after the children this afternoon, has a house in town with a *casita*. We're there. Dave comes in to visit the children and I bring them out to Cedar Crest for the day on Saturday and Sunday."

Now Ethan understands. She needs the loan for herself. "If you don't mind my asking, how are you getting by financially, with all this?"

"Oh, now that I've broken up with Dave, my mother is happy to help. She's a psychiatrist. In Chicago. She's never been a big fan of Dave. She thought Dave's gentleness was actually laziness. I'm sorry it turned out she was right."

Tamsin comes by: "How is everything, guys?"

Ethan says, "Fine. No, we'll pour the champagne ourselves, thanks."

"No problem."

Ethan tops up their glasses. "If there's any way I can be of help. Perhaps I could talk to Dave or—"

"I don't think I'm looking for reconciliation. But thank you."

Ethan feels exhausted. Boston, the flight, Stucic, drinking all this so fast… With his fork, he moves a piece of goat cheese through a grove of lamb's lettuce. To sleep with his head along Jeanie's neck, just there. She wants coffee. He orders two coffees. The coffees come. She stirs the spoon around in her cup.

She looks up and says, "I guess you haven't asked about my writing because you must be tired of people bugging you. I don't know. But I'm serious about writing. And I don't know if I have any right to ask. I don't have any claim on your time, but here's what I wanted to say. What I would like more than anything else is to study under you."

Ethan is charmed by the way she puts this. He says, "I don't know. Maybe we could work something out."

"That would be wonderful." She hands him a slip of paper. "Here's my phone and email. And please let this be my treat."

"No, this was my idea, and most of the bill is my drinks, so let me insist."

She puts her hand across on his and squeezes it. "Thank you. For this and whatever you're able to work out. I know you're busy with the book and land bill—I've seen you on the news—but any time you could give me, I'd really love it."

He walks Jean to her car, at the far end of the parking lot, between two cottonwoods. Should he kiss her? Tell her how beautiful she is? Hold her wonderful body close? He says, "It was good seeing you," holds out his hand and leans to kiss her cheek. She pulls into him and tips her head back and they're kissing, open mouthed, tasting, tongues, vodka, champagne, his hand slid into her open coat. He pushes away. She says, "I think I've had too much champagne. Thank you, Ethan. This has been wonderful. Are you near where you're going?"

"Where I'm going? Oh, yes, it's not far."

He stands with his hand on the cottonwood, watching her back out, wave to him, and drive out of the parking lot. Not until he sees her turn on Corales Road does he go to the Jeep. Maybe she's parked out there, waiting to follow him to his hideaway. What is he thinking? Rancho Escondido. He must be nuts.

On the drive back to Lucy's house, he makes selections from Jeanie's conversation: She'd really love it; she wants to study under him. And, when she first came in, did she not say she was dripping wet? He edits his selections: She loves it dripping wet under him, and reconciliation with Dave is not what she's looking for.

Next thing he knows, he's at Las Lomas and Lucy is in her doorway, kissing him. "Where have you been? I've been calling your apartment, Stucie, Charlie, everyone."

He says, "I had to see someone. I didn't know where you were. I drank too much at lunch. I need to sleep."

She takes his coat in the hall. "Who did you see?"

"Someone I met on one of my trips. In Cedar Crest. I helped her husband a little. Nice people." He walks down the hallway. Lucy follows.

She says, "Is she pretty? Did you kiss her? Is she in love with you?"

He says, "What?"

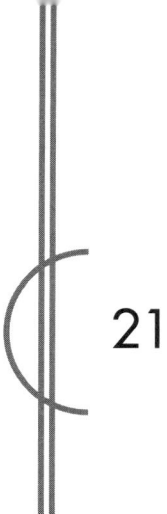

21

"OH, OF COURSE SHE IS," says Lucy. "You're the best looking man in Albuquerque, in North Central New Mexico."

Ethan hugs her. She says, "Did you know that another of my attractive qualities, besides being old and plain, is that I'm murderously jealous?"

He puts an arm around her waist and pulls her into the bedroom and onto the bed on top of him and falls asleep.

He wakes at one in the morning, still fully dressed. Lucy is sleeping. He remembers dreaming about his mother but can't hold on to it. In the bathroom, he takes off his clothes and stands in front of the mirror. He says to his reflected image, "What is your problem?" He says, "Where is your energy? Where is your passion? Hey, come on, a little pepper, here!" He says, "Your good looks sicken me. Your good looks can't write." He says, "Your dark almond eyes have slayed me, suddenly, soddenly. I can no longer bear my beauty. How did Meyer manage with those looks to do so much work, considering his compulsions? Maybe he thought the physical inheritance plus the carpets would slay me suddenly, for sure. Is that why I need to give it to Lucy and Emmy?" In the mirror, he sees the bathroom door move. "Lucy?"

"I was outside, listening." She's naked. She nudges him to the side and runs cold water into her cupped hands and drinks. When she straightens, they see in the mirror the water drip from her chin to her chest, above her breasts.

She says, "I know that Chaucer poem, the Triple Roundel to Beauty. That was the first part, about love. But the second part goes, 'So hath your beauty from your heart chased/ Pity, that it doesn't avail me to complain,/ For Danger halts your mercy in his chain.'"

He says, "The archaic meaning of danger, the power to hurt."

She says, "Aren't we two naked smartasses."

He says, "As well as two lonely babes in the wood," and sings, "so lady be good"—as she sings, "so mister be good—to me."

He says, "I'm putting my hand on your smart ass to swear you are and always will be enough for me."

Her hand goes onto Ethan's buttocks. "I know that. The question is, am I too much?"

They put robes on and have tea and toast in the kitchen. "Feeling better now?" she asks.

"The worst of the hangover is gone. I like it that you don't mind being quiet with me. Sometimes, when I felt he wasn't ignoring me, I liked that in Meyer. Meyer... That's right. I remember the dream I just had."

"I'd ask you to tell me about it, if you didn't mind me breaking my quiet with you."

He takes her smile for playfulness and says, "I was walking with Meyer on a white street. It was Oaxaca. We turned into the yard of Carmen's so-called family house. It was empty. We sat on a bench and Meyer told me I'd let myself be bullied by the police in Oaxaca because I felt guilty and wanted to be punished. He said that attitude would kill me. I didn't like hearing this, so I stood and went into the house, but Meyer called after me that even if I hadn't been in Oaxaca, Carmen would have been beaten by the three Americans. I walked down the narrow corridor. In the gloom of the first room I saw a woman. It was Marion, my mother. I wanted to go to her, but she had such a sad smile that I couldn't bear it. I continued down the corridor and there in the shadow of the next room stood my mother again, with the same unbearable smile. Then I knew the corridor was endless, each room with my sad mother looking at me endlessly. That's the dream."

Lucy says, "What do you make of it?"

"I don't know: Meyer seems pretty obviously the id. The ego energizer. You know, just do it, forget the others, forget social mores, even morality, and do what you have to. And there's my mother in me saying look what happens when you do. Of course, I have no way of knowing how happy or unhappy she was in her life. But that was the dream."

"Do you think it's about your writing?"

"My writing?" he asks, as if this were the furthest interpretation from his mind. "Yes, certainly about my writing. How did you know?"

"Because all those years I couldn't see what was happening right in front of my nose to Emmy. Because at some level I was afraid that if I let myself see, it would threaten my writing. And I went on doing this even though friends—Roberta, and Charlie, even sweet Doc—told me in so many words what I was up to."

"There it is," he says.

"No, that's not it. Look, maybe what attracted me to you besides your looks was thinking that we would recognize each other's need to live as writers. That we wouldn't have to justify or explain that. And now you say you can't write. That's not literally so, because your writing for Charlie's book is really good. But, I know, it's not fiction. I understand. But the choice your dream suggests to you is false. It's not either write and be a selfish bastard or don't write and be nice. Nice! If you stopped writing and it made you miserable, you wouldn't be nice, you'd probably be a bastard. But going on and on, unable to do what you want is also no good for your self-esteem or happiness. All I can say is if you should stop being a novelist—if you decided—I wouldn't think less of you. I'm perfectly selfish about it: the more unhappy you are with yourself, the less you can love me or like me, no matter how many ranches you buy me and Emmy. How's that for being quiet?"

He slides his chair over, puts his arm around her, and is quiet. She has never been so open with him, so real. He believes Lucy knows it, too. Yet he can't tell her of what his mother's image at its deepest suggests: what kept him from going to her in those dark dream rooms was not so much his guilt as his terror. She was not merely dead, she was death, his own death, his suicide. He kisses Lucy's ear to forget.

Two weeks before Christmas, the day before the land-use bill is voted on, Lucy drives out on I-40 West with Ethan and Emmy to look at a property Doc N has found. They meet Doc and Hosteen Charlie at the Wauneka family set-up outside Crownpoint and then follow Doc's pickup east on Navajo 48, leaving the rez at State 509. The land is dry and rocky, and Ethan looks at Lucy with disappointment and shakes his head. He turns to see Emmy in the back seat smiling out the window. The land rises, trees and grass appear, and they follow the pickup east onto a track. They come over a low ridgeline into a small valley. It ends in rolling hills. Beyond, under the bright blue of early afternoon, are higher mesas, pale red and pale yellow. "Hmm," says Lucy, comfortably. Ethan shrugs. Halfway along the valley floor they drive through an open gate in a low wire fence. Lucy pulls up by Doc's stopped truck.

Hosteen Charlie leans out the window. "From the fence to that first ridge, that's the spread. Buildings up the top end. The ridge is East Hills and part of the Cibola Forest beyond." Ethan sees some faraway buildings. Hosteen Charlie says, "Place is called Little Coyote Valley, so I guess this is Little Coyote Ranch." Doc N gets out of the pickup and comes to Ethan's window. He says, "Some Californians bought this. They thought they'd turn it into a fancy dude ranch. When they came out and looked close, they got spooked. Yuh, it was too far from anywhere rich, too close to a lot of poor Indians. It makes you feel a little bad for them." He brings his thumb and index finger together: "About this much. The word is they want out fast and will take an offer considerably less than the asking price."

Hosteen Charlie points down the track: "You got a main house and a little house, not that little. There's a barn. We been there. The siding's no good but the beams and rafters are, and there's lots of good tongue-in-groove inside. You also got some falling-down stables. But you got to look past all that, cause what you got here is almost three hundred acres with two good wells and a pretty good stream down there. Water is why I figure this is a good buy."

When they get to the buildings, Doc and Hosteen Charlie leave the three of them to walk around. The houses are shut up, but it's obvious that the main, two storey house is large and solid. Lucy and Ethan say, almost at once, that it needs a porch around it. When they walk around the small, single storey house, Emmy says, "This would be—Could I have this? This would be cool. The cottonwoods out there and the hills. Probably there are lots of wild animals. I could have a dog, a golden retriever." "And what would you call it?" Ethan asks. "Him," she says. "I'd call him Lucky."

Later, when Ethan and Lucy are walking through the barn on their own, he says, "Emmy already has a name for her dog."

Lucy says, "Looks like we'll just have to buy the place, won't we?"

"I could make a good workroom out here."

"The house and cottage are situated perfectly with the stream and cottonwoods. It's really beautiful, Ethan. Do you like it?"

"So much I wouldn't call it after the carpets. Little Coyote Ranch is fine."

"We'd fix it up with the money from the sale of the house. My workroom would be on the second floor of the house, at the back, with the view to the East Hills ridge."

He says, "Let's check it out again with Emmy and go from there."

Before they can ask her, Emmy says, "The first thing we have to do is post the land."

He says, "Right after getting the name of the real estate agent from Doc."

Before leaving, they walk up the hill path behind the barn. Emmy, too, her arm on Lucy's arm. They stop a few hundred paces up and look down on the trees, fields, and buildings.

Lucy says, "If we get this place—"

"We'll get this place," says Ethan.

"Yes," Lucy says. "Will we be happy here?"

"Yes," he says.

Emmy says, "Yeah, well, we damn well better be."

They drive back with the sun setting behind them. It's not until the outskirts of the city, when Ethan imagines the fine workroom he might have in the barn, that he realizes he still won't be able to write a novel.

Next day, the Land Use bill is defeated by two votes in the State Senate. But what should be his great joy if he is to be part of this land is no more than a pleasure that fades as soon as Lucy and Emmy and he finish hugging, as soon as he hangs up the phone after Charlie Lavery calls. He's invited with Charlie, and Lucy, of course, up to Santa Fe for a celebration lunch, guest of the key legislators who fought the bill. Much toasting of each other and of many places in the saved environments goes on in the smart Canyon Road restaurant. Besides this general image, what Ethan most remembers is a drunken senator pulling him to a corner of a table saying, "C'mere, you wanna know the God's honest. You wanna?"

"I do, honestly," says Ethan.

"Is this: okay, okay, okay, we won this one, sure. But if that asshole governor of Texas gets to be president, you mark my words, you can kiss all our good work goodbye, goodbye. Goodbye, know what I mean? I mean two years down the line in Washington, this deregulation shit's gonna come up for all the federal land, thousand times more of it here than state land, and all tucked into some fuckin' innocuously—hey, not so drunk I can't say that—hidden in some *innocuously* worded rider to some federal appropriation bill that's fuckin' got to pass. So what you think of that?"

Ethan says, "It sounds plausible, Senator." He remembers how well this man's prediction fit his own mood.

Three days before Christmas, Ethan's big present arrives by registered mail: a bank draft from the Corporation of the Boston Museum of Fine Arts for $771,480. The accompanying note from Alex Goulatis says, first, that Ethan might be wondering about the peculiarly unrounded sum. It says, second, that he shouldn't even ask. Ethan then phones the real estate agent, introduces himself, and says he'd like to make an offer on Little Coyote Ranch, in McKinley County. The agent says she can't seem to find his name. He says he's never registered. She says she can arrange a visit to the property. He says he's been to the property and repeats that he'd like to make an offer. At this point, she begins to hear him, because she says it's a really nice property with a lot of development potential. He says he doesn't want to develop it. He wants to live there. He says he's offering $750,000 for the property. The agent laughs and says that's an unrealistically low offer on an asking price of one point one million. He says he's offering $750,000 and it's not a bargaining position, but it will be cash, no mortgage involved. She says, yes, that is a point in his favor. He asks if she'll make his offer to her clients. She says she will, because it's her job to do so. He says nothing. She says that actually her clients are very eager to sell, and since he's making an offer on the entire property, and since there won't be financing problems, well, who knows, he might be lucky. He says nothing. She says as a matter of fact, and this is strictly between them, she's going to do what she can to make her clients consider his offer very seriously. He thanks her, gives her his details, and asks for her to proceed as quickly as possible.

When he puts down the phone, he tells Lucy what the agent has said. She asks, "What do you think?"

"Since everything she said fit with what Doc and Hosteen Charlie told us, I think we'll get it."

"It's good to hear you so positive,"

He laughs. "I can be positive." About the unimportant things, he thinks.

On December 30, the agent calls to say that by working hard, she has convinced her clients to accept his offer. He says good. She says he must be very pleased to have made such a good buy. He says yes and asks what next. She says she'll bring the papers to him on the second. He needs to write a check then for $75,000 and then, when the title company completes its search, pay the remaining $675,000. She wishes him a very happy and prosperous New Year and knows with this property it will be. He says yes and wishes her the same.

Dick Palmer calls to tell Ethan and Lucy that Roberta has come down with an awful flu, so they have to cancel their Millennium shindig. There are two other parties they've been asked to, but when Lucy says she'd rather make it a quiet night in—Emmy will be overnight with Elena and friends—Ethan is relieved. There is too much ungraspable about the big, round 2000; severe anti-climax seems built in.

So they watch TV fireworks circle the Earth towards them. Sydney, Tokyo, Hong Kong, Singapore, New Delhi, Istanbul, Moscow, Budapest, Berlin, Paris, London. Then, while midnight crosses the unilluminated Atlantic, they make supper and afterwards find dance music on the radio and dance together in the living room and through the long hall into the kitchen and back through the dining room and out to the porch room. And a while after this they watch the fireworks in New York City and Miami. They nod off on the sofa, but then there's the fireworks in Chicago and New Orleans, and soon Ethan brings the best bottle of champagne from the fridge and the fireworks come to Las Lomas Road, fireworks on television and outside on the street. They go out into the garden to see them. The night is cold. They kiss and toast: Lucy hopes the strangely numbered new year brings Ethan what he wants, the start of a new novel. This—not just the Tattinger—touches him. He hopes for Lucy that Emmy is well and happy, that they all are happy in their new home together. Lucy says, "Don't you dare not wish me good writing."

In late January, as Ethan hands in the final section of his text to the Institute, the purchase of Little Coyote Ranch goes through. Emmy insists on taking them out to dinner where she toasts the ranch, invites them to dinner in her cottage there when it's finished, "because," she says, "I'm going to use my trust to make it just what I want, a small but devastatingly cool place." And after they drink to this she says, "I have another toast, if you're allowed to have two in a row. To you, Mom, for biting your tongue all these months you knew I was writing, and to you, Ethan, for being an unbelievably patient teacher. And, I guess, to me, because that story 'Vanishing Cream' has been accepted by an Arizona literary magazine called *Big Saguaro*."

Even while Ethan is hugging and kissing Lucy and Emmy, and Lucy again, he knows that if Emmy survives she'll write her novel before he writes his. The selfishness of this thought brings tears to his eyes, which he uses to seem happy, the awareness of which brings more tears to his eyes, so conscience and consciousness doth make cry-babies of us all.

In March, in the midst of final proofs and publicity photos and going back and forth to the ranch to deal with the contractors, Ethan decides it's only fair to set up a meeting about her writing with Jeanie Brown at Copper Place. He decides this out of the blue of blue films tinged with all shades of gray rationale. She's sent him three stories. One is way over the top, one is flatly under the bottom, but one is just right, almost, a hard story of cracks in a rock-solid marriage. The meeting is on a day when Lucy has a full teaching schedule, but Jeanie brings Billy and baby Lee with her, a last minute screw-up with her babysitter, she says. The infant sleeps in her carry cot. Billy drinks orange juice and looks at his picture books and some art books of Ethan's.

Ethan tells Jeanie he's only going to discuss the good story; when he has, she can infer what's not there in the other two. She nods. She takes notes. He talks sternly of the qualities of structure and language which characterize the story. He points out a few places where there's some over-writing spoiling, as he puts it, her chilly abilities. Jeanie keeps her head down over her notes. All this time, sitting so close, nobody touches anyone else, nor even looks at the other. When Jeanie gets up to wake Billy, asleep on the sofa, and leave, she smiles at Ethan and says, "Chilly abilities, huh?" and gives him a peck on the cheek, hardly a peck, a pecklet. He says, "Jesus, Jeanie," and they're kissing, hands on each other's backs, legs, buttocks, moving each other to the bedroom, shoes, skirt, trousers and shirt off, onto the bed, bra off, his underpants off, her underpants off (her underpants, her underpants, he smells and tastes her now remembering her underpants in the trailer) and fucking sweetly, wildly fucking, his mouth at the side of her neck tasting and smelling her; when she comes he comes looking into her brown eyes, jumping into them feeling he can do anything shivering full, everything, he can write novels; he stays inside her still hard, full. "The kids," she says, and he rolls out of her, she jumps out of bed, stops, looks at him, says, "Oh, my. Oh, my," picks up her underwear, darts out to the bathroom.

What? He asks himself. What? Her skin, for one. She is so beautiful, for two, enjoyable, for three, for four, for five thousand. Jeanie, the way her hips and buttocks curved as she went out the door. Her face, hair, neck. Jesus. If Lucy were to suddenly materialize at his bedside, he could only shrug and smile; no point in denying Jeanie. Lucy would understand. He knows this is the daydream of a man who's certain that Lucy won't appear. His hands smell of sex. Of unprotected sex. He collects his clothes and, kissing Jeanie as she come out of the bathroom, he goes in. When he comes out dressed, she's holding the carry cot in one hand, Billy's hand in the other. Billy says, "Ian."

"Ethan," Jeanie says. Billy says, "Eton."

Ethan puts his hand on Billy's soft hair. "I didn't think to use anything."

"No, it's okay. I've been on the pill since we met for lunch. Hoping."

He says, "That was wonderful. You delight me."

She drops Billy's hand and stokes Ethan's cheek. She says, "Will I see you pretty soon? I know you're with Lucy Evans."

"Yes," he says. "Yes, pretty soon."

In Early April, on a Thursday, a week before the publication of *New Mexico Now*, Ethan picks up the ringing phone at Copper Place and hears Bud Brandon say, "Baum, I want to see you and Lavery. To finish the hunt business. This Saturday, at noon. Out at your place, Little Coyote Ranch. Just you and Lavery. You don't have builders out there on Saturday, right?"

"Right." That's all it seems worth saying.

When he calls Lavery, he finds Brandon has already called him. Ethan says, "What do you think about this not telling anyone?"

"It's okay with me. I guess the fewer we are, the fewer asses he gets to whup."

"Right," says Ethan.

He thinks of Lavery's bleak reasoning on Saturday. A cold front sits over northern New Mexico. Snow has fallen overnight. From up on East Hills, its powder intensifies the outline of every rock and ridge and hill below in Little Coyote Valley, so that the eye is tricked into seeing everything in perfect focus at once: the juniper bush six feet away, the veins of root back down the trail, the loose scatter of boulders across the valley floor, its earth marbled with blown snow, the stands of bare cottonwood and the house and barn and cottage roofs etched white on reddish-brown, the hill-line behind like a flash-frozen breaker at a beach, and, finally, the squared ends of the mesas flattening to the north horizon, which is the clearest line of all, as if seeing not the real valley but its Ansel Adams photograph.

He and Charlie Lavery sit on a piñon log up near the southeast boundary of the ranch. He's taken Charlie up to view the property while they wait for Brandon. Ethan says, "It's cold."

Lavery says, "Not really, for this time of year."

"Ah, then I must be shivering from fright."

"Keep thinking of the land. After Min died, I figured what was I married to if not the land? What would this nice place of yours be like if they deregulated? Just north of the horizon out there is a billion tons of low grade coal those bastards are aching to strip mine."

Ethan's thinking of what satisfaction it might be to know he could be killed and buried on his nice, un-ruined land. "Ten to twelve," he says. "I guess we should go down. I can't believe Brandon would try something dumb like physically attacking us. Everyone would know. On the other hand, he had me beaten up on a whim of Carlos."

They walk down the path. Lavery says, "Well, we have our cell phones." Ethan looks at the grayed leaves of gambel oak under his feet. Cell phones aren't as fast as bullets. On the last rise before the valley floor, they pause. The ranch looks good. Scaffolding is up around the barn. He spots dust up from the road to the south. As they reach the bottom of the trail, Brandon's Ferrari roars up to the barn, spins in a great arc of brown earth, and stops inches from the scaffolding. If the idea of this trick is to get him to pay attention, it's worked. Ethan is paying great attention to Brandon getting out of the car, walking twenty feet from it, and waiting for them, hands in his coat pockets, gigantic, impassive, another boulder on the valley floor.

Except this boulder is wearing a blue knit ski cap with a red tassel. Ethan concentrates on the slight silliness of this hat atop the long black ponytail and long black leather coat. A little closer, he makes out a pattern in the cap: snowflakes and some sort of flower. Edelweiss, he decides, also an endangered species. He and Lavery stop about six feet away.

Brandon says, "Anyone else around?"

Ethan is thinking stupid answers, like Just us mice. He's having trouble finding his voice.

Lavery says, "No. What you see is what's here."

Ethan wishes he'd said that.

Brandon looks from one to the other. "You have any idea what you've done to Carlos?"

Ethan says, "Did he send you?"

"No, you piece of shit. Of course not. You don't know the first fucking thing about Carlos. You know where he is now?"

Lavery says, "In Spain, like the papers say."

"In Spain, yeah," Brandon says. "In Seville, Spain, staying with Celia's relatives. Eight thousand miles away because you shamed him so much, you fucks. Do you have any idea who this man is? I would have still been stealing cars, or worse, in prison or dead, without him taking an interest in me. But forget about me. Do you know how many hundreds, no, thousands, of poor New Mexican barrio kids he's helped? The charities he founded? The millions he's given? Do you?"

Lavery kicks some pebbles. "Yes, I know. Carlos has always made sure everyone knows about every dime he donates."

"Are you making fun of him, Lavery, you wise fuck?"

"No, just saying he makes his good deeds known."

"Good deeds," says Brandon. "What kind of fucking good deed was what you did to Carlos, Baum?"

Ethan finds it particularly uncomfortable to be yelled at on his nice un-spoiled ranch. He shrugs. "Whatever happened, Carlos did it himself by lying and sticking to his lies."

Brandon says, "Bullshit. He has the right to protect his private life."

"Not when it illegally interferes with other people's rights."

"People? You mean fucking elks?"

"No, people who don't want elks shot on their land, people who want a decent respect towards the environment, and, yes, I guess I mean the rights of elks, too. The rights of fucking elks!"

"Baum, you're not only a complete asshole, you're an asshole who owed Carlos. You owed him, man."

"What did I owe him for, having you beat me up?"

"That? That thing last summer, off Carlisle?" Brandon shakes his head. "That was nothing. Hey, the man wanted you hurt, believe me, you'd stay hurt. What you did was the worst: you hurt Carlos's *spirit*. You know what I'm saying?"

Ethan looks at Lavery. Lavery shakes his head. The word "spirit" out of Brandon's mouth strikes Ethan like a fly rising off dogshit. It's not that Ethan's brave. He knows he's not as he walks up to Brandon; it's that he has to somehow tell him that he can't use the word like that, not do such violence to language.

"Oh, a tough guy," Brandon says. He grabs Ethan's jacket and, though Ethan does not believe this as it happens, he finds himself looking Brandon straight in the eye, which he knows means his feet are three inches off the ground. Ethan is thinking that he's slim, but at six-five weighs around 195 pounds and is still being held by one hand, off the ground. This and the word "spirit" and it being on his own nice old new ranch is intolerable. Ethan does the only thing he can in this position: he draws his head back and head-butts Brandon.

Then, though it seems the same moment, he's on the ground with a terrible pain in his forehead and Brandon is laughing over him.

Lavery comes to help Ethan up, but Ethan needs to stay sitting on the ground some.

Lavery says, "Spirit, Brandon? You and Carlos and Everets, you three thieving fucks destroying this state and hunting elks with helicopters and Hummers, and you have the balls to talk about *spirit*?"

There is a silence. Ethan winces and looks up. Brandon has a gun in his hand. Ethan says, "Let it go, Charlie."

Lavery says, "No, I'm not going to be threatened and lectured about *spirit* by this outsized Gucci gangster."

Even with his headache, Ethan wishes he'd said this.

Lavery walks away from Ethan, turns to Brandon, and spreads out his arms. "What are you going to do, big man, shoot me?"

Brandon shoots him.

Ethan sees Lavery grab his shin and fall. Maybe a ricochet. It could have been that Brandon shot down at the pebbles and one hit Lavery. Or the bullet did. Lavery is a guest on his ranch.

Ethan gets to his feet. There's some blood on Lavery's trouser cuff and sock. Ethan says, "You can't stop there, Bud. Shoot me, too, and shoot Doc N and—and remember showing me photos of your kids? Shoot them, too. This is their land, too." Ethan sees Lavery hobbling out around Brandon. "What about your kids' spirit? What's supposed to feed their spirit in the wasteland of over-mining and over-logging and over-grazing of public land? Public land is your kids' land, Bud. We've spoiled too much of it. There are too many people wanting—"

Bud levels the gun at him. "Two less of you would make a good fucking start."

Lavery hits Brandon over the head with a length of pipe. Brandon turns slowly and Lavery hits him over the head again. Brandon goes down to one knee and drops the gun. Lavery kicks it towards Ethan, and Ethan bends for it but goes dizzy, falls, and clutches the gun in both hands, sitting down.

"Way to go, Charlie," he hears. "I should have got here sooner."

It's Doc N. He kneels by the now kneeling Lavery. Doc is wearing his Harvard tennis sweater with a long crimson and white scarf around his neck. He looks preposterous. Ethan laughs and clutches his headache with the gun in his hands.

Doc N says, "The good news is your ankle seems to have been hit by a piece of flying rock. A surface wound, a bad bruise at worst. Let's look at the other patient."

He goes to Brandon, now stretched out, moaning. Doc asks if he can hear him. Brandon says, "Yes." Doc helps him up to a sitting position and asks if he's nauseous and how many fingers he sees held up. Brandon waves him away, but Doc takes off the ski cap and feels his head. "Better have it x-rayed."

Brandon says, "What are you doing here?"

"Just out for a walk on East Hills. Thought I'd look in here, see how the work was coming. I see the barn roof is almost finished. Yuh, but I didn't expect to see my clinic's chief benefactor out here in the boonies. Too bad about Charlie tripping like that. He's lucky nothing's broken."

"Tripping," Brandon says.

"Ethan," says Doc, "did you know Bud is also a major donor to the children's clinic I run on the rez?"

Ethan shakes his head. Brandon says, "Well, kids…"

Lavery says, "So, have we finished our discussion?"

Brandon shakes his head, blinking. "Hey, I just see one of everything now. Yeah, I guess we've made our positions clear. Like they say, agree to disagree."

Doc helps him up. Brandon looks at Ethan: "I'll take my gun." Ethan looks at Doc, who nods. He gives the gun to Brandon, who locks it and puts it into a holster under his coat. He touches his head and puts on his knit cap.

Doc says, "I don't advise driving."

Brandon walks slowly to his car. "I'm okay, Doc. Always good behind the wheel. I'll drive straight to the hospital." He gets in, starts the car, turns it in a slow, wide semi-circle and then roars off, pluming dirt.

Lavery says, "My god, I hit him twice on the head with all my might and he wasn't even knocked out."

Ethan says, "You had that pipe on you all the time and you told Doc about this, didn't you?"

"Of course. Do you think I'd be foolish enough to meet Brandon out here unarmed and alone?"

Ethan looks to Doc, but Doc's smiling sweetly as he might at a fool.

22

BY THE MIDDLE OF JUNE, Ethan, Lucy, and Emmy have moved to Little Coyote Ranch. Emmy is still in the main house; her renovation of the cottage has evolved into its total reconstruction as a small, though devastatingly cool, adobe-style house. *New Mexico Now*, both photos and text, is a critical success, but it's not selling in numbers likely to reach the unbelievers and convert them to environmentalists.

Ethan spends each morning at the desk of his fine new workroom in the barn, putting down a few words or otherwise doodling on sheet after sheet of paper. Sometimes, after reading a page or two from a book drawn almost randomly from the shelves, he writes down an idea that swims against the numbing current of his mind; the effort makes it lie inert on the page, beyond resuscitation. Once or twice his eyes go up to the heavy beam above his desk. This can be reached by standing on a chair placed on the desk. Less often, but often enough, he checks, between the back of the desk and the wall, the quantity of strong rope saved from the barn's re-roofing. He knows from the example of Stucic at Cimarron that if you wish to succeed you cannot take too much care in these matters. Each evening, Lucy, fresh from the, he guesses, triumphant struggles with her fiction, asks him, "How did the writing go today, darling?" Perhaps he adds the "darling" for bathetic effect. Among the variants of his dishonest answer, the one that most satisfies him goes, with its grimace, "Not easy, but I'm hanging in there."

And now, late June, the bitty grass of the outfield burnt to the sand-color of the earth, Ethan is saying goodbye to his ballplayers. He shakes the hand of each boy and girl. They wear tags so he can learn their names faster. The tags and handshakes are his ideas. The boys and girls, aged ten to thirteen, are from Doc N's clinic, part of its summer sports program. They are spindle-legged or big-bellied or round-shouldered or no-necked, or any compound of these deformities. Never mind, they like playing ball, which is neither baseball nor softball. Ethan is coaching Eastern Navajo Little League Kickball. A soccer ball is rolled from the pitcher's mound to the kicker, who stands two steps behind home plate (two steps only are allowed as runup into the kick). The fielding is like baseball, except the fielder may throw out a base-runner by hitting her or him with the ball when the runner is off base. Ethan enjoys this: the kids are fun; what's more, at his suggestion, they call themselves the Red Sox. His final handshake is with George Begay, one of the round-shouldered, a kid he's tossed a real baseball with, who could be a good ballplayer despite his need to keep around him a stash of candy bars and insulin syringes. For a moment, Ethan thinks of going to the clinic, but getting into a conversation with Doc might keep him from going through with it.

He drives out to Navajo 48 and heads home. It's a comfortable forty-minute drive. No rush, it's Lucy's grad student day: she won't be back until ten at night. And though her Jeep isn't there, Ethan superstitiously walks the house, softly calling "Lucy?" as he enters the more and less likely rooms. She isn't there. He shaves, takes a shower, and puts on fresh clothes. If something's to be done, it should be done well. Is that from Emerson's "Self-Reliance" or the foaming rant of some right-wing general? Ah, the pursuit of anything done well. Of happiness. The God-given, inalienable pursuit of hap-pi-ness.

On his way out, he looks in at Emmy's room, having planned this for when she has her afternoon nap. There she is, head propped on pillows, under a knit blanket, despite the heat. Her pup Lucky lifts his head to Ethan, but seeing no sign to come play, drops it again against Emmy's side, a side that still makes hardly a bump beneath the blanket. Though Emmy seems to eat more, the only sign he sees of increased weight is false: her face is puffed from the new drugs she's on. And who, seeing her, would take her for a teenager, eyes sunk so deep behind the watery sacs of skin? When she's awake, she writes and writes. A real writer. He quietly closes her door.

He walks the hundred and fifty yards to the barn, and at the side door, his workroom door, he turns to look back at the house in its grove of cottonwood. The new porch timber doesn't quite fit, but it will weather. He can't see, but imagines the garden in back. All three of them are working on it. Strange how he loves the place, loves—he supposes—Emmy and Lucy. Strange how he can't write. He goes into the barn and locks the door, and goes to his desk under the beam. Through the windows, he sees the old, empty corral and behind it the reds, tans, and greens of the hillside. His hillside. Ethan Baum lives on a ranch in the West. He can remember the sound of the wolves up in the Cimarron Range, their wild, sad, shadow tones. Enough, he thinks. It's time.

And yet—

He opens the bottom desk drawer and reaches under the paper for the note. He only touches it, he knows it so well. In a week, Jeanie's mother, Grace, is taking the children for two weeks. He's met Grace, forty-eight, only two years older than Lucy. A beautiful woman. So, Jeanie, in a week, for two weeks. Weak? It's only, after all, what both his late beloved father and mother would wish, what Jeanie's very lively mother seems to wish, his inalienable right, every American's, to pursue that happiness, pursue it with good looks and charm or out of the barrel of a gun, at home with elks or in inalienably alien lands with others.

He closes the drawer. He goes to the side of the desk and reaches behind and brings out the thick coil of rope. He pulls back the desk chair, stands on it, and steps up onto the desk. He looks up at the beam.

Ethan says, "Fucking Boston, fucking Albuquerque, fucking Slava Stucic! Fucking XHelen, fucking Cambridge, fucking Thoreau! Fucking Sandy Milocic, fucking Lucy Evans, fucking Gustav Klimt, fucking Bobby Doer!"

He's speaking loudly now: "Fucking Wolfe Tone, fucking Henry Gratton, fucking William Shakespeare! Fucking Franz Schubert, fucking Roberta Palmer, fucking Caresse Crosby! Fucking Embrace Evans, fucking Gary Cooper, fucking Montgomery Clift! Fucking President Klotz, fucking Carlos Alvarado, fucking Willie Dixon, fucking Herman Melville!"

He's starting to shout: "Fucking Meyer Baum, fucking Somerville, fucking Jacques Derrida, fucking Jackson Pollock, fucking Joan Miró, fucking Lee Krasner, fucking Conrad Hilton! Fucking Kit Carson, fucking General Carleton, fucking Eileen Smith, fucking Elena Stucic! Fucking Flaubert, fucking Kafka, fucking Buster Keaton!"

Now he's shouting: "Fucking Celia Alvarado, fucking Roland Everets, fucking Willard Van Orman Quine, fucking Congreve, fucking Socrates! Fucking D.H. Lawrence, fucking Taos, fucking Oswald Spengler, fucking Errol Flynn! Fucking Stravinsky, fucking Virgil Thompson, fucking Grinling Gibbons, fucking Gerard Manley Hopkins, fucking Wordsworth, fucking Nina Ricci, fucking John Keats, fucking Mies van der Rohe, fucking Big Joe Turner!"

Ethan's screaming, "Fucking Saint Exupéry, fucking Enrico Fermi, fucking Stan Getz, fucking Marcel Proust, fucking Bertrand Russell! Fucking Catullus, fucking Ludwig Wittgenstein, fucking Mary Keegan, fucking Charlie Lavery, fucking Ingrid Bergman, fucking Hitler, fucking Rilke!"

His screaming grows shrill: "Fucking Bud Brandon, fucking Søren Kierkegaard, fucking Georg Buchner, fucking Derek Walcott! Fucking Buck Rogers, fucking Adam Smith, fucking Jeremy Bentham, fucking Emanuel Kant! Fucking Walt Whitman, fucking Percy Shelley, fucking Jeanie Brown! Fucking Horace, fucking Horace Gregory, fucking Hobbes, fucking Cicero, fucking Wyatt Earp, fucking Antony Caro!"

His screaming gets hoarse: "Fucking Mother Teresa, fucking Yves St. Laurent, fucking Lew Wallace, fucking William Cody, fucking John Dewey, fucking Yang Chou, fucking Tom and Jerry! Fucking Oaxaca, fucking Carmen, fucking Xavier, fucking Meyer, fucking Estella Rosen, fucking Diego Rivera, fucking Detective Otero! Fucking Lenin, fucking Mussolini, fucking John Millington Synge!"

He's croaking, "Fucking Jesse James, fucking e.e. cummings, fucking Rabbi Weissman, fucking Ralph Waldo Emerson, fucking Edward Arlington Robinson! Fucking Tom Yawkey, fucking Ted Williams, fucking Geoffrey Jacobs, fucking Geoffrey Chaucer! Fucking Hegel, fucking Husserl, fucking Jean Harlow, fucking Heidegger! Fucking St. Simone, fucking Jane Austen, fucking Louis Tiffany, fucking T.S. Eliot, fucking Thomas Mann!"

His voice is a small scratch: "Fucking Doc N, fucking Lucy, fucking Emmy, fucking Little Coyote Ranch, fucking house, fucking cottage, fucking barn, fucking chair, fucking desk!"

He stretches up his arms and whispers, "Fucking beam, fucking rope, fucking me!"

And then, because there is nothing left for Ethan to fuck, he gets off the desk, drops the rope, sits on the chair and begins to write:

> My flight to Albuquerque was annoying, but at least it was daytime. I hated night flights. Flying in daylight, I could still imagine my country having countryside. I seemed to see vast spaces without roads or houses